Praise for #1 *New York Times*
and *USA TODAY* **bestselling author**

NORA ROBERTS

"When Roberts puts her expert fingers on the
pulse of romance, legions of fans feel the heartbeat."
—*Publishers Weekly*

"You can't bottle wish fulfillment, but Nora Roberts
certainly knows how to put it on the page."
—*New York Times*

"Roberts is indeed a word artist, painting her story
and her characters with vitality and verve."
—*Los Angeles Daily News*

"Characters that touch the heart, stories that intrigue,
romance that sizzles—Nora Roberts has mastered it all."
—*Rendezvous*

"With clear-eyed, concise vision and a sure pen,
Roberts nails her characters and settings with awesome
precision, drawing readers into a vividly rendered world
of family-centered warmth and unquestionable magic."
—*Library Journal*

"Her stories have fueled the dreams of
twenty-five million readers."
—*Entertainment Weekly*

"Roberts' style has a fresh, contemporary snap."
—*Kirkus Reviews*

Dear Reader,

The West can be a very seductive setting, and the incomparable Nora Roberts makes the very best of the opportunity for romance in her two classic novels, *Song of the West* and *Boundary Lines*. These are the stories of two women who are not only captivated by the beauty of the land—but also by a couple of irresistible cowboys who call it home.

Sure, Wyoming is magnificent, but Samantha Evans had planned on getting back to city life as soon as her sister was well. Of course, that was before handsome cowboy Jake Tanner moseyed on into her life, with his easy confidence and careless smile. Suddenly she is listening to a sweet, sultry *Song of the West,* and the range is starting to look like home!

When Jillian Baron returned to the family ranch after her grandfather fell ill, she was determined to make Utopia the best spread in Montana! But a long-standing family feud soon threatens to reignite when Jillian finds herself falling for the enemy, Aaron Murdock. She is confident she would never let her heart rule her head—would she? Suddenly Jillian's beginning to wonder if some *Boundary Lines* are actually meant to be crossed!

We hope you enjoy these stories of love—cowboy style!

The Editors
Silhouette Books

NORA ROBERTS

Western Skies

Silhouette Books

Published by Silhouette Books
America's Publisher of Contemporary Romance

SILHOUETTE BOOKS

Recycling programs
for this product may
not exist in your area.

WESTERN SKIES

ISBN-13: 978-0-373-28152-7

Copyright © 2009 by Harlequin Books S.A.

The publisher acknowledges the copyright holder
of the individual works as follows:

SONG OF THE WEST
Copyright © 1982 by Nora Roberts

BOUNDARY LINES
Copyright © 1985 by Nora Roberts

All rights reserved. Except for use in any review, the reproduction
or utilization of this work in whole or in part in any form by any
electronic, mechanical or other means, now known or hereafter
invented, including xerography, photocopying and recording, or in
any information storage or retrieval system, is forbidden without
the written permission of the editorial office, Silhouette Books,
233 Broadway, New York, NY 10279 U.S.A.

This is a work of fiction. Names, characters, places and incidents are
either the product of the author's imagination or are used fictitiously, and
any resemblance to actual persons, living or dead, business establishments,
events or locales is entirely coincidental.

This edition published by arrangement with Harlequin Books S.A.

For questions and comments about the quality of this book please contact us
at Customer_eCare@Harlequin.ca.

® and TM are trademarks of Harlequin Books S.A., used under license.
Trademarks indicated with ® are registered in the United States Patent
and Trademark Office, the Canadian Trade Marks Office and in other
countries.

Visit Silhouette Books at www.Harlequin.com

Printed in U.S.A.

CONTENTS

SONG OF THE WEST

Chapter One

The land in southeast Wyoming is a magnificent paradox. Spreading plains and rolling hills coexist with rocky mountains and thick velvet pines. From the kitchen window, the view was astounding, and Samantha Evans halted in her duties for a moment to drink it in.

The Rockies dominated the vast curtain of sky, their peaks laced with snow, though it was late March.

Samantha wondered if she would still be in Wyoming the following winter. She dreamed of long walks with the air biting and sharp on her cheeks, or wild rides on a spirited mount with hooves kicking up a flurry of white. But none of that could happen until her sister was well enough to be left alone.

A frown creased her smooth brow. Sabrina was her reason for being in Wyoming, with its majestic mountains and quiet plains, rather than in the more familiar surroundings of Philadelphia's tall buildings and traffic-choked streets.

The two sisters had always been close, with that special, magical intimacy that twins share. They were not identical. Though they were the same in height and build, Samantha's eyes were a dark cornflower blue, widely set, with thick, spiky lashes, while Sabrina's eyes were a light gray. Both faces were oval set with small, straight noses and well-shaped mouths, but while Samantha's rich brown hair, with its highlights of gold, was shoulder length with a fringe of bangs, Sabrina's ash blond was short, framing her face with delicate curls. The bond between them was strong and enduring. Even when Sabrina had married Dan Lomax and moved so many miles away to settle on his ranch in the Laramie Basin, their devotion had remained constant and unwavering.

They kept in touch by phone and letter, which helped to mitigate Samantha's aching loneliness. And she was happy in her sister's delight in the coming baby. The two women had laughed and planned together over the phone. But that was before Dan's call. Samantha had been aroused from a deep predawn sleep by the shrill ringing of the phone. She reached groggily for it, but was instantly alerted by the anxious tone of her brother-in-law's voice. "Sam," he said without any preamble, "Bree's been very ill. We did manage to save the baby, but she has to be very careful for a while now. She will have to stay in bed and have constant round-the-clock care. We are trying to find someone to—"

Samantha had only one thought—her sister, the person she loved best in the world. "Don't worry, Dan, I will come immediately."

She was on the plane to Wyoming less than twenty-four hours later….

The whistle of the kettle brought Samantha back to

the present. She began to brew the herbal tea, placing delicate floral cups on a silver tray.

"Teatime," she called as she entered the living room. Sabrina was propped up with pillows and comforters on the long wood-edged sofa. Though her smile was warm, her cheeks still retained a delicate pallor.

"Just like the movies," Sabrina commented as her sister set a tray on the pine table. "But the role of Camille is getting to be a bore."

"I imagine so." Samantha poured the fragrant tea into cups. "But you may as well get used to it, Bree, you've got the part for a month's run." She transferred a large gray-striped cat from Sabrina's lap to her own, offered Sabrina a steaming cup and sat on the rug. "Has Shylock been keeping you company?"

"He's a terrible snob." With a wry smile, Sabrina sipped at her tea. "He did graciously allow me to scratch his ears. I have to admit, I'm glad you brought him with you, he's my biggest entertainment." She sighed and lay back against the pillows, regarding her sister seriously. "I'm ashamed to be lying here feeling sorry for myself. I'm lucky." She rested her hand on her stomach in a protective gesture. "I shall have my baby, and I sit here moaning about your waiting on me."

"You're entitled to moan a bit, Bree," said Samantha, immediately sympathetic. "You're used to being active and busy."

"I've no right to complain. You gave up your job and left home to come out here and take care of me." Another deep sigh escaped, and her gray eyes were dangerously moist. "If Dan had told me what you were planning to do, I would never have allowed it."

"You couldn't have stopped me." Samantha attempted to lighten the mood. "That's what older sisters are for."

"You never forget those seven minutes, do you?" Sabrina's eyes cleared, and a reluctant smile curved her generous mouth.

"Nope, it gives me seniority."

"But your job, Sam."

"Don't worry." Samantha made another dismissive gesture. "I'll get another job in the fall. There's more than one high school in the country, and they all have gym teachers. Besides, I needed a vacation."

"Vacation!" Sabrina exclaimed. "Cleaning, cooking, caring for an invalid. You call that a vacation?"

"My dear Sabrina, have you ever tried to teach an overweight, totally uncoordinated teenager the intricacies of the parallel bars? Well, the stories I could tell you about vacations."

"Sam, what a pair we are. You with your teenagers and me with my preadolescent Mozarts. Lord knows how many times I cleaned peanut butter off the keys of that old Wurlitzer before Dan came along and took me away from scales and infant prodigies. Do you think Mom expected us to come to this when she dragged us to all those lessons?"

"Ah, but we're well-rounded." Samantha's grin was faintly wicked. "Aren't you grateful? She always told us we'd be grateful one day for the ballet and the piano lessons."

"The voice lessons and the riding lessons," Sabrina continued, ticking them off on her fingers.

"Gymnastics and swimming lessons," Sabrina concluded with a giggle.

"Poor Mom." Samantha shifted Shylock to a more comfortable position. "I think she expected one of us to marry the president, and she wanted us to be prepared."

"We shouldn't make fun." Sabrina wiped her eyes with a tissue. "The lessons did give us our living."

"True. And I can still whip up a mean spinach souf-flé."

"Ugh." Sabrina grimaced, and Samantha lifted her brows.

"Exactly."

"You have your medals," Sabrina reminded her. Her smile warmed with pride and a trace of awe.

"Yes, I have the medals and the memories. Sometimes, it feels like yesterday instead of nearly ten years ago."

Sabrina smiled. "I can still remember my terrified excitement when you first swung onto the uneven bars. Even though I'd watched the routine countless times, I couldn't quite believe it was you. When they put that first Olympic medal around your neck, it was one of the happiest moments of my life."

"I remember thinking just before that competition, after I'd botched the balance beam so badly, that I couldn't do it. My legs felt like petroleum jelly, and I was mortally afraid I was going to be sick and disgrace myself. Then I saw Mom in the stands, and it ran through my mind how much she'd sacrificed. Not the money. The bending of those rather strange values of hers to allow me those years of training and those few heady moments of competition. I had to prove it was justified, I had to pay her back with something, even though I knew she'd never be able to say she was proud of me."

"You proved it was justified." Sabrina gave her twin a soft smile. "Even if you hadn't won on the bars and the floor exercises, you'd proved it by just being there. And she was proud of you, even if she didn't say it."

"You've always understood. So get over the idea I'm doing you a favor coming here. I want to be here. I *belong* here."

"Sam." Sabrina held out a hand. "I don't know what I'd do without you. I don't know what I *ever* would have done without you."

"You'd manage," Samantha returned, giving the frail hand a squeeze. "You have Dan."

"Yeah, I do." The smile became soft. "This is the time of day that I miss him most. He should be home soon." Her gaze wandered to the glass-domed anniversary clock on the mantel above the fire.

"He said something about checking fences today. I can't quite get away from the image of him chasing rustlers or fighting off renegade Indians."

With a light laugh, Sabrina settled back among the cushions. "City slicker. You know, Sam, sometimes I can't even remember what Philadelphia looks like. Jake Tanner was riding along with Dan today to make sure the boundary fences were in good repair."

"Jake Tanner?" Samantha's question was idle.

"Oh, that's right, you haven't met him yet. The northwest corner of the ranch borders his. Of course, the Lazy L would fit into one corner of his ranch. He owns half the county."

"Ah, a land baron," Samantha concluded.

"A very apt description," Sabrina agreed. "The Double T, his ranch, is the most impressive I've seen. He runs it like clockwork, super efficient. Dan says he's not only an incredible rancher, but a very crafty businessman."

"Sounds like a bore," Samantha commented, wrinkling her nose. "Steel-gray hair around a leathered face, a handlebar mustache drooping over his mouth and a generous belly hanging over his belt…"

Sabrina's laughter rang out, high and sweet.

"You're about as far off the mark as you can get. Jake Tanner is anything but a bore, and speaking from the safety of marital bliss, he's a fascinating man to look at. And, being rich, successful and unattached, all the females under forty buzz around him like bees around honey."

"Sounds like a good catch," Samantha said dryly. "Mom would love him."

"Absolutely," Sabrina agreed. "But Jake has eluded capture so far. Though from what Dan says, he does enjoy the chase."

"Now he sounds like a conceited bore." Samantha tickled Shylock's smooth belly.

"You can hardly blame him for taking what's offered." Sabrina defended the absent Jake Tanner with a vague movement of her shoulders. "I imagine he'll settle down soon. Lesley Marshall—her father's ranch borders the other side of the Double T—has her sights set on him. She's a very determined woman, as well as being more than a little spoiled, and dreadfully rich."

"Sounds like a perfect match."

"Mmm, maybe," Sabrina murmured. Her face creased in a small frown. "Lesley's nice enough when it suits her, and it's about time Jake had a wife and family. I'm fond of Jake. I'd like to see him set up with someone with more warmth."

"Listen to the old married woman." Samantha addressed a dozing and unconcerned Shylock. "A year of nuptial bliss, and she can't stand to see anyone unattached."

"True. I'm going to start on you next."

"Thanks for the warning."

"Wyoming's full of good-looking cowboys and handsome ranchers." Sabrina continued to smile as her sister grimaced. "You could find a worse place to settle down."

"I have no objection to settling here, Bree. I've become quite attached to the wide open spaces. But—" she paused significantly "—cowboys and ranchers are not among my immediate plans for the future." She rose from the floor in a fluid motion. "I've got to check on that roast. Here." She handed her sister the novel that rested on the table. "Read your love stories, you incurable romantic."

"You won't be so cynical when you fall in love," Sabrina predicted with the wisdom of experience.

"Sure." Samantha's grin was indulgent.

"There'll be bells ringing and fireworks shooting and trumpets blaring." She patted her sister's hand and strolled from the room, calling over her shoulder. "Angels singing, flames leaping…"

"Just you wait," Sabrina shouted after her.

Samantha busied herself preparing vegetables for the evening meal, clucking her tongue at her sister's nonsense. *Love,* she sniffed derisively. Her only experience with that complex emotion had been fending off unwanted attentions from eager males. Not once had any man lit an answering spark in her. But whatever this love was, it worked for Bree. The younger twin had always been more delicate, softer and more dependent. And though Sabrina was trying to be brave and strong, her sister knew the fear of miscarriage still lurked in the back of her mind. She needed Dan's support and love, and right now, she needed to feel his arms around her.

Like the answer to a prayer, Samantha spotted two figures on horseback approaching from the lower pasture. Grabbing her heavy jacket from the hook by the back door, she scurried out of the kitchen and into the cold March air.

As Dan and his companion drew closer, Samantha greeted him with a smile and a wave. She had noticed, even at a distance, Dan's expression of concern. But a smile relaxed his features when he spotted Samantha.

"Sabrina's all right?" he asked as he reined in next to her.

"She's fine," Samantha assured him. "Just a trifle restless, and tremendously lonely for her husband."

"Did she eat better today?"

Samantha's smile warmed, lighting her face with a quick flash of astonishing beauty.

"Her appetite was much better. She's trying very hard." Samantha lifted a hand to stroke the smooth flank of the gelding he rode. "What she needs now is you."

"I'll be in as soon as I stable my horse."

"Oh, Dan, for heaven's sake. Let your hand do it, or I'll do it myself. Bree needs you."

"But…"

"'S all right, boss," the other horseman interrupted, and Samantha spared him a brief glance. "I'll tend to your horse. You go on and see the missus."

Dan flashed his companion a wide grin and dismounted. "Thanks," he said simply as he handed over the reins and turned to Samantha. "Coming in?"

"No." She shook her head and hunched her shoulders in the confines of her jacket. "You two could use some time alone, and I'd like some air."

"Thanks, Sam." He pinched her cheek with brotherly affection and moved off toward the house.

Waiting until the door closed behind him, Samantha walked over and dropped wearily onto the stump used for splitting wood. Resting her back against the fence, she breathed deeply, devouring the brisk, cold air. The strain of caring for her sister in addition to running the house and cooking the meals, including, over his objection, Dan's predawn breakfast, had taken its toll.

"A few more days," she whispered as she closed her eyes. "A few more days and I'll have adjusted to the routine and feel more like myself." The heavy corded jacket insulated her from the bite of the cold, and she tilted back her head, allowing the air to play on her cheeks as her mind drifted on the edge of exhaustion.

"Funny place to take a nap."

Samantha sat up with a jerk, confused and disoriented by sleep. Her eyes traveled up to the speaker's face. It was a lean face, skin bronzed by the sun and stretched tightly over cheekbones, all lines and shadows, hollows and angles. The eyes were arresting, deep-set and heavily lashed. But it was their color, a deep, pure jade that caught and held her attention. His dusky gold hair curled from under a well-battered Stetson.

"Evening, ma'am." Though he touched the brim of his hat with due respect, his extraordinary eyes were faintly mocking.

"Good evening," she returned, struggling for dignity.

"Person could catch a bad chill sitting out too long after the sun's low. Wind's picking up, too." His speech was slow and thickly drawled. His weight was distributed evenly on both legs, hands deep in pockets. "Oughtn't to be out without a hat." His comment was accompanied by a fractional movement of his head toward her unadorned one. "Hat helps keep the heat in."

"I'm not cold." She feared for a moment her teeth would chatter and betray her. "I was…I was just getting some air."

"Yes, ma'am." He nodded in agreement, glancing behind her at the last, dying brilliance of sun as it slipped behind circling peaks. "Fine evening for setting out and watching the sunset."

Her eyes flashed at the teasing. She was embarrassed to have been caught sleeping. He smiled a slow, careless smile that crept unhurried across his face. The movement of his lips caused the hollows to deepen, the shadows to shift. Unable to resist, Samantha's lips curved in response.

"All right, I confess. You caught me napping. I don't suppose you'd believe I was just resting my eyes."

"No, ma'am." His answer was grave, with just a hint of apology.

"Well." She rose from her seat and was dismayed at how far she still had to look up to meet his eyes. "If you keep quiet about it, I'll see to it that you get a piece of the apple pie I baked for dinner."

"That's a mighty tempting offer." He considered it with a long-fingered hand reaching up to stroke his chin. "I'm partial to apple pie. Only one or two things I'm more partial to." His eyes roamed over her in a thorough and intense study that caused her heart to pound with unaccustomed speed.

There was something different about this man, she thought swiftly, something unique, a vitality at odds with lazy words and careless smiles. He pushed his hat back farther on his head, revealing more disorderly curls. "You've got yourself a deal." He held out his hand to confirm the agreement, and she placed her small hand in his.

"Thanks." The single word was breathless, as she found her speech hampered by the currents running up her arm. Abruptly, she pulled her hand away, wondering what it was about him that disturbed her equilibrium. "I'm sorry if I was short before, about Dan's horse." She spoke now in a rush, to conceal a reaction she could not understand.

"No need to apologize," he assured her, and the new soft texture in his tone both warmed and unnerved her. "We're all fond of Mrs. Lomax."

"Yes, well, I…" she stammered, suddenly needing to put a safe distance between herself and this slow-talking man. "I'd better go inside. Dan must be hungry." She looked past him and spotted his horse, still saddled, waiting patiently. "You didn't stable your horse. Aren't you finished for the day?" Hearing the concern in her own voice, she marveled at it. Really, she thought, annoyed, why should I care?

"Oh, yes, ma'am, I'm finished." There was laughter in his voice now, but Samantha failed to notice. She began to study the mount with care.

It was a magnificent animal, dark, gleaming chestnut, at least sixteen hands, she estimated, classic lines, fully flowing mane and proud, dished face. Arabian. Samantha knew horses and she recognized a full-blooded Arabian stallion when she saw one. What in the world…? "That's an Arabian." Her words interrupted her thoughts.

"Yes, ma'am," he agreed easily, entirely too easily. Her eyes narrowed with suspicion as she turned to him.

"No ranch hand is going to be riding around on a horse that's worth six months' pay." She stared at him and he returned the steady survey with a bland, poker face. "Who are you?"

"Jake Tanner, ma'am." The slow grin appeared again, widening, deepening, then settling as he lifted the brim of his hat at the introduction. "Pleased to meet you."

The land baron with the women at his feet, Samantha's brain flashed. Anger darkened her eyes.

"Why didn't you say so?"

"Just did," he pointed out.

"Oh." She tossed back her thick fall of hair. "You know very well what I mean. I thought you were one of Dan's men."

"Yes, ma'am." He nodded.

"Stop *ma'aming* me," she commanded. "What a mean trick! All you had to do was open your mouth and say who you were. I would have stabled Dan's horse myself."

"I didn't mind." His expression became annoyingly agreeable. "It wasn't any trouble, and you had a nice rest."

"Well, Mr. Tanner, you had a fine laugh at my expense. I hope you enjoyed it," she said coldly.

"Yes, ma'am." The grin widened without seeming to move at all. "I did."

"I told you to stop…" She halted, biting her lip with frustration. "Oh, forget it." Tossing her head, she took a few steps toward the house, then turned back crossly. "I notice your accent has modified quite a bit, Mr. Tanner."

He did not reply, but continued to stand negligently, his hands in his pockets, his face darkened by the late-afternoon shadows. Samantha spun back around and stomped toward the house.

"Hey," he called out, and she turned toward him before she could halt the reflex. "Do I still get that pie?"

She answered his question with a glare. His laughter, deep and rich, followed her into the house.

Chapter Two

The sound of the slamming door reverberated through the ranch house as Samantha struggled out of her jacket and marched into the living room. At the sight of her sister's face Sabrina slipped down into the pillows, picked up the novel lying on her lap and buried her nose in its pages. Dan, however, did not recognize the storm warning in his sister-in-law's blue eyes and flushed cheeks. He greeted her with a friendly, ingenuous smile.

"Where's Jake?" His gaze slid past her. "Don't tell me he went home without a cup of coffee?"

"He can go straight to the devil without his coffee."

"I expect he wanted to get home before dark," Dan concluded. His nod was sober, but his eyes were brilliant with merriment.

"Don't play innocent with me, Dan Lomax." Samantha advanced on him. "That was a rotten trick, letting me think he was one of your hands, and…" A giggle escaped from behind the paperback. "I'm glad you think it's amusing that your sister's been made a fool of."

"Oh, Sam, I'm sorry." Warily, Sabrina lowered the book. "It's just hard to believe anyone could mistake Jake Tanner for a ranch hand." She burst out laughing, and Samantha was torn between the pleasure of seeing her sister laugh and irritation at being the brunt of the joke.

"Well, really, what makes him so special?" she demanded. "He dresses like every other cowboy I've seen around here, and that hat of his has certainly seen better days." But, she remembered, there *had* been something special about him that she had not quite been able to define. She firmly dismissed this disquieting thought. "The nerve of him." She rounded on Don again. "Calling you boss, and ma'aming me in that exaggerated drawl."

"Reckon he was just being polite," Dan suggested. His smile was amiable and pure. Samantha sent him the look that terrified her students.

"Men." Raising her eyes, she searched the ceiling in hopes of finding the answer there. "You're all alike, and you all stick together." She bent and scooped up the sleeping Shylock and marched into the kitchen.

Time at the ranch passed quickly. Though her days were full and busy, Samantha fretted for some of the physical outlet that had so long been part of her life. At times, the confinement of the house was suffocating. Years of training and discipline had left her with an inherent need for activity.

Unconsciously, she separated her life into three categories: the pre-Olympic years, the Olympic years and the post-Olympic years.

The pre-Olympic years were a blur of lessons, piano teachers, dance instructors, her mother's gentle but inescapable admonishments to "be a lady." Then, the first time she had gripped the lower bar of the unevens, the new chapter had begun.

By the time she was twelve years old, she had remarkable promise. The gymnastics instructor had informed her mother, who was more distressed than pleased at the praise. Though her mother had objected to more intense training, Samantha had ultimately prevailed.

The hours of training became months, county meets became state meets, and national competitions became international competitions. When Samantha was picked for the Olympic team, it was just another step down a road she was determined to follow. Weariness and aching muscles were accepted without hesitation.

Then it was over, and at fifteen she had found it necessary to alter what had become a way of life. College had to be considered, and earning a living. The years passed into the post-Olympic period, and she remembered her days of athletic competitions as a dream. Now her life was shifting again, though she was unsure as to the direction. The mountains and plains were calling to her, inviting her to explore, but she buried her desires, remaining indoors to see to her sister's needs. Dan is a busy man, she thought as she prepared lunch, and Bree needs someone within calling distance during this critical period. When she's better, there will be plenty of time to see the country.

She arched her back and rubbed a small spot of tension at the base of her neck. The kitchen door opened and Dan burst in, accompanied by Jake Tanner. Samantha met the amused green eyes levelly, though once more she felt treacherously at a disadvantage.

Her hair had been carelessly scooped on the top of her head that morning, and now, with their usual abandonment, stray locks were beginning to escape confinement. She was dressed in a black ribbed sweater that had seen too many washings and ancient jeans, splattered, faded, patched and too tight. She resisted the urge to raise her hand to her tumbling hair, forced a smile and turned to her brother-in-law.

"Hello, Dan. What are you doing home this time of day?" Purposefully, she ignored the tall figure beside him.

"Wasn't too far out," Dan explained. Slipping off his jacket and hat, he tossed both over the hooks provided. "Jake was giving me a hand, so I figured it was only neighborly to bring him back for lunch."

"Hope I'm not imposing, ma'am." The slow smile spread, once more rearranging the angles of his face.

"No imposition, Mr. Tanner. But you'll have to settle for potluck."

"My favorite dish—" he paused, giving her a cheeky wink "—next to apple pie."

Samantha sent him a withering glance and turned away to warm the previous evening's stew.

"I'll just go tell Sabrina I'm home," Dan announced to the room in general, and strode away. Samantha did her best to ignore Jake's disturbing presence. She stirred the stew busily.

"Smells good." Jake moved over to the stove and lounged against it. Samantha went to the cupboard to get the bowls.

When she turned back to place them on the round kitchen table, she noticed that he had shed his outdoor clothing. The slim-fitting jeans, snug and low on narrow hips, accentuated his leanness. His flannel shirt fitted over his broad shoulders and hard chest before tapering down to a narrow waist. The athlete in her immediately responded to the firm, well-proportioned body; there was not an ounce of spare flesh on him.

"Don't talk much, do you?" The drawl was there again, the exaggerated twang of the previous evening. Samantha turned her head, prepared to freeze him with her eyes.

His face was barely inches from hers as he slouched by the stove. For a moment, her mind ceased to function.

"I really have nothing to say to you, Mr. Tanner." She struggled to keep her voice cold and detached, but she could feel the blood rush to her face.

"Well, now, we'll have to see if we can change that." He spoke with easy confidence as he straightened to his full height. "We're not much on formalities around here. Just make it Jake." Though his words were spoken with his usual lazy delivery, there was an undertone of command. Samantha's chin rose in defense.

"Maybe I prefer to keep things formal between us, Mr. Tanner."

His lips were curved in his careless smile, but in his eyes she now recognized that special something that separated him from an ordinary ranch hand. *Power.* She wondered how she had missed it at their first meeting.

"I don't think there's much chance of that." He paused and tugged at a loose lock of his hair before adding with irritating emphasis, "Ma'am. Nope, I don't think there's much chance of that at all."

Samantha was saved from coming up with a suitable rebuttal by Dan's reappearance. She began to spoon the stew into ceramic bowls, noting to her dismay that her hands were not altogether steady. This man was infuriating her with his arrogantly lazy confidence. I have never met a more irritating male, she thought. He thinks he can switch on that rugged cowboy charm and women will drop in droves at his feet. Well, maybe some do, but not this one.

"Okay, Sam?" Dan's voice shattered the electric silence.

"What? I'm sorry, I wasn't listening."

"You'll keep Jake company over lunch, won't you? I'll have mine in the living room with Sabrina."

She swore silently. "Of course," she answered with an impersonal smile.

Within a short time, Samantha found herself sitting across from the man she wanted most to avoid.

"You've a fine hand with dumplings, Sam." Her brows rose involuntarily at his easy use of her nickname, but she kept her voice even.

"Thank you, Mr. Tanner. It's just one of my many talents."

"I'm sure it is," he agreed with an inclination of his head.

"You haven't changed much from the girl in the picture in Sabrina's parlor." Samantha was astonished.

"You'd have been about fifteen," he continued. "A bit skinnier than you are now, but your hair was the same, not quite willing to stay bundled on top of your head." Samantha's blank expression had turned to a frown at the word skinnier. She remembered the photo clearly.

"You'd just finished winning your second medal." She had indeed been fifteen. The picture had been snapped at the moment she had completed her floor routine. It had captured the look of stunned triumph, for she had known in that instant that a medal was hers.

"Sabrina's just about as proud of you as you are

worried about her." Samantha said nothing, only staring into the lean, handsome features. His brows rose ever so slightly, a movement that would have gone unnoticed had she not been so intent on his face. For a moment, she forgot the thread of the conversation, caught up suddenly in a series of small, irrelevant details: the curling gold which spilled over his brow, the tiny white scar on his jawline, the thickness of his long lashes. Confused, she dropped her eyes to her bowl and struggled to bring her thoughts to order.

"I'd forgotten Bree had that picture," she said. "It was a long time ago."

"So now you teach. You don't look like any gym teacher I ever knew."

"Oh, really?"

"No, ma'am." He shook his head slowly and considered her through another mouthful of stew. "Don't look strong enough or old enough."

"I assure you, Jake, I'm both strong enough and old enough for my profession."

"What made you become a gym teacher?" His sudden question caught her off balance, and she stared at him.

"Well, I…" Her shoulders moved restlessly. "Our mother was a fanatic on lessons when Bree and I were growing up." She smiled in spite of herself. "We took lessons in everything, Mom's theory on being well-rounded. Anyway, Bree found her talent in music and I developed a knack for the physical. For a while, I focused on gymnastics, then, when the time came to work, it seemed natural. Bree taught little people to play the classics, and I teach bigger people to tumble."

"Do you like your work? Are you happy with it?"

"As a matter of fact, I do," she retorted. "I like the activity, I like being involved in a physical type of work. It can be frustrating at times, of course. Some of the girls I teach would rather be flirting with their boyfriends than learning gymnastics, I suspect."

"And you yourself are more interested in calisthenics than men?" The question was delivered with a broad masculine smile.

"That's hardly relevant," she snapped, annoyed that she had lowered her guard.

"You don't think so?"

Samantha scraped back her chair and moved to the stove. "Coffee?"

"Yes, ma'am, black." It was unnecessary to turn around; she felt the slow grin crease his face as clearly as if she had witnessed it with her eyes. She set the cup down on the table with a bang. Before she could spin back to pour her own, her hand was captured in a firm grip. There was nothing soft about the hand. It was hard and masculine.

Completely outmatched in the short battle that ensued, Samantha discovered that under the lean, lanky exterior lay an amazing strength. Deciding that it was undignified to grapple in her sister's kitchen, she allowed her hand to rest quietly in his, meeting his laughing eyes with a resentful glare. Her heart began to pound uncomfortably against her ribs.

"What do you want?" Her voice came out in a husky whisper. His eyes left hers to travel slowly down to the generous curve of her mouth, lingering until she could taste the heat on her lips, as real as a kiss. Taking his time, he moved his gaze back to her eyes.

"You're jumpy." His observation was laconic, as if none of the heat had touched him, though she herself was beginning to suffocate. "Powerful strong for such a little bit of a thing."

"I'm not little," she retorted. "You're just so big." She began to tug at her hand again, feeling a near desperate urgency to shake off the contact that was infusing her with an unexplained weakness around the knees.

"Your eyes are fabulous when you're angry, Sam." His tone was conversational. "Temper agrees with you. You grow beautiful with it." He laughed and pulled her closer.

"You're insufferable," she said, still struggling to escape his grasp.

"For telling you you're beautiful? I was just stating the obvious. I'm sure it's been mentioned to you once or twice before."

"You men are all the same." She ceased her struggles long enough to aim a lethal glare. "Always grabbing and groping."

"I don't grope, Samantha." His drawl was feather-soft. For an instant, the cocky cowboy vanished, and she glimpsed the man, shrewd and ruthless, beneath. Here was a man who not only expected to have his own way, but would. "And the next time I grab you, it won't only be to hold your hand." Releasing her, he leaned back in his chair. "You have been warned."

Later, as Sabrina napped and the house grew still around her, Samantha found herself staring blankly at the pages of a novel. Scowling, she tossed it aside and rose from the sofa to pace to the window. What an infuriating man. Obviously, he considers himself irresistible. She began to wander the room, attempting to block out the effect his blatant virility had had on her.

It was too bad, she decided on her fourth circle, that all those good looks, all that strength and appeal, had to belong to such a rude, arrogant man.

Deciding that a brisk walk was just what she needed to get Jake Tanner out of her mind, she stopped her pacing and grabbed a warm jacket. Moments later she was out the door, gazing around her in delight at the beauty of the starlit Wyoming night. Her breath puffed out in thin white mists as she moved. The air, tinged with frost, carried the aroma of pine, and she drank it in greedily, enjoying the mixed scent of hay and horses and aged wood. She could hear the lonely sound of a coyote calling to the full silver moon. And suddenly she realized that she had fallen in love with Wyoming. The spell of the mountains and plains was on her, and she was inexplicably glad she had come.

"Goodness, you were out a long time," her sister commented as Samantha plopped down in a wing-backed chair in front of the fire a few minutes later. "You must be frozen."

"No." Samantha stretched out her legs and sighed. "I love it out there. It's fantastic! I never realized how big the sky was before, and I don't think I'll ever get used to the space, the openness."

She turned her attention to the powerfully built man sitting next to her sister on the sofa. "I wonder if you appreciate it, Dan, living here all of your life. Even your letters, Bree, didn't do justice to that world out there." Running her fingers through her hair, she made a small sound of pleasure. "To someone used to traffic-choked streets and huge buildings, all this…" Her hands moved in an inadequate gesture.

"You haven't had much of a chance to see anything since you've been here," Dan observed. "You've been with us a month and you haven't gone a quarter mile away from the house. And that's been mostly to fetch the mail in the mornings."

"I'll have plenty of time to explore later. I'll be around through the summer."

"Just the same, we're not having you tied to the house while you're here, Sam," Dan announced, and sat back against the cushions. "Even the most devoted sister is entitled to a day off."

"Don't be silly. You make it sound as though I were slaving from dawn to dusk. Half the time I'm not doing anything."

"We know how hard you're working, Sam," Sabrina said quietly, glancing up at Dan before returning her gaze to her twin. "And I know the lack of activity is harder on you than the work. I also know how you disrupted your life to come out here and take care of me."

"Oh, Bree, for heaven's sake," Samantha began, shifting uncomfortably. "I never would have found out how much I love Wyoming if I hadn't come."

"Don't try to shrug if off, Sam." Dan grinned at the embarrassed motion of her shoulders. "We're grateful, and you'll just have to get used to us telling you so. But tomorrow, we're going to show we're grateful instead of just talking about it. We're kicking you out for the day."

"Huh?" Blankly, Sam blinked at the bland smile before shifting her gaze to Sabrina's serene one.

"That's right." His grin widened as she drew her brows together. "Tomorrow's Sunday, and I'm staying home with my wife. And you…" He pointed a warning finger at his sister-in-law. "You're going to have your pick of the horses and take off."

Samantha sprung up from her slouched position. "Do

you mean it?" Her face was glowing with pleasure, and Dan's smile warmed with affection.

"Yes, little sister, I mean it. It should be more."

"The dapple-gray gelding," she began in a rush, ignoring the last part of his comment. "Can I take him?"

"Already inspected the stock, and it appears you know your horses." Dan chuckled and shook his head. "Spook's a good mount. A little frisky, but from what Sabrina's told me, you can handle him."

"Oh, I can, and I promise I'll be careful with him." She sprang from her chair and crossed the room, flinging her arms around his neck. "Thanks, Dan. You are absolutely my favorite brother-in-law, bar none."

"I think she likes the idea, Sabrina," Dan commented as he met his wife's eyes over Samantha's head. "In fact, I'd say she's downright pleased about it."

"And I thought I hid my emotions so effectively." She gave his cheek a loud, smacking kiss.

"You be ready to start out about nine." He patted Samantha's slim shoulder. "Jake'll be around, then."

"Jake?" Samantha repeated. Her smile froze.

"Yeah, he'll be riding out with you. Actually," Dan continued, "he suggested the idea this afternoon. He thought it would do you good to get out of the house for a while." He sighed and scratched his dark head, managing to appear sheepish, for all his size. "I'm ashamed I didn't think of it first. I guess I've been a bit preoccupied and didn't notice you were looking a littled tired and hemmed in."

"I'm not tired," she denied automatically.

"Hemmed in?" Sabrina offered with a knowing smile.

"A little, maybe, but I'm hardly in the last stages of cabin fever. I'm sure it's very kind of Mr. Tanner to be so concerned about my welfare." She managed to say his name in a normal voice. "But there's certainly no need for him to go with me. I know he has hundreds of more important things to do with his Sunday."

"Well, now, he didn't seem to think so," Dan said. "It was his suggestion, and he seemed keen on the idea, too."

"I don't know why he would be," she muttered. "Besides, I don't want to impose on him. We're practically strangers. I can just go by myself."

"Nonsense." Dan's refusal was good-natured but firm. "I couldn't possibly let you ride out by yourself just yet, no matter how good you are on a horse. You don't know the country, and it's easy to get lost. There's always the possibility of an accident. Besides," he added, and his grin was expansive, "you're part of the family, and I grew up with Jake, so you're not strangers. If anyone knows his way around this part of Wyoming, he does." He shrugged and rested his back against the cushions. "He owns half of it, anyway." Samantha glanced at her sister for help. Sabrina, however, appeared to be engrossed in her needlepoint.

Frowning at the lack of support, Samantha stewed over her predicament. If she refused Jake's company, she would not only forfeit the opportunity to ride the Wyoming countryside, but she would spoil Sabrina's and Dan's plans for a day alone together. She shrugged in resignation and offered a smile.

"I'll be ready at nine." She added to herself, If Jake Tanner can stand a day in my company, I guess I can stand a day in his.

Chapter Three

Sunday dawned with a sky as cold and clear as sapphire. The sun offered thin light and little warmth. To her annoyance, Samantha had overslept. Hurriedly, she showered and dressed in forest-green cords and a chunky beige pullover.

Her riding boots clattered on the parquet floor as she hurried from her room and down the hall to the kitchen. She frowned as she reached the doorway. Jake was sitting at the table, enjoying a cup of coffee with the air of one very much at home.

He was, she noted with illogical irritation, every bit as attractive as she remembered.

"Oh, you're here." Her greeting was hardly welcoming, but he returned it with his slow smile.

"Morning, ma'am."

"Don't start ma'aming me again," she said.

He remained silent as she clattered the cups in the cupboard and filled one with the steaming liquid from the pot on the stove.

"Sorry." She popped a piece of bread in the toaster and turned to offer a peace-offering smile. "My! I overslept. I hope you haven't been waiting long."

"I've got all day," he answered, leaning back in his chair as if to emphasize his words.

She drew a slab of bacon and a carton of eggs from the refrigerator. "Have you eaten?" she asked in invitation.

"Yeah, thanks." He rose, poured himself another cup of coffee and resumed his position at the table. "Dan's already seen to breakfast for himself and Sabrina. They're having it in their room."

"Oh." She replaced the items and pulled out the butter.

"Aren't you going to eat?"

"Toast and coffee. I'm not much on breakfast."

"If you always eat like that," he observed over the rim of his cup, "it's no wonder you never grew any bigger."

"For goodness' sake." She whirled around, brandishing the butter knife. "I'm hardly a midget. I'm five-four, that's tall enough for anybody."

He held up his hands in mock surrender. "I never argue with an armed woman.

"Ready?" He rose when she had finished both the toast and another cup of coffee.

When she mumbled her assent, he plucked her jacket from its hook, holding it out so that she had no choice but to allow him to help her into it. She stiffened as his hands touched her shoulders and turned her to face him. Her pulses responded immediately. As if he were aware of her reaction, he began to do up her leather buttons with slow care. She jerked back, but his hold on the front of her coat prevented her from a clean escape.

"You're a pretty little thing," he drawled, completing

his task with his eyes directly on hers. "Can't have you catching cold." He reached out and plucked Sabrina's dark wide-brimmed hat from a peg and placed it neatly on her head. "This'll keep your head warm."

"Thanks." She pushed the hat firmly in place.

"Anytime, Sam." His face was unperturbed as he pulled his own sheepskin jacket over his flannel shirt and jeans.

On the way to the stables, Samantha increased her pace to a trot to keep up with Jake's long, careless stride. Despite herself, she admired the confident, loose-limbed grace of his movement. He took his time, she noted, deciding he probably did nothing quickly, and more than likely still finished ahead of everyone else.

The dapple gray had been saddled and led outside by a smiling ranch hand.

"Howdy, ma'am. Dan said to have Spook ready for you."

"Thanks." She returned his friendly smile and patted the gelding's neck. "But I could have done it. I don't like to give you extra work."

"No trouble, ma'am. Dan said you weren't to do a lick of work today. You just go and have yourself a good time, and I'll rub old Spook down when you get back."

Samantha vaulted easily onto the horse's back, happy to feel a mount beneath her again. Riding was an old pleasure, to be enjoyed only when finances allowed.

"Now, you take good care of Miss Evans, Jake," the cowboy admonished with a conspirator's wink Samantha failed to catch. "Dan sets great store by this little lady."

Little again, Samantha thought.

"Don't you worry about Miss Evans, Lon." Jake mounted his stallion with a fluid motion. Again

Samantha noticed that he wasted no time on superfluous movement. "I intend to keep a close eye on her."

Samantha acknowledged Jake's statement with a wrinkled nose, then, following the direction his hand indicated, set off in a brisk canter.

As the neat cluster of ranch buildings was left behind, her irritation vanished. The rushing air was exciting, filling her lungs and whipping roses into her cheeks. She had almost forgotten the sense of liberation riding gave her. It was the same sensation that she had experienced many times when flying from top to bottom or springing high in a double twist.

They rode in silence for a quarter of an hour. Jake allowed her to fill her being with the thrill of movement and the beauty of the countryside. Wild peaks jutted arrogantly into the sky. The rolling plains below were yellow-green with winter. They rode by Herefords, white-faced and sleek, who noted their passing with a lazy turn of the head before resuming their grazing.

A shape darted across an open field, and Samantha slowed her horse to a walk and pointed. "What's that?"

"Antelope," Jake answered, narrowing his eyes against the sun.

"Oh!" She halted her mount and watched the animal's graceful, bounding progress until it streaked over a hill and out of her view. "It must be marvelous to run like that, graceful and free." She turned her unguarded face to the man beside her and found him regarding her intently. His eyes held an expression she did not understand. A strange tingling raced along her spine, like warm fingers on cold skin. The tingling increased, the sensation spreading to settle somewhere in her stomach. Suddenly, his expression changed. The shadows of his face shifted as his lips moved into a smile.

"Someday you will be caught, little antelope."

She blinked at him, totally disoriented, trying to re-member what they had been talking about. His grin increased. He pointed to a large, bare-limbed tree a quarter of a mile away.

"Race you." There was challenge under the lazy dare.

Her eyes brightened with excitement. "Fine chance I'd have against a horse like that. What handicap do I get?"

Jake pushed his hat back as if to view her more com-pletely. "From the look of you, I'd say you've got a good fifty-pound advantage. That should balance the odds some."

"No head start?"

"No, ma'am."

She pouted for a moment, then grinned. "All right, Jake Tanner, I'll give you a run for your money."

"Whenever you say, Sam." He pulled the brim of his hat low over his forehead.

"Now!"

She met the gelding's sides with her heels and spurted forward in a gallop. The quiet morning air vibrated with the thunder of hooves. Samantha, her hair flow-ing behind her, gave herself over to the thrill of the race. She reached the finish just ahead of her competitor and reined in, filling the morning with dusty, breathless laughter.

"Oh, that was wonderful, absolutely wonderful."

"Any time you want to give up teaching, Sam, you can work for me. I can use a hand who rides like you."

"I'll keep that in mind, even though I know you let me beat you."

"Now what makes you think that?" He leaned his arm on the horn of his saddle and watched her thoughtfully.

"I'm not stupid." Her grin was good-natured and friendly. "I couldn't beat that Arabian in a million years. You, maybe," she added with a touch of arrogance, "but not that horse."

"Pretty sharp, aren't you?" he returned, answering her grin.

"As a tack," she agreed. "And," she continued, brushing her hair from her shoulders, "I am not a weak female who needs to be placated. With my background, I know how to compete, I know how to lose, and—" she grinned and lifted her brows "—I know how to win."

"Point taken." He tilted his head as if to view her from a different angle. "From now on, Sam, we play head-to-head." He smiled, and she was no longer sure they were talking about the same thing. "I know how to win, too," he added slowly. They continued at a leisurely pace for a time, crossing a narrow branch of the Medicine Bow River. They paused there for the horses to quench their thirst in the icy water that forced its way over shining rocks with hisses and whispers. At Samantha's request, Jake began to identify the surrounding mountains.

Pointing to the long fingers of peaks at the south, the Laramie Range, he told her they extended from eastern Colorado. The middle section was the Medicine Bow Range, and the Sierra Madre loomed to the west. The vast ranges were separated by broad tongues of the Wyoming Basin. Silver-blue, they gleamed in the sunlight, lacings of snow trembling from their summits.

She had reined in without being aware of her action. "I can never look at them long enough. I suppose you're used to them."

"No." There was no laughter or mockery in his tone. "You never get used to them."

She smiled a bit uncertainly, not at all sure she could deal with this side of him.

"Are there bears up there?" she asked.

He glanced up at the mountains, smiled, then looked back at her. "Black bear and grizzly," he informed her. "Elk, coyotes, mountain lions…"

"Mountain lions?" she repeated, a little nervously.

"You're not likely to run into one down here," he returned with an indulgent smile.

She ignored the mockery in his voice and looked around her, again awed by the miles of open space. "I wonder if this looked the same a century ago."

"Some of it. Those don't change much." He indicated the Rockies with an inclination of his head. "The Indians are gone," he continued, as if thinking aloud. "There were Arapaho, Sioux, Cheyenne, Crow, Shoshone, all roaming free over the state before the first white man set foot here. Then trappers came, trading with Indians, dressing like them, living like them, and the beaver was nearly driven into extinction." He turned back to her, as if suddenly remembering she was there. "You're the teacher." His smile appeared. "You should be telling me."

Samantha shook her head in mock despair. "My knowledge of Wyoming's history is limited to late-night westerns." They were walking their horses slowly, side by side. She had completely forgotten her aversion to the man beside her. "It's impossible to believe the killing and cruelty that must have gone on here. It's so serene, and so vast. It seems there would have been room enough for everyone."

This time it was Jake who shook his head. "In 1841 more than a hundred and fifty thousand people crossed the South Pass going west, and a few years later, fifty thousand more came through on their way to California looking for gold. This was Indian land, had been Indian land for generations. Game disappeared, and when people get hungry, they fight. Treaties were signed, promises made by both sides, broken by both sides." He shrugged.

"In the 1860s, they tried to open the Bozeman Pass from Fort Laramie to Montana, and open war broke out. The trail ran through the Sioux hunting ground. The fighting was of the worst kind, massacres, indiscriminate killing of women and children, butcheries by both white and Indian. More treaties were signed, more misunderstandings, more killing, until the whites outnumbered the Indians, drove them away or put them on reservations."

"It doesn't seem fair," Samantha whispered, feeling a wave of sadness wash over her.

"No, it doesn't." He heard the wistful note in her voice and turned to regard her. "Life isn't always fair, though, is it, Samantha?"

"I suppose not." She sighed. "You seem to know quite a bit about what happened here. You must have had a good history teacher."

"I did." He held her curious look with a teasing half-smile on his lips. "My great-grandmother lived to be ninety-eight. She was Sioux."

Samantha lifted her brows in surprised interest. "Oh, I'd love to have met her. The things she must have seen, the changes in nearly a century of living."

"She was quite a woman." His smile faded a moment. "She taught me a lot. Among other things, she told me that the land goes on no matter who walks on it, that life moves on whether you fight against it or flow with it, that when you want something, you go after it until it's yours."

Suddenly, she felt he was leading her out of her depth, reaching for something she was not sure she possessed. She turned from the directness of his eyes to search the land.

"I'd like to have seen all this before there were any fences, before there was any fighting."

Jake pointed skyward. Glancing up, Samantha watched the graceful flight of an eagle. For a timeless moment, it soared overhead, the undisputed sovereign of the skies. They moved off again, in companionable silence. "I hope you're getting some fun out of this trip, some compensation for taking care of your sister," Jake said at last.

"I don't need any compensation for taking care of Bree, she's my sister, my…"

"Responsibility?"

"Well…yes. I've always looked out for Bree, she's more delicate, more…dependent than I am." She shrugged and felt uncomfortable without knowing why. "Dad always joked that I took my share of strength and half of Bree's while we were still in the womb. She needs me," she added, feeling compelled to defend what she had always taken for granted.

"She has Dan," Jake reminded her. "And she's a grown woman now—just as you are. Did it ever occur to you that you have your own life to lead now that Sabrina has a husband to care for her?"

"I'm not trying to take over for Dan," she said quickly. "Perhaps you can figure out how he could see to her needs and tend to the house and the ranch all at the same time, but I can't." She glared at him, half in anger, half in exasperation. "What do you expect me to do? Sit up in Philadelphia teaching kids to jump on a tramp while my sister needs help?"

"No, Samantha." He met her eyes with a quiet patience that was more disturbing than angry words and shouts. "What you're doing is very kind and unselfish."

"There's nothing kind or unselfish about it," she interrupted, shrugging the words away. "We're sisters. More than that, we're twins. We shared life from its beginning. You can't understand the kind of bond that creates. I'd give up a hundred jobs to help Bree if she needed me."

"No one's condemning your loyalty, Samantha. It's an admirable trait." He gave her a long, level look. "Just a word of advice. Don't become so involved that you forget who Samantha Evans is, and that she just might have the right to her own woman's life."

Samantha drew herself up to her full height in the saddle. "I hardly need your advice on how to run my life. I've been managing nicely for some time now."

His face creased in a lazy smile. "Yes, ma'am, I'm sure you have."

Chapter Four

Samantha had been riding the dapple gray in stubborn silence for nearly thirty minutes when she noticed more cattle. Her guide seemed unperturbed by her silence and slowed his Arabian's gait to the gelding's meandering walk. She would never have admitted to the man at her side that his words had disturbed her peace of mind.

What business was it of his how she chose to run her life? What gave Jake Tanner the right to question her relationship with Sabrina? No one asked him for his advice. And why in heaven's name should anything he said matter in the first place?

They were approaching a large ranch house. A redwood porch skirted the building's front, graced by evergreen shrubs. A gray wisp of smoke rose in a welcoming spire from the chimney. Ranch buildings sat neat and unobtrusive in the background.

"Welcome to the Double T, ma'am."

Jake drew her eyes with the uncharacteristic formality

in his tone. She turned to see him smile and touch the brim of his well-worn Stetson.

"Thank you, Mr. Tanner. I can honestly say your ranch is spectacular. But what, may I ask, are we doing here?"

"Well, now…" Jake shifted in the saddle to face her directly. "I don't know about you, but nearly three hours in the saddle gives me a powerful appetite. I figured here we might do a bit better than beef jerky."

"Three hours?" Samantha repeated, and pushed Sabrina's hat from her head so it lay against her back. "Has it really been that long?"

The angles of his face moved slowly with his grin, and she found herself once more intrigued by the process. "I'll take that to mean you were so delighted with my company, time stood still."

She answered with a toss of her head. "I hate to tread on your ego, Jake, but the credit goes to Wyoming."

"Close enough for now." Reaching over, he plopped the brimmed hat back in place on Samantha's head and urged his mount into a canter.

Samantha stared after him in exasperation, watching the confidence with which he rode the Arabian. They moved like one form rather than horse and man. Scowling, she pressed her heels to the gelding's side and raced forward to join him.

As she reached his side, he skirted the ranch house and rode toward the buildings in the rear, following the left fork on a long, hard-packed road. A large, sleepy-eyed Saint Bernard rose from his siesta and romped forward to greet them. A deep, hoarse bark emitted from his throat. Jake halted in front of the stables. He slid off the Arabian's back, running his hand through the dog's thick fur as he hit the ground.

"Wolfgang's harmless." He acknowledged the loving, wet kisses with another brief caress and moved to the gelding's side. "He's just a puppy."

"A puppy," Samantha repeated. "You don't see many hundred-and-fifty-pound puppies." Tilting her head, she gave the overgrown baby a thorough examination before she brought her leg over the saddle to dismount.

Jake gripped her waist as she made her descent, holding her off the ground a moment as if she were weightless. As her boots touched earth, she was turned around and drawn against a hard chest. She tilted her head to inform him that his assistance was unnecessary, but saw only a brief blur of his face before his lips captured hers.

Her mind whirled with the touch and scent of him. She felt as though she were falling into a deep well and her heart began to beat a mad tempo against her ribs. She clutched at his jacket in defense. Perhaps the kiss was brief. It could have lasted no more than a portion of a minute, but it felt like forever. She knew his mouth was warm and sure on hers while decades flew into centuries.

The strange sensations of timelessness and loss of control frightened her. She stiffened and began to struggle against his grasp. He released her immediately, staring down at her clouded blue eyes with a satisfied smile. The smile transformed terror into fury.

"How dare you?"

"Just testing, ma'am." His answer was complacent, as though the kiss had been no more than that, a traditional touching of lips.

"Testing?" she repeated, running an agitated hand through her hair. "Testing what?"

"I've always wanted to kiss a teacher." Grinning, he

gave her a friendly pat on the cheek. "I think there're some holes in your education."

"I'll show you holes, you conceited, high-handed—" her mind searched for something appropriately derogatory and settled on a generality "—*man*. If I didn't consider that kiss so insignificant, you'd be lying on your back checking out the sky."

He surveyed her as she trembled with a mixture of fury and wounded pride. He rubbed his chin thoughtfully. "You know, Sam, I almost believe you could do it."

"You can bank on it," she confirmed with an arrogant toss of her head. "And the next time you…" Feeling her arm sharply pulled, she glanced down to see the sleeve of her jacket captured in the awesome jaws of the Saint Bernard. "What'd you do, teach him to eat unwilling females?"

"He just wants to make your acquaintance," Jake laughed, as he led the horses to the stable to turn them over to one of his men.

Samantha was not normally timid, and her pride refused to allow her to call Jake to untangle her from the teeth of his puppy. She swallowed and spoke to her canine captor.

"Hello…Wolfgang, wasn't it?" she muttered. "I'm Sam. You, ah, wouldn't consider letting go of my jacket, would you?" The dog continued to stare with droopy, innocent eyes. "Well, that's all right," she said, trying out magnanimity. "It's just an old one, anyway. I'm very fond of dogs, you know." Tentatively, she brought her free hand up to touch the fur on his huge head. "Well, actually, I have a cat," she admitted in apology, "but I have absolutely no prejudices."

Though his expression did not alter, she decided it

was prudent to give him time for consideration. Her patience was rewarded when he released her sleeve and bathed her hand with his enormous tongue.

"Well, I see you two have made friends," Jake drawled, coming up behind her.

"No thanks to you," she said. "He might have eaten me alive."

"Not you, Sam," Jake disagreed, taking her hand and striding toward the house. "Too tough for Wolfgang's taste."

Jake led her to the back entrance through a paneled, tiled-floor mudroom and into the kitchen. A large square room, it was bright and cheery with tangerine curtains framing the wide windows. The pleasant-looking woman who stood by the sink smiled at Samantha. "Jake, you scoundrel, have you had this poor little lady out in the cold all this time?" Samantha met the warm brown eyes with a returning smile.

Jake grinned, unabashed. "Samantha Evans, meet Annie Holloway, my cook, housekeeper and best girl."

"Don't you try soft soaping me, you young devil." She brushed off his words with indulgent affection, but pleased color rose to her pudgy cheeks. "Thinks he can get around me with sweet talk. Pleased to meet you, Miss Evans." Samantha found her hand enclosed in a firm grip.

"Hello, Miss Holloway, I hope I'm not putting you out."

"Putting me out?" Annie let out a rich, full laugh, her ample bust heaving with the sound. "Isn't she the sweet one? Don't you be silly, now, and you just call me Annie like everyone else."

"Thank you, Annie." Samantha's smile warmed. "Everyone calls me Sam."

"Now that's a pretty thing," Annie commented, peering candidly into Samantha's face. "Yes, sir, a right pretty thing. You two run along," she commanded with an attempt at sternness. "Out of my kitchen. Lunch will be along, and I'll bring you in some tea to warm you up. Not you," she said with a scowl as Jake grimaced. "For the little lady. You don't need any warming up."

"Annie runs things," Jake explained as he led Samantha down a wide hall into the living room.

"I can see she does, even when she's securely wrapped around your little finger."

For a moment, his smile was so boyish and full of mischief, she nearly gave in to the urge to brush the curls from his forehead.

The paneling in the living room was light. The expanse of wood was broken by a large stone fireplace and wide windows framed with cinnamon-colored sheers. The dark gleaming furniture had been upholstered in gold, burnt sienna and rich browns. There was a comfortable hodgepodge of Hepplewhites and Chippendales with piecrust tilt-top tables and Pembrokes, ladder-back chairs and candlestands. In the center of the hardwood floor lay a wide rug of Indian design, so obviously old and handworked, that Samantha wondered if it had been his great-grandmother's fingers that had hooked it perhaps nearly a century ago. The room reflected a quiet, understated wealth, a wealth she somehow did not associate with the rangy, brash cowboy side of Jake.

A Charles Russell painting caught her eye. She turned to study it, attempting to sort out her new impressions of this complex man. Turning back, she found him watching her reaction with unconcealed amusement.

"I have a feeling you were expecting bearskins and oilcloth."

Samantha focused her attention on the inviting fire. "I never know what to expect from you," she muttered.

"No?" He dropped his lanky form into a wing-backed chair and pulled out a long, thin cigar. "I thought you were pretty bright."

Samantha seated herself in the chair across from him, keeping the warmth and hiss of the fire between them. "This is a lovely room, very appealing and very warm."

"I'm glad you like it." If he noticed her blatant change of subject, he gave no sign. Lighting his cigar, he stretched out his legs and looked totally relaxed and content.

"I have a weakness for antiques," she continued, deciding the topic was safe and impersonal.

He smiled, the smoke curling lazily above his head. "There's a piece in one of the bedrooms you might like to see. A blanket chest in walnut that was brought over from the East in the 1860s."

"I'd like that very much." She returned his smile and settled back as Annie wheeled a small tea cart into the room.

"I brought you coffee," she said to Jake, and passed him a cup. "I know you won't take tea unless you douse it with bourbon. Something not quite decent about doing that to a good cup of tea."

"Tea is an old ladies' drink," he stated, ignoring her rapidly clucking tongue.

"How do you think Sabrina looks?" Samantha asked him when Annie had bustled back to the kitchen.

"I think you worry too much about her."

She bristled instinctively before replying. "Perhaps you're right," she surprised herself by admitting. "Our mother always said Bree and I were mirror images, meaning, I discovered after a while, opposites."

"Right down to Sabrina being right-handed, and you being left."

"Why, yes." She looked at him in faint surprise. "You don't miss much, do you?" He merely shook his head and gave her an enigmatic smile. "Well," she plunged on, not sure she liked his expression, a bit like a cat who already had the mouse between his paws. "I suppose the summary of my discrepancies was that I could never keep the hem in my white organdy party dress. You'd have to know my mother to understand that. She would have Bree and me all decked out in these frilly white organdy dresses and send us off to a party. Bree would come back spotless, pure and angelic. I'd come back with dirt on my frills, bloody knees and a trailing hem."

During her story, Jake's smile had widened. The coffee in his cup cooled, unattended as he watched her. "There're doers and there're watchers, Samantha. I imagine you had fun scraping up your knees."

As ridiculous as it seemed, she felt she'd just been complimented, and was both pleased and faintly embarrassed.

"I suppose you're a doer, too." She dropped her eyes. "You couldn't run a ranch like this and not be. Cattle ranching sounds romantic, but I imagine it's long hours, hot summers and cold winters. I don't suppose it's really all that different from the way it used to be a hundred years ago."

"The range isn't open anymore," he corrected. "You don't find cowboys going off to Texas to punch cattle with a ten-dollar horse and a forty-dollar saddle." He shrugged and set his empty cup on the table beside him. "But some change slow, and I'm one who likes to take my time."

She was frowning into his smile when Annie announced lunch. It was not until they were settled in the dining room that she spoke directly to him again, pressing him for more details on how the ranch was run.

He explained how roundups, which had once been accomplished on the vast open range with only men and horses, were now aided by fences and technology. But it was still men and ponies who moved the cattle into corrals. Over a few states there were still strongholds of riders and ropers, men who cultivated the old technique and blended it with the new. On the Double T, Jake employed the best of both.

"If roundups aren't what they once were, they still accomplish the same end. Getting the cattle together and branding them."

"Branding?" Samantha interrupted, and shuddered.

"Your Philadelphia's showing, Sam." He grinned. "Take my word for it, branding is a good deal more unpleasant for the branders than the brandees."

She decided to ignore his comments and changed the subject abruptly. "Bree told me your ranch borders Dan's. This place must be huge for it to have taken us three hours to get here."

Jake's deep, rich laughter filled the room, and she decided unwillingly that she liked the sound very much. "It's a pretty big spread, Sam, but if you take the straight road north for the Lazy L, you can be here in twenty minutes on horseback. I took you on a big circle today," he explained. "Just a small taste of our part of the Laramie Basin."

They lingered over coffee, relaxed in each other's company.

"We'd better get started back," Jake said after a while. He rose and extended his hand. Her own slipped without hesitation into it as he pulled her to her feet. When she looked up at him, her smile was warm and spontaneous.

"Annie was right, that's a pretty thing." He lifted his hand and traced his fingers over the curve of her mouth. She started. "Now don't go skittish on me, Sam, I'm not going to use spurs and a whip."

His mouth lowered, gentle and persuasive. One hand held hers while the other circled the back of her neck to soothe with coaxing fingers. She had only to sway forward to feel his body against hers, had only to lift her hand to bring his mouth firmer and warmer on hers. Before the choice could be made, he drew her away and the decision was taken out of her hands.

"Sam." He shook his head as if exasperated and lightly amused. "You're enough to try a man's patience."

With this, he pulled her through to the kitchen.

"Well, so you're off again." Annie wiped one hand on her apron and wagged the other at Jake. "And don't be keeping her out in that cold too long."

"No, ma'am," Jake returned with suspicious respect.

"Thank you, Annie," Samantha broke in. "Lunch was wonderful."

"Well, now, that's fine, then." She gave Samantha a friendly pat on the cheek. "You just come back real soon, and you say hi to Sabrina for me, and that young rascal Dan, too. As soon as she's fit again, I'll be coming by to see her. Oh, Jake, I clean forgot." Annie turned to him and sighed at her absentmindedness. "Lesley Marshall called earlier, something about dinner tonight. I told her you'd give her a call, then it went straight out of my mind."

"No problem," Jake said easily. "I'll get back to her later. Ready, Sam?"

"Yes, I'm ready." She kept her smile in place, though

a large black cloud seemed to have suddenly smothered the sunshine.

Lesley Marshall, she mused, automatically going through the motions of securing her hat and coat. That was the woman Bree had predicted would marry Jake when he decided to settle down. Why should it matter to me? She straightened her spine and accompanied Jake to the waiting horses. I have absolutely no interest in Jake Tanner's affairs.

He's probably had dozens of girlfriends. Well, it's no concern of mine. Vaulting into the saddle, she followed as he set off down the hard-packed road.

They spoke little on the return journey. Samantha pretended an engrossment with the scenery that she was far from feeling. Unhappily, she realized Wyoming's magic was not quite enough to lift her flagging spirits. Snow-capped peaks glistened just as brightly in the late afternoon sun, and the land still spread and beckoned, but as she surveyed them now she felt strangely depressed.

It had been an unusual day, she concluded. Jake had annoyed her, charmed her, angered her and delighted her, all in a handful of hours. His kiss had aroused excitement and a deeper feeling she could not explain.

The knowledge that he was dining with another woman that evening depressed her beyond belief. She stole a sidelong look at his lean, tanned features.

He was undeniably attractive, she admitted, pulling her eyes away from him before he could sense her study. There was a powerful aura of virility about him, which alternately intrigued her and made her wary. Perhaps it would be wise to avoid his company. He confused her, and Samantha liked to know precisely where she stood with a man. She wanted to call the shots, and she realized that this man would never allow anyone to call the shots but himself.

She would keep her distance from now on. Let him spread his charm over this Lesley Marshall, or any of the other women who were undoubtedly thirsting for his attention. Samantha Evans could get along very easily without him. As the Lazy L grew closer, she resolved to be polite and casually friendly to her escort. After all, she reflected, there was no reason to be rude. He was perfectly free to dine with whomever he chose; his life was most assuredly his own. Besides, she added to herself, if she had anything to say about it, they would be seeing very little of each other in the future.

When they reached the ranch, she dismounted, handing Spook's reins to a waiting cowboy. "I had a wonderful time, Jake." Samantha's smile was faultless in its social politeness as he walked her toward the ranch house, leading his stallion behind him. "I appreciate your time and hospitality."

Jake's mouth lifted at one corner. "It was my pleasure, ma'am."

If there was a mockery in his tone, Samantha chose to ignore it. Reaching the back door, she turned to smile at him again as he stood, tall and lean, beside the gleaming chestnut.

"Would you like some coffee before you go?" she invited, determined to be polite.

"No, thanks, Sam." He continued to watch her, his eyes shaded by the brim of his hat. "I'd best be getting along."

"Well." She breathed a small sigh of relief when her hand touched the doorknob and safety was in easy reach. "Thanks again."

"Sure." He nodded briefly and turned to his horse,

paused and turned back to look at her with a penetrating intensity that turned her legs to water. When he spoke, it was soft and final. "I mean to have you, you know."

Several moments of silence passed before she could summon up an answer.

"D-Do you?" Her voice was a shaky whisper, unlike the coolly flippant tone she would have wished for.

"Yes, ma'am." He vaulted onto the chestnut's back and pushed the Stetson back on his head so that she had a disturbingly clear view of his eyes. "I do," he confirmed, turning his mount and galloping away.

Chapter Five

Often over the next few days, Samantha told herself that her reaction to Jake's kiss had been merely a passing physical attraction. She was a normal woman, wasn't she? So why feel guilty about it?

Jake Tanner *was* a very attractive man. *Too attractive,* she added to herself. And he knew too much about charming women. The fact that Jake was abrasive, smug and irritating had nothing to do with the way she had acted. It had just been a passing fancy. *And would certainly not occur again.*

Finally Sabrina was allowed up from the confinement of her bed. Samantha decided it was safe to leave her sister for a few hours. With a light heart, she saddled Spook and set off from the ranch at a brisk canter. For a while she enjoyed the feeling of Spook's hooves pounding the hard road. The sky hung low above her, and heavy, leaden gray clouds draped the distant mountains in mysterious gloom. There was a stillness, a waiting in the air, unnoticed by Samantha in her eagerness to escape the close confines of the house.

She rode swiftly past the bored, white-faced cattle and the stretches of barbed wire, eager to explore new territory, tasting the joy of motion and freedom. The mountains, grim sentinels above her, stood stone-gray under the unbroken sky. Remembering Dan's instructions, Samantha took care to mark her route, choosing a clump of rocks, a cottonwood tree with a broken limb, and a gnarled stump as landmarks for her return trip.

She led her mount to a crest of a hill, watching as a jackrabbit, startled by her intrusion, darted across the road and out of sight.

Nearly an hour passed before the first flakes began to drift lazily from sky to earth. She stopped and watched their progress in fascination. The snow fell slowly. Lifting her face, she let it caress her cheeks and closed lids. The air was moist, coming to life around her, and she stirred herself out of her dream.

"Well, Spook, this is my first Wyoming snow. I'd like to stay here all day and watch it fall, but duty calls. We'd better head back." Patting the horse's neck, she turned back toward the ranch.

They rode slowly. Samantha was enchanted with the fairyland that was forming around her. Cottonwoods and aspens were draped in white, their branches a stark contrast to the brilliant etchings of snow. The ground was cloaked quickly. Though the beauty was breathtaking, Samantha began to feel uncomfortably alone.

She took Spook into a canter. The sound of his hooves was soft and muffled. The quiet surrounding her was unearthly, almost as though the world had ceased to breathe. She shivered, suddenly cold in the warm confines of her jacket. To her annoyance, she saw that in her preoccupation with the landscape she had taken a wrong turn, and she began to backtrack, berating herself for carelessness.

The snow increased, plunging down from a sky she could no longer see. She cursed herself for having come so far, fighting down a sudden surge of panic. "Don't be silly, Sam," she spoke aloud, wanting the reassurance of her own voice. "A little snow won't hurt you."

The cold became more intense, piercing the layers of her skin. Samantha tried to concentrate on steaming coffee and a blazing fire as she looked around for a familiar landmark. Nothing was the same as it had been. She clamped her lips tight to still the chattering of her teeth, telling herself that it was impossible that she could be lost. But it was a lie. The trees and hills around her were strangers blanketed in white.

The snow fell thickly, a blinding white wall blocking her vision. A wind had sprung up, breaking the silence with its moans and tossing snow, hard and bitter, into her face. She was forced to slow the gelding to a walk, afraid of tangling with the sharp teeth of barbed wire she was unable to see. Her teeth savaged her lips in an effort to control a growing terror.

It's so cold, she thought as she began to shiver convulsively, so unbelievably cold.

The snow had soaked through the wool of her slacks and slipped mercilessly down the neck of her coat. She hunched her shoulders against the driving wind. Snow was everywhere, blocking her in and seeping into her clothing.

She let the reins hang limp, praying that the horse's instinct would guide him back to the warm shelter of his stables. They trudged on, the vortex of white that had begun so innocently now whirling around her. Time and direction had lost all meaning, and though she tried calling out, her voice was soundless against the fierce breath of the wind.

Now she felt the cold. Her body was numbed into submission. Her mind was following suit. The swirling snow was hypnotic, and a growing lethargy was creeping over her. In a small part of her mind, she knew her survival depended on remaining alert.

Horse and rider plodded on. There was no time, no world beyond the unbroken curtain of white. Samantha felt her eyelids growing heavy, but she willed them open with all her strength. The snow piled onto her back, weighing her down until she slumped onto the gelding's mane and clung to him. Staring down at the gelding's front hoof, she began to count each drudging step that Spook took as he continued his slow progress through the blinding storm.

Samantha's concentration on the horse's halting steps began to fade.

If I close my eyes, she thought dimly, I won't see all that white and I can sleep. Oh, how I want to sleep....

The snow was talking, she mused deliriously. Well, why not? It's alive. Why should it sound like Jake? Helplessly, she began to giggle. Well, why shouldn't it? *They both play to win.*

"Samantha!" The snow was shouting at her. "Open your eyes. Stop that insane laughing and open your eyes!"

Wearily, she forced herself to obey the command. Dimly she saw the blur of Jake's features through the flurries of snow. "You would be the last thing I see before I die." With a moan, she closed her eyes again and sought the silence.

"Tell Dan we've found her," Jake shouted against the howl of the wind. "I'm taking her back to the Double T."

The darkness was comforting. Samantha gave herself over to it, feeling herself falling slowly into a hole with no bottom. She burrowed deeper into it. Her consciousness swam to the surface.

Bemused, she looked around a dimly lit room. The snow that pooled around her was not snow at all, but a bed with a thick, warm quilt. She allowed her heavy lids to close again.

"Oh, no, you don't." The lids opened fractionally, and Samantha saw Jake standing in the open doorway.

"Hello."

His mouth thinned as he advanced to the bed to tower over her. It seeped through the misty reaches of her brain that he was angry. She stared at him with lazy fascination.

"What in heaven's name were you doing out in such a storm? I've seen some dumb stunts, but taking a joyride in the middle of a blizzard tops them all."

She wanted to ask him to stop shouting at her, but lacked the energy. "Where am I?" was all she could find to say.

Sitting on the edge of the bed, he drew her head from the pillow, then held a cup to her lips. "Here, drink this first, then we'll talk."

The brandy was warm and strong, and she sputtered and gasped as he poured it down her throat. Its power spread through her, pushing back the mists of unconsciousness.

"Now, to answer your question, you're at the Double T." Jake set the empty cup aside, and laid her head back on the mound of pillows.

"Oh."

"Is that all you can say?" He was shouting again. He took her shoulders as if to shake her. "Just 'Oh'? What in heaven's name were you doing out there?"

"It seems so long ago." She frowned in concentration, closing her eyes with the effort. "It wasn't snowing when I left," she said in weak defense.

"Wasn't snowing?" Jake repeated, incredulous. "Samantha, didn't you see the sky? Where are your brains?"

"There's no excuse for insults," she retorted with a small flash of spirit.

"No excuse for insults? Are you stark raving mad? Do you realize what nearly happened to you?" His hands retreated to his pockets, as though he could barely prevent them from throttling her. "Out here in the middle of a blizzard, half-frozen and helplessly lost! It was a miracle we found you. A little longer, and you'd be lying somewhere buried in it, and no one would have found what was left until spring. Dan was half out of his mind when he got through to me and told me you'd gone out in this."

"Bree?"

"Knew nothing." He whirled to face her again. "She was taking a nap. It never occurred to her that you had gone out with a storm brewing." He laughed harshly.

The memory of the snow and the terror washed over her, and she began to shake. "I'm sorry," she managed through the tears that threatened to flow. With a brief oath, Jake ran a hand through his hair. He closed the distance between them and gathered her in his arms. "Samantha," he murmured against her hair. "What hell you put us all through."

"I'm sorry," she repeated, and she began to sob in earnest. "I was so scared, so cold."

He rocked and murmured words she could not understand, his lips brushing through her hair and over her damp cheeks until they met hers. The kiss mingled with the salt of her tears. "I've gotten your shirt all wet," she murmured after a while.

He let out a deep breath. She saw his smile begin to spread before he rested his brow against hers. "That is without doubt the worst calamity of the day."

"It's dark," she said with sudden realization. "How long...?"

"Too long. What you need now is rest."

"Spook?" she began as he lay her down on the pillows.

"Is sleeping off his adventure in the stables. He looks a lot better than you, I might add."

"I want to thank you for everything." Samantha reached for his hand. In that instant, she discovered there was nothing covering her save sheets and blankets. "M-My clothes," she stammered, drawing the quilt higher in a purely feminine gesture that caused Jake's mouth to twitch.

"Soaked through, Sam." Rising, he stood, rocking gently on his heels. "It was necessary to get you warm and dry."

"Did Annie?" she managed a smile at the thought of the matronly presence of Jake's housekeeper. "I seem to have put everyone to a lot of trouble. Will you thank her for me?"

"Well, Sam, I'd like to oblige you, but Annie left yesterday for Colorado to spend a week with her nephew." Jake's grin broadened.

"Then who—?" The question caught in her throat, and her eyes became round and impossibly dark. "Oh, no," she whispered, closing her eyes in humiliation.

"No need to be embarrassed, Sam, you have a beautiful body."

"Oh, no." With a moan, she squeezed her eyes tighter.

"Now, don't you fret." His tone took on the light insolence of the cowboy she'd met a month before in the cold March sunset. "When I took off your clothes and rubbed you down, it was strictly medical. I'd do as much for any stray." He patted her hand, and her eyes opened warily at his touch.

"Yes, of course." Moistening her lips, she attempted to see the practical side. "I, well…thank you."

"'S all right, don't give it a thought." He moved toward the door, then paused and turned back. "Now, the next time I get your clothes off, my purpose'll be completely different."

He strolled casually from the room, leaving a speechless Samantha.

Chapter Six

Samantha looked around her. She remembered with a shock that she was in Jake's house—and, worse yet, *naked* in bed. She was debating the wisdom of wrapping the quilt around her and searching for more appropriate attire when footsteps sounded down the hall outside her room. She pulled the covers to her chin as Jake strode through the open door.

"So, you're awake. How do you feel?"

"Fine." Her respiratory system behaved erratically as he continued toward her and dropped onto the bed. "I'm just fine," she repeated, then added unnecessarily, "It's still snowing."

"So it is," he agreed without taking his eyes from her face. "Slowing down, though."

"Is it?" She forced herself to look out the window.

"The worst'll be over by midday." He reached up and pried one of her hands loose from the death grip on the blankets. "Calm down, Sam, I'm not going to ravish you, I'm going to check your pulse."

"I'm fine," she repeated again.

"Far from fine, Samantha," he corrected. His fingers brushed against her cheek, as if to test its substance. "The first thing is to get some food into you." Rising, he held out a large flannel robe that he had dropped at the foot of the bed. "You'd probably feel better if you had something on." His smile was gently mocking. "Can you manage to get into this by yourself?"

"Of course." Plucking it from him, she kept a cautious grip on the blankets. "I'm not an invalid."

"You best think like one. Put that on, then get back in bed. I'll bring you some breakfast."

"I don't..."

"Don't argue." The two words were swift and final. He was gone before she could say another word.

He had shut the door, however, and grateful for the concession, Samantha tossed back the covers and slipped her arm into the robe. When she stood, the room swayed and spun around her. She sank back onto the bed and slipped her other arm into its sleeve, pulling the robe around her before attempting to stand again. Her limbs felt heavy and weak, and she noted with puzzlement that her ankle was throbbing lightly. Gripping one poster of the bed until the room steadied, she rolled up the sleeves of the robe several times until her hands became visible, then moved to the bathroom to study herself in the mirror.

The sight of her own face caught at her breath. Her skin seemed nearly transparent, her eyes darker and larger in contrast. The breath of color that resulted when she pinched her cheeks faded instantly. She ran a hand through her hair falling on the shoulders of the dark green robe.

It must be his, she realized, looking down at the sleeves, which swallowed her arms, and the hem, which fell nearly to her ankles. A strange sensation flowed over her as she felt the material on her skin. Turning away from the mirror, she studied the bed.

"I'm not getting in there again," she muttered, and with a small gesture of defiance belted the robe more securely. "I can eat at the table like a normal person."

After a moment, her progress down the hall seemed more of a crawl than a walk. Her legs were heavy with a weakness which infuriated her. The stillness of the house vibrated around her, playing havoc with her nerves, and the need to hear the natural, everyday movements of another human being became increasingly important. She cursed the waves of giddiness that swam around in her head, forcing her to stop time after time to rest her hand against the wall.

"This is ridiculous."

"You're right."

The harsh agreement came from behind as Jake's hands gripped her shoulders.

"What are you doing out of bed?"

"I'm all right." She swayed against his chest. He gripped her waist to support her, and she rested her hands on his arms.

"I'm just a bit wobbly, and I'm having some trouble with my ankle."

He let his gaze travel down to rest on her bare feet. "Probably turned it when you fell off the horse."

"I fell off Spook?" Her expression was incredulous.

"You were unconscious at the time. Now, get back in

bed and stay there." Effortlessly, he swept her into his arms, and she laid her head against his shoulder.

"Jake, don't make me go back to bed. It's so quiet in there, and I don't feel like being alone now."

He bent and brushed lips that parted in confusion. "If you think you can sit in a chair without sliding on your face, you can come in the kitchen."

She nodded, sighed and closed her eyes. "I hate being so much trouble."

She felt him shift her in his arms before he began the journey down the hall. "I knew you were trouble the minute I set eyes on you."

"Don't tease, Jake, I'm trying to thank you."

"What for?"

She lifted a hand to his cheek, turning his face so that he would look at her. "For my life."

"Then take better care of it in the future," he suggested.

"Jake, please, I'm serious. I owe you…"

"Nothing, you owe me nothing." His voice had hardened with annoyance. "I don't want your gratitude." They had reached the kitchen, and he placed her in a chair at the table. "Which ankle did you hurt?" He crouched down by her feet.

"The left one. Jake, I— Ouch!"

"Sorry." He grinned up at her, then rested his hand with friendly ease on her knee. "It's not swollen."

"It still hurts," she said stubbornly.

"Keep off it, then," he advised with simple logic, and turned away to finish breakfast.

"You've got some bedside manners, Dr. Tanner," she observed sharply.

"Yes, ma'am, so I've been told." When he turned

to face her, his smile was bland. "Tell me, Sam, does Sabrina have a mole on her left hip, too?"

Color flooded her face. "You…you…" she faltered, and clutched the robe tight at her throat.

"Around here, we call that locking the barn door after the cow's got loose. Have some coffee," he invited with sudden graciousness, pouring a cup and setting it on the table. "Start on this bacon," he ordered, sliding a plate in front of her. "That color didn't last long, you're pale as a ghost again. When did you eat last?"

"I…at breakfast yesterday, I guess."

"Toast and coffee, I imagine," he said disgustedly. "It's a wonder you can manage to sit up at all. Eat." He plucked a piece of bacon from the plate and held it out to her. "I'll have some eggs ready in a minute."

Obediently, she accepted the bacon and took a bite. "Are you going to have something?"

"In a minute," he answered absently, involved with breaking and beating eggs in a bowl.

With the first bite of bacon, Samantha realized she was ravenous. Through her preoccupation with food, she watched Jake cook with a deftness that amused and surprised her.

In a moment, he sat across from her, his plate piled high. She wondered how he could eat with such abandon and remain hard and lean.

She watched him under the cover of her lashes, and the thought came unbidden into her mind that never before had she shared the breakfast table with a man. The intimacy of their situation washed over her; the scent of bacon and coffee drifting through the air, the house quiet and empty around them, the soft flannel of his robe against her skin, the faint masculine scent of him clinging to it. It was as if they were lovers, she thought suddenly, as if they had shared the night, and now they were sharing the morning. Her face grew warm.

"I don't know what thought put roses back in those cheeks, Sam, but keep it up."

Her eyes lifted to his, and she had the uncomfortable feeling that he knew very well what road her thoughts had taken. She dropped her eyes to her plate. "I should call Bree and let her know I'm all right."

"Phones are out," he said simply, and her eyes flew back to his.

"The phones are out?" she repeated.

No telephone, her mind said again. Without a telephone, they might as well be on an island a thousand miles from anyone. Their isolation was complete, and the snow was still falling as though it would never stop.

"With a storm like this, it's not surprising to lose the phones. Power's out, too. We're on generator. Don't worry about Sabrina, she knows you're with me." His words did nothing to erase her tension.

"When…when do you think I'll be able to get back?"

"Couple of days," he returned with an easy shrug, and sipped his coffee. "The roads'll have to be cleared after the storm lets up, and you're not in any shape to travel through a mess like that yet. In a day or two, you'll be more up to it."

"A couple of days?"

He leaned back comfortably in his chair, his voice smooth as a quiet river. "Of course, by then you'll be hopelessly compromised, not a scrap of your sterling reputation left. Alone with me for two or three days, without Annie to add a thread of decency to the situation." His eyes traveled down her slim figure. "Wearing my bathrobe, too." He shook his head. "Not too many years back, I'd have had to marry you."

"Thank goodness for progress," she retorted smartly.

"Oh, I don't know, Sam." His sigh was convincing. "I'm an old-fashioned sort of man."

"It's only a matter of circumstance that we're alone here in the first place." With great dignity, she folded her arms. "And I've hardly been compromised, as you so quaintly put it."

"No?" He watched her through lazily narrowed eyes. "So far, I've undressed you, tucked you in and fixed your breakfast. Who knows what that might lead to?"

His smile might have been lazy, but it was full of meaning. Suddenly Samantha found it difficult to swallow.

"Relax, Sam." His laugh was full of arrogant enjoyment. "I told you I mean to have you, but it's not in my plans to take on a pale child who barely has the strength to stand." He paused, lit one of his long, thin cigars and blew smoke at the ceiling. "When I make love to you, I want you to have your wits about you. I don't want you passing out in my arms."

The man's arrogance was amazing! "You conceited mule," she began. "How dare you sit there and tell me you're going to make love to me? You seem to think you're irresistible! Well, you have another think coming—"

"I'm going to remind you of that one day, Sam," Jake said mildly as he crushed out his cigar. "Now, I think you better lie down again. You're not quite up to sparring with me yet."

"I do not have to lie down. And I certainly don't need you carting me around. I can manage." She stood up, then was forced to grasp the table as the room revolved around her.

"You don't look ready to turn cartwheels, teacher," Jake observed as he took her arm.

"I'm all right." Her hand, which she had lifted to push him away, lay weakly on his chest for support. He tilted her chin, and he was no longer smiling. "Samantha, sometimes you have to be strong enough to let someone else take care of things. You're going to have to hand over the reins to me for a couple of days. If you fight it, you're only going to make it harder on yourself."

With a sigh, she allowed her head to fall against his chest, not protesting as his arms encircled her. "Do I have to like it?"

"Not necessarily." He gave a short laugh and lifted her easily and carried her back to bed.

Her small spurt of energy deserted her. With an odd feeling of contentment, she settled down under the covers. She was asleep even before his lips had lightly touched her forehead in a farewell kiss…

"I was beginning to think you'd sleep through the night."

She turned her head quickly. Jake was sitting across the room, the smoke of his cigar spiraling upward, the flickering lights from the fire shooting specks of gold into his eyes. Samantha brushed the tousled hair from her face and struggled into a sitting position.

"It's dark," she said. "What time is it?"

He glanced at the gold watch on his wrist and took a slow drag from his cigar. "It's a bit past six."

"Six? I've slept for hours. I feel as if I've slept for weeks."

"You needed it." Tossing the stub of his cigar into the

mouth of the fire, Jake rose and moved toward her. His concerned eyes roamed over her sleep-flushed cheeks and heavy eyes. Gradually, his expression lightened, the angles of his face moving into a satisfied smile. "Your color's coming back." He took her wrist, and her eyes dropped from his to study the dancing flames of the fire. "Pulse's a bit jumpy." The smile reflected in his voice. "Strong though. Hungry?"

"I shouldn't be." She forced her eyes to meet his. "I've done nothing but lie around all day, but I'm starved."

He smiled again, lifting her without comment. She felt small and vulnerable in his arms, a sensation that was both pleasant and disturbing. She found it difficult to resist the impulse to rest her head against the strong curve of his shoulder. Instead, she concentrated on the sharp, clean lines of his profile.

"I'm sure I can walk. I really feel fine."

"I doubt it." She could feel his warm breath on her face. "Besides, you seem to fit in my arms pretty well."

Finding no quick comeback to this comment, she took the journey to the kitchen in silence.

Leaning back in her chair, replete and content, Samantha sipped the cool white wine in her glass and gave Jake a nod of approval.

"You're going to make some woman a terrific husband. You're an outstanding cook."

"I think so." He nodded smugly. "My wife wouldn't have to be a gourmet cook," he added with casual consideration. "I'd demand other qualities."

"Adoration," Samantha suggested. "Obedience, unswerving loyalty, solicitude."

"That's all right for a start."

"Poor woman."

"Of course, I don't want her to be a doormat. Let's say I like a woman who knows how to think, one who doesn't pretend to be anything but who she is. Of course," he added, finishing off his wine, "I'm also partial to good looks."

"Well, so far it doesn't sound as though you're asking for much," Samantha giggled. "Just perfection."

"The woman I have in mind can handle it." He smiled broadly as he rose to pour coffee. Samantha stared at his back, feeling as though her heart had been dropped into a deep hole. *Lesley Marshall.* Her mind flashed the name like a neon sign in bright red letters.

Jake squelched her offer to do the dishes and swooped her from her chair and deposited her on the living room sofa.

"I feel useless," she muttered, helplessly cocooned by blankets and pillows. "I'm not made for lying around. I'm never sick." She gave Jake a sulky glare as if the entire matter was his fault. "I don't know how Bree coped with this sort of thing for a month."

"Could be you got her share of strength, and she got your share of patience," he considered, then shrugged. "Of course, I could be wrong." She heard his chuckle and the quiet click of his lighter as he lit a cigar.

Well, Samantha, she chided herself, you've really done it this time. Not only are you isolated with a man who constantly confuses you, but you can't even stand on your own feet. They say people learn about each other quickly when they live together, but I think it's going to take much more than one day to learn what this man is all about. *Living together,* she repeated, finding herself more amused than embarrassed. If Momma could see me now, we'd need a gallon of smelling salts.

Chapter Seven

Dawn was breaking. Pink and gold streaks split the hazy blue of the sky, and light tumbled through to rest on Samantha's closed lids.

Morning? Sitting up with a start, she shook her head vigorously to dispel the last remnants of sleep. Pulling on the borrowed robe, she set her feet on the floor, took three deep breaths and stood. When both the room and her head remained stable, she let out a long sigh of relief. Her legs were weak, but they no longer felt as if they would melt from under her, and the stiffness in her ankle had disappeared.

Mobility, she thought with arrogant glee. I've never truly appreciated it until now. Coffee. One thought followed swiftly on the trail of the other, and she deserted the room with the intention of making fantasy fact. A door opened as she passed it, and with a cry of surprise, she fell against the opposite wall.

Jake stood in the doorway, rubbing a towel briskly

through his damp hair, a terry-cloth robe tied loosely around his waist. "Morning, ma'am."

"You startled me." She swallowed, over-powered by the lean, bronzed maleness that the terry cloth did little to hide. He took a step toward her, and her breath caught instinctively. "I—I'm much better." She began to babble, unconsciously cowering against the smooth paneling. "I can actually walk a straight line."

Her voice died to a whisper as he stood directly in front of her. Her eyes were on a line with the tanned column of throat revealed by the open neck of the robe. His hand lifted her chin, and she trembled.

"Relax, Sam." His laughter sounded deep in his throat. "I just want to look you over. You must have the constitution of an elephant," he concluded with unflattering candor. "You look as though you've been on vacation instead of battling blizzards. One day's rest after nearly freezing to death. Most women would have been stretched out for a week."

"I'm not most women." She pushed his hand away from her face. "I'm not fragile and delicate, and I'm not going back to bed. I'm going to fix breakfast." She nudged him out of her path and started down the hall.

"Coffee's already on," he called after her.

Samantha had breakfast under way by the time Jake joined her. Clad in the less disturbing attire of corded jeans and flannel shirt, he watched her prepare the meal as he silently sipped at his coffee at the kitchen table.

"I'm getting used to having a pretty face across from me at breakfast," he commented when she sat down to join him.

"I'm sure I'm not the first," she commented with studied indifference. Nor, she added to herself, will I be the last.

"Nope," he agreed easily, "but there's something to be said for big blue eyes first thing in the morning."

"Blue eyes are common enough," she muttered, and lowered them to the contents of her plate. "Besides, this is hardly a long-term arrangement." He did not speak for a moment, and her fork moved restlessly among her eggs.

"We should have the road clear enough sometime tomorrow."

"Tomorrow?" she repeated. A hollow feeling spread through her stomach.

"There's a lot of snow out there, some of the drifts are small mountains. It's going to take a little time to move it."

"I see."

"Do you think you could manage on your own for a while today?"

"What? Oh, sure, I'll be fine."

"There's a lot I should see to. My foreman was in charge yesterday, but the men need all the help they can get." He was frowning. "Cattle need hay brought out to them. They haven't the sense to dig through to the grass. They'll just stand there and starve to death."

"I suppose the storm did a lot of damage."

"It's only minor from the reports I've gotten. We were hit worse a couple years ago."

"Reports?"

"One of my men came by yesterday afternoon to fill me in." Pouring more coffee in his cup, he reached for the cream. "You were asleep."

"Oh." Strange, she thought, there had been a ripple in their isolation and she had been totally unaware of it.

Lifting his cup, he studied her over the rim. "I don't like leaving you alone, especially with the phones out."

Her shoulders moved. "Don't worry about me, I'll be fine." Glancing up, she met his speculative gaze.

"I don't know how long I'll be gone."

"Jake, stop fussing. I feel fine."

He tilted his head to the side, his eyes still narrowed. "Stand up. I want to see how you feel for myself."

Before she realized his intent, his arms were around her, and his mouth was on hers. Her legs buckled.

His mouth was light, teasing, his teeth nibbling at the fullness of her bottom lip until she moaned from the exquisite agony. She gripped his shoulders as a dim light of control seeped into the darkness. Pulling away she shook her head in refusal.

"Now, Sam..." His voice was soft and persuasive, but the hands that descended to her hips were firm. "You wouldn't send a man out in the cold without something warm to remember, would you?"

Insistently, he brought her closer, molding her hips, exploring the soft roundness until she was pressed against him with exciting intimacy. His mouth closed over her protest, his tongue moving with slow devastation to tease hers until she felt the room spinning as wildly as it had the day before. Slowly, his hands ascended, his thumbs circling the side of her breasts while his mouth and tongue destroyed all resistance. She was straining against him, moving against him, reason forgotten. Her body heated urgently at his touch. Her sigh was a moan as his mouth descended to her throat. His lips tasted, lingered, traveled to new territories, the tip of his tongue moist and warm against her skin, erotic and devastating against her ear, until her mouth was desperate for its return to hers.

Her mouth was to go unsatisfied. He pulled her away

with the same arrogance as he had pulled her to him. Dazed and limp, she could do no more than stare up at him as her body throbbed with a myriad of newly discovered desires.

"You're learning fast, Sam. That was enough to keep any man moving through a six-foot snowdrift."

Furious, and humiliated by her own response, she drew back her hand.

"Now, Sam." He caught her wrist easily, holding it aloft, ignoring her efforts to escape. "You're not strong enough yet for wrestling. Give yourself a couple more days." Turning her hand over, his lips brushed her palm, causing her struggles to cease abruptly. "I'm going to bring in Wolfgang to keep an eye on you. Take it easy today, and try to remember, you're not as tough as you'd like to think."

Ruffling her hair as though she were a child, he disappeared into the adjoing mudroom.

Later Samantha indulged in a hot, steaming shower, attempting to forget, as she soaped her skin, the feel of Jake's hands running over her. In the bedroom, she noticed her clothes piled neatly on the spoon-back chair. She slipped them on and wandered through the house in aimless exploration, the Saint Bernard lumbering at her heels.

The house abounded in small, delightful treasures, an oak rolltop desk, a wall box with Friesian carving, a Windsor cradle. With a small sigh, she wondered if the latter had rocked the baby Jake. Opening yet another door, she found Jake's library.

It smelled of leather and age, and her fingers ran over volume after volume. She pulled out a small volume of love poetry and opened the cover. Light, feminine hand-writing adorned the top corner, and her mouth turned down at the inscription.

Darling Jake... To remind you.
> *Love, Lesley*

Shutting the book with a snap, Samantha held it for one heat-blinded movement over the wastebasket, then, grinding her teeth, stuck it firmly back in place.

"It makes no difference to me," she informed Wolf-gang. "She can give him a hundred books of poetry, she can give him a thousand books of poetry. It's her privi-lege."

She nudged the big dog with her toe. "Come on, Wolf-gang, let's get moving."

She returned to the living room and built up the fire, which had burned down to a hissing pile of embers. She curled up beside it.

One hour slipped into two, two slipped into three. Surely, Jake should be home by now, she told the silent clock as the hands crept past six. It was getting dark. Rising, Samantha stared out into the diminishing light.

What if something had happened to Jake? Her throat went dry, fear creeping along her skin. Nothing could happen to him, she told herself, running her hands over her arms to combat the sudden chill. He's strong and self-reliant.

But why am I so worried about him?

"Because," she said aloud, slowly, *"I love him. I've lost my mind and fallen in love with him."* Her hands lifted to cover her eyes as the weight of the knowledge crushed down on her. "Oh, how could I be so stupid?

Of all the men in the world, I had to fall in love with this one."

A man, she remembered, *who had chosen Lesley Marshall to be his wife.* Is that why I've felt pulled in two? Is that why I responded to him when I've never responded to anyone else? Looking out into the darkness, she shuddered. I might as well admit that I don't care about anything except his getting home....

When finally the sound of the outside door slamming reached her ears, she ran into the mudroom and threw herself at an astonished, snow-covered Jake.

"Sam, what's going on?" He tried to pull her away from his cold, wet jacket.

"I was afraid something had happened to you." Her voice was muffled against his chest, her cheek oblivious to the frigid dampness.

"Nothing's happened, except I'm half-frozen and soaked to the skin." Firmly now, he took her shoulders, disentangling himself from her arms. "You're getting covered with snow." His grip was gentle. She stared up at him with huge, swimming eyes. "I'm sorry I was gone so long, but things were piled up, and it's slow working in a mess like this."

Embarrassed by her outburst, she backed away. "You must be exhausted. I'm sorry, it was stupid to go on like that. It must come from being alone in the house all day." As she babbled, she was backing purposefully toward the door. "You probably want a shower and something hot to drink. I—I've got dinner on."

"Something smells good," he commented. His eyes roamed over her flushed face, and a smile spread over his features.

"S-Spaghetti," she stammered and despised herself. "I'll go finish it up."

Retreating into the kitchen, Samantha kept her back toward him when he emerged and announced casually that he would have a hot shower before dinner. She mumbled a vague reply, pretending a complete involvement with her dinner preparation. Listening to his receding footsteps, she let out a long, pent-up breath.

"Oh, idiot that I am," she sighed, and pushed her hair from her face in an angry gesture. The type of behavior she had displayed in the mudroom would only lead to trouble. She took a solemn oath to keep her emotions on a tight leash as long as Jake Tanner was around.

Tomorrow, she remembered, with a mixture of relief and disappointment, she would be back with her sister, and avoiding Jake would be a great deal easier. She had only to get through one more evening without making a fool of herself, and then she would sort out her thinking.

She was setting the table when Jake returned.

"If that tastes as good as it smells, I'll die a happy man." He lifted the lid on the pot and gave a sigh of approval. Grinning, he disappeared for a moment, then returned with a bottle of wine just as she was placing the pot on the table.

"A nice burgundy," he said, opening the bottle and setting out two glasses.

"Samantha, this is fantastic." He broke off eating long enough to give her a smile. "Where'd you learn to cook like this?"

"More of my mother's famous lessons."

"What else can you do?"

"Well, let's see. I do a rather superb swan dive, a very graceful arabesque, I can walk on my hands as easily as some walk on their feet, whip up an incredible quiche, and waltz without counting the time."

"I am suitably impressed. How did a woman of your talents spend the day?"

She sighed and grimaced and began to toy with her spaghetti. "Sleeping, mostly."

"Hmm." His cough did not quite cover his laugh.

After dinner, Samantha insisted on seeing to the washing up herself. She wanted to avoid the intimacy of working side by side with him in the confines of the kitchen.

When the last signs of the man had vanished, she walked down the hall to the living room. Jake was adding another log to the low, shifting blaze. As she entered, he turned to smile at her. "Want some brandy?"

"No, no, thank you." She took a deep breath and willed her legs to carry her to the sofa.

"Not in training, are you?" He moved from the hearth to join her on the sofa.

Smiling, she shook her head. "The fire's wonderful." Grasping the first topic that came to mind, she riveted her eyes on the flames. "I always wanted one in my apartment. We had one at home, and Bree and I used to pop corn over it. We'd always burn it, and…"

The rest of her rush of words was lost as Jake placed his finger under her chin and turned her face to his. His face moved closer, and when she jerked back in defense, his brow lifted in amusement. He bent toward her again, and again she started.

"I'm only going to kiss you, Samantha." His grip tightened on her chin. Sliding from her chin, his hand framed her face as his lips moved over hers, soft as a whisper. In spite of herself, she relaxed against him. Her lips parted, inviting him to explore, begging him to take.

"Samantha." Her name was a sigh.

"Kiss me again," she whispered slowly as she lifted her mouth to his.

With a low groan, he brought his lips down on hers. She clung to him, her body throbbing with heat, her heart desperate against his, while a part of her looked on, aghast, as she answered his kiss.

Her mouth clung, avid and sweet, to his. Dormant passion exploded into life until there remained only man and woman and the need, older than time, to love and be loved, to possess and be possessed.

He opened her shirt and claimed her breast. The first desperation mellowed into slow exploration as his fingers trailed lightly, drugging her with a new, delirious languor. His mouth moved to sample the taste of her neck, his face buried in the spreading lushness of her hair. She pressed against the rippling muscles of his back as his mouth and tongue and hands raged fire over her.

She felt rather than heard him say her name against her mouth, sensed rather than felt the tension enter his body before her lips were set free. Dimly, she heard the strident insistence of bells ringing as she groped to bring heaven back within reach.

"Hell of a time for them to fix the phones." She opened her eyes, dark as sapphires, and stared without comprehension. "There's nothing I'd like more than to ignore it, Samantha, but it might be important." Her lids fluttered in confusion. She could feel the warm raggedness of his breath against her cheek. "The phones have been out for two days, and there's a lot of damage out there."

His body left hers and took the warmth with it. She struggled to sit up, pulling her shirt closed. The hands that worked at the buttons were unsteady and, rising on weak legs, she sought the warmth of the fire. Pushing at tumbled hair, she wrapped her arms around her body and closed her eyes.

What had she done, losing herself that way? Tossing away pride like damaged goods! What if the phone hadn't rung? Her arms closed tighter. Does love always hurt? Does it always make a fool of you?

"Samantha." She whirled at the sound of her name, her arms still tight in protection. "It's Sabrina." Dropping her eyes from his, she moved into the hall.

Samantha picked up the phone and swallowed. "Hi, Bree." Her voice sounded strangely high-pitched to her ears, and her fingers gripped hard on the receiver.

"Sam, how are you?"

Taking a deep breath, she answered. "Fine. How *you* are is more important."

"Stronger every minute. I'm so glad you had the sense to head for the Double T when the snow started. The thought of you getting caught in that blizzard makes my blood turn cold."

"That's me, a steady head in a crisis." Samantha nearly choked on a gurgle of hysterical laughter.

"Are you sure you're all right? You sound strange. You aren't coming down with a cold, are you?"

"It's probably the connection."

"I thought they'd never get the phones fixed! I guess I just couldn't really relax until I'd talked to you and made sure you were safe! Of course, I know Jake would take care of you, but it's not the same as hearing your voice. I won't keep you, Sam, we'll see you tomorrow. By the way, I think Shylock misses you."

"Probably indigestion. Tell him I'll see him tomorrow." After replacing the receiver, she stared at it for a full minute.

"Samantha." She whirled again at Jake's voice, finding him watching her from the living room archway.

"I...ah...Bree seems fine." She avoided his eyes and toyed with the ink pot by the phone. She took a step backward as Jake advanced. "She said she thought Shylock misses me. That's quite an accomplishment, he's so self-sufficient and aloof."

"Samantha. Come, sit down." He held out his hand for hers. She knew if he touched her, she would be lost.

"No, no, I think I'll go to bed, I'm still not quite myself." Her color had ebbed again, leaving pale cheeks and darkened eyes.

"Still running, Sam?" The anger in his tone was well controlled.

"No, no, I..."

"All right, then, for the moment we seem to be at a stalemate." He captured her chin before she could avoid the gesture. "But we haven't finished by a long shot. Do you understand?"

She nodded, then broke away to flee to the sanctuary of her room.

Chapter Eight

As each day passed, Sabrina became more cheerful. Her features took on a roundness that gave her a contented appearance. And as Samantha watched her, she wondered if Sabrina possessed more strength than she had ever given her credit for. It was a sobering experience to see her usually dreamy sister grabbing life with determination and purpose while she herself couldn't seem to stop day-dreaming. Jake Tanner, she had to admit, was disturbing her days and sneaking into her dreams.

Stuffing her hands in her pockets, she scowled and continued her morning trudge to the mailbox. He meant to have her, did he? Well, Samantha Evans had no intention of being had by anyone, especially some annoying cowboy with too much charm for his own good…and fascinating green eyes, and that beautiful mouth….

Now the days began to lengthen. The sun grew in strength. Spring began to drift over the basin, greening the grass and teasing the crocuses to push their heads from the earth.

Scurrying down the hall as the doorbell interrupted her latest project—painting the nursery—Samantha wiped a few streaks of canary yellow on her jeans and opened the door.

The woman in the doorway smiled, her almond-shaped dark eyes making a thorough survey. "Hello, you must be Samantha. I'm Lesley Marshall."

The introduction was unnecessary, for with an instinct she had been unaware of possessing, Samantha had recognized the woman instantly. "Please, come in. It's still rather cold, isn't it?" She smiled, refusing to acknowledge the effort it cost her, and shut the nippy May air outside.

"I'm so glad to meet you at last." The dark eyes swept down, then up Samantha briefly. "I've heard so much about you." There was light amusement in her voice.

"Oh, really? I'm afraid I can't say the same." Her smile was faintly apologetic. "But, of course, I've been rather busy."

"I would have been by sooner, but I wanted to wait until Sabrina was more up to company."

"Bree's feeling much better these days. I'm sure she'll be glad to see you. Let me take your coat." Samantha hung the soft fur in the hall closet. Turning back to her visitor, she needed all her willpower to keep the social smile in place. The oatmeal slacks accentuated Lesley's sleekness; the trim cerise blouse set off her delicately feathered ebony hair and the perfect ivory of her skin. Desperately, Samantha wished a miracle would transform her navy sweatshirt with its Wilson High School banner and her paint-streaked jeans into something smart and sophisticated. As usual, her hair was escaping from its pins. She resisted the urge to bring her hand up to it and jam them in tightly.

"Bree's in the living room," she announced, knowing the pale gray eyes had studied her and found her wanting. "I was just about to make some tea."

Sabrina appeared at that moment, and Samantha gladly relinquished the role of hostess and escaped to the kitchen.

"So, she's beautiful," she grumbled to an unconcerned Shylock as she set the kettle on to boil. "So, she's smooth and sophisticated and makes me feel like a pile of dirty laundry." Turning, she lowered her face to his and scowled. "Who cares?" Shylock scowled back and went to sleep. Her thoughts wandered on. "I don't imagine he's ever laughed at her and patted her head as though she were a slow-witted child," she muttered as she gathered up the tea tray.

"Sabrina, you look wonderful," Lesley commented sometime later, sipping from a dainty china cup. "I'm sure having your sister with you must be very good for you. I don't have to tell you how concerned everyone has been."

"No, and I appreciate it. Sam's made everything so easy. I didn't have anything to do but sit and heal." She shot her sister an affectionate glance. "I don't know what we would have done without her these past two months."

Lesley followed her gaze. "Jake was telling me that you're a gym teacher, Samantha," she purred, managing to make this sound faintly disgusting.

"Physical education instructor," Samantha corrected, slipping into a vague southern drawl.

"And you were in the Olympics, as well. I'm sure it must have been fascinating. You don't look the sturdy, athletic type." The shrug of her shoulders was elegant, as was the small gesture of her hand. "I suppose one can never tell." Samantha gritted her teeth against a biting retort and was vastly relieved when, glancing at a slender gold watch, Lesley suddenly rose from her chair. "I must run now, Sabrina, I have a dinner engagement." Turning to Samantha, she offered a small smile. "So happy to have met you. I'm sure we'll be seeing each other again soon."

She left amidst a swirl of fur and the drifting scent of roses. Samantha sat back in the cushioned chair, relaxing for the first time in more than an hour.

"Well, what did you think of Lesley?" Sabrina questioned, shifting into a more comfortable position on the sofa.

"Very sophisticated."

"Come on, Sam." Sabrina grinned, her hands folding across the mound of her belly. "This is Bree."

"I don't know why I should have to comment, since you seem to be reading me so well. But—" her mouth curved into a rueful smile "—I suppose she's a bit smooth for my taste, and I didn't much care for the way she looked down that aristocratic nose at me."

"Actually, you really don't appear very sturdy." The observation was made with wide-eyed innocence. Samantha grimaced, pulling pins from her hair with a sharp tug until a cascade of golden brown tumbled in confusion about her shoulders.

"She'd have gotten her own back on that one if you hadn't sent me that 'Don't make a scene' look."

"Oh, well, Lesley can be nice enough when it suits her. Her father spoils her dreadfully. Her mother died when she was barely into her teens, and he transferred all his attention to Lesley. An overabundance of clothes, the best horses, and, as she grew older, cars and European tours and so on. Whatever Lesley wants, Lesley gets."

"Poor thing." The sarcasm caused her to feel spiteful and unjust. She sighed. "I suppose too much is as bad as too little. It was nice of her to come and see how you were getting along."

Sabrina's laughter floated through the room. "Sam, darling, I've never known you to be so slow." At her sister's puzzled expression, she continued. "Lesley didn't come to see me, she came to get a look at you."

"At me?" Finely etched brows disappeared under a fringe of bangs. "What for? I wouldn't think a lowly gym teacher from Philadelphia would interest Lesley Marshall."

"Any teacher who caught Jake Tanner's attention the way you have would interest Lesley. He wouldn't have gone out of his way to show just anyone around the ranch, you know."

A light color rose in Samantha's cheeks. "I think Miss Marshall's mind was put to rest after she got a good look." Her hand moved expressively down her sweat-shirt and jeans. "She'd hardly see any danger here."

"Don't underestimate yourself, Sam."

"No false modesty." Samantha's sigh came from no-where. "If a man's attracted to silk and champagne, cotton and beer are no competition. I'm cotton and beer, Bree," she murmured. Her voice trailed away with her thoughts. "I couldn't be anything else if I wanted to."

The following day, Samantha's continuing battle with her paints and brushes was interrupted by a more welcome visitor. Annie Holloway arrived at the ranch's kitchen door with a beaming smile and a chocolate cake.

"Hi." Samantha opened the door wide in welcome. "It's nice to see you again, and bearing gifts, too."

"Never like to come empty-handed," Annie announced, handing the thickly frosted cake to Samantha. "Dan always had a partiality for chocolate cake."

"Me, too." She eyed the cake hungrily. "He's not here right now, and I was just going to make some coffee. Do you suppose we could start without him?"

"Good idea." Setting herself comfortably in a chair, Annie waved a wide-palmed hand. "I reckon it wouldn't hurt for us to have a slice or two."

"Bree's taking a nap," Samantha explained as she put down the mugs of steaming coffee. "The doctor says she still has to lie down every day, but she's beginning to grumble about it a bit. Very quietly, of course."

"You're keeping an eye on her." Annie nodded and added two generous spoons of sugar to her coffee. "Dan says she's up to company now."

"Oh, yes, people have been dropping by now and again. Ah…" Samantha added cream to her own cup. "Lesley Marshall was by yesterday."

"I wondered how long it would be before Lesley hauled herself over to get a look at you."

"You sound like Bree." Sipping her coffee, Samantha shook her head. "I don't know why Lesley Marshall would want to meet me."

"Easy. Lesley's a mite stingy with her possessions, and she'd like to group Jake among them. She hasn't figured out yet that Jake is his own man, and all her daddy's money can't buy him for her. When my Jake picks his woman, he'll decide the time and place. He's always been an independent rascal. He was barely twenty when he lost his folks, you know." Samantha lifted her eyes to the warm brown ones. "It wasn't an easy time for him, they'd been close. They were a pair, Jake's folks, always squabbling and loving. You're a bit like her when she was a young thing." Annie smiled, her head tilting with it as Samantha remained silent. "Nobody's going to ride roughshod over you, at least not for long. I saw that straight off. She was stubborn as a mule with two heads, and there's times, though it's been better than ten years, I still miss her."

"It must have been hard on Jake, losing his parents and having all the responsibility of the ranch when he was still so young," Samantha murmured.

"Seemed to change from boy to man overnight, just out of college and still green. 'Course," she continued, "he'd been in the saddle since childhood and what he hadn't learned about ranching from his father and that fancy college, he learned from doing. He picked up the reins of that ranch with both hands. There's not a man who works for him wouldn't wrestle a long-horned bull if he asked them to. He can fool you with that easygoing way of his, but nobody gets the better of Jake Tanner. He runs the ranch like his life, and Lesley's going to find him a hard steer to rope and brand."

"Maybe it's more the other way around," Samantha suggested. Annie's response was prevented by the appearance at the kitchen door of the man in question.

He entered with the easy familiarity of an old friend.

"Howdy, ma'am." He broke the silence with a cocky smile, removed his battered Stetson and glanced at her attire. "Been painting?"

"Obvious, isn't it?" Samantha said sharply.

"Nice colors." He helped himself to a cup of coffee. "Are you going to part with another piece of that cake?"

"Jake Tanner!" Annie exclaimed in disgust. "You

should be ashamed, gobbling Dan's cake when you've got a perfectly good one of your own at home."

"Somebody else's always tastes better, Annie." He slipped off his jacket, tossing it over a hook, and grinned boyishly. "He won't miss it, anyway. I brought you and the cake over, didn't I? You're not going to begrudge me one little piece?"

"Don't waste those eyes on me, you young devil." Annie attempted to sniff and look indignant. "I'm not one of your fillies."

Jake's appearance had successfully shattered Samantha's peace of mind. After a reasonable period of politeness, she excused herself to Annie and Jake and went back to her job in the nursery.

Samantha's artistic talent was decidedly impressionistic. The floor, protected by plastic, was splotched and splattered, but the walls were coming to life with a joy of brilliant colors. Of the four walls, two were yellow and two were white, and each was trimmed with its opposite's color. On the one wall that was unbroken by door or windows, she had begun the construction of a wide, arching rainbow, carefully merging blues into pinks into greens.

Time passed, and in the quiet concentration of her work she forgot her preoccupation with Jake. Sitting on the ladder's top step, she paused, brushing the back of her hand across her cheek absently as she viewed the results.

"That's a mighty pretty sight."

She jolted, dropping the brush with a clatter, and would have fallen from the ladder had Jake's arms not gripped her waist and prevented the tumble.

"Sure spook easy," Jake commented, removing the dangerously sloshing paint bucket from her hand.

"You shouldn't come up behind a person like that," she complained. "I might have broken my neck." She wiped her hands on the legs of her jeans. "Where's Annie?"

"With your sister. She wanted to show Annie some things she's made for the baby." He set the bucket on the floor and straightened. "I didn't think they needed me."

"No, I'm sure they didn't. I need that paint, though, and the brush you made me drop." She glanced down, but his eyes remained on hers.

"I like the blue, especially that spot on your cheek," Jake said.

She rubbed at the offending area in annoyance. "If you'd just hand those things back to me, I could finish up."

"Green's nice, too," he said conversationally, and ran a finger over a long streak on her thigh. "Wilson High." His eyes lowered to the letters on her shirt. "Is that where you taught back east?"

"Yes." She shifted, uncomfortable that the name was prominent over her breasts. "Are you going to hand me my things?"

"What are your plans for tonight?" he countered easily, ignoring her request. She stared, completely thrown off balance by his unexpected question.

"I, ah, I have a lot of things to do." She searched her mind for something vital in her schedule.

"Things?" he prompted. His smile grew as his finger began to twist through a stray curl that had escaped its confines.

"Yes, things," she retorted, abandoning the attempt

to elaborate. "I'm going to be very busy, and I really want to finish this room."

"I suppose I could let you get by with that, even though we both know better. Well." He smiled and shrugged. "Come down and kiss me goodbye, then. I've got to get back to work."

"I will not kiss you goodbye…." she began, the words trailing off as he gripped her waist. Her hands automatically went to his arms, and he plucked her from her perch.

He lowered her slowly, his eyes never leaving hers, and her mouth was roughly claimed before her feet could reach the floor. His hands slipped under her shirt to roam the smooth skin of her back, pressing her closer as her body betrayed her and dissolved against his. Slowly he explored her soft, firm breasts, subtly rounded hips, lean thighs.

Every time, every time, her mind murmured. Every time he kisses me, I go under deeper, and one day I'll never find my way back. His teeth moved to nip at her ear and neck, searching and finding new vulnerabilities before returning to ravage her mouth again. Without will, without choice, she rested in his arms, surrendering to forces she could never defeat.

He drew her away, breaking the intimacy, but his mouth returned to hers to linger briefly before he spoke. "About tonight, Samantha."

"What?" she murmured as his tongue traced the softness of her lips.

"I want to see you tonight."

Jerking herself back into reality, she pressed her hands against his chest, but did not manage to break away. "No, no, I'm busy. I told you."

"So you did," he acknowledged, and his eyes narrowed in speculation.

His words were cut off by the sound of Sabrina's laughter drifting down the hall. Samantha wiggled against Jake's hold. "Let me go, will you?"

"Why?" He was grinning now, enjoying the flood of color in her cheeks.

"Because…"

"Don't ever play poker, Sam." The warning was curt. "You'd lose your shirt."

"I…I…"

"Sabrina's due in September, right?"

The sudden question caused her to blink in confusion. "Well, yes, she…"

"That gives you a little breathing space, Samantha." He leaned down, and his kiss was hard and brief and to the point. "After that, don't expect to get away so lightly."

"I don't know what…"

"You know exactly what I mean," he said interrupting. "I told you I meant to have you, and I always get what I want."

Her eyes flashed. "If you think I'm going to let you make love to me just because you say so, then you…"

The suggestion she would have made died as his mouth took hers again. She went rigid telling herself she would not amuse him with a response this time. As she told herself she would not, her arms circled his neck. Her body became pliant, her lips parted with the hunger she had lived with all through the past month. As he took, she offered more; as he demanded, she gave. Her own mouth was mobile, her own hands seeking, until it seemed the month of fasting had never been.

"I want you, I don't have to tell you that, do I?"

She shook her head, trying to steady her breathing as his eyes alone caused her pulse to triple its rate.

"We'll settle this in September, unless you decide to come to me sooner." She began to shake her head again, but the fingers on the back of her neck halted the movement. "If you don't come to me, I'll wait until after the baby's born and you've got that much off your mind. I'm a patient man, Sam, but…" He stopped talking as Annie and Sabrina stepped into the room.

"Well." Annie shook her head at the two of them. "I can see he's been giving you a hard time." She turned to Sabrina with a half-exasperated shrug. "He's always been fresh as a new-laid egg. This is going to be a beautiful room, Sam." She glanced around at Samantha's handiwork, nodding in approval. "Let go of the little lady now, Jake, and take me back home, I've got dinner to fix."

"Sure. I've already said what I came to say." He released Samantha with a last, penetrating look and strode from the room, calling a goodbye over his shoulder.

"Fresh as a new-laid egg," Annie reiterated, and echoing his goodbye, followed him.

When the guests had departed, Samantha began to gather up paint buckets and brushes.

"Sam." Walking over, Sabrina placed a hand on her sister's arm. "I had no idea."

"No idea about what?" Bending, she banged the lid securely on rose pink.

"That you were in love with Jake." The truth she had avoided for so long was out in the open now: She had fallen hopelessly, irrevocably in love with Jake Tanner! Standing, Samantha searched in vain for words of denial.

"We know each other too well, Sam," Sabrina said before she could answer. "How bad is it?"

Samantha lifted her hands and let them fall to her sides. "Terminal."

"Well, what are you going to do about it?"

"Do about it?" Samantha repeated. "What can I do about it? After the baby comes, I'll go back east and try to forget about him."

"I've never known you to give up without a fight," Sabrina spoke sharply. At the unexpected tone, Samantha's brows rose.

"I'd fight for something that belonged to me, Bree, but I don't move in on someone else's territory."

"Jake's not engaged to Lesley Marshall. Nothing's official."

"I'm not interested in semantics." Samantha began to fiddle with the paint cans. "Jake wants an affair with me, but he'll marry Lesley Marshall."

"Are you afraid to compete with Lesley?" Bree asked.

Samantha whirled around, eyes flashing. "I'm not afraid of anyone," she stormed. Sabrina's lips curved in a smug smile. "Don't try your psychology on me, Sabrina! Lesley Marshall and I don't belong in the same league, but I'm not afraid of her. I *am* afraid of getting hurt, though." Her voice wavered and Sabrina's arm slipped over her shoulders.

"All right, Sam, we won't talk about it any more right now. Leave those brushes, I'll wash them out. Go take a ride. You know the only way to clear your head is to go off by yourself."

"I'm beginning to think you know me too well." With a wry smile, Samantha wiped her hands on her jeans.

"I know you, all right, Samantha." Sabrina patted her cheek and urged her from the room. "I just haven't always known what to do about you."

Chapter Nine

During the months since their first meeting, Samantha had grown to know Jake Tanner, and to realize that when he wanted something, he made certain he got it. And she knew he wanted her.

If, when she rode out on horseback, she kept closer to the ranch than had been her habit, she told herself it was not fear of encountering Jake that prompted the action, but simply her desire to spend more of her free time with Sabrina. Now Sabrina was growing cumbersome in her pregnancy, there was a grain of truth to this, so Samantha found it easy to accept the half-truth.

Every day she fell more under the spell of Wyoming. Bare branches were now fully cloaked in green. The cattle grew sleek and fat. The land was fully awakened and rich.

"I think you may just have twins in there, Bree," Samantha commented as the two sisters took advantage of golden sun and fragrant warmth. Sabrina glanced down to where Samantha sat cross-legged on the wide front porch. "Dr. Gates thinks not." She patted the mound in question. "He says there's only one, and I'm just getting fat. One of us should have twins, though."

"I'm afraid that's going to be up to you, Bree. I think I'll revive the tradition of old-maid schoolteachers."

Sabrina was sensitive to the wistfulness in the words. "Oh, no, you'll have to get married, Sam. You can't let all those lessons go to waste."

This brought the light laugh it had intended. "I'm perfectly serious. Remember what Madame Dubois always said, 'Von must reach for ze stars.'"

"Oh, yes, Madame Dubois." Samantha smiled at the memory of their former ballet teacher. "You know, of course, that accent was a phony. She came from New Jersey."

"I'm suitably crushed. She did think she had a genuine protégé in you."

"Yes, I was magnificent." Samantha sighed with exaggerated pride.

"Let's see a few of your famous leaps now, Sam."

"Not on your life!"

"Come on, cutoffs are as good as a tutu any day. I'd join you in a pas de deux, but it would actually be a pas de trois."

Samantha rose reluctantly from her seat on the porch. "All right, I don't mind showing off a little."

With quiet dignity, Sabrina began to hum a movement from *Swan Lake,* and Samantha lowered into a purposefully dramatic body sweep before exploding with an energetic series of grand jetés, stage leaps and cabrioles. She concluded the performance with a group of pirouettes, ended by dropping in a dizzy heap on the grass.

"That's what you get," she said, closing her eyes and

shaking her head at the giddiness, "when you forget to spot focus."

"Is this show open to the public?"

Samantha glanced sharply toward the sound of the all-too-familiar voice.

"Dan!" Sabrina exclaimed. "I didn't expect you back so early."

"Ran into Lesley and Jake out on the north boundary," he explained, striding over and planting a firm kiss. "I thought you and Sam might like some company."

"Hello, Lesley, Jake." Sabrina included them both in her smile. "Have a seat, I'll bring out something cool."

Samantha had been sitting, praying without result for the ground to open up and swallow her. "I'll do it, Bree." She jumped at the opportunity to escape. "Don't get up."

"I'm up," Sabrina pointed out, disappearing inside before Samantha could argue.

"Do you teach ballet, as well, Samantha?" Lesley asked. She surveyed Samantha's outfit of semiragged cutoffs and T-shirt with dark, mocking eyes.

"No, no," Samantha muttered, feeling once more desperately at a disadvantage next to the slim woman in elegantly tailored breeches and silk shirt.

"I thought it was real nice," Dan commented, innocently turning the knife.

"Samantha's just full of surprises," Jake said.

Now that he had spoken again, Samantha was forced to give Jake a portion of her attention. He looked devastatingly male, the denim shirt rolled past his elbows to expose bronzed, corded arms, the low-slung belt in his jeans accentuating his leanness. She concentrated on a spot approximately six inches to the left of his face, in order to avoid the smile that had already mastered his face.

"Yeah," she returned. "I'm just a bushel of surprises."

"Anything you can't do, Sam?"

"A few things." She attempted a cool sophistication.

"You're so energetic," Lesley commented, slipping her hand through Jake's arm. "You must be horribly strong and full of bulging muscles."

For one heady moment, Samantha considered flight. She was opening her mouth to make her excuses when Dan effectively cut off all hope.

"Sit down, Sam, I want to talk over a little idea with you and Sabrina." Sinking down on the porch steps, Samantha avoided any glimpse of Jake's face. "Do you think Sabrina's up to a little party?" Samantha looked up at Dan's question and attempted to marshal her thoughts.

"A party?" she repeated, drawing her brows together in concentration. "I suppose so. Dr. Gates says she's doing very well, but you could always ask to be sure. Did you want to go to a party?"

"I was thinking of having one," he corrected with a grin. "There're these twins I know who have this birthday in a couple of weeks." Bending over, he tugged at Samantha's loosened locks. "Seems like a good excuse for having a party."

"Oh, our birthday." Samantha's response was vague. The impending anniversary had slipped her mind.

"Did I hear someone say party?" Sabrina emerged through the screen door with a tray of iced tea.

Samantha sipped the cool, sweet tea her sister handed her and watched Sabrina's face light up with anticipation.

"A birthday party, Sam." She turned to her sister, eyes shining with excitement. "When's the last time we had one?"

"When we were twelve and Billy Darcy got sick all over Mom's new carpet." Leaning back against the porch rail, Samantha unwittingly lifted her face to Jake's.

"Well, then, it's high time for another," Dan said. "What do you say, Sam? I know it means extra work for you."

"Huh." Tearing her eyes from Jake's smile, she endeavored to pick up the threads of the conversation. "What? Oh, no, it's no trouble. It'll be fun." Concentrating on Dan's face, she blocked out the sight of Lesley lounging intimately against Jake. "How many people did you have in mind?"

"Just neighbors and friends." He reached up to rub his chin. "About thirty or forty, I'd say. What do you think, Lesley?"

The full mouth pouted a moment in thought. "If you want to keep it small, Dan," she agreed after a short deliberation. Samantha's eyes grew wide. These people definitely had a different idea of small than she did.

"Oh, Lesley, come take a look at this punch bowl I've got, see if you think we should use it." Rising, Sabrina took Dan's hand. "Come, get it down for me, Dan." Throwing her sister an innocent smile, Sabrina disappeared inside and left her alone with Jake.

"How's the painting coming?" Jake stretched both arms over the back of the swing.

"Painting? Oh, the nursery. It's finished."

That, she recalled with a frown, was just one of many times he had come upon her in a ridiculous situation. Sleeping on stumps, covered with paint, and now leaping across the lawn like some crazed ballerina. Samantha, she told herself, you have class.

"What do you want for your birthday, Sam?" He prodded her with the toe of his boot and earned a scowl.

Blowing a wisp of hair from her eyes, she moved her shoulders. "Fur, diamonds."

"No, you're not the type for furs." Taking out a cigar, he lit it and blew a lazy stream of smoke. "You'd be thinking about all the little minks that were scalped to make it. And diamonds wouldn't suit you."

"I suppose I'm more the quartz type." She rose, irritated.

"No, I was thinking more of sapphires." He caught her wrist. "To go with your eyes, or maybe rubies to go with your temper."

"I'll be sure to put both on my list. Now, if you'll excuse me." She glanced at her captured hand, then back at him. "I've got to go feed my cat." She gestured to where Shylock lay on the far side of the porch.

"He doesn't look very hungry."

"He's pretending to be dead," she muttered. "Shylock, let's eat."

Amber eyes opened and blinked. Then, to her pleasure, Shylock rose and padded toward her. However, upon reaching his mistress, he gave her a disinterested stare, leaped into Jake's lap and began to purr with wicked enjoyment.

"No, ma'am." Jake glanced down at the contented cat. "He doesn't look hungry at all."

With a final glare, Samantha turned, stalked to the door and slammed the screen smartly behind her.

The sun shone warm and friendly on the morning of the twins' birthday. Samantha carried a large parcel into the kitchen. Dumping her burden on the table where her sister was enjoying a cup of tea, she nudged Shylock away with her foot. She had not yet decided to forgive him for his treacherous advances to Jake.

"This just came, it's from the folks."

"Open it, Sam." Sabrina poked an experimental finger at the package. "Dan refuses to give me my present yet, and I've searched everywhere I can think of."

"I bet it's six books on child rearing for you, and six on etiquette for me."

"A present's a present," Sabrina stated, and tore the mailing paper from the box.

"Here's a note." After breaking the seal, Samantha produced a sheet of paper and read aloud.

"To Samantha and Sabrina:
    A very happy birthday and our love to you both. Sabrina, I do hope you are taking good care of yourself. As you know, proper diet and rest are essential. I'm sure having Samantha with you during the last weeks of your confinement is a great comfort. Samantha, do look after your sister and see that she takes the necessary precautions. However, I hope you're not overlooking your own social life. As your mother, it is my duty to remind you that you are long past the marriageable age. Your father and I are looking forward to seeing you and our first grandchild in a few weeks. We will be in Wyoming the first part of September, if Dad's schedule holds true.

With love,
Mom and Dad

"There's a postscript for you, Bree.

"Sabrina, doesn't Daniel know any suitable men for your sister?"

With a sigh, Samantha folded the letter and dropped

it on the table. "She never changes." Dipping into the box, Samantha plucked out a smaller one with Sabrina's name on it and handed it to her. "Marriageable age," she muttered, and shook her head.

"Did you peek in here before?" Sabrina accused, dumping out volumes on infant and child care.

"No," Samantha denied with a superior smirk. "I just know Mom." Drawing out her own package, she ripped off the concealing paper. "Good grief." She let the box drop to the table and held up a brief black lace negligee.

"I thought I knew Mom." Both sisters burst into laughter. "She must be getting desperate," Samantha concluded, holding the negligee in front of her.

"Now that's a pretty thing," Jake observed as he and Dan entered the kitchen. "But it's even prettier with something in it." Samantha bundled the garment behind her and flushed scarlet.

"Presents from Mom and Dad," Sabrina explained, indicating her stack of books.

"Very suitable." Dan grinned as he glanced through the volumes.

"Doesn't look like Sam feels the same about hers." Jake smiled. Samantha felt her already alarming color deepen. "Let's see it again."

"Don't tease, Jake." Sabrina turned to her husband. "Mom says they'll be here the first part of September."

"I'll put this stuff away." Samantha tossed the gown into the box and began to bury it under books.

"Leave that till later." Dan took her hand and pulled her away. "I need you outside for a minute."

She went willingly. Escape was escape. Imagining it had something to do with Sabrina's gift, she was surprised when Dan slowed his pace and allowed his wife to join them in their walk toward the ranch buildings.

He kept her involved in a running conversation about the party until they came to a halt at the paddock fence.

"Happy birthday, Sam." Sabrina kissed her sister's cheek as Samantha's eyes focused on the golden Arabian mare.

"Oh." She could manage no more.

"She's from a good line," Dan informed her, his arm slipping around Sabrina's shoulders. "She's out of the Double T stock, no finer in Wyoming."

"But I..." Words faltered, and she swallowed and tried to begin again.

"What do you give someone who packs their own life away for six months without hesitation, without asking for anything in return?" Dan's free arm slipped around Samantha and pulled her to his side.

"We figured if you insisted on going back east, we'd always have a hold on you. You'd have to come visit us to ride your mare."

"I don't know how to thank you."

"Then don't," Dan ordered. "Go try her out."

"Now?"

"Now's as good a time as any." Not needing a second urging, Samantha was over the fence, stroking the mare and murmuring.

"We may convince her to stay yet," Dan commented, watching as she slipped into the saddle and took the mare around the paddock. "I could have a word with Jake."

Sabrina shook her head. "No, Sam would be furious if we interfered. She'd bolt back to Philadelphia before we could take a breath. For now, we'd better keep out of it." She lowered her voice as a beaming Samantha trotted around to them and slipped off the little mare.

"She's a real beauty," she sighed. "I don't know how I can ever bear to leave her..."

Sabrina's eyes met her husband's in silent satisfaction. Perhaps it will not be necessary, their unspoken message said.

"Come, little sister," Dan said. "If you can tear yourself away from your new friend, I sure could use a cup of coffee now."

As the trio trooped back toward the house, Jake swung through the back door. "Delivery just came. It's in the living room."

"Oh," Dan murmured, looking entirely too innocent. "Come on, Sabrina, we'd best see what it is."

"Is it the piano?" Sam asked Jake, as Dan and Sabrina disappeared inside.

"Looked like one to me. I guess that's another present that'll go over big. Walk to the truck with me," Jake commanded, and captured her hand before she could protest.

"Really, Jake, I have a million things to do." She trotted to keep pace with his loose, lanky stride.

"I know, you're indispensable." Stopping by his truck, he reached in the cab and produced a package. "But this seems to be the time for gift giving. I thought I'd let you have your present now."

"You didn't have to get me anything."

"Samantha." His drawl was lazy, but his eyes narrowed in annoyance. "I never do anything unless I want to." Taking her hand from behind her back, he placed the box in it. "Open it."

Lifting the statue from its tissue bedding, she examined it in silent amazement. The alabaster was smooth and cool in her hands, carved into the shape of a horse and rider in full gallop. The artist had captured the fluid grace, the freedom of motion. She ran a hesitant finger over the delicate features.

"It looks like me." She lifted her eyes to Jake's.

"And so it should," he answered easily. "It's supposed to be you."

"But how?" She shook her head, torn between pleasure and confusion.

"A man I know does this kind of thing. I described you to him."

For the second time that day, Samantha found herself at a loss for words.

"Why?" The question was out before she could swallow it.

Slowly, a smile drifted across his face. He pushed back his hat. "Because it suits you better than furs and diamonds."

She braced herself to meet his eyes again. "Thank you."

He nodded, his face solemn. He took the box from her hands and placed it on the hood of the truck. "I think a birthday kiss is traditional."

Swallowing, she took an instinctive step in retreat, but he gripped her arms and held her still. She offered her cheek, and his laughter broke out, full and rich on the summer air. "Sam," he turned her face to his, and his eyes sparkled with humor, "you're incredible."

His lips met hers. His hands moved from her arms to her hips, drawing her firmly against the hard lines of his body. She submitted to the embrace, as long as his arms held her, as long as they were mouth to mouth, as long as the heat from his body infused hers, he owned her, and she could not run.

Finally he drew her away, bringing his hands to her shoulders while hers rested on his chest for support.

"Happy birthday, Sam."

"Thank you," she managed, still breathless from the impact of his embrace.

He lifted the box from the hood of the truck and placed it in her hands before sliding into the cab. "See you tonight." With a salute, he started the engine. The truck moved down the road, leaving her staring after it.

Chapter Ten

Party sounds filled the house. Laughter and voices and music mingled and drifted through open windows to float on the night air.

On this evening, the twins were dramatically different in their appearance. Sabrina's pale blue gown floated around her, cunningly disguising her pregnancy. Her hair was a glinting halo around rose-tinted cheeks. Samantha's black-striped satin clung to her body, her halter neckline plunging deep to a wide, gathered waist. Her hair was free and thick around her shoulders.

As she moved and mingled with the crowd, Samantha searched for a tall, lanky form, noting with increasing despair and a gnawing jealousy that a slim, dark woman had also as yet failed to put in an appearance.

Cornered by an enthusiastic young cowboy, Samantha was feeling her attention begin to wander from a detailed account of horse breeding when her eyes met dark jade across the room.

He was standing with two men she did not recognize, and Lesley Marshall stood beside him. She was elegant in an oyster-white gown. Her fine-boned ivory hand was placed from time to time on Jake's arm, as if, Samantha thought grimly, she were flaunting her possession.

Furious with the sudden feeling of inadequacy, Samantha turned to her companion with a dazzling smile. He stammered over his lecture, his words grinding to a halt. She tucked her arm in his and used her eyes without shame.

"Howdy, Tim." Jake appeared from nowhere and placed a hand on the young man's shoulder. "I'm going to steal this little lady for a moment." He paused and smiled easily into Samantha's mutinous face. "There's a couple of people she hasn't met yet."

Without waiting for an assent, he had her unwilling hand in his, propelling her through the crowd. "Tim won't be the same for weeks," he whispered close to her ear. "A woman could get run out of town for using her eyes that way on susceptible young boys," he warned, pulling her through the sea of people.

"You don't have to drag me."

"I know a stubborn mule when I see one," he countered, without bothering to lower his voice. Her furious retort was swallowed as Jake presented her to the two men who flanked Lesley.

"Sam, I'd like you to meet George Marshall, Lesley's father." Samantha's hand was enveloped in a hearty grip. "And Jim Bailey," he continued, nodding toward the second man.

"Jim only works with cattle on paper. He's a lawyer."

"My, this is a mighty pretty girl!" George Marshall boomed. Giving Jake a sly wink, he patted his daughter's shoulder.

"You always manage to rope in the pick of the herd, don't you, Jake?"

Jake slipped his hands easily into his pockets. "I do my best. But then, roping them's one thing, getting them's another."

"Well, now, little lady," George's genial voice continued, "Les tells me you're a gym teacher."

"That's right, Mr. Marshall."

"Now, you just call me George," he instructed, squeezing her shoulder with a genial affection. "Tell me, why isn't a pretty little thing like you married and settled down instead of running around some gymnasium?"

Jake was grinning with obvious enjoyment. Samantha tossed her hair behind her back, but before she could think of a suitable answer, George's laughter boomed through the room.

"I like this girl," George announced to the group. "Looks like she has spirit. You come over to our ranch any time, little lady, any time at all."

In spite of herself, Samantha found herself liking his expansive hospitality. "If you'll excuse me now, I've got…got to get a tray out of the kitchen." She gave the group an all-encompassing smile and melted into the crowd.

In the kitchen, she pulled a tray from the refrigerator to give her excuse credibility and was glad she had when Jake followed her in a moment later.

"George is a good man. He has the right ideas when it comes to women." Smiling knowingly at her, he leaned against the door watching her every move.

"That's your opinion," she returned tartly, bustling around the kitchen in an attempt to ignore him.

"Sit down a minute, Sam."

She glanced up, immediately wary, then lifted the tray as a defense. "No, I've got to get back."

"Please."

Despite herself, she lowered the tray to the table and herself into a chair.

"I ran into Jack Abbot, the school principal, the other day."

"Oh?"

"He told me the girls' phys ed instructor isn't coming back next term." Leaning back in his chair, Jake studied her. "He's going to offer you the job."

"Oh," she repeated before she could stop herself.

"He wants you pretty bad. He really needs someone this fall. I told him I'd be seeing you, and that I'd mention it. He's going to call you officially, of course."

How simple, Samantha thought.

How simple it would all be if I didn't love this man. I could stay where I want to stay, work where I want to work. But now, I've got to refuse, I've got to go away.

"I appreciate your telling me, and I appreciate Mr. Abbot wanting me, but…"

"Don't appreciate it, Samantha, think about it."

"You don't know what you're asking me to do."

He rose to pace the room, his hands seeking the depths of his pockets. "I'm just asking you to think about it. You like it here. You've made friends. You like being near your sister. You'd still have the satisfaction of doing what you feel you're suited for. Is it so much to ask that you consider it?"

"Yes, it's quite a lot. Jake, I don't want to argue with you. There are things I have to do, the same way there are things you have to do."

"All right." He nodded, then repeated slowly, as if coming to a decision. "All right, there *are* things I have to do." Moving over, he captured her chin between his thumb and fingers.

His arms slipped around her waist to bring her close, his mouth lowering to brush her cheeks and the corners of her lips. "Come home with me now, Samantha. We can be alone there." His voice had become low and seductive, as his fingers trailed over the bare skin of her back.

"No, please don't." She turned her face away.

"I want to make love to you. I want to feel your skin under my hands, all of you. I want to hear you sigh when I touch you."

"Jake, please." She dropped her head to his chest. "It's unfair, here, like this."

"Then come home with me."

"No, I can't." She shook her head without raising it. "I won't."

"All right, Samantha." He framed her face and brought it up to his. "I said I'd give you until the baby was born. We'll stick to that. We won't argue tonight. Let's call it a truce for your birthday. Agreed?"

He kissed her once, briefly, and turned to lift the tray. "Then we'll both do what we have to do when the time comes."

Leaving her confused, Jake moved through the doorway.

Rejoining the festivities, Samantha moved from group to group, but her thoughts were only about Jake. Why was he so interested in her career choices? Why did he want her to take the job in Wyoming? *Maybe he cared for her.* For a brief moment, she allowed hope to shimmer. Her eyes swept the room to find him. Finally she spotted him. He was dancing with Lesley. The shining cap of her raven hair brushing his cheek, the ivory of her hand entwined with the bronze of his. Samantha winced as he threw back his head and laughed at something Lesley had said for his ears alone.

Care for me? her mind repeated in a scathing whisper. Grow up, Samantha, *caring* and *wanting* don't always mean the same thing. In a few weeks, she comforted herself, she would no longer be subjected to this constant pain. When the ache had eased, she could visit Bree again. Jake would probably be too busy with his wife to spare time for visits to the Lazy L. Samantha felt her heart contract with pain.

She turned away and bumped solidly into Jim Bailey.

"Sorry." He took her shoulders to steady her. "I didn't see you."

"It's all right," she returned, offering a smile. "Besides, I think I ran into you."

"Well, no harm done either way." She watched his eyes slide past her and focus on Jake and Lesley. "They look nice together, don't they?"

Embarrassed that he must have seen her staring at them, Samantha nodded, and looked down at her empty glass. "Come on, we better get you a refill."

A few moments later, they joined the group around the piano as Sabrina played.

"So, you're a lawyer." She smiled at Jim. "I don't think I've ever met a lawyer before."

Jim returned her smile. "And you're a gymnast."

"No, actually, I'm a gym teacher now."

He lifted his glass in a toast and drank. "I remember you. I've always been an avid fan of the Olympics. I thought you were fabulous."

"Well, that's nice to hear after a decade."

He tapped his glass to hers. "Well, Olympic star, would you like to dance?"

"I'd love to."

Samantha enjoyed Jim Bailey's easy conversation. She learned during their two dances that he was interested in getting into politics. His dark good looks and ready wit would certainly be assets, she decided.

"Sam." Sabrina motioned to her as they moved back toward the piano. "It's your turn. Union rules."

"Okay," Samantha agreed, sliding onto the bench.

She played with practiced ease, moving from one song to the next. Time slipped through her fingers. As in a dream, she was aware of the voices behind her, the faint, drifting breeze of Wyoming through the open windows.

Someone sat beside her. Recognizing the lean fingers that lifted to turn the page of her sheet music, she faltered and missed a note.

"You and Jim seem to have hit it off." Samantha heard the click of his lighter over the sounds of the party.

"He's a very nice man. Have you known him long?"

"Oh, only since we were about eight and I gave him a black eye and he loosened a few of my teeth."

"Sounds like a loving friendship."

Jake again turned the page before she could do so herself. "Well, after that we sort of stuck together." He pushed the curtain of hair behind her shoulder, and Samantha struggled not to break the thread of the melody. "The two of you seemed to have a lot to talk about."

"He's very charming, and we have a few mutual interests."

"Hmm." Jake shifted slightly in his seat. His thigh brushed hers, and her fingers responded by hitting three wrong notes.

"You play very well."

Was he being ironic? She turned to look at him, but found no mockery in his jade eyes.

"Pleasantly," she corrected. "I get the general melody, but the details are a bit fuzzy."

"I've noticed that you have a tendency to shrug off your own capabilities. Are you aware of that?"

"That's not true. I just know what I do well and what I don't."

"You're a very tough critic, and you're inclined to underestimate."

"Honesty," she countered, finishing the song with a flourish. "I am a totally honest person."

"Are you, Samantha?" he said softly. "That's what I plan to find out."

Chapter Eleven

The days grew hot and sultry. The skies were improbably blue, rarely softened by clouds.

Long hours in the sun had deepened the honey of Samantha's skin, teasing out the gold in her hair. As long as she was occupied, she had no time for soul searching. She could enjoy the long summer days without thinking of the fall. As Sabrina wilted like a thirsty rose in the searing heat, Samantha confined her own activities to the early-morning hours. In the long, hot haze of the afternoon, Sabrina moved slowly through the house, her body clumsy. Samantha did not dare leave her. The baby was due in two weeks, and Samantha wanted to remain within calling distance of her sister as much as possible.

One particularly humid afternoon, the two women were sitting idly in the living room. Sabrina got up heavily from her chair to look out the window. "Sam," she said, "before Dan left for town, he said a storm was brewing. From the looks of the sky, I'd say he was right."

Before Samantha could answer, there was a sudden flash of lightning. A blast of thunder rolled in on the wind, and the rain began to fall in sheets.

"It's coming down fast," Samantha agreed. "It should cool us off a bit." She looked sympathetically at her sister's bulky form.

The storm built in power. Jagged flashes of lightning illuminated the room and an angry wind hurled the rain against the windows. The two women watched in fascination as the storm exhausted itself. Soon rain dripped tentatively from the eaves and the thunder was a mere grumble in the distance.

The sun struggled to reappear, breaking through the gloom with a hazy promise of light.

"That," Sabrina commented with an enormous sigh, "was a mean one."

Samantha turned from her place by the window and again slumped into a chair. "Remember when you used to hide in the closet whenever we had a thunderstorm?"

"All too well." She gave her sister a pained smile. "And you used to stand on the porch, loving every minute of it, until Mom dragged you in, soaking wet. On that note from the past," Sabrina announced, "I'm going to take a nap, Sam." She turned at the doorway and studied the woman slouched in the chair, bare legs and feet stretched out in unconscious grace. "I love you."

With a rather puzzled smile, Samantha watched her walk away.

Wandering out to the porch, Samantha drank in the rain-fresh air. Everything sparkled. Raindrops clung like jewels to blossoms and leaves. Though the flowers had drooped with the weight of the storm, their colors had been washed into brilliant life. A bird, flying by on a shaft of light, trilled above her. She could hear the steady dripping of the rain off the eaves above the whisper of the dying wind. Satisfied, she curled up on a porch rocker and instantly fell asleep.

She had no idea how long she had drifted in the soft twilight world when, with reluctance, she woke at the touch of a hand on her shoulder. She looked up drowsily and yawned. "Oh, Bree, I must have fallen asleep. It's so wonderfully cool out here."

"Sam, I think the baby's decided to put in an unscheduled appearance."

"Huh? Oh!" Springing to her feet, she was instantly awake. "Right now? Dan's not here, and it's not time yet. Sit down, sit," she ordered, running agitated fingers through her hair.

"I think the first thing to do is to calm down," Sabrina suggested.

"You're right. I'm not going to fall apart, it was just a shock. I wasn't expecting this for another week or two."

"Neither was I." Sabrina's smile was half amused, half apologetic.

"All right, how long have you been having contractions, and how far apart are they?"

"Only for an hour or so."

"That should give us plenty of time." Samantha patted Sabrina's hand.

"But they've been getting awfully strong, and…" Breaking off, she closed her eyes and began to breathe in a deep, methodical rhythm. "And," she continued, after a final long breath, "awfully close together."

"How close?" Samantha asked, feeling new tension at the base of her neck.

"Ten minutes."

"Ten minutes," Samantha repeated. "I'd better get

you to the hospital. I'll bring the car around. Stay put," she told her sister, and raced to the garage.

Upon reaching Sabrina's compact and sliding behind the wheel, Samantha was horrified to find the engine unresponsive to the turn of the key. The little car sputtered, emitted an apologetic groan and died.

"You can't," she insisted, and smacked the steering wheel. "We just had you fixed."

There was no use wasting more time trying to figure out what was wrong with the car. It was clearly not going to start, and Samantha hadn't the first idea of where to look for the problem.

Rushing back to the house, she picked up the phone in the kitchen. At least she could call Dr. Gates. A groan of despair was wrenched from her when she heard the dead silence on the line. Oh, no, the storm must have knocked out the phones!

Forcing herself to appear calm, she returned to the living room where Sabrina was waiting for her.

Reaching her sister again, Samantha knelt down so their eyes were level. "Bree, the car won't start. All the trucks and jeeps are out with the men, and the storm must have knocked down the phone lines."

"Looks like we've got a few problems." Sabrina took a deep breath.

"It's going to be all right." Samantha took her hand in reassurance. "I'll help you get into bed, and then I'll take a horse and ride toward the Double T. If I don't see any of the men on the way, I'll get a truck there and bring it back. Most of them have radios, and I can call ahead to the doctor."

"Sam, it's going to take time for you to get there, and to get back. I don't think I'll make it in time to get to the hospital after that. You'll have to have the doctor come here."

"Here?" Samantha repeated. Her throat closed on the word. Sabrina nodded. "All right. Don't worry, I won't be long. I'll be back as soon as I can." Samantha raced off to the stables, and without wasting the time for a saddle, she leaped on her mare's back.

The familiar landscape was a blur, as she urged more speed out of the powerful horse. The sound of her own breath was masked by the sound of thudding hooves. Every minute she took was a minute longer that Sabrina was alone. She crouched lower on the horse and dug in bare heels.

When Samantha spotted the men on horseback, she spurred the Arabian over the fence in a fluid leap. As her hooves touched earth, she met the horse's sides again. They streaked across the field, scattering annoyed cattle.

When she reached the group, she reined in sharply. The mare reared, nearly unseating her. Her breath came in gasps as she struggled to keep her seat.

"What are you trying to do, break your neck?" Furiously Jake snatched the reins from her hands. "If you're stupid enough not to care about yourself, think of your horse. What do you mean riding like a fool and jumping fences? Where's your saddle? Have you lost your mind?"

"Bree," she managed at last between giant gulps of air. "The baby's coming, and the phone's out. The car wouldn't start, and there's nobody around. Dan's in town. Bree says there's no time to get her to the hospital now, and I have to call the doctor." She felt tears of fear burning at her eyes and bit her lip.

"All right, take it easy." Twisting in the saddle, Jake called out to one of his men. "Get back to the ranch and get hold of Dr. Gates on the CB radio. Tell him Sabrina Lomax is in labor and to get to the Lazy L in a hurry." Turning back, he handed the reins to Samantha. "Let's go."

"Are you coming back with me?" Flooded with relief, she gripped tight on the leather.

"What do you think?"

Together, they sprang forward in a gallop.

Speed and thundering hooves were all Samantha ever remembered of the ride back. There was no time for conversation, no time for thought. She was sliding to the ground before she came to a full stop and Jake once more secured her reins.

"Keep your head, Samantha," he ordered, watching her bound up the steps and through the front door.

The house was silent. Her stomach tightened as she rushed to the master bedroom. Sabrina sat up in bed, propped by a mound of pillows and greeted her with a cheerful smile.

"That was quick, did you fly?"

"Just about," Samantha returned, faint with relief.

"We've sent for the doctor. Everything's under control." She sat down on the bed, taking her sister's hand. "How are you doing?"

"Not too bad." Her hand closed over Samantha's, as much to reassure as seeking reassurance. "I'm glad you're back. Here comes another one."

Samantha looked on with unfamiliar helplessness. Her fingers grew tighter over her twin's, as if to steal some of her pain.

"We can thank Mom for that book on natural childbirth." Sabrina gave a long, shaky sigh and relaxed against the pillows.

"Don't look so worried, I'm doing fine. Oh, hello,

Jake." Glancing at the doorway, Sabrina greeted him with friendly cheerfulness. "I didn't know you were here. Come in. It's not contagious."

He advanced into the room, looking tall, male and out of place. His hands retreated to his pockets. "How're you doing?"

"Oh, well, you've seen a cow in labor before, I don't imagine there's much difference." The small hand tightened on Samantha's. "Here we go again."

Samantha lifted the hand to her cheek. *Where was the doctor?* Sabrina should be in the hospital, surrounded by experts.

"This baby's in a big hurry," Sabrina announced with a small moan. "I'm sorry, Sam, it's not going to wait much longer."

I don't know anything about childbirth, Samantha thought in a moment of terror. *What am I going to do? What do I do first?*

Standing, she turned to Jake. "Go sterilize some towels, lots of them, and some string and scissors."

"All right." His hand rested on her shoulder a moment. "If you need me, give a call."

Nodding, she moved into the adjoining bath and scrubbed her hands and arms until they hurt.

"You're going to be fine," she stated as she reentered the bedroom.

"Yes, I am." Sabrina lay back on the pillows and closed her eyes. "I'm going to have this baby, Sam, and I'm going to do a good job of it. You can't do this for me, I have to be strong."

"You are strong." Brushing away the hair from Sabrina's cheeks, she realized with a sudden jolt that it was true. "You're stronger than I ever knew."

Her calm had returned, and she took over the duties

of midwifery with an instinct as old as time. She wiped moisture from her sister's face, working with her, breathing with her, uttering soothing encouragements. Sabrina had not gone through all she had to lose now, and Samantha would not allow anything to go wrong.

"All right." Wiping beads of sweat from her own brow, Samantha straightened. "I think she's going to come this time, it's almost over. You have to help."

Sabrina nodded, her face pale and composed. Her hair had darkened with dampness. She shuddered and moaned with the final pang of childbirth. A thin, shrill cry pierced the stillness of the room. Samantha held new life in her hands.

"Oh, Bree." She stared down at the tiny, wriggling form.

Dan burst into the room two steps ahead of the doctor.

Suddenly, it was all so simple, Dan standing by Sabrina's side, his large hand clutching hers, the small, fresh form swaddled in the curve of her mother's arms.

"Only one." Sabrina sighed, her eyes luminous. "You'll have to handle the twins, Sam. One at a time is enough for me."

Sometime later, Samantha shut the door behind her and walked toward the kitchen. Jake looked up at her approach.

"A girl." She lowered herself into a chair. "The doctor says she's perfect, almost seven pounds. Bree's fine." She pushed at her tumbled hair and ran a hand across her brow. "I want to thank you."

"I didn't do anything."

"You were here." She lifted her eyes, and they were young and vulnerable. "I needed to know you were here."

"Samantha." He smiled and shook his head. "You sure find a man's weak points. I'll get you a drink."

He was back in a moment with a decanter of brandy and two snifters. Sitting across from her, he filled both generously. "It's not champagne, but it'll do." Lifting his glass, he touched it solemnly to hers. "To mother and child, and to Samantha Evans." He paused, his smile fading into seriousness. "She's one hell of a woman."

Samantha folded her arms on the table, laid her head on them and burst into tears.

"I was so scared." She found her voice muffled against his shoulder as he brought her against him. "I've never been so scared. I thought I would lose them both."

He tilted her chin as one hand rubbed the small of her back. "You're a survivor, Sam, and too stubborn to let anything happen to Sabrina or the baby."

Her forehead dropped to his chest as she struggled to stem the flow of tears.

"I always seem to fall apart in front of you."

"Don't much care for that, do you?" She felt his lips descend to her hair and allowed herself the joy of being cradled in his arms. "Most people don't look for perfection, Sam, they find it boring. You," he said, framing her face with his hands, "are never boring."

She sniffed and smiled. "I guess that was a compliment." Giving in to impulse, she leaned over and rested her cheek against his. "I don't think you're boring, either."

"Well." He stroked her hair a moment, and his voice was curiously soft. "That's about the nicest thing you've ever said to me.

"Now drink some of that." He pushed her gently away and handed her the brandy.

Obeying, she allowed the warm strength to seep into

her veins and relaxed with a sigh. "Bree certainly came through this better than I did." She drank again. Jake straddled a chair, leaning his arms on the back. "When I left her, she was lying there with the baby, looking like she'd just finished having a picnic. Dan looked like he was about to keel over, I was ready for someone to cart me away. Yet Bree lies there, glowing like a rose."

"Your sister's quite a woman."

"I know." Her eyes dropped to the surface of the table. "She said she has someone to depend on her now. I guess the time's come to stop playing big sister. She doesn't need that anymore."

"So, what will you do now?" His voice was casual.

"I'll stay around a couple of weeks, then I'll go on." She struggled, seeing only a void.

"To what?"

Her fingers tightened on her glass. "To my work, to my life." She drank, and the brandy was bitter.

"Still set on leaving?" He lifted his own glass, swirling the liquid. Amber danced under the kitchen light. "You haven't seen Wyoming in the autumn."

"No, I haven't," she answered, evading his prior question. "Maybe I'll come back next year." She stared down at her hands, knowing she never would.

"She's hungry!" Dan charged into the kitchen, his grin threatening to split his face. "Just had a baby, and she says she's hungry. Sam, I love you." Plucking her from her chair, Dan tossed her into the air. Her laughter ended on a shriek as she clutched at him on her journey down. The shriek was strangled as she was smothered by a bear hug. "I swear, if bigamy wasn't against the law, I'd marry you."

"If I was still all in one piece," she managed, turning her face and gulping for air.

"I ask you, Jake." He consulted the other man as his arms threatened to destroy the alignment of Samantha's rib cage. "Have you ever known another like this one?"

"Can't say that I have." She heard the smile in his voice, though it was impossible in her position to see his face. "I'd say Samantha is unique. One of a kind."

Rising, he lifted his brandy and toasted them both.

Chapter Twelve

"Sam, you're going to spoil her."

"Impossible." Sitting in the front porch rocker with the week-old Jennifer, Samantha smiled at her sister. "She's much too intelligent to be spoiled. Anyway, it's an aunt's privilege."

As she continued to rock, her lips strayed to Jennifer's soft tuft of dark hair. *I won't be able to do this much longer.* She looked to the massive peaks gleaming silver-blue in the afternoon sun. A light breeze stirred the air, bringing the sweet scent of freshly mowed grass. She breathed it in, and the soft scent of Jennifer's talc mingled with it. A sigh escaped.

She had not realized such a small creature could wrap her way around the heart so completely. *Another love to leave behind. In just a week, I'll have to say goodbye to all the things that matter: Bree, Dan, Wyoming, and now Jennifer.*

Dents and bruises, she thought again, *but not the open*

wound that comes from leaving the man. Arrogant and gentle, demanding and kind, hot-tempered and easy; the parts that made up Jake Tanner were complicated and many, but to Samantha, it was a simple equation of love.

Blast you, Jake Tanner, if it weren't for you, I could stay. I belong here. I felt it from the first time I saw the mountains. There's nothing for me in Philadelphia. You've left me without anything to go back to.

"Looks like Lesley's coming to pay a visit," Sabrina observed. Samantha jerked back to the present with a snap.

She watched the late-model compact winding down the drive. Ignoring the flare of impossible jealousy, she set her features in casual lines.

"Sabrina, how well you look." Lesley's greeting was obviously tinged by surprise. "It's only been a week, and you look positively…" She hesitated, searching for a word.

"Radiant?" Sabrina suggested, and laughed. "I just had a baby, Lesley, not open-heart surgery."

"But to go through all that here, and without a doctor." She turned to Samantha. "I heard from Jake that you were marvelous and handled everything."

Samantha shrugged, uncomfortable at hearing Jake's praise from Lesley's lips. "It was nice of him to say so, but Sabrina did all the work."

"Well, having a baby is not a prospect I look forward to." Lesley shivered delicately. "I certainly intend to put it off as long as possible." Gliding over, she bent her head over the sleeping infant. "She is quite lovely, Sabrina. Very sweet."

"Would you like to hold her?" Samantha offered.

"Oh, no." Lesley stepped back. "I'm afraid I'm not very good with babies."

As she moved, Samantha caught the glint of the large square-cut diamond on her left hand. Lesley followed her gaze, and held out her hand. "You didn't know I was engaged, did you, Sabrina?"

"No." Sabrina cast a quick glance at her sister. "We hadn't heard."

"Well, you have been rather busy." She moved her fingers, enjoying the changing lights. "And we haven't made any formal announcement yet. We're planning a bit of a party for next week. As a matter of fact, I'm just on my way into town to begin shopping for my trousseau. Of course, I'll have to make a trip into New York for some proper clothes, but I'll just have to make do locally for the time being. We've set the wedding for the end of September." She smoothed her perfectly groomed hair with a well-manicured hand. "I could have done with a bit more time, but men have no idea how difficult things are to arrange properly." She smiled again. "Well, I must fly. I have so much to do. I do hope you'll be able to make it to the wedding, Samantha."

Sabrina glanced again at her sister. "Sam won't be here in September, Lesley."

"Oh, too bad." The regret in Lesley's voice was mild. Her mind had already run ahead to her wardrobe. She opened the door of the compact and slid behind the wheel. Lifting a slim arm in farewell, she drove away.

Rising, Sabrina took the sleeping Jennifer from her sister's arms and went into the house. When she returned, she sat on the arm of the rocker and laid her hand on Samantha's shoulder.

"I knew it was going to happen," Samantha murmured. "I just didn't want to be here when it did. I didn't think it would hurt this much. Oh, Bree." She looked up at her twin with helpless, swimming eyes. "What am I going to do?"

For the first time in their relationship, their situations were reversed, and Samantha was vulnerable, seeking comfort and advice.

"Sam, you can't go on like this. Why don't you talk to him?" Sabrina stroked the thick fall of her sister's hair. "Something is wrong here, and the two of you have to talk things out."

"No. I won't give him the opportunity to feel sorry for me."

"Pride can be a very cold companion," Sabrina murmured.

Samantha stood up. "I'm going back early, Bree. I can have everything arranged by the day after tomorrow, maybe even by tomorrow night."

"Sam, you can't run away from this."

"Just watch me."

"Mom and Dad won't be here for a few more days. They'll be disappointed."

"I'm sorry, I hate to miss them, but I can't handle this." Pausing, she repeated, the admission surprising her, "I *really* can't handle this."

"But, Sam…" Sabrina joined her at the porch rail. "You should at least talk to Jake. Don't you want to know how he feels? You can't just go flying off without speaking to him, without saying goodbye. Something's not right about all this. I've thought about the two of you. I've seen the way he looks at you."

Shaking her head, Samantha moved toward the door. "No, he hasn't shown his face since the baby was born, and Lesley Marshall has his ring on her finger. A diamond. He has what he wants."

* * *

Samantha spent the evening packing, while Shylock watched her in silent accusation from his habitual place in the center of her bed.

Once in bed, she spent most of the night staring at a moon-washed ceiling. When the first pale light of dawn crept into the room, she rose. The mauve shadows under her eyes were a sad tribute to the restless hours.

The house slept on, and she deserted it, making her way to the stables. She saddled her mount with quick, deft movements, then galloped over the faint mist of morning.

As the sky lightened, the air came to life with the sweet song of birds. Sadly, she listened to the song of the west, for she knew that the melody would linger forever in her heart. She watched the mountains transformed by the dawn. Ribbons of rose and gold melted into blue until the peaks were no longer silhouettes, but stood proud in the full glory of the sun. She stayed for a last look at the white-faced Herefords grazing on the short, coarse grass. She knew now that her love for this wild, free country was forever bound up with her love for Jake. In saying goodbye to one, she was saying goodbye to the other. Straightening her shoulders, she turned the little mare back to the Lazy L.

When she returned to the house, she greeted her sister with bright chatter, the meaningless words no disguise for sleep-starved eyes. Sabrina made no comment, and shortly disappeared into the bedroom to tend to the baby.

Alone, Samantha wandered aimlessly from window to window. Tonight, she thought, slipping her hands into the pockets of her jeans, I'll be on a plane. And tomorrow morning, all this will just be a dream.

"Morning, ma'am."

She whirled, nearly upsetting a vase of roses with the movement. Jake leaned against the door frame, legs crossed at the ankles, as if he had been watching for some time.

"What are you doing here?"

He took a few strides into the room. "Well, now, I came to fetch you." This information was imparted in an irritatingly slow drawl.

"Fetch me? What are you talking about? I'm not a dog or a maverick calf to be fetched."

"Maverick calf sounds pretty close. You're always running off in the wrong direction." Reaching out, he took her arm. "Come on, we're going for a ride." His voice was pleasant, but the steel was there. She jerked away, angry with his arrogance, wary of his tone.

"I have no intention of going anywhere with you. Why don't you just go away and leave me alone?"

"Now, I can't do that, Sam," he returned in a reasonable tone. "We have some unfinished business to attend to. Your time's up."

The fire in her eyes flickered and died. "You can't be serious."

"I'm dead serious."

"What…what about Lesley?"

"She's not invited," he returned simply.

"I'm not going with you," she said, somewhere between terror and fury. "You can't make me."

Stopping, he looked down at her from his overpowering height. "Sure I can," he corrected with easy confidence. With a swift movement, he swung her over his shoulder. "See?" He walked effortlessly down the hall. "Nothing to it."

"Let me down!" Furious fists beat against his back. "This is crazy, it's illegal. I'll have you thrown in jail!"

"No kidding? Sam, you're scaring me to death."

He continued easily down the hall, as if he carried an empty sack, rather than an irate woman who was thumping against his back. Pausing, he touched the brim of his hat as Sabrina appeared in the bedroom doorway, the baby in her arms.

"Morning, Sabrina." His greeting was genial, and he cocked his head to get a better view of Jennifer. "She's a real beauty."

"Thank you, Jake. We certainly think so." She shifted the baby and smiled. "Are you two going out?"

"Thought we'd go for a little ride," Jake informed her. "We may be gone some time."

"It's a fine day for it, hardly a cloud in the sky."

"Bree." Samantha's voice was desperate. "Don't just stand there, *do* something." She pushed at the hair that hung over her face. "Don't you see what he's doing? He's kidnapping me. Call the police, call Dan." She continued to plead as Jake touched the brim of his hat once more and moved down the hall. "Bree, say something."

"Have a good time" was her sister's surprising response.

Samantha's mouth fell open in dumb astonishment. A stream of imaginative curses was hurled on Jake's unperturbed head as he took the reins of his mount from a grinning cowboy.

"Looks like you got yourself a real handful there, Jake."

"No more than I can handle," he countered, swinging into the saddle with Samantha still held over his shoulder. With a speed that defied his easygoing manner, he had her in front of him in the saddle, spurring the horse into a gallop, before she could think of escape.

"You're going to pay for this," Samantha promised, clutching the saddle horn to keep her balance. "You can't just run off with me this way!"

"I didn't see anybody try to stop me," Jake pointed out.

He followed the road for some time without decreasing his pace, then cut across an open field. At a small grove of trees, he reined in, gripping Samantha around the waist when she attempted to wiggle down.

"Now, don't do that, Sam," he warned in a friendly voice. "I'd just have to catch you, and I throw a mean lasso."

He slid from the chestnut, and before her feet could touch the ground, she was back over his shoulder. Without ceremony, she was dumped under the fragile, bending leaves of a willow while he towered over her, grinning with obvious enjoyment.

"You're going to be sorry," she predicted, smoldering with fury. "I'm going to…" The rest of her words slipped back down her throat as he dropped down next to her. "You—you can't do this, Jake. You're not the kind of man who forces himself on a woman."

"Who says?" Pushing her back on the soft grass, he covered her body with his.

Her body betrayed her with instant response. Her skin tingled as his mouth brushed over it. "You're not really going to do this."

"I told you once—" his mouth moved to her ear, and his words were warm and soft against it "—not to forget your own words. There are some things you just have to do."

His kiss was long and lingering.

When her mouth was free, she drew in a deep breath and spit out with all her strength, "What kind of man are you, to make love to one woman and plan to marry another?"

His eyes lazily narrowed. He propped himself on one elbow, his other arm pinning her down. Lifting his head from his elbow, he undid the top button of her blouse. "Suppose," he continued, moving down to the next button, "you tell me whom I'm supposed to marry."

His fingers trailed a slow line from her throat, down the smooth skin her open blouse revealed, and rested on the next button. The blood began to pound in her ears. His eyes alone held her still as he spread her blouse apart. Slowly, his fingers roamed up the warmth of her skin, moving with casual possession over her. Her eyes clouded with growing need as he explored.

"Tell me who I'm going to marry, Samantha." His body shifted again, molding to hers. His shirt was warm against her naked flesh.

"L-Lesley," she stammered.

"No." His mouth lowered to the curve of her throat, his tongue teasing the vulnerable skin.

She felt the waist of her jeans loosen under his hand. His finger pushed away the material and moved along her hip. With her last claim to lucidity, she pushed against his chest.

"Please stop."

"Now I just can't do that, Sam." His hands teased the curve of her hip, trailing back up to the side of her breast. "I've waited a good long time to get you where I want you."

"I'm not staying… Did you say you weren't marrying Lesley?"

He frowned down in consideration, winding her hair

around his finger. "Seems to me I did mention that. I don't know why you're always piling your hair on top of your head when it looks so good spread all over."

"But she was wearing your ring."

"Not mine," Jake corrected, still concentrating on the hair around his finger. "Your hair's gotten lighter these past few weeks, you haven't been wearing a hat. Les has a diamond, doesn't she? I told you once diamonds don't suit you. They're cold, and they don't have much imagination. But that's Les." He shrugged and began to move his mouth over her face again. "It doesn't seem to matter to Jim."

Valiantly, Samantha attempted to follow his words. Her head shook with the effort.

"Les is engaged to Jim Bailey. I'm sure you remember Jim Bailey, you spent enough time with him at the party."

"Yes, but…"

"No buts," he interrupted. "Les likes to have a couple of fish on the line, and when she got it through her head I wasn't in season, she netted Jim without a struggle."

"But I thought…"

"I know what you thought." He cut her off again and smiled. "Running away a few days early, weren't you?"

"I wasn't running. How did you know I was leaving?"

"Sabrina told me."

"Bree?" Samantha whispered. Bree did that?

"Yeah, yesterday. She came to see me while you were packing. I like this spot right here," he stated, planting his lips against the hollow of her throat. "I've had a devil of a time putting things in order since then, so I could take time for a honeymoon. Busy time of year for a cattleman."

"Honeymoon?" Her skin was trembling where his lips continued to taste.

"I've got a good foreman," he continued, as if thinking aloud. "I reckon he can manage things for a while. I could use another day or two. I had a nice long honeymoon in mind, someplace quiet." He brought his attention back to her stunned face. "You've never been to Bora Bora, have you?"

"Are you talking about getting your ranch in order so you can take time off to marry me?" She attempted to speak slowly and clearly while her emotions whirled like a summer tornado.

"Just being practical," he explained with a bland smile.

"Why you conceited, overbearing... Just what makes you think I'll marry you? You sit back and make all these plans and expect me to run off to Bora Bora with you like a passive little puppy. Of all the chauvinist—"

"How about Antarctica?" he suggested, willing to be reasonable. "Not too many people there, either."

"You're crazy. I never said I'd marry you. What makes you think..." Her tirade was cut off effectively as his mouth coaxed her silence. When he let her breathe, her voice had lost its strength. "That's not going to help you. I'm not in love with you."

"Seems to me I recall someone telling me she was a totally honest person." His gaze was disconcertingly direct. He held her chin, preventing her face from turning away. "You want to look at me and tell me that again? You've been fighting me all along, and I think I've just about used up my patience." His lips were teasing hers again, and his hands moved over her with more urgency. "Mmm, but you have a nice body. I can't take much more of this waiting around. Six months is a long time, Sam. I've wanted you from the minute you stood there ordering Dan to have his man tend to the horses."

"Yes, you let me know very early what you wanted." She no longer struggled, but lay passive in his arms.

"Gave you something to think about. Of course, you didn't know I wanted you to be my wife, too. It was easy to tell you I wanted you, but a bit difficult to tell you I loved you. Sam, look at me." She shook her head, but the fingers on her chin tightened in authority. "Look at me." She obeyed, her lids opening to reveal eyes veiled with tears. "You stubborn little idiot. Listen carefully, I've never said this to another woman, and I've had to wait too long to say it to you. If you don't marry me soon, I'm going to lose my mind." His mouth took hers, spinning the world into nothing. Her arms flew around him as pain evaporated into unspeakable joy. "Samantha." He buried his face in the lushness of her hair. "It's been quite a race."

"I don't understand." She brought his face back to hers, needing to see the truth in his eyes. "Why didn't you tell me before?"

"I didn't think you'd believe that a man had nearly been knocked off his feet by a picture of a girl less than half his age, then had completely lost his balance when he saw the woman she'd become. If you hadn't been so wrapped up in Sabrina those first few minutes, you'd have seen how a man looks when he gets hit by lightning."

"Just like that?" Stunned, she traced the angles of his face to assure herself she was not dreaming.

"Just like that," he agreed, bringing her palm to his lips. "Then, after I'd recovered a bit, I knew I had to work around your dedication to Sabrina until you'd figured out there was room in your life for someone else.

Then you stood there telling me you were going back home as soon as the baby was born. I nearly strangled you." His fingers tightened on her hand as he brought his eyes back to hers. "How was I supposed to tell you that I loved you, that I wanted to marry you, wanted you to stay in Wyoming? The night of the party, in the kitchen, I made up my mind I wasn't letting you go, no matter what I had to do to keep you."

"But I never wanted to leave." She shook her head in brisk denial, as if he should have realized it all along. "It was just that I couldn't bear to see you married to Lesley."

"You know, things might have gotten even more complicated if Sabrina hadn't come by and laid things out for me. She's got a bit more of you in her than I had thought." Laughing, he lifted his face from hers. "She told me to sit down and listen. She'd never seen two people run around in circles so long and get nowhere."

"It's not like Bree to interfere."

"She interfered beautifully. First thing she did was ask me what business I had getting engaged to Lesley. I must have stared at her like she'd lost her mind. After I managed to tell her I was definitely not engaged to Lesley, she let me have it with both barrels. Mixed with the buckshot was the information that you were miserable about going home, and that I was a fool for not seeing it myself. Then she folded her arms, stuck out her chin exactly like someone else has a habit of doing and asked me what the devil I intended to do about it."

Samantha stared up at him and shook her head in astonishment. "I wish I could have seen that."

He smiled and lowered his mouth. "Just look in the mirror sometime." Flesh met flesh with no barriers, and with a small sound of desperation he savaged her mouth.

The hard lines of his chest pressed into her breasts. "Let me hear you say it, Samantha," he murmured, unable to resist the curve of her neck. "I need to hear you say it."

"I love you." Her mouth searched for his, her arms urging him closer. "I love you. I love you." Her lips found their objective, and her silence told him again.

"I need you, Samantha." His mouth and hands continued to seek, growing wilder, possessive, demanding. "I never knew I could need anyone the way I need you. I want you for myself for a while, no distractions, no complications, just you. We've got six months of loving to make up for. I'm going to keep you fully occupied for a very long time." Lifting his face, he smiled down at her, running his hand through the hair spread over the grass. "A very long time."

She smiled back, running her hands up his chest to circle his neck. "I intend to keep you occupied, as well. Your cows are going to get very lonely." Removing his hat, she tossed it carelessly aside, then turned back to him with raised brows. "Okay, cowboy." Her arms lifted to lock around his neck, fingers tangling possessively in his hair. "Start occupying."

"Yes, ma'am." With a polite nod, he lowered his mouth and followed orders.

* * * * *

BOUNDARY LINES

For Ruth Langan,
for all the years.

Chapter One

The wind whipped against her cheeks. It flowed through her hair, smelling faintly of spring and growing things. Jillian lifted her face to it, as much in challenge as in appreciation. Beneath her, the sleek mare strained for more speed. They'd ride, two free spirits, as long as the sun stayed high.

Short, tough grass was crushed under hooves, along with stray wildflowers. Jillian gave no thought to the buttercups as she crossed to the path. Here the soil was hard, chestnut in color and bordered by the silver-gray sage.

There were no trees along this rough, open plain, but Jillian wasn't looking for shade. She galloped by a field of wheat bleaching in the sun with hardly a stray breeze to rustle it. Farther on there was hay, acres of it, nearly ready for the first harvesting. She heard and recognized the call of a meadowlark. But she wasn't a farmer. If someone had termed her one, Jillian would have laughed or bristled, depending on her mood.

The crops were grown because they were needed, in the same way the vegetable patch was sown and tended. Growing your own feed made you self-reliant. There was nothing more important than that in Jillian's estimation. In a good year there were enough crops left over to bring in a few extra dollars. The few extra dollars would buy more cattle. It was always the cattle.

She was a rancher—like her grandfather had been, and his father before him.

The land stretched as far as she could see. Her land. It was rolling and rich. Acre after acre of grain sprouted up, and beyond it were the plains and pastures where the cattle and horses grazed. But she wasn't riding fence today, counting head, or poring over the books in her grandfather's leather-and-oak office. Today she wanted freedom, and was taking it.

Jillian hadn't been raised on the rugged, spacious plains of Montana. She hadn't been born in the saddle. She'd grown up in Chicago because her father had chosen medicine over ranching, and east over west. Jillian hadn't blamed him as her grandfather had—it was a matter of choice. Everyone was entitled to the life they chose. That was why she'd come here, back to her heritage, five years before when she'd turned twenty.

At the top of the hill Jillian stopped the mare. From here she could see over the planted fields to the pastures, fenced in with wire that could hardly be seen from that distance. It gave the illusion of open range where the cattle could roam at will. Once, it would've been like that, she mused as she tossed her hair back over her shoulder. If she narrowed her eyes, she could almost see it—open, free—the way it had been when her ancestors had first come to settle. The gold rush had brought them, but the land had kept them. It kept her.

Gold, she thought with a shake of her head. Who needed gold when there was priceless wealth in space alone? She preferred the spread of land with its isolated mountains and valleys. If her people had gone farther west, into the higher mountains, her great-great-grand-parents might have toiled in the streams and the mines. They might have staked their claim there, plucking out nuggets and digging out gold dust, but they would never have found anything richer than this. Jillian had under-stood the land's worth and its allure the first moment she'd seen it.

She'd been ten. At her grandfather's invitation— command, Jillian corrected with a smirk—both she and her brother, Marc, had made the trip west, to Utopia. Marc had been there before, of course. He'd been six-teen and quietly capable in the way of their father. And no more interested in ranching than his father had been.

Her first glimpse of the ranch hadn't surprised her, though it wasn't what many children might've expected after years of exposure to western cinema. It was vast, and somehow tidy. Paddocks, stables, barns, and the sturdy charm of the ranch house itself. Even at ten, even after one look, Jillian had known she hadn't been meant for the streets and sidewalks of Chicago, but for this open sky and endless land. At ten, she'd had her first experience with love at first sight.

But it wasn't love at first sight with her grandfather. He'd been a tough, weathered, opinionated old man. The ranch and his herd had been his life. He hadn't the least idea what to do with a spindly girl who happened to be his son's daughter. They'd circled each other warily for days, until he'd made the mistake of letting out some caustic remark about her father and his choice of pills and needles. Quick tempered, Jillian had flown to her father's defense. They'd ended up shouting at each other, Jillian red-faced and dry-eyed even after being threatened with a razor strap.

They'd parted at the end of that visit with a combination of mutual respect and dislike. Then he'd sent her a custom-made, buff-colored Stetson for her birthday. And it began…

Perhaps they'd grown to love one another so deeply because they'd taken their time about it. Those sporadic weeks during her adolescence he'd taught her everything, hardly seeming to teach at all: how to gauge the weather by the smell of the air, the look of the sky; how to deliver a breech calf; how to ride fence and herd a steer. She'd called him Clay because they'd been friends. And when she'd tried her first and only plug of tobacco, he'd held her head when she'd been sick. He hadn't lectured.

When his eyes had grown weak, Jillian had taken over the books. They'd never discussed it—just as they'd never discussed that her move there in the summer of her twentieth year would be permanent. When his illness had begun to take over, she'd gradually assumed the responsibilities of the ranch, though no words had passed between them to make it official.

When he died, the ranch was hers. Jillian hadn't needed to hear the will read to know it. Clay had known she would stay. She'd left the east behind—and if there were memories from there that still twisted inside her, she buried them. More easily than she'd buried her grandfather.

It was herself she grieved for, and knowing it made her impatient. Clay had lived long and hard, doing as he chose the way he chose. His illness had wasted him, and would have brought him pain and humiliation had it continued. He would have hated that, would have railed at her if he could have seen how she'd wept over him.

God Almighty, girl! What're you wasting time here for? Don't you know there's a ranch to run? Get some hands out to check the fence in the west forty before we've got cattle roaming all over Montana.

Yes, she thought with a half smile. He'd have said something like that—cursed her a bit, then would've turned away with a grunt. Of course, she'd have cursed right back at him.

"You mangy old bear," she muttered. "I'm going to turn Utopia into the best ranch in Montana just to spite you." Laughing, she threw her face up to the sky. "See if I don't!"

Sensing her change of mood, the mare began to dance impatiently, tossing her head. "All right, Delilah." Jillian leaned over to pat her creamy neck. "We've got all afternoon." In a deft move she turned the mare around and started off at an easy lope.

There weren't many free hours like this, so they were prized. As it was, Jillian knew she'd stolen them. That made it all the sweeter. If she had to work eighteen hours tomorrow to make up for it, she'd do it without complaint. Even the bookwork, she thought with a sigh. Though there was that sick heifer that needed watching, and the damn Jeep that'd broken down for the third time this month. And the fence along the boundary line. The Murdock boundary line, she thought with a grimace.

The feud between the Barons and the Murdocks stretched back to the early 1900s when Noah Baron, her great-grandfather, came to southeast Montana. He'd meant to go on, to the mountains and the gold, but had stayed to homestead. The Murdocks had already been there, with their vast, rich ranch. The Barons had been peasants to them, intruders doomed to fail—or to be driven out. Jillian gritted her teeth as she remembered the stories her grandfather had told her: cut fences, stolen cattle, ruined crops.

But the Barons had stayed, survived, and succeeded. No, they didn't have the amount of land the Murdocks did, or the money, but they knew how to make the best use of what they did have. If her grandfather had struck oil as the Murdocks had, Jillian thought with a smirk, they could have afforded to specialize in purebred beef as well. That had been a matter of chance, not skill.

She told herself she didn't care about the purebred part of it. Let the Murdock clan wave their blue ribbons and shout about improving the line. She'd raise her Herefords and shorthorns and get the best price for them at the Exchange. Baron beef was prime, and everyone knew it.

When was the last time one of the high-and-mighty Murdocks rode the miles of fence, sweating under the sun while checking for a break? When was the last time one of them had eaten dust on a drive? Jillian knew for a fact that Paul J. Murdock, her grandfather's contemporary, hadn't bothered to ride fence or flank cattle in more than a year.

She let out a short, derisive laugh. All they knew about was the figures in the account books and politicking. By the time she was finished, Utopia would make the Double M look like a dude ranch.

The idea put her in a better mood, so that the line between her brows vanished. She wouldn't think of the Murdocks today, or of the back-breaking work that promised to begin before the sun came up tomorrow. She would think only of the sweetness of these stolen hours, of the rich smell of spring…and the endless hard blue of the sky.

Jillian knew this path well. It ran along the westernmost tip of her land. Too tough for the plow, too stubborn for grazing, it was left alone. It was here she always came when she wanted both a sense of solitude and excitement. No one else came here, from her own ranch or from the Murdock spread that ran parallel to it. Even the fence that had once formed the boundary had fallen years before, and had been forgotten. No one cared about this little slice of useless land but her, which made her care all the more.

Now there were a few trees, the cottonwood and aspen just beginning to green. Over the sound of the mare's hooves she heard a warbler begin to sing. There might be coyotes too, and certainly rattlesnakes. Jillian wasn't so enchanted she didn't remember that. There was a rifle, oiled and loaded, strapped to the back of her saddle.

The mare scented the water from the pond, and Jillian let her have her head. The thought of stripping off her sweaty clothes and diving in appealed immensely. Five minutes in that clear, icy water would be exhilarating, and Delilah could rest and drink before they began the long trip back. Spotting the glistening water, Jillian let the reins drop, relaxing. Her grandfather would have cursed her for her lack of attention, but she was already thinking about the luxury of sliding naked into the cold water, then drying in the sun.

But the mare scented something else. Abruptly she reared, plunging so that Jillian's first thought was rattler. While she struggled to control Delilah with one hand, she reached behind for the rifle. Before she could draw a breath, she was hurtling through space. Jillian only had time for one muttered oath before she landed bottom first in the pond. But she'd seen that the rattlesnake had legs.

Sputtering and furious, she struggled to her feet, wiping her wet hair out of her eyes so that she could glare at the man astride a buckskin stallion. Delilah danced nervously while he held the glistening stallion still.

He didn't need to have his feet on the ground for her to see that he was tall. His hair was dark, waving thick and long beneath a black Stetson that shadowed a raw-boned, weathered face. His nose was straight and aristocratic, his mouth well shaped and solemn. Jillian didn't take the time to admire the way he sat the stallion—with a casual sort of control that exuded confidence and power. What she did see was that his eyes were nearly as black as his hair. And laughing.

Narrowing her own, she spat at him, "What the hell are you doing on my land?"

He looked at her in silence, the only movement a very slow lifting of his left brow. Unlike Jillian, he was taking the time to admire. Her fiery hair was darkened almost to copper with the water and clung wetly to accent the elegance of bone and skin—fine boned, honey-toned skin. He could see the flash of green that was her eyes, dark as jade and dangerous as a cat's. Her mouth, clamped together in fury, had a luxuriously full, promising lower lip that contrasted with the firm stubborn chin.

Casually he let his gaze slide down. She was a long one, he thought, with hardly more curves than a boy. But just now, with the shirt wet and snug as a second skin… Slowly his gaze climbed back to hers. She didn't blush at the survey, though she recognized it. There wasn't apprehension or fear in her eyes. Instead, she shot him a hard look that might have withered another man.

"I said," Jillian began in a low, clipped voice, "what the hell are you doing on my land?"

Instead of answering he swung out of the saddle—the move smooth and economic enough to tell her he'd been in and out of one most of his life. He walked toward her with a loose, easy stride that still carried the air of command. Then he smiled. In one quick flash his face changed from dangerously sexy to dangerously charming. It was a smile that said, you can trust me…for the moment. He held out a hand.

"Ma'am."

Jillian drew in one deep breath and let it out again. Ignoring the offered hand, she climbed out of the water by herself. Dripping, cold, but far from cooled off, Jillian stuck her hands on her hips. "You haven't answered my question."

Nerve, he thought, still studying her. She's got plenty of that. Temper and—he noticed the way her chin was thrown up in challenge—arrogance. He liked the combination. Hooking his thumbs in his pockets, he shifted his weight, thinking it was a shame she'd dry off quickly in the full sun.

"This isn't your land," he said smoothly, with only a hint of a western drawl. "Miss…"

"Baron," Jillian snapped. "And who the hell are you to tell me this isn't my land?"

He tipped his hat with more insolence than respect.

"Aaron Murdock." His lips twitched at her hiss of breath. "Boundary runs straight up through here." He looked down at the toes of his boots inches away from the toes of hers as if he could see the line drawn there. "Cuts about clean down the middle of the pond." He brought his gaze back to hers—mouth solemn, eyes laughing. "I think you landed on my side."

Aaron Murdock, son and heir. Wasn't he supposed to be out in Billings playing in their damn oil fields? Frowning, Jillian decided he didn't look like the smooth college boy her grandfather had described to her. That was something she'd think about later. Right now, it was imperative she make her stand, and make it stick.

"*If* I landed on your side," she said scathingly, "it was because you were lurking around with that." She jerked her thumb at his horse. Gorgeous animal, she thought with an admiration she had to fight to conceal.

"Your hands were slack on the reins," he pointed out mildly.

The truth of it only added fuel to the fire. "His scent spooked Delilah."

"Delilah." A flicker of amusement ran over his face as he pushed back his hat and studied the smooth clean lines of Jillian's mare. "Must've been fate," he murmured. "Samson." At the sound of his name the stallion walked over to nuzzle Aaron's shoulder.

Jillian choked back a chuckle, but not in time to conceal the play of a small dimple at the side of her mouth. "Just remember what Samson's fate was," she retorted. "And keep him away from my mare."

"A mighty pretty filly," Aaron said easily. While he stroked his horse's head his eyes remained on Jillian. "A bit high strung," he continued, "but well built. She'd breed well."

Jillian's eyes narrowed again. Aaron found he liked the way they glinted through the thick, luxurious lashes. "I'll worry about her breeding, Murdock." She planted her feet in the ground that soaked up the water still dripping from her. "What're you doing up here?" she demanded. "You won't find any oil."

Aaron tilted his head. "I wasn't looking for any. I wasn't looking for a woman either." Casually he reached over and lifted a strand of her heavy hair. "But I found one."

Jillian felt that quick, breathless pressure in her chest and recognized it. Oh, no, she'd let that happen to her once before. She let her gaze drop down to where his long brown fingers toyed with the ends of her hair, then lifted it to his face again. "You wouldn't want to lose that hand," she said softly.

For a moment, his fingers tightened, as if he considered picking up the challenge she'd thrown down. Then, as casually as he'd captured her hair, he released it. "Testy, aren't you?" Aaron said mildly. "But then, you Barons've always been quick to draw."

"To defend," Jillian corrected, standing her ground.

They measured each other a moment, both surprised to find the opposition so attractive. Tread carefully. The command went through each of their minds, though it was an order both habitually had trouble carrying out.

"I'm sorry about the old man," Aaron said at length. "He'd have been your—grandfather?"

Jillian's chin stayed up, but Aaron saw the shadow that briefly clouded her eyes. "Yes."

She'd loved him, Aaron thought with some surprise. From his few run-ins with Clay Baron, he'd found a singularly unlovable man. He let his memory play back with the snatches of information he'd gleaned since his return to the Double M. "You'd be the little girl who spent some summers here years back," he commented, trying to remember if he'd ever caught sight of her before. "From back east." His hand came back to stroke his chin, a bit rough from the lack of razor that morning. "Jill, isn't it?"

"Jillian," she corrected coldly.

"Jillian." The swift smile transformed his face again. "It suits you better."

"Miss Baron suits me best," she told him, damning his smile.

Aaron didn't bother to acknowledge her deliberate unfriendliness, instead giving in to the urge to let his gaze slip briefly to her mouth again. No, he didn't believe he'd seen her before. That wasn't a mouth a man forgot. "If Gil Haley's running things at Utopia, you should do well enough."

She bristled. He could almost see her spine snap straight. "I run things at Utopia," she said evenly.

His mouth tilted at one corner. "You?"

"That's right, Murdock, me. I haven't been pushing papers in Billings for the last five years." Something flashed in his eyes, but she ignored it and plunged ahead. "Utopia's mine, every inch of ground, every blade of grass. The difference is I work it instead of strutting around the State Fair waving my blue ribbons."

Intrigued, he took her hands, ignoring her protest as he turned them over to study the palms. They were slender, but hard and capable. Running his thumb over a line of callus, Aaron felt a ripple of admiration—and desire. He'd grown very weary of pampered helpless hands in Billings. "Well, well," he murmured, keeping her hands in his as he looked back into her eyes.

She was furious—that his hands were so strong, that they held hers so effortlessly. That her heartbeat was roaring in her ears. The warbler had begun to sing again and she could hear the gentle swish of the horses' tails as they stood.

He smelled pleasantly of leather and sweat. Too pleasantly. There was a rim of amber around the outside of his irises that only accented the depth of brown. A scar, very thin and white, rode along the edge of his jaw. You wouldn't notice it unless you looked very closely. Just as you might not notice how strong and lean his hands were unless yours were caught in them.

Jillian snapped back quickly. It didn't pay to notice things like that. It didn't pay to listen to that roaring in your head. She'd done that once before and where had it gotten her? Dewy-eyed, submissive, and soft-headed. She was a lot smarter than she'd been five years before. The most important thing was to remember who he was—a Murdock. And who she was—a Baron.

"I warned you about your hands before," she said quietly.

"So you did," Aaron agreed, watching her face. "Why?"

"I don't like to be touched."

"No?" His brow lifted again, but he didn't yet release her hands. "Most living things do—if they're touched properly." His eyes locked on hers abruptly, very direct, very intuitive. "Someone touch you wrong once, Jillian?"

Her gaze didn't falter. "You're trespassing, Murdock."

Again, that faint inclination of the head. "Maybe. We could always string the fence again."

She knew he hadn't misunderstood her. This time, when she tugged on her hands, he released them. "Just stay on your side," she suggested.

He adjusted his hat so that the shadow fell over his face again. "And if I don't?"

Her chin came up. "Then I'll have to deal with you." Turning her back, she walked to Delilah and gathered the reins. It took an effort not to pass her hand over the buckskin stallion, but she resisted. Without looking at Aaron, Jillian swung easily into the saddle, then fit her own damp, flat-brimmed hat back on her head. Now she had the satisfaction of being able to look down at him.

In a better humor, Jillian leaned on the saddle horn. Leather creaked easily beneath her as Delilah shifted her weight. Her shirt was drying warm on her back. "You have a nice vacation, Murdock," she told him with a faint smile. "Don't wear yourself out while you're here."

He reached up to stroke Delilah's neck. "Now, I'm going to try real hard to take your advice on that, Jillian."

She leaned down a bit closer. "Miss Baron."

Aaron surprised her by tugging the brim of her hat down to her nose. "I like Jillian." He grabbed the string tie of the hat before she could straighten, then gave her a long, odd look. "I swear," he murmured, "you smell like something a man could just close his eyes and wallow in."

She was amused. Jillian told herself she was amused while she pretended not to feel the quick trip of her pulse. She removed his hand from the string of her hat, straightened, and smiled. "You disappoint me. I'd've thought a man who'd spent so much time in college and the big city would have a snappier line and a smoother delivery."

He slipped his hands into his back pockets as he looked up at her. It was fascinating to watch the way the sun shot into her eyes without drawing out the smallest fleck of gold or gray in that cool, deep green. The eyes were too stubborn to allow for any interference; they suited the woman. "I'll practice," Aaron told her with the hint of a smile. "I'll do better next time."

She gave a snort of laughter and started to turn her horse. "There won't be a next time."

His hand was firm on the bridle before she could trot off. The look he gave her was calm, and only slightly amused. "You look smarter than that, Jillian. We'll have a number of next times before we're through."

She didn't know how she'd lost the advantage so quickly, only that she had. Her chin angled. "You seem determined to lose that hand, Murdock."

He gave her an easy smile, patted Delilah's neck, then turned toward his own horse. "I'll see you soon, Jillian."

She waited, seething, until he'd swung into the saddle. Delilah sidestepped skittishly until the horses were nearly nose to nose. "Stay on your own side," Jillian ordered, then pressed in her heels. The straining mare lunged forward.

Samson tossed his head and pranced as they both watched Jillian race off on Delilah. "Not this time," Aaron murmured to himself, soothing his horse. "But soon." He gave a quick laugh, then pointed his horse in the opposite direction. "Damn soon."

Jillian could get rid of a lot of anger and frustration with the speed and the wind. She rode as the mare wanted—fast. Perhaps Delilah needed to outrace her blood as well, Jillian thought wryly. Both male animals had been compelling. If the stallion had belonged to anyone but a Murdock, she would've found a way to have Delilah bred with him—no matter what the stud fee. If she had any hope of increasing and improving Utopia's line of horses, the bulk of the burden rested with her own mare. And there wasn't a stallion on her ranch that could compare with Murdock's Samson.

It was a pity Aaron Murdock hadn't been the smooth,

fastidious, boring businessman she'd envisioned him. That type would never have made her blood heat. A woman in her position couldn't afford to acknowledge that kind of attraction, especially with a rival. It would put her at an immediate disadvantage when she needed every edge she could get.

So much depended on the next six months if she was going to have the chance to expand. Oh, the ranch could go on, making its cozy little profit, but she wanted more. The fire of her grandfather's ambition hadn't dimmed so much with age as it had been transferred to her. With her youth and energy, and with that fickle lady called luck, she could turn Utopia into the empire her ancestors had dreamed about.

She had the land and the knowledge. She had the skill and the determination. Already, Jillian had poured the cash portion of her inheritance back into the ranch. She'd put a down payment on the small plane her grandfather had been too stubborn to buy. With a plane, the ranch could be patrolled in hours, stray cattle spotted, broken fences reported. Though she still believed in the necessity of a skilled puncher and cow pony, Jillian understood the beauty of mixing new techniques with the old.

Pickups and Jeeps roamed the range as well as horses. CBs could be used to communicate over long distances, while the lariat was still carried by every hand—in the saddle or behind the wheel. The cattle would be driven to feed lots when necessary and the calves herded into the corral for branding, though the iron would be heated by a butane torch rather than an open fire. Times had changed, but the spirit and the code remained.

Above all, the rancher, like any other country person, depended on two things: the sky and the earth. Because the first was always fickle and the second often unyielding, the rancher had no choice but to rely, ultimately, on himself. That was Jillian's philosophy.

With that in mind, she changed directions without changing her pace. She'd ride along the Murdock boundary and check the fences after all.

She trotted along an open pasture while broadrumped, white-faced Herefords barely glanced up from their grazing. The spring grass was growing thick and full. Hearing the rumble of an engine, she stopped. In almost the same manner as her mount, Jillian scented the air. Gasoline. It was a shame to spoil the scent of grass and cattle with it. Philosophically she turned Delilah in the direction of the sound and rode.

It was easy to spot the battered pickup in the rolling terrain. Jillian lifted her hand in half salute and rode toward it. Her mood had lifted again, though her jeans were still damp and her boots soggy. She considered Gil Haley one of the few dyed-in-the-wool cowboys left on her ranch or any other. A hundred years before, he'd have been happy riding the range with his saddle, bedroll, and plug of tobacco. If he had the chance, she mused, he'd be just as happy that way today.

"Gil." Jillian stopped Delilah by the driver's window and grinned at him.

"You disappeared this morning." His greeting was brusque in a voice that sounded perpetually peppery. He didn't expect an explanation, nor would she have given one.

Jillian nodded to the two men with him, another breed of cowhand, distinguished by their heavy work shoes. Gil might give in to the pickup because he could patrol fifty thousand acres quicker and more thoroughly than on horseback, but he'd never give up his boots. "Any problem?"

"Dumb cow tangled in the wire a ways back." He shifted his tobacco plug while looking up at her with his perpetual squint. "Got her out before she did any damage. Looks like we've got to clear out some of that damn tumbleweed again. Knocked down some line."

Jillian accepted this with a nod. "Anyone check the fence along the west section today?"

There was no change in the squint as he eyed her. "Nope."

"I'll see to it now, then." Jillian hesitated. If there was anyone who knew the gossip, it would be Gil. "I happened to run into Aaron Murdock about an hour ago," she put in casually. "I thought he was in Billings."

"Nope."

Jillian gave him a mild look. "I realize that, Gil. What's he doing around here?"

"Got himself a ranch."

Gamely Jillian hung on to her temper. "I realize that too. He's also got himself an oil field—or his father does."

"Kid sister married herself an oil man," Gil told her. "The old man did some shifting around and got the boy back where he wants him."

"You mean…" Jillian narrowed her eyes. "Aaron Murdock's staying on the Double M?"

"Managing it," Gil stated, then spit expertly. "Guess things've simmered down after the blowup a few years back. Murdock's getting on, you know, close on to seventy or more. Maybe he wants to sit back and relax now."

"Managing it," Jillian muttered. So she was going to be plagued with a Murdock after all. At least she and the old man had managed to stay out of each other's way. Aaron had already invaded what she considered her private haven—even if he did own half of it. "How long's he been back?"

Gil took his time answering, tugging absently at the grizzled gray mustache that hung over his lip—a habit Jillian usually found amusing. "Couple weeks."

And she'd already plowed into him. Well, she'd had five years of peace, Jillian reminded herself. In country with this much space, she should be able to avoid one man without too much trouble. There were other questions she wanted to ask, but they'd wait until she and Gil were alone.

"I'll check the fence," she said briefly, then turned the mare and rode west.

Gil watched her with a twinkle. He might squint, but his eyesight was sharp enough to have noticed her damp clothes. And the fire in her eyes. Ran into Aaron Murdock, did she? With a wheeze and a chuckle, he started the pickup. It gave a man something to speculate on.

"Keep your eyes front, son," he grumbled to the young hand who was craning his neck to get a last look of Jillian as she galloped over the pasture.

Chapter Two

The day began before sunrise. There was stock to be fed, eggs to be gathered, cows to be milked. Even with machines, capable hands were needed. Jillian had grown so accustomed to helping with the early morning chores, it never occurred to her to stop now that she was the owner. Ranch life was a routine that varied only in the number of animals to be tended and the weather in which you tended them.

It was pleasantly cool when Jillian made the trip from the ranch house to the stables, but she'd crossed the same ground when the air had been so hot and thick it seemed to stick to her skin, or when the snow had been past her boot tops. There was only a faint lessening in the dark, a hint of color in the eastern sky, but the ranch yard already held signs of life. She caught the scent of grilled meat and coffee as the ranch cook started breakfast.

Men and women went about their chores quietly, with an occasional oath, or a quick laugh. Because all of them had just been through a Montana winter, this sweet spring morning was prized. Spring gave way to summer heat, and summer drought too quickly.

Jillian crossed the concrete passageway and opened Delilah's stall. As always, she would tend her first before going on to the other horses, then the dairy cows. A few of the men were there before her, measuring out grain, filling troughs. There was the click of boot heels on concrete, the jingle of spurs.

Some of them owned their own horses, but the bulk of them used Utopia's line. All of them owned their own saddles. Her grandfather's hard-and-fast rule.

The stables smelled comfortably of horses and hay and sweet grain. By the time the stock had been fed and led out to the corrals, it was nearly light. Automatically, Jillian headed for the vast white barn where cows waited to be milked.

"Jillian."

She stopped, waiting for Joe Carlson, her herdsman, to cross the ranch yard. He didn't walk like a cowboy, or dress like one, simply because he wasn't one. He had a smooth, even gait that suited his rather cocky good looks. The early sun teased out the gold in his curling hair. He rode a Jeep rather than a horse and preferred a dry wine to beer, but he knew cattle. Jillian needed him if she was to make a real success out of what was now just dabbling in the purebred industry. She'd hired him six months before over her grandfather's grumbles, and didn't regret it.

"Morning, Joe."

"Jillian." He shook his head when he reached her, then pushed back the powder-gray hat he kept meticulously clean. "When are you going to stop working a fifteen-hour day?"

She laughed and started toward the dairy barn again, matching her longer, looser stride with his. "In August, when I have to start working an eighteen-hour day."

"Jillian." He put a hand on her shoulder, stopping her at the entrance of the barn. His hand was neat and well shaped, tanned but not callused. For some reason it reminded her of a stronger hand, a harder one. She frowned at the horizon. "You know it's not necessary for you to tie yourself down to every aspect of this ranch. You've got enough hands working for you. If you'd hire a manager…"

It was an old routine and Jillian answered it in the usual way. "I am the manager," she said simply. "I don't consider the ranch a toy or a tax break, Joe. Before I hire someone to take over for me, I'll sell out."

"You work too damn hard."

"You worry too much," she countered, but smiled. "I appreciate it. How's the bull?"

Joe's teeth flashed, straight, even, and white. "Mean as ever, but he's bred with every cow we've let within ten feet of him. He's a beauty."

"I hope so," Jillian murmured, remembering just what the purebred Hereford bull had cost her. Still, if he was everything Joe had claimed, he was her start in improving the quality of Utopia's beef.

"Just wait till the calves start dropping," Joe advised, giving her shoulder a quick squeeze. "You want to come take a look at him?"

"Mmmm, maybe later." She took a step inside the barn, then shot a look over her shoulder. "I'd like to see that bull take the blue ribbon over the Murdock entry in July." She grinned, quick and insolent. "Damned if I wouldn't."

By the time the stock had been fed and Jillian had

bolted down her own breakfast, it was full light. The long hours and demands should have kept her mind occupied. They always had. Between her concerns over feed and wages and fence, there shouldn't have been room for thoughts of Aaron Murdock. But there was. Jillian decided that once she had the answers to her questions she'd be able to put him out of her mind. So she'd better see about getting them. She hailed Gil before he could climb into his pickup.

"I'm going with you today," she told him as she hopped into the passenger's seat.

He shrugged and spit tobacco out the window. "Suit yourself."

Jillian grinned at the greeting and pushed her hat back on her head. A few heavy red curls dipped over her brow. "Why is it you've never gotten married, Gil? You're such a charmer."

Beneath his grizzled mustache his lips quivered. "Always was a smart aleck." He started the engine and aimed his squint at her. "What about you? You might be skinny, but you ain't ugly."

She propped a booted foot on his dash. "I'd rather run my own life," she said easily. "Men want to tell you what to do and how to do it."

"Woman ain't got no business out here on her own," Gil said stubbornly as he drove out of the ranch yard.

"And men do?" Jillian countered, lazily examining the toe of her boot.

"Men's different."

"Better?"

He shifted, knowing he was already getting out of his depth. "Different," he said again and clamped his lips.

Jillian laughed and settled back. "You old coot," she said fondly. "Tell me about this blowup at the Murdocks'."

"Had a few of them. They're a hardheaded bunch."

"So I've heard. The one that happened before Aaron Murdock went to Billings."

"Kid had lots of ideas when he come back from college." He snorted at education in the way of a man who considered the best learning came from doing. "Maybe some of them were right enough," he conceded. "Always was smart, and knew how to sit a horse."

"Isn't that why he went to college?" Jillian probed. "To get ideas?"

Gil grunted. "Seems the old man felt the boy was taking over too quick. Rumor is the boy agreed to work for his father for three years, then he was supposed to take over. Manage the place like."

Gil stopped at a gate and Jillian climbed out to open it, waiting until he'd driven through before closing and locking it behind her. Another dry day, she thought with a glance at the sky. They'd need some rain soon. A pheasant shot out of the field to her right and wheeled with a flash of color into the sky. She could smell sweet clover.

"So?" she said when she hopped into the truck again.

"So when the three years was up, the old man balked. Wouldn't give the boy the authority they'd agreed on. Well, they got tempers, those Murdocks." He grinned, showing off his dentures. "The boy up and quit, said he'd start his own spread."

"That's what I'd've done," Jillian muttered. "Murdock had no right to go back on his word."

"Maybe not. But he talked the boy into going to Billings 'cause there was some trouble there with the books and such. Nobody could much figure why he did it, unless the old man made it worth his while."

Jillian sneered. Money, she thought derisively. If

Aaron had had any guts, he'd've thumbed his nose at his father and started his own place. Probably couldn't handle the idea of starting from the ground up. But she remembered his face, the hard, strong feel of his hand. Something, she thought, puzzled, just didn't fit.

"What do you think of him, Gil—personally?"

"Who?"

"Aaron Murdock," she snapped.

"Can't say much," Gil began slowly, rubbing a hand over his face to conceal another grin. "Was a bright kid and full of sass, like one or two others I've known." He gave a hoot when Jillian narrowed her eyes at him. "Wasn't afraid of work neither. By the time he'd grown whiskers, he had the ladies sighing over him too." Gil put a hand to his heart and gave an exaggerated sigh of his own. Jillian punched him enthusiastically in the arm.

"I'm not interested in his love life, Gil," she began and then immediately changed gears. "He's never married?"

"Guess he figured a woman might want to tell him what to do and how to do it," Gil returned blandly.

Jillian started to swear at him, then laughed instead. "You're a clever old devil, Gil Haley. Look here!" She put a hand on his arm. "We've got calves."

They got out to walk the pasture together, taking a head count and enjoying one of the first true pleasures of spring: new life.

"These'd be from the new bull." Jillian watched a calf nurse frantically while its mother half dozed in the sun.

"Yep." Gil's squint narrowed further while he skimmed over the grazing herd and the new offspring. "I reckon Joe knows what he's about," he murmured and rubbed his chin. "How many younguns you count?"

"Ten and looks like twenty more cows nearly ready

to drop." She frowned over the numbers a moment. "Wasn't there—" Jillian broke off as a new sound came over the bored mooing and rustling. "Over there," she said even as Gil started forward.

They found him collapsed and frightened beside his dying mother. A day old, no more than two, Jillian estimated as she gathered up the calf, crooning to him. The cow lay bleeding, barely breathing. The birth had gone wrong. Jillian didn't need Gil to tell her that. The cow had survived the breech, then had crawled off to die.

If the plane had been up…Jillian thought grimly as Gil walked silently back to the pickup. If the plane had been up, someone would've spotted her from the air, and… She shook her head and nuzzled the calf. This was the price of it, she reminded herself. You couldn't mourn over every cow or horse you lost in the course of a year. But when she saw Gil returning with his rifle, she gave him a look of helpless grief. Then she turned and walked away.

One shudder rippled through her at the sound of the shot, then she forced herself to push the weakness away. Still carrying the calf, she went back to Gil.

"Going to have to call for some men on the CB," he told her. "It's going to take more than you and me to load her up." He cupped the calf's head in his hand and studied him. "Hope this one's got some fight in him or he ain't going to make it."

"He'll make it," Jillian said simply. "I'm going to see to it." She went back to the truck, murmuring to soothe the newborn in her arms.

By nine o'clock that evening she was exhausted. Antelope had raced through a hay field and damaged half an acre's crop. One of her men fractured his arm when his horse was spooked by a snake. They'd found three breaks in the wire along the Murdock boundary and some of her cows had strayed. It had taken the better part of the day to round them up again and repair the fence.

Every spare minute Jillian had been able to scrape together had been dedicated to the orphaned calf. She'd given him a warm, dry stall in the cattle barn and had taken charge of his feeding herself. She ended her day there, with one low light burning and the scent and sound of animals around her.

"Here, now." She sat cross-legged on the fresh hay and stroked the calf's small white face. "You're feeling better." He let out a high, shaky sound that made her laugh. "Yes, Baby, I'm your momma now."

To her relief he took the nipple easily. Twice before, she'd had to force feed him. This time, she had to take a firm hold on the bottle to prevent him from tugging it right out of her hand. He's catching on, she thought, stroking him as he sucked. It's a tough life, but the only one we've got.

"Pretty Baby," she murmured, then laughed when he wobbled and sat down hard, back legs spread, without releasing the nipple. "Go ahead and be greedy." Jillian tilted the bottle higher. "You're entitled." His eyes clung to hers as he pulled in his feed. "In a few months you'll be out in the pasture with the rest of them, eating grass and raising hell. I've got a feeling about you, Baby," she said thoughtfully as she scratched his ears. "You might just be a real success with the ladies."

When he started to suck air, Jillian pulled the nipple away. The calf immediately began to nibble at her jeans. "Idiot, you're not a goat." Jillian gave him a gentle shove so that he rolled over and lay, content to have her stroke him.

"Making a pet out of him?"

She whipped her head around quickly and stared up at Aaron Murdock. While he watched, the laughter died out of her eyes. "What are you doing here?"

"One of your favorite questions," he commented as he stepped inside the stall. "Nice-looking calf." He crouched beside her.

Sandalwood and leather. Jillian caught just a whiff of it on him and automatically shifted away. She wanted no scent to creep up and remind her of him when he was gone. "Did you take a wrong turn, Murdock?" she asked dryly. "This is my ranch."

Slowly, he turned his head until their eyes met. Aaron wasn't certain just how long he'd stood watching her— he hadn't intended to watch at all. Maybe it had been the way she'd laughed, that low, smoky sound that had a way of rippling along a man's skin. Maybe it had been the way her hair had glistened—firelike in the low light. Or maybe it had just been that softness he'd seen in her eyes when she'd murmured to the calf. There'd been something about that look that had had tiny aches rushing to the surface. A man needed a woman to look at him like that—first thing in the morning, last thing at night.

There was no softness in her eyes now, but a challenge, a defiance. That stirred something in him as well, something he recognized with more ease. Desire was so simple to label. He smiled.

"I didn't take a wrong turn, Jillian. I wanted to talk to you."

She wouldn't allow herself the luxury of shifting away from him again, or him the pleasure of knowing how badly she wanted to. She sat where she was and tilted her chin. "About what?"

His gaze skimmed over her face. He was beginning to wish he hadn't stayed in Billings quite so long. "Horse breeding—for a start."

Excitement flickered into her eyes and gave her away even though she schooled her voice to casual disinterest. "Horse breeding?"

"Your Delilah." Casually he wound her hair around his finger. What kind of secret female trick did she use to make it so soft? he wondered. "My Samson. I'm too romantic to let a coincidence like that pass."

"Romantic, my foot." Jillian brushed his hand aside only to find her fingers caught in his.

"You'd be surprised," Aaron said softly. So softly only a well-tuned ear would have heard the steel in it. "I also know a—" his gaze skimmed insolently over her face again "—prime filly when I see one." He laughed when her eyes flashed at him. "Are you always so ready to wrestle, Jillian?"

"I'm always ready to talk business, Murdock," she countered. *Don't be too anxious.* Jillian remembered her grandfather's schooling well. *Always play your cards close to your chest.* "I might be interested in breeding Delilah with your stallion, but I'll need another look at him first."

"Fair enough. Come by tomorrow—nine."

She wanted to jump at it. Five years in Montana and she'd never seen the Murdock spread. And that stallion… Still, she'd been taught too well. "If I can manage it. Middle of the morning's a busy time." Then she was laughing because the calf, weary of being ignored, was butting against her knee. "Spoiled already." Obligingly she tickled his belly.

"Acts more like a puppy than a cow," Aaron stated, but reached over to scratch the calf's ears. It surprised her how gentle his fingers could be. "How'd he lose his mother?"

"Birthing went wrong." She grinned when the calf licked the back of Aaron's hand. "He likes you. Too young to know better."

Amused, Aaron lifted a brow. "Like I said, it's a matter of touching the right way." He slid one lean hand over the calf's head and massaged its neck. "There's one technique for soothing babies, another for breaking horses, and another for gentling a woman."

"Gentling a woman?" Jillian sent him an arch look that held humor rather than annoyance. "That's a remarkable phrase."

"An apt one, in certain cases."

She watched as the calf, satisfied, his belly full, curled up on the hay to sleep. "A typical male animal," Jillian remarked, still smiling, "Apparently, you're another."

There wasn't any heat in the comment, but an acceptance. "Could be," he agreed, "though I wouldn't say you were typical."

Unconsciously relaxed, Jillian studied him. "I don't *think* you meant that as a compliment."

"No, it was an observation. You'd spit a compliment back in my face."

Delighted, Jillian threw back her head and laughed. "Whatever else you are, Murdock, you're not stupid." Still chuckling, she leaned back against the wall of the stall, bringing up one knee and circling it with her hands. At the moment she didn't want to question why she was pleased to have his company.

"I have a first name." A trick of the angle had the light slanting over her eyes, highlighting them and casting her face in shadow. He felt the stir again. "Ever thought of using it?"

"Not really." But that was a lie, she realized. She already thought of him as Aaron. The real trouble was that she thought of him at all. Yet she smiled again, too comfortable to make an issue of it. "Baby's asleep," she murmured.

Aaron glanced over, grinning. Would she still call him Baby when he was a bull weighing several hundred pounds? Probably. "It's been a long day."

"Mmmm." She stretched her arms to the ceiling, feeling her muscles loosen. The exhaustion she dragged into the barn with her had become a rather pleasant fatigue. "They're never long enough. If I had just ten hours more in a week, I'd catch up."

With what? he wondered. Herself? "Ever heard of overachievement, Jillian?"

"Ambition," she corrected. Her eyes met his again and held. "I'm not the one who's willing to settle for what's handed to her."

Temper surged into him so quickly he clenched at the hay under him. It was clear she was referring to his father's ranch and his own position there. His expression remained completely passive as he battled back the need to strike out where he was struck. "Each of us does what he has to do," Aaron said mildly and let the hay sift through his hands.

It annoyed her that he didn't defend himself. She wanted him to give her his excuses, his reasons. It shouldn't matter, Jillian reminded herself. He shouldn't matter. He didn't, she assured herself with something perilously close to panic. Of course he didn't. Rising, she dusted off her jeans.

"I've got paperwork to see to before I turn in."

He rose too, more slowly, so that it was too late when she realized she was backed into the corner of the stall. "Not even going to offer me a cup of coffee, Jillian?"

There was a band of tension at the back of her neck, a thudding at her ribs. She recognized the temper in his eyes, and though she wondered that she hadn't noticed it before, it wasn't his temper that worried her. It was her own shaky pulse. "No," she said evenly. "I'm not."

He hooked his thumbs through his belt loops and studied her lazily. "You've got a problem with manners."

Her chin came up. "Manners don't concern me."

"No?" He smiled then, in a way that made her brace herself. "Then we'll drop them."

In a move too quick for her to evade, he gathered her shirtfront in one hand and yanked her against him. The first shock came from the feel of that long, hard body against hers. "Damn you, Murdock—" The second shock came when his mouth closed over hers.

Oh, no… It was that sweet, weak thought that drifted through her mind even as she fought back like a tiger. Oh, no. He shouldn't feel so good, taste so wonderful. She shouldn't want it to go on and on and on.

Jillian shoved against him and found herself caught closer so that she couldn't shove again. She squirmed and only succeeded in driving herself mad at the feel of her body rubbing against his. Stop it! her mind shouted as the fire began to flicker inside her. She couldn't—wouldn't—let it happen. She knew how to outwit desire. For five years she'd done so with hardly an effort. But now…now something was sprinting inside her too fast, twisting and turning so that she couldn't grab on and stop it from getting further and further out of her reach.

Her blood began to swim, her hands began to clutch. And her mouth began to answer.

He'd expected her temper. Because his own had peaked, he'd wanted it. He'd known she'd be furious, that she'd fight against him for outmaneuvering her and taking something without her permission. His anger demanded that she fight, just as his desire demanded that he take.

He'd expected her mouth to be soft. Why else would he have wanted to taste it so badly that he'd spent two days thinking of little else? He'd known her body would be firm with only hints of the subtle dips and curves of woman. It fit unerringly to his as though it had been fashioned to do so. She strained away from him, shifting, making his skin tingle at the friction her movements caused.

Then, abruptly, her arms were clasped around him. Her lips parted, not in surrender but with an urgency that rocked him. If her passion had been simmering, she'd concealed it well. It seemed to explode in one blinding white flash of heat that came from nowhere. Shaken, Aaron drew back, trying to judge his own reaction, fighting to keep his own needs in perspective.

Jillian stared up at him, her breath coming in jerks. Her hair streamed behind her back, catching the light while her eyes glinted in the dark. Her mind was reeling and she shook her head as if to clear it. Just as she began to draw her first coherent thought, he swore and crushed his mouth to hers again.

There was no hint of struggle this time, nor any hint of surrender. Passion for passion she met him, matching his need with hers, degree by degree. Sandalwood and leather. Now she drew it in, absorbed the aroma as she absorbed the hard, relentless texture of his lips. She let her tongue toy with his while she drank up all those hot, heady male tastes. There was something unapologetically primitive in the way he held her, kissed her. Jillian reveled in it. If she was to take a man, she neither needed nor wanted any polish or gloss that clouded or chipped away so easily.

She let her body take control. How long had she yearned for this? To have someone hold her, spin her away so that she couldn't think, couldn't worry? There were no responsibilities here, and the only demands were of the flesh. Here, with a warm, moist mouth on hers, with a hard body against her, she was finally and ultimately only a woman. Selfishly a woman. She'd forgotten just how glorious it could feel, or perhaps she'd never fully known the sensation before.

What was she doing to him? Aaron tried to pull himself back and found his hands were trapped in the thick softness of her hair. He tried to think and found his senses swimming with the scent of her. And the taste... A low sound started in his throat as he ravaged her mouth. How could he have known she'd taste like this? Seductive, pungent, alluring. Her flavor held all the lushness her body lacked, and the combination was devastating. He wondered how he'd ever lived without it. With that thought came the knowledge that he was getting in much too deep much too fast.

Aaron drew away carefully because the hands on her shoulders weren't as steady as he'd have liked.

Jillian started to sway and caught herself. Good God, what was she doing? What had she done? As the breath rushed swiftly and unevenly through her lips, she stared up at him. Those dark, wicked looks and clever mouth... She'd forgotten. She'd forgotten who she was, and who he was. Forgotten everything but that heady feeling of freedom and heat. He'd use that against her, she thought grimly. If she let him. But something had happened when—

Don't think now! she ordered herself. Just get him out of here before you make a complete fool of yourself. Very carefully, Jillian brushed Aaron's hands from her shoulders. Tilting her chin, she prayed her voice would be steady.

"Well, Murdock, you've had your fun. Now clear out."

Fun? he thought, staring at her. Whatever had happened it didn't have anything to do with fun. The room was tilting a bit, like it had when he'd downed his first six-pack of beer a hundred years before. That hadn't been much fun either, but it'd been a hell of an experience. And he'd paid for it the next day. He supposed he'd pay for this one as well.

He wouldn't apologize, he told himself as he forced himself to relax. Damned if he would, but he would back off while he still could. Casually he bent down to pick up the hat that had fallen off when her fingers had combed through his hair. He took his time putting it on.

"You're right, Jillian," he said mildly—when he could. "A man would have a hard time resisting a woman like you." He grinned at her and tipped his hat. "But I'll do my best."

"See that you do, Murdock!" she called out after him, then hugged herself because she'd begun to tremble.

Even after his footsteps died away, she waited five full minutes before leaving the barn. When Jillian stepped outside, the ranch yard was dark and quiet. She thought she could just hear the murmur of a television or radio from the bunkhouse. There were a few lights farther down the road where her grandfather had built quarters for the married hands. She stopped and listened, but couldn't hear the engine of whatever vehicle Aaron had used to drive from his ranch to hers.

Long gone, she thought, and turned on her heel to stride to the house. It was a two-story stone-and-wood structure. All native Montana material. The rambling building had been constructed on the site of the original homestead. Her grandfather had been fond of bragging that he'd been born in a house that would have fit into the kitchen of this one. Jillian entered by the front door, which was still never locked.

She'd always loved the space, and the clever use of wood and tile and stone that made up the living area. You could roast one of Utopia's steers in the fireplace. Her grandmother's ivory lace curtains still hung at the windows. Jillian often wished she'd known her. All she knew was that she'd been an Irishwoman with dainty looks and a strong back. Jillian had inherited her coloring and, from her grandfather's accounting, her temper. And perhaps, Jillian thought wryly as she climbed the stairs, her back.

God, she wished she had a woman to talk to. Halfway up the stairs she paused and pressed her fingers to her temple. Where did that come from? she wondered. As far back as she could remember, she'd never sought out the company of women. So few of them were interested in the same things she was. And, when there was no niggling sexual problem to overcome, she found men easier to deal with.

But now, with the house so empty around her, with her blood still churning, she wished for a woman who might understand the war going on inside her. Her mother? With a quiet laugh, Jillian pushed open the door to her bedroom. If she called her mother and said she was burning up with desire and had no place to put it, the gentle doctor's wife would blush crimson and stammer out a recommendation for a good book on the subject.

No, as fond as she was of her mother, she wasn't a woman who would understand—well, cravings, Jillian admitted, stripping out of her work shirt. If she was going to be honest, that's what she'd felt in Aaron's arms. Perhaps it was all she was capable of feeling. Frowning, she dropped her jeans into a heap on top of her work shirt and walked naked to the bath.

She should probably be grateful she'd felt that. With a jerk of the wrist, she turned the hot water on full, then added a trickle of cold. She'd felt nothing at all for any man in years. Five years, Jillian admitted and dumped in bath salts with a lavish hand. With an expert twist and a couple of pins, she secured her hair to the top of her head.

It was a good thing she remembered Kevin and that very brief, very unhappy affair. Did one night in bed equal an affair? she wondered ruefully, then lowered herself into the steaming water. Whatever you called it, it had been a fiasco. That's what she had to remember. She'd been so young. Jillian could almost—almost—think of it with amusement now.

The young, dewy-eyed virgin, the smooth, charming intern with eyes as clear as a lake. He hadn't talked her into bed, hadn't pressured her. No, Jillian had to admit that she'd wanted to go with him. And he'd been gentle and sweet with her. It had simply been that the words *I love you* had meant two different things to each of them. To Jillian, they'd been a pledge. To him, they'd been a phrase.

She'd learned the hard way that making love didn't equal love or commitment or marriage. He'd laughed at her, perhaps not unkindly, when she'd naively talked of their future together. He hadn't wanted a wife, or even a partner, but a companion willing to share his bed from time to time. His casualness had devastated her.

She'd been willing to mold herself into whatever he'd wanted—a tidy, socially wise doctor's wife like her mother; a clever, dedicated housewife; an organized marriage partner who could juggle career and family. It had taken her months before she'd realized that she'd made a fool of herself over him, taking every compliment or sweet word literally, because that's what she'd wanted to hear. It had taken more time and several thousand miles of distance before she'd been able to admit that he'd done her a favor.

Not only had he saved her from trying to force her personality into a mold that would never have fit, but he'd given her a solid view of the male species. They weren't to be trusted on a personal level. Once you gave them your love, the power to hurt you, you were lost, ready to do anything to please them even at the loss of self.

When she was young, she'd tried to please her father that way and had failed because she was too like her grandfather. The only man she'd ever loved who'd accepted her for what she was had been Clay Baron. And he was gone.

Jillian lay back, closed her eyes, and let the hot water steam away her fatigue. Aaron Murdock wasn't looking for a partner and neither was she. What had happened between them in the barn was a mistake that wouldn't be repeated. He might be looking for a lover, but she wasn't.

Jillian Baron was on her own, and that's the way she liked it.

Chapter Three

He wondered if she would come. Aaron drove back from a line camp on a road that had once been fit only for horses or mules. It wasn't in much better shape now. The Jeep bucked along much like a bad-tempered bronc might, dipping into ruts, bounding over rocks. He rather liked it. Just as he'd enjoyed the early morning visit with five of his men at the line camp. If he could spare the time, he would appreciate a few days at one of the camps in unabashedly male company. Hard, sweaty work during the day, a few beers and a poker game at night. Riding herd far enough from the ranch so that you could forget there was civilization anywhere. Yes, he'd enjoy that, but...

He appreciated the conservative, traditional ways of his father—particularly when they were mixed with his own experimental ideas. The men would still rope and flank cattle in the open pasture, but two tractors dragging a cable would clear off more brush in a day than axmen could in a month. And a plane...

With a wry smile Aaron remembered how he'd fought six years before for the plane his father had considered a foolish luxury. He'd ended up paying for it himself and flying it himself. His father had never admitted that the plane had become indispensable. That didn't matter to Aaron, as long as it was used. He had no desire to push the cowboy out of existence, just to make him sweat a little less.

Downshifting for the decline, he let the Jeep bump its way down the hill. The differences with his father that had come to a head five years before had eased, but not vanished. Aaron knew he'd have to fight for every change, every improvement, every deviation. And he'd win. Paul Murdock might be stubborn, but he wasn't stupid. And he was sick. In six months…

Aaron rammed the Jeep back into fourth. He didn't like to dwell on the battle his father was losing. A battle Aaron could do nothing about. Helplessness was something Aaron wasn't accustomed to. He was too much like his father. Perhaps that's why they spent most of their time arguing.

He pushed his father and mortality out of his mind and thought of Jillian. There was life, and youth, and vitality.

Would she come? Grinning, Aaron sped past a pasture covered with mesquite grass. Damn right she would. She'd come if for no other reason than to prove to him that she couldn't be intimidated. She'd throw her chin up and give him one of those cool go-to-hell looks. No wonder he wanted her so badly it caused an ache in the pit of his belly. The ache had burned like fire when he'd kissed her.

There hadn't been a female who'd made him come so close to stammering since Emma Lou Swanson had initiated him into life's pleasures in the hayloft. It was one thing for a teenager to lose the power of speech and reason with soft arms around him, and quite another for it to happen to a grown man who'd made a study of the delights and frustrations of women. Aaron couldn't quite account for it, but he knew he was going to have to have more. Soon.

She was a typical Baron, he decided. Hotheaded, stubborn, opinionated. Aaron grinned again. He figured the main reason the Barons and Murdocks had never gotten on was that they'd been too much alike. She wasn't going to have an easy time taking over the ranch, but he didn't doubt she'd do it. He didn't doubt he was going to enjoy watching her. Almost as much as he was going to enjoy bedding her.

Whistling between his teeth, Aaron braked in front of the ranch house. Over near the cattle barn a dog was barking halfheartedly. Someone was playing a radio by the feed lot—a slow, twangy country lament. There were asters popping up in the flower bed and not a weed in sight. As he climbed out of the Jeep he heard the porch door open and glanced over. His mother walked out, lips curved, eyes weary.

She was so beautiful—he'd never gotten used to it. Very small, very slender, Karen Murdock walked with the gliding step of a runway model. She was twenty-two years younger than her husband, and neither the cold winters nor the bright sun of Montana had dimmed the luster of her skin. His sister had those looks, Aaron mused, the classic blond beauty that went on and on with the years. Karen wore slimming slacks, a rose-colored blouse, with her hair loosely coiled at the neck. She could've walked into the Beverly Wilshire without changing a stitch. If the need had arisen, she could've saddled up a horse and ridden out to string wire.

"Everything all right?" she asked him, holding out a hand.

"Fine. They've rounded up the strays we were losing through the south fence." Studying her face, Aaron took her hand. "You look tired."

"No." She squeezed his fingers as much for support as reassurance. "Your father didn't sleep well last night. You didn't come by to see him."

"That wouldn't've made him sleep any better."

"Arguing with you is about all the entertainment he has these days."

Aaron grinned because she wanted him to. "I'll come in later and tell him about the five hundred acres of mesquite I want to clear."

Karen laughed and put her hands on her son's shoulders. With her standing on the porch and him on the ground, their eyes were level. "You're good for him, Aaron. No, don't raise your brow at me," she told him mildly.

"When I saw him yesterday morning, he told me to go to the devil."

"Exactly." Her fingers kneaded absently at his shoulders. "I tend to pamper him, even though I shouldn't. He needs you around to make him angry enough to live a bit longer. He knows you're right—that you've been right all along. He's proud of you."

"You don't have to explain him to me." The steel had crept into his voice before he could prevent it. "I know him well enough."

"Almost well enough," Karen murmured, laying her cheek against Aaron's.

When Jillian drove into the ranch yard, she saw

Aaron with his arms around a slim, elegant blonde. The surge of jealousy stunned, then infuriated her. He was a man after all, she reminded herself, gripping the steering wheel tightly for a moment. It was so easy for a man to enjoy quick passion in a horse stall one evening, then a sweet embrace in the sunshine the next day. True emotion never entered into it. Why should it? she thought, setting her teeth. She braked sharply beside Aaron's Jeep.

He turned, and while she had the disadvantage of the sun in her eyes, she met his amused look with ice. Not for a moment would she give him the satisfaction of knowing she'd spent a restless, dream-disturbed night. Jillian stepped out of her aging compact and managed not to slam the door.

"Murdock," she said curtly.

"Good morning, Jillian." He gave her a bland smile with something sharper hovering in his eyes.

She walked to him, since he didn't seem inclined to drop the blonde's hand and come to her. "I've come to see your stud."

"We talked about manners last night, didn't we?" His grin only widened when she glared at him. "I don't think you two have met."

"No, indeed." Karen came down the porch steps, amused by the gleam in her son's eye, and the fire in the woman's. "You must be Jillian Baron. I'm Karen Murdock, Aaron's mother."

As her mouth fell open Jillian turned to look at Mrs. Murdock. Soft, elegant, beautiful. "Mother?" she repeated before she could stop herself.

Karen laughed, and rested a hand on Aaron's shoulder. "I think I've just been given a wonderful compliment."

He grinned down at her. "Or I have."

Laughing again, she turned back to Jillian. Karen filed away her quick assessment. "I'll leave you two to go about your business. Please, stop in for coffee before you go if you've time, Jillian. I have so little opportunity these days to talk with another woman."

"Yes, ah—thank you." With her brows drawn together, Jillian watched her go back through the porch door.

"I don't think you're often at a loss for words," Aaron commented.

"No." With a little shake of her head she looked up at him. "Your mother's beautiful."

"Surprised?"

"No. That is, I'd heard she was lovely, but…" Jillian shrugged and wished he'd stop looking down at her with that infernal smile on his face. "You don't look a thing like her."

Aaron swung his arm around her shoulders as they turned away from the house. "You're trying to charm me again, Jillian."

She had to bite down on her lip to keep the chuckle back. "I've better uses for my time." Though the weight felt good, she plucked his arm away.

"You smell of jasmine," he said lazily. "Did you wear it for me?"

Rather than dignify the question with an answer, Jillian stopped, tilted her chin, and gave him one long icy look that only wavered when he began to laugh. With a careless flick he knocked the hat from her head, pulled her against him, and gave her a hard, thorough kiss. She felt her legs dissolve from the knees down.

Though he released her before she'd even thought

An Important Message from the Editors

Dear Nora Roberts Fan,

Because you've chosen to read one of our fine novels, we'd like to say "thank you!" And, as a **special** way to thank you, we're offering to send you <u>two more</u> of the books you love so well **plus** two exciting Mystery Gifts — absolutely <u>FREE!</u>

Please enjoy them with our compliments…

Lift here

Pam Powers

NR-ROM-11C

For Your Romance Reading Pleasure...

2 FREE BOOKS that will fuel your imagination
with intensely-moving stories about life, love and relationships.

NEW YORK TIMES AND
USA TODAY BESTSELLING AUTHOR

ROBYN CARR

A VIRGIN RIVER NOVEL

HARVEST MOON

Returning to Virgin River is always a pleasure
—RT Book Reviews

NEW YORK TIMES AND USA TODAY BESTSELLING AUTHOR

SUSAN MALLERY

Already Home

A Novel

FREE!

Your 2 free books have a combined cover price
of $15.98 in the U.S. and $19.98 in Canada.

And remember...just for accepting the Editor's Free Gifts Offer,
we'll send you 2 books and 2 gifts, ABSOLUTELY FREE!

YOURS FREE!

We'll send you two fabulous surprise gifts
worth about $10, absolutely FREE,
just for trying our Romance books!

Visit us at
www.ReaderService.com

The Editor's "Thank You" Free Gifts Include:
- *2 Romance books!*
- *2 exciting mystery gifts!*

Yes! I have placed my
Editor's "Thank You" seal in the
space provided at right. Please send
me 2 free books and 2 fabulous
mystery gifts. I understand I am
under no obligation to purchase
any books, as explained on the
back of this card.

PLACE
FREE GIFTS
SEAL
HERE

194/394 MDL FJF2

FIRST NAME

LAST NAME

ADDRESS

APT.#   CITY

STATE/PROV.   ZIP/POSTAL CODE

Thank You!

NR-ROM-11C

▶ Detach card and mail today. No stamp needed. ▶

The Reader Service - Here's How It Works:

to demand it, Jillian gathered her wits quickly enough. "What the hell do you think—"

"Sorry." His eyes were laughing, but he held his hands up, palms out in a gesture of peace. "Lost my head. Something comes over me when you look at me as though you'd like to cut me into small pieces. *Very* small pieces," he added as he took the hat from where it hung at her back and placed it back on her head.

"Next time I won't just look," she said precisely, wheeling away toward the corral.

Aaron fell into step beside her. "How's the calf?"

"He's doing well. Vet's coming by to check him over this afternoon, but he took the bottle again this morning."

"Was he sired by that new bull of yours?" When Jillian sent him a sharp look, Aaron smiled blandly. "Word gets around. As it happens, you snatched him up from under my nose. I was making arrangements to go to England to check him out for myself when I heard you'd bought him."

"Really?" It was news—and news she couldn't help but be pleased to hear.

"Thought that might make your day," Aaron said mildly.

"Nasty of me," Jillian admitted as they came to the corral fence. Resting a foot on the lower rail, she smiled at him. "I'm not a nice person, Murdock."

He gave her an odd look and nodded. "Then we'll deal well enough together. What's the nickname your hands have dubbed that bull?"

Her smile warmed so that the dimple flickered. He was going to have to find out what it felt like to put his lips just there. "The Terror's the cleanest in polite company."

He chuckled. "I don't think that was the one I heard. How many calves so far?"

"Fifty. It's early yet."

"Mmm. Are you using artificial insemination?"

Her eyes narrowed. "Why?"

"Just curious. We are in the same business, Jillian."

"That's not something I'll forget," she said evenly.

Annoyance tightened his mouth. "Which doesn't mean we have to be opponents."

"Doesn't it?" Jillian shifted her hat lower on her forehead. "I came to look at your stud, Murdock."

He stood watching her a moment, long enough, directly enough, to make Jillian want to squirm. "So you did," Aaron said quietly. Plucking a halter from the fence post, he swung lithely over the corral fence.

Rude, Jillian condemned herself. It was one thing to be cautious, even unfriendly, but another to be pointedly rude. It wasn't like her. Frowning, Jillian leaned on the fence and rested her chin in her open hand. Yet she'd been rude to Aaron almost continually since their first encounter. Her frown cleared as she watched him approach the stallion.

Both males were strong and well built, and each was inclined to want his own way. At the moment the stallion wasn't in the mood for the halter. He pranced away from Aaron to lap disinterestedly at his water trough. Aaron murmured something that had Samson shaking his head and trotting off again.

"You devil," she heard Aaron say, but there was a laugh in his voice. Aaron crossed to him again, and again the stallion danced off in the opposite direction.

Laughing, Jillian climbed the fence and sat on the top rung. "Round 'em up, cowboy," she drawled.

Aaron flashed her a grin, then shrugged as though

he'd given up and turned his back on the stallion. By the time he'd crossed the center of the corral, Samson had come up behind him to nudge his head into Aaron's back.

"Now you wanna make up," he murmured, turning to ruffle the horse's mane before he slipped on the halter. "After you've made me look like a greenhorn in front of the lady."

Greenhorn, hell, Jillian thought, watching the way he handled the skittish stallion. If he cared about impressing anyone, he'd have made the difficult look difficult instead of making it look easy. With a sigh, she felt her respect for him go up another notch.

Automatically she reached out to stroke the stallion's neck as Aaron led him to her. He had a coat like silk, and eyes that were wary but not mean. "Aaron…" She glanced down in time to see his brow lift at her voluntary use of his name. "I'm sorry," she said simply.

Something flickered in his eyes, but they were so dark it was difficult to read it. "All right," he said just as simply and held out a hand. She took it and hopped down.

"He's beautiful." Jillian ran her hands along Samson's wide chest and sleek flank. "Have you bred him before?"

"Twice in Billings," he said, watching her.

"How long have you had him?" She went to Samson's head, then passed under him to the other side.

"Since he was a foal. It took me five days to catch his father." Jillian looked up and caught the light in his eyes. "There must've been a hundred and fifty mustangs in his herd. He was a cagey devil, damn near killed me the first time I got a rope around him. Then he busted down the stall and nearly got away again. You should've seen him, blood spurting out of his leg, fire in his eyes. It took six of us to control him when we bred him to the mare."

"What did you do with him?" Jillian swallowed, thinking how easy it would be to breed the wild stallion again and again, then geld him. Break his spirit.

Aaron's eyes met hers over Samson's withers. "I let him go. Some things you don't fence."

She smiled. Before she realized it, she reached over Samson for Aaron's hand. "I'm glad."

With his eyes on hers, Aaron stroked a thumb over her knuckles. The palm of his hand was rough, the back of hers smooth. "You're an interesting woman, Jillian, with a few rather appealing soft spots."

Disturbed, she tried to slip her hand from his. "Very few."

"Which is why they're appealing. You were beautiful last night, sitting in the hay, crooning to the calf, with the light in your hair."

She knew about clever words. Why were these making her pulse jerky? "I'm not beautiful," she said flatly. "I don't want to be."

He tilted his head when he realized she was perfectly serious. "Well, we can't have everything we want, can we?"

"Don't start again, Murdock," she ordered, sharply enough that the stallion moved restlessly under their joined hands.

"Start what?"

"You know, I wondered why I always end up being rude to you," she began. "I realize it's simply because you don't understand anything else. Let go of my hand."

His eyes narrowed at her tone. "No." Tightening his hold, he gave the stallion a quick pat that sent him trotting off, leaving nothing between himself and Jillian. "I wondered why I always end up wanting to toss you over my knee—or my shoulder," he added thoughtfully. "Must be for the same reason."

"Your reasons don't interest me, Murdock."

His lips curved slowly, but his eyes held something entirely different from humor. "Now, I might've believed that, Jillian, if it hadn't been for last night." He took a step closer. "Maybe I kissed you first, but, lady, you kissed me right back. I had a whole long night to think about that. And about just what I was going to do about it."

Maybe it was because he'd spoken the truth when she didn't care to hear it. Maybe it had something to do with the wicked gleam in his eyes or the insolence of his smile. It might have been a combination of all three that loosened Jillian's temper. Before she had a chance to think about it, or Aaron a chance to react, she'd drawn back her fist and plunged it hard into his stomach.

"That's what *I* intend to do about it!" she declared as he grunted. She had only a fleeting glimpse of the astonishment on his face before she spun on her heel and strode away. She didn't get far.

Jillian's breath was knocked out of her as he brought her down in a tackle. She found herself flat on her back, pinned under him with a face filled with fury rather than astonishment looming over hers. It only took her a second to fight back, and little more to realize she was outmatched.

"You hellion," Aaron grunted as he held her down. "You've been asking for a thrashing since the first time I laid eyes on you."

"It'll take a better man than you, Murdock." She nearly succeeded in bringing her knee up and scoring a very important point. Instead he shifted until her position was only more vulnerable. Heat that had nothing to do with temper surged into her stomach.

"By God, you tempt me to prove you wrong." She squirmed again and stirred something dangerous in him. "Woman, if you want to fight dirty, you've come to the right place." He closed his mouth over hers before she could swear at him. At the instant of contact he felt the pulse in her wrist bound under his hands. Then he felt nothing but the hot give of her mouth.

If she was still struggling beneath him, he wasn't aware of it. Aaron felt himself sinking, and sinking much deeper than he'd expected. The sun was warm on his back, she was soft under him, yet he felt only that moist, silky texture that was her lips. He thought he could make do with that sensation alone for the rest of his life. It scared him to death.

Pulling himself back, he stared down at her. She'd stolen the breath from him much more successfully this time than she had with the quick jab to the gut. "I ought to beat you," he said softly.

Somehow in her prone position she managed to thrust her chin out. "I'd prefer it." It wasn't the first lie she'd told, but it might have been the biggest.

She told herself a woman didn't want to be kissed by a man who tossed her on the ground. Yet her conscience played back that she'd deserved that at the least. She wasn't a fragile doll and didn't want to be treated like one. But she shouldn't want him to kiss her again…want it so badly she could already taste it. "Will you get off me?" she said between her teeth. "You're not as skinny as you look."

"It's safer talking to you this way."

"I don't want to talk to you."

The gleam shot back in his eyes. "Then we won't talk."

Before Jillian could protest, or Aaron could do what he'd intended, Samson lowered his head between their faces.

"Get your own filly," Aaron muttered, shoving him aside.

"He's got a smoother technique than you," Jillian began, then choked on a laugh as the horse bent down again. "Oh, for God's sake, Aaron, let me up. This is ridiculous."

Instead of obliging he looked back down at her. Her eyes were bright with laughter now, her dimple flashing. Her hair spread like fire in the dust. "I'm beginning to like it. You don't do that enough."

She blew the hair out of her eyes. "What?"

"Smile at me."

She laughed again and he felt the arms under his hands relax. "Why should I?"

"Because I like it."

She tried to give a long-winded sigh, but it ended on a chuckle. "If I apologize for hitting you, will you let me up?"

"Don't spoil it—besides, you won't catch me off guard again."

No, she didn't imagine she would. "Well, in any case you deserved it—and you paid me back. Now, get up, Murdock. This ground's hard."

"Is it? You're not." He lifted a brow as he shifted into a more comfortable position. He wondered if her legs would look as nice as they felt. "Anyway, we still have to discuss that remark about my technique."

"The best I can say about it," Jillian began as Aaron

pushed absently at Samson's head again, "is that it needs some polishing. If you'll excuse me, I really have to get back. Some of us work for a living."

"Polishing," he murmured, ignoring the rest. "You'd like something a little—smoother." His voice dropped intimately as he brushed his lips over her cheek, light as a whisper. He heard the quick, involuntary sound she made as he moved lazily toward her mouth.

"Don't." Her voice trembled on the word so that he looked down at her again. Vulnerability. It was in her eyes. That, and a touch of panic. He hadn't expected to see either.

"An Achilles' heel," he murmured, moved, aroused. "You've given me an advantage, Jillian." Lifting a hand, he traced her mouth with a fingertip and felt it tremble. "It's only fair to warn you that I'll use it."

"Your only advantage at the moment is your weight."

He grinned, but before he could speak a shadow fell over them.

"Boy, what're you doing with that little lady on the ground?"

Jillian turned her head and saw an old man with sharp, well-defined features and dark eyes. Though he was pale and had an air of fragility, she saw the resemblance. Astonished, she stared at him. Could this bent old man who leaned heavily on a cane, who was so painfully thin, be the much feared and respected Paul Murdock? His eyes, dark and intense as Aaron's, skimmed over her. The hand on the cane had the faintest of tremors.

Aaron looked up at his father and grinned. "I'm not sure yet," he said easily. "It's a choice between beating her or making love."

Murdock gave a wheezing laugh and curled one hand around the rail of the fence. "It's a stupid man who wouldn't know which choice to make, but you'll do neither here. Let the filly up so I can have a look at her."

Aaron obliged, taking Jillian by the arm and hauling her unceremoniously to her feet. She slanted him a killing glare before she looked back at his father. What nasty twist of fate had decided that she would meet Paul J. Murdock for the first time with corral dust clinging to her and her body still warm from his son's? she wondered as she silently cursed Aaron. Then she tossed back her hair and lifted her chin.

Murdock's face remained calm and unexpressive. "So, you're Clay Baron's granddaughter."

She met his steady hawklike gaze levelly. "Yes, I am."

"You look like your grandmother."

Her chin lifted a fraction higher. "So I've been told."

"She was a fire-eater." A ghost of a smile touched his eyes. "Hasn't been a Baron on my land since she marched over here to pay her respects to Karen after the wedding. If some young buck had tried to wrestle with her, she'd have blackened his eye."

Aaron leaned on the fence, running a hand over his stomach. "She hit me first," he drawled, grinning at Jillian. "Hard."

Jillian slipped her hat from her back and meticulously began to dust it off and straighten it. "Better tighten up those muscles, Murdock," she suggested as she set the hat back on her head. "I can hit a lot harder." She glanced over as Paul Murdock began to laugh.

"I always thought I should've thrashed him a sight more. What's your name, girl?"

She eyed him uncertainly. "Jillian."

"You're a pretty thing," he said with a nod. "And it

doesn't appear you lack for sense. My wife would be glad for some company."

For a minute she could only stare at him. This was the fierce Murdock—her grandfather's archrival—inviting her into his home? "Thank you, Mr. Murdock."

"Come in for coffee, then," he said briskly, then shot a look at Aaron. "You and I have some business to clear up."

Jillian felt something pass between the two men that wasn't entirely pleasant before Murdock turned to walk back toward the house. "You'll come in," Aaron said as he unlatched the gate. It wasn't an invitation but a statement. Curious, Jillian let it pass.

"For a little while. I've got to get back."

They walked through the gate together and relatched it. Though they moved slowly, they caught up with Murdock as he reached the porch steps. Seeing his struggle to negotiate them with the cane, Jillian automatically started to reach out for his arm. Aaron grabbed her wrist. He shook his head, then waited until his father had painstakingly gained the porch.

"Karen!" It might have been a bellow if it hadn't been so breathless. "You've got company." Murdock swung open the front door and gestured Jillian in.

It was more palatial than Utopia's main building, but had the same western feel that had first charmed a little girl from Chicago. All the wood was highly polished— the floor, the beams in the ceilings, the woodwork—all satiny oak. But here was something Utopia lacked. That subtle woman's touch.

There were fresh flowers arranged in a pottery bowl, and softer colors. Though Jillian's grandfather had kept the ivory lace curtains at the windows, his ranch house had reverted to a man's dwelling over the years. Until she walked into the Murdock home and felt Karen's presence, Jillian hadn't realized it.

There was a huge Indian rug spread over the floor in the living area and glossy brass urns beside the fireplace that held tall dried flowers. A seat was fashioned into a bow window and piled with hand-worked pillows. The room had a sense of order and welcome.

"Aren't either of you men going to offer Jillian a chair?" Karen asked mildly as she wheeled in a coffee cart.

"She seems to be Aaron's filly," Murdock commented as he lowered himself into a wing-backed chair and hooked his cane over the arm.

Jillian's automatic retort was stifled as Aaron nudged her onto the sofa. Gritting her teeth, she turned to Karen. "You have a lovely home, Mrs. Murdock."

Karen didn't attempt to disguise her amusement. "Thank you. I believe I saw you at the rodeo last year," she continued as she began to pour coffee. "I remember thinking you looked like Maggie—your grandmother. Do you plan to compete again this year?"

"Yes." Jillian accepted the cup, declining cream or sugar. "Even though my foreman squawked quite a bit when I beat his time in the calf roping."

Aaron reached over to toy with her hair. "That tempts me to enter myself."

"It'd be a pretty sorry day when a son of mine couldn't rope a calf quicker than a female," Murdock muttered.

Aaron sent him a bland look. "That would depend on the female."

"You might be out of practice," Jillian said coolly as she sipped her coffee. "After five years behind a desk."
As soon as she'd said it, Jillian felt the tension between

father and son, a bit more strained, a bit more unpleasant than she'd felt once before.

"I suppose things like that are in the blood," Karen said smoothly. "You've taken to ranch life, but you were raised back east, weren't you?"

"Chicago," Jillian admitted, wondering what she'd stirred up. "I never fit in." It was out before she realized it. A frown flickered briefly in her eyes before she controlled it. "I suppose ranching just skipped a generation in my family," she said easily.

"You have a brother, don't you?" Karen stirred the slightest bit of cream into her own coffee.

"Yes, he's a doctor. He and my father share a practice now."

"I remember the boy—your father," Murdock told her, then chugged down half a cup of coffee. "Quiet, serious fellow who never said three words if two would do."

Jillian had to smile. "You remember him well."

"Easy to understand why Baron left the ranch to you instead." Murdock held out his cup for more coffee, but Jillian noticed that Karen only filled it halfway. "Guess you can't do much better than Gil Haley for running things."

Her dimple flickered. It was, she supposed, a compliment of sorts. "Gil's the best foreman I could ask for," Jillian said mildly. "But I run Utopia."

Murdock's brows drew together. "Women don't run ranches, girl."

Her chin angled. "This one does."

"Nothing but trouble when you start having cowboys in skirts," he said with a snort.

"I don't wear them when I'm hazing cattle."

He set down his cup and leaned forward. "Whatever

I felt about your grandfather, it wouldn't sit well with me to see what he worked for blown away because of some female."

"Paul," Karen began, but Jillian was already rolling.

"Clay wasn't so narrow-minded," Jillian shot back. "If a person was capable, it didn't matter what sex they were. I run Utopia, and before I'm done you'll be watching your back door." She rose, unconsciously regal. "I've got work to do. Thank you for the coffee, Mrs. Murdock." She shot a look at Aaron, who was still lounging back on the sofa. "We still have to discuss your stud."

"What's this?" Murdock demanded, banging his cane.

"I'm breeding Samson to one of Jillian's mares," Aaron said easily.

Color surged into Murdock's pale face. "A Murdock doesn't do business with a Baron."

Aaron unfolded himself slowly and stood. "I do business as I please," Jillian heard him say as she started for the door. She was already at her car when Aaron caught up with her.

"What's your fee?" she said between her teeth.

He leaned against the car. If he was angry, she couldn't see it. "You spark easily, Jillian. I'm usually the only one who can put my father in a rage these days."

"Your father," she said precisely, "is a bigot."

With his thumbs hooked idly in his pockets, Aaron studied the house. "Yeah. But he knows his cows."

She let out a long breath because she wanted to chuckle. "About the stud fee, Murdock."

"Come to dinner tonight, we'll talk about it."

"I haven't time for socializing," she said flatly.

"You've been around long enough to know the advantages of a business dinner."

She frowned at the house. An evening with the Murdocks? No, she didn't think she could get through one without throwing something. "Look, Aaron, I'd like to breed Delilah with Samson—if the terms are right. I'm not interested in anything more to do with you or your family."

"Why?"

"There's been bad blood between the Barons and Murdocks for almost a century."

He gave her a lazy look under lowered lids. "Now who's a bigot?"

Bull's-eye, she thought and sighed. Putting her hands on her hips, she tried to bring her temper to order. Murdock was an old man, and from the looks of him, a sick one. He was also, though she'd choke rather than admit it, a great deal like her grandfather. She'd be a pretty poor individual if she couldn't drum up some understanding. "All right, I'll come to dinner." She turned back to him. "But I won't be responsible if it ends up with a lot of shouting."

"I think we might avoid that. I'll pick you up at seven."

"I know the way," she countered and started to push him aside to open her door. His hand curled over her forearm.

"I'll pick you up, Jillian." The steel was back, in his eyes, his voice.

She shrugged. "Suit yourself."

He cupped the back of her head and kissed her before she could prevent it. "I intend to," he told her easily, then left her to walk back into the house.

Chapter Four

Jillian was still smarting when she returned to Utopia. Murdock's comments, and Aaron's arrogance, had set her back up. She wasn't the sort of woman who made a habit of calming down gracefully. She told herself the only reason she was going back to the Double M to deal with the Murdocks again was because she was interested in a breeding contract. She wanted to believe it.

Dust flew out from her wheels as she drove up the hard-packed road to the ranch yard. It was nearly deserted now at mid-morning, with most of the men out on the range, others busy in the outbuildings. But even an audience wouldn't have prevented her from springing out of her car and slamming the door with a vicious swing. She'd never been a woman who believed in letting her temper simmer if it could boil.

The sound of the door slam echoed like a pistol shot.

Fleetingly she thought of the paperwork waiting for her in the office, then brushed it aside. She couldn't deal with ledgers and numbers at the moment. She needed something physical to drain off the anger before she tackled the dry practicality of checks and balances. Spinning on her heel, she headed for the stables. There'd be stalls to muck out and tack to clean.

"Anybody in particular you'd like to mow down?"

With her eyes still sparkling with anger, Jillian whipped her head around. Joe Carlson walked toward her, his neat hat shading his eyes, a faint, friendly smile on his lips.

"Murdocks."

He nodded after the short explosion of the word. "Figured it was something along those lines. Couldn't come to an agreement on the stud fee?"

"We haven't started negotiating yet." Her jaw clenched. "I'm going back this evening."

Joe scanned her face, wondering that a woman who played poker so craftily should be so utterly readable when riled. "Oh?" he said simply and earned a glare.

"That's right." She bit off each word. "If Murdock didn't have such a damn beautiful horse, I'd tell him to go to the devil and to take his father with him."

This time Joe grinned. "You met Paul Murdock, then."

"He gave me his opinion on cowboys in skirts." Her teeth shut with an audible click.

"Really?"

The dry tone was irresistible. Jillian grinned back at him. "Yes, really." Then she sighed, remembering how difficult it had been for Paul Murdock to climb the four steps to his own porch. "Oh, hell," she murmured, cooling off as quickly as she'd flared. "I shouldn't have let him get under my skin. He's an old man and—"

She broke off, stopping herself before she added *ill.* For some indefinable reason she found it necessary to allow Murdock whatever illusions he had left. Instead she shrugged and glanced toward the corral. "I suppose I'm just used to the way Clay was. If you could ride and drive cattle, he didn't care if you were male or female."

Joe gave her one sharp glance. It wasn't what she'd started to say, but he'd get nothing out of her by probing. One thing he'd learned in the past six months was that Jillian Baron was a woman who did things her way. If a man got too close, one freezing look reminded him how much distance was expected.

"Maybe you'd like to take another look at the bull now, if you've got a few minutes."

"Hmm?" Abstracted, she looked back at him.

"The bull," Joe repeated.

"Oh, yeah." Hooking her thumbs in her pockets, she began to walk with him. "Gil told you about the calves we counted yesterday?"

"Took a look in the south section today. You've got some more."

"How many?"

"Oh, thirty or so. In another week all the calves should be dropped."

"You know, when we were checking the pasture yesterday, I thought the numbers were a little light." Frowning, she went over the numbers in her head again. "I'm going to need someone to go out there and see that some of the bred cows haven't strayed."

"I'll take care of it. How's the orphan?"

With a grin Jillian glanced back toward the cattle barn. "He's going to be fine." Attachments were a mistake, she knew. But it was already too late between her and Baby. "I'd swear he's grown since yesterday."

"And here's Poppa," Joe announced as they came to the bull's paddock.

After angling the hat farther over her eyes, Jillian leaned on the fence. Beautiful, she thought. Absolutely beautiful.

The bull eyed them balefully and snorted air. He didn't have the bulk or girth of an Angus but was built, Jillian thought, like a sleek tank. His red hide glistened as he stood in the full sun. She didn't see boredom in his expression as she'd seen in so many of the steers or cows, but arrogance. His horns curved around the wide white face and gave him a sense of dangerous royalty. It occurred to her that the little orphan she had sheltered in the cattle barn would look essentially the same in a year's time. The bull snorted again and pawed the ground as if daring them to come inside and try their luck.

"His personality's grim at best," Joe commented.

"I don't need him to be polite," Jillian murmured. "I just need him to produce."

"Well, you don't have any problem there." His gaze skimmed over the bull. "From the looks of the calves in this first batch, he's already done a good job for us. Since we're using artificial insemination now, he should be able to service every Hereford cow on the ranch this spring. Your shorthorn bull's a fine piece of beef, Jillian, but he doesn't come up to this one."

"No." Smiling, she rested her elbows on the rail. "As a matter of fact, I found out today that Aaron Murdock was interested in our, ah, Casanova. I can't help but pat myself on the back when I remember how I sent off to England for him on a hunch. Damned expensive hunch," she added, thinking of the hefty dent in the books. "Aaron told me today that he was planning on going over to England to take a look at the bull himself when he learned we'd bought him."

"That was a year ago," Joe commented with a frown. "He was still in Billings."

Jillian shrugged. "I guess he was keeping his finger in the pie. In any case, we've got him." She pushed away from the rail. "I meant what I said about the fair in July, Joe. I can't say I cared much about competition and ribbons before. This year I want to win."

Joe brought his attention from the bull and studied her. "Personal?"

"Yeah." She gave him a grim smile. "You could say it's personal. In the meantime, I'm counting on this guy to give me the best line of beef cattle in Montana. I need a good price in Miles City if I'm going to keep the books in the black. And next year when some of his calves are ready…" She trailed off with a last look at the bull. "Well, we'll just take it a bit at a time. Get back to me on those numbers, Joe. I want to take a look at Baby before I go into the office."

"I'll take care of it," he said again and watched her walk away.

By five Jillian had brought the books up to date and was, if not elated with the figures, at least satisfied. True, the expenses had taken a sharp increase over the last year, but by roundup time, she anticipated a tidy profit from the Livestock Auction Saleyard in Miles City. The expenses had been a gamble, but a necessary one. The plane would be in use within the week and the bull had already proved himself.

Tipping back in her grandfather's worn leather chair, she studied the ceiling. If she could find the time, she'd like to learn how to fly the plane herself. As owner she felt it imperative that she have at least a working knowledge of every aspect of the ranch. In a pinch she could shoe a horse or stitch up a rent hide. She'd learned to operate a hay baler and a bulldozer during a summer visit when she'd still been a teenager—the same year she'd wielded her first and last knife to turn a calf into a steer.

When and if she could afford the luxury, she thought, she'd hire someone to take over the books. Grimacing, she closed the ledger. She had more energy left after ten hours on horseback than she did after four behind a desk.

For now it couldn't be helped. She could justify adding another puncher to the payroll, but not a paper pusher. Next year... She laughed at herself and rested her feet on the desk.

Trouble was, she was counting too heavily on next year and too many things could happen. A drought could mean the loss of crops, a blizzard the loss of cattle. And that was just nature. If feed prices continued to rise, she was going to have to seriously consider selling off a larger portion of the calves as baby beef. Then there was the repair bill for the Jeep, the vet bill, the food bill for the hands. The bill for fuel that would rise once the plane was in use. Yes, she was going to need top dollar in Miles City and a blue ribbon or two wouldn't hurt.

In the meantime she was going to keep an eye on her spring calves. And Aaron Murdock. With a half smile, Jillian thought of him. He was an arrogant son of a bitch, she mused with something very close to admiration, and sharp as they came. It was a pity she didn't trust him enough to discuss ranch business with him and kick around ideas. She'd missed that luxury since her grandfather died. The men were friendly enough, but you didn't talk about your business with a hand who might be working for someone else next year. And Gil was…Gil was Gil, she thought with a grin. He was fond of her, even respected her abilities, though he wouldn't come out and say so. But he was too steeped in his own ways to talk about ideas and changes. So that left—no one, Jillian admitted.

There had been times in Chicago when she could have screamed for privacy, for solitude. Now there were times she ached just to have someone to share an hour's conversation with. With a shake of her head she rose. She was getting foolish. She had dozens of people to talk to. All she had to do was go down to the barn or the stables. Wherever this sudden discontent had come from it would fade again quickly enough. She didn't have time for it.

Her boots clicked lightly on the floor as she walked through the house and up the stairs. From outside she could hear the ring of the triangle, those quick three notes that ran faster and faster until it was one high sound. Her hands would be sitting down to their meal. She'd better get ready for her own.

Jillian toyed with the idea of just slipping into clean jeans and a shirt. The deliberate casualness of such an outfit would be pointedly rude. She was still annoyed enough at both Aaron and his father to do it, but she thought of Karen Murdock. With a sigh, Jillian rejected the idea and hunted through her closet.

It was a matter of her own choice that she had few dresses. They were relegated to one side of her closet, and she rooted them out on the occasions when she entertained other ranchers or businessmen. She stuck with simple styles, having found it to her advantage not to call her femininity to attention. Standing in a brief teddy, she skimmed over her options.

The oversized white cotton shirt wasn't precisely masculine in cut, but it was still casual. Matched with a full white wrap skirt with yards of sash, it made an outfit she thought not only suitable but understated. She made a small concession with a touch of makeup, hesitated over jewelry, then, shrugging, clipped small swirls of gold at her ears. Her mother, Jillian thought, would have badgered her to do something more sophisticated with her hair. Instead she ran a brush through it and left it down. She didn't need elegant styles to discuss breeding contracts.

When she heard the sound of a car drive up outside, she stopped herself from going to the window to peer out. Deliberately she took her time going back downstairs.

Aaron wasn't wearing a hat. Without it Jillian realized he still looked like what he was—a rugged outdoorsman with touches of the aristocracy. He didn't need the uniform to show it.

Looking at him, she wondered how he had found the patience to sit in Billings behind a desk. Trim black slacks and a thin black sweater fit him as truly as his work clothes, yet they seemed to accent the wickedness of his dark looks. She felt an involuntary stir and met his eyes coolly.

"You're prompt," she commented and let the door swing shut behind her. It might not be wise to be alone with him any longer than necessary.

"So are you." He let his gaze move over her slowly, appreciating the simplicity of her outfit—the way the sash accented her small waist and narrow hips, the way the unrelieved white made her skin glow and her hair spark like fire. "And beautiful," he added, taking her hand. "Whether you like it or not."

Because her pulse reacted immediately, Jillian knew

she had to tread carefully. "You keep risking that hand of yours, Murdock." When she tried to slip hers from it, he merely tightened his fingers.

"One thing I've learned is that nothing's worth having if you don't have trouble getting it." Very deliberately he brought her hand to his lips, watching her steadily.

It wasn't a gesture she expected from him. Perhaps that was why she did nothing but stare at him as the sun dipped lower in the sky. She should've jerked her hand away—she wanted to spread her fingers so that she could touch that high curve of cheekbone, that lean line of jaw. She did nothing—until he smiled.

"Maybe I should warn you," Jillian said evenly, "that the next time I hit you, I'm going to aim a bit lower."

He grinned, then kissed her hand again before he released it. "I believe it."

Because she couldn't stop her own smile, she gave up. "Are you going to feed me, Murdock, or not?" Without waiting for an answer, she walked down the steps in front of him.

His car was more in tune with the oil man she'd first envisioned. A low, sleek Maserati. She admired anything well built and fast and settled into her seat with a little sigh. "Nice toy," she commented with a hint of the smile still playing around her mouth.

"I like it," Aaron said easily when he started the engine. It roared into life, then settled down to a purr. "A man doesn't always like to take a woman out in a Jeep or pickup."

"This isn't a date," she reminded him but skimmed her fingers over the smooth leather of the upholstery.

"I admire your practical streak—most of the time."

Jillian turned in her seat to watch the way he handled the car. As well as he handles a horse, she decided. As well as she was certain he handled a woman. The smile curved her lips again. He was going to discover that she wasn't a woman who took to being handled. She settled back to enjoy the ride.

"How does your father feel about me coming to dinner?" she asked idly. Those last slanting rays of the sun were tipping the grass with gold. She heard a cow moo lazily.

"How should he feel about it?" Aaron countered.

"He was amiable enough when I was simply Clay Baron's granddaughter," Jillian pointed out. "But once he found out I was *the* Baron, so to speak, he changed his tune. You're fraternizing with the enemy, aren't you?"

Aaron took his eyes off the road long enough to meet her amused look with one of his own. "So to speak. Aren't you?"

"I suppose I prefer to look at it as making a mutually advantageous bargain. Aaron…" She hesitated, picking her way carefully over what she knew was none of her business. "Your father's very ill, isn't he?"

She could see his expression draw inward, though it barely changed at all. "Yes."

"I'm sorry." Jillian turned to look out the side window. "It's hard," she murmured, thinking of her grandfather. "It's so hard for them."

"He's dying," Aaron said flatly.

"Oh, but—"

"He's dying," he repeated. "Five years ago they told him he had a year, two at most. He outfoxed them. But now…" His fingers contracted briefly on the wheel, then relaxed again. "He might make it to the first snow, but he won't make it to the last."

He sounded so matter-of-fact. Perhaps she'd imagined that quick tension in his fingers. "There hasn't even been a rumor of his illness."

"No, we intend to keep it that way."

She frowned at his profile. "Then why did you tell me?"

"Because you understand about pride and you don't play games."

Jillian studied him another moment, then turned away. No soft words or whispered compliments could have moved her more than that brisk, emotionless statement. "It must be difficult for your mother."

"She's tougher than she looks."

"Yes." Jillian smiled again. "She'd have to be to put up with him."

They drove under the high-arched *Double M* at the entrance to the ranch. The day was hovering at dusk when the light grew lazy and the air soft. Cattle stood slack-hipped in the pasture to the right. She saw a mother licking patiently to clean her baby's hide while other calves were busy at their evening feeding. In another few months they'd be heifers and steers, the maternal bond forgotten, but for now they were just babies with awkward legs and demanding stomachs.

"I like this time of day," she murmured, half to herself. "When work's over and it isn't time to think about tomorrow yet."

He glanced down at her hand that lay relaxed against the seat. Competent, unpampered, with narrow bones and slender fingers. "Did you ever consider that you work too hard?"

Jillian turned and met his gaze calmly. "No."

"I didn't think you did."

"Cowboys in skirts again, Murdock?"

"No." But he'd made a few discreet inquiries. Jillian Baron had a reputation for working a twelve-hour day—on a horse, in a pickup, on her feet. If she wasn't riding fence or hazing cattle, she was feeding her stock, overseeing repairs, or poring over the books. "What do you do to relax?" he asked abruptly. Her blank look gave him the answer before she did.

"I don't have a lot of time for that right now. When I do there are books or the toy Clay bought a couple years ago."

"Toy?"

"Videotape machine," she said with a grin. "He loved the movies."

"Solitary entertainments," Aaron mused.

"It's a solitary way of life," Jillian countered, then glanced over curiously when he stopped in front of a simple white frame house. "What's this?"

"It's where I live," Aaron told her easily before he stepped from the car.

She sat where she was, frowning at the house. She'd taken it for granted that he lived in the sprawling main house another quarter mile or so up the road. Just as she'd taken it for granted that they were having dinner there, with his parents. Jillian turned her head as he opened her door and sent him an uncompromising look. "What are you up to, Murdock?"

"Dinner." Taking her hand, he pulled her from the car. "Isn't that what we'd agreed on?"

"I was under the impression we were having it up there." She gestured in the general direction of the ranch house.

Aaron followed the movement of her hand. When he turned back to her, his mouth was solemn, his eyes amused. "Wrong impression."

"You didn't do anything to correct it."

"Or to promote it," he countered. "My parents don't have anything to do with what's between us, Jillian."

"Nothing is."

Now his lips smiled as well. "There's a matter of the horses—yours and mine." When she continued to frown, he stepped closer, his body just brushing hers. "Afraid to be alone with me, Jillian?"

Her chin came up. "You overestimate yourself, Murdock."

He saw from the look in her eyes that she wouldn't back down no matter what he did. The temptation was too great. Lowering his head, he nipped at her bottom lip. "Maybe," he said softly. "Maybe not. We can always ride on up to the main house if you're—nervous."

Her heart had already risen to the base of her throat to pound. But she knew what it was to deal with a stray wildcat. "You don't worry me," she said mildly, then turned to walk to the house.

Oh, yes, I do, Aaron thought, and admired her all the more because she was determined to face him down. He decided, as he moved to open the front door, that it promised to be an interesting evening.

She couldn't fault his taste. Jillian glanced around his living quarters, wondering just how much she could learn about him from his choice of furnishings. Apparently, he had his mother's flair for style and color, though there were no subtle feminine touches here. Buffs and creams were offset by a stunning wall hanging slashed with vivid blues and greens. He favored antiques and clean lines. Though the room was small, there was no sense of clutter. Curious, she wandered to a curved mahogany shelf and studied his collection of pewter.

The mustang at full gallop caught her attention, though all the animals in the miniature menagerie were finely crafted. For a moment she wished he wasn't a man who appreciated what appealed to her quite so much. Then, remembering the stand she had to take, she turned around. "This is very nice. Though it is a bit simple for a man who grew up the way you did."

His brow lifted. "I'll take the compliment. How do you like your steak?"

Jillian dipped her hands in the wide pockets of her skirt. "Medium rare."

"Keep me company while I fix them." He curled a hand around her arm and moved through the house with her.

"So, I get Murdock beef prepared by a Murdock." She shot him a look. "I suppose I should be complimented."

"We might consider it a peace offering."

"We might," Jillian said cautiously, then smiled. "Providing you know how to cook. I haven't eaten since breakfast."

"Why not?"

He gave her such a disapproving look that she laughed. "I got bogged down in paperwork. I can't work up much of an appetite sitting at a desk. Well, well," she added, glancing around his kitchen. Its simplicity suited the house, with its hardwood floor and plain counters. There wasn't a crumb out of place. "You're a tidy one, aren't you?"

"I lived in the bunkhouse for a while." Aaron uncorked a bottle of wine that stood on the counter next to two glasses. "It either corrupts or reforms you."

"Why the bunkhouse when—" She cut herself off, annoyed that she'd begun to pry again.

"My father and I deal together better when there's some distance." He poured wine into both glasses. "You'd have heard by now that we don't always agree."

"I heard you'd had a falling-out a few years ago, before you went to Billings."

"And you wondered why I—buckled under instead of telling him to go to hell and starting my own place."

Jillian accepted the wine he handed her. "All right, yes, I wondered. It's none of my business."

He looked into his glass a moment, as if studying the dark red color of the wine. "No." Aaron glanced back up and sipped. "It's not."

Without another word he turned to take two hefty steaks out of the refrigerator. Jillian sipped her wine and remained quiet, watching him as he began preparation of the meal with the deft, economical moves that were characteristic of him. Five years ago they'd given his father a year, perhaps two, to live. Aaron had told her that without even a hint of emotion in his voice. And he'd gone to Billings five years before.

To wait his father out? she wondered and winced at the thought. No, she couldn't believe that of him—a man cool and calculating enough to wait for his father to die? Even if his feelings for his father didn't run deep, it was too cold, too heartless. With a shudder, Jillian took a deep swallow of her wine, then set it down. She wouldn't believe it of him.

"Anything I can do?"

Aaron glanced over his shoulder to see her calmly watching him. He knew what direction her thoughts had taken—the logical direction. Now he saw she'd decided in his favor. He told himself he didn't give a damn one way or the other. It wasn't just astonishing to find out he did, it was enervating. He could feel the emotion stir, and drain him. To give himself a moment to settle, he slipped the steaks under the broiler and turned it on.

"Yeah, there's something you can do." Crossing to

her, Aaron framed her face in his hands, seeing her eyes widen in surprise just before his mouth closed over hers. He meant to keep it hard and brief. A gesture—a gesture only to rid him of whatever emotion had suddenly sprung up in him. But as his lips moved over hers the emotion swelled, threatening to take over as the kiss lingered.

She stiffened, and lifted her hands to his chest in automatic defense. Aaron found he didn't want the struggle that usually appealed to him, but the softness he knew she'd give to very few. "Jillian, don't." His fingers tangled in her hair. His voice had roughened with feelings—mysterious, unnamed—he didn't pause to question. "Don't fight me—just this once."

Something in his voice, that quiet hint of need, had her hands relaxing against him before the thought to do so had registered. So she yielded, and in yielding brought herself a moment of sweet, mindless pleasure.

His mouth gentled on hers even as he took her deeper. Her hands crept up to his shoulders, her head tilted back so that he might take what he needed and bring her more of that soft, soft delight she hadn't been aware existed. With a sigh that came from discovery, she gave.

He hadn't known he was capable of tenderness. There'd never been a woman who'd drawn it from him before. He hadn't been aware that desire could ever be calm and easy. Yet while the need built inside of him, he felt a quiet wave of contentment. Aaron basked in it until it made him light-headed. Shaken, he eased her away, studying her face like a man who had seen something he didn't quite understand. And wasn't sure he wanted to.

Jillian took a step back, regaining her balance by

placing her palm down on the scrubbed wooden table. She found sweetness in the last place she expected to. There was nothing she was more determined to fight. "I came here for dinner," she began, eyeing him just as warily as he was eyeing her. "And to talk business. Don't do that again."

"You've got a point," he murmured before he turned back to the stove to tend the steaks. "Drink your wine, Jillian. We'll both be safer."

She did as he suggested only because she wanted something to calm her nerves. "I'll set the table," she offered.

"Dishes're up there." Aaron pointed to a cabinet without looking up. The steaks sizzled when he flipped them. "There's salad in the refrigerator."

They finished up the cooking and preparation in silence, with only the sound of sizzling meat and frying potatoes. Jillian finished off her first glass of wine and looked at the food with real enthusiasm.

"Either you know what you're doing, or I'm starved."

"Both." Aaron passed her some ranch dressing. "Eat. When you're skinny you can't afford to miss meals."

Unoffended, she shrugged. "Metabolism," she told him as she speared into the salad. "It doesn't matter how much I eat, nothing sticks."

"Some people call it nervous energy."

She glanced up as he tilted more wine into her glass. "I call it metabolism. I'm never nervous."

"Not often, in any case," he acknowledged. "Why did you leave Chicago?" Aaron asked before she could formulate a response.

"I didn't belong there."

"You could have, if you'd chosen to."

Jillian gave him a long neutral look, then nodded.

"I didn't choose to, then. I felt at home here the first summer I visited."

"What about your family?"

She laughed. "They didn't."

"I mean, how do you feel about you living here, running Utopia?"

"How should they feel?" Jillian countered. She frowned into her wine a moment, then shrugged again. "I suppose you could say my father feels about Chicago the way I feel about Montana. It's where he belongs. You'd think he'd been born and raised there. And of course, my mother was, so... We just never worked out as a family."

"How?"

Jillian dashed some salt on her steak and cut into it. "I hated my piano lessons," she said simply.

"As easy as that?"

"As basic as that. Marc—my brother—he just melded right in. I suppose it helped that he developed an interest in medicine early, and he loves opera. My mother's quite a fan," she said with a smile. "Anyway, I still cringe a bit when I have to use a needle on a cow, and I've never been able to appreciate *La Traviata*."

"Is that what it takes to suit as a family?" Aaron wondered.

"It was important in mine. When I came here the first time, things started to change. Clay understood me. He yelled and swore instead of lecturing."

Aaron grinned, offering her more steak fries. "You like being yelled at?"

"Patient lecturing is the worst form of punishment."

"I guess I've never had to deal with it. We had a wood shed." He liked the way she laughed, low, appreciative. "Why didn't you come out to stay sooner?"

She moved her shoulders restlessly as she continued to eat. "I was in college. Both my parents thought
a degree was vital, and I felt it was important to try to
please them in that if nothing else. Then I got involved
with—" She stopped herself, stunned that she'd almost
told him of her relationship with that long-ago intern.
Meticulously she cut a piece of steak. "It just didn't
work out," she concluded, "so I came out here."

The someone who touched her wrong, Aaron decided. The astonishment in her eyes had been brief,
her cover-up swift and smooth, but not smooth enough.
He wouldn't probe there, not on a spot that was obviously tender. But he wondered who it had been who
had touched her, and hurt her while she'd still been too
young to build defenses.

"I think my mother was right," he commented. "Some
things are just in the blood. You belong here."

There was something in the tone that made her look
up carefully. She wasn't certain at that moment whether
he referred to the ranch or to himself. His eyes reminded
her just how ruthless he could be when he wanted something. "I belong at Utopia," she said precisely. "And I
intend to stay. Your father said something today too,"
she reminded him. "That a Murdock doesn't do business with a Baron."

"My father doesn't run my life, personally or profes-
sionally."

"Are you going to breed your stallion with Delilah
to spite him?"

"I don't waste time with spite." It was said very
simply, with that undercurrent of steel that made her
think if he wanted revenge, he'd choose a very direct
route. "I want the mare—" his dark eyes met hers and
held "—for reasons of my own."

"Which are?"

Lifting his wine, he drank. "My own."

Jillian opened her mouth to speak, then shut it again. His reasons didn't matter. Business was business. "All right, what fee are you asking?"

Aaron took his time, calmly watching her face. "You seem to be finished."

Distracted, Jillian looked down to see that she'd eaten every bite on her plate. "Apparently," she said with a half laugh. "Well, I almost hate to admit it, Murdock, but it was good—almost as good as Utopia beef."

He answered her grin as he rose to clear off the table. "Why don't we take the wine in the other room, unless you'd like some coffee."

"No." She got up to help him stack the dishes. "I drank a full pot when I was fooling with the damn books."

"Don't care for paperwork?" Aaron picked up the half-full bottle of wine as they walked out of the kitchen.

"Putting it mildly," she murmured. "But someone has to do it."

"You could get a bookkeeper."

"The thought's crossed my mind. Maybe next year," she said with a move of her shoulders. "I've gotten used to keeping my finger on the pulse, let's say."

"Rumor is you rope a steer with the best of them."

Jillian sat on the couch, the full white skirt billowing around her. "Rumor's fact, Murdock," she said with a cocky smile. "Anytime you want to put some money on it, we'll go head to head."

He sat down beside her and toyed with the end of her sash. "I'll keep that in mind. But I have to admit, it isn't a hardship to look at you in a skirt."

Over the rim of her glass she watched him. "We

were talking stud fees. What'd you have in mind for Samson?"

Idly he twisted a lock of her hair around his finger. "The first foal."

Chapter Five

For a moment there was complete silence in the room as they measured each other. She'd thought she had him pegged. It infuriated her to realize he was still a step ahead of her. "The first—" Jillian set down her glass of wine with a snap. "You're out of your mind."

"I'm not interested in cash. Two guaranteed breedings. I take the first foal, colt or filly. You take the second. I like the looks of your mare."

"You expect me to breed Delilah, cover all the expenses while she's carrying a foal, lose the use of her for three to four months, deal with the vet fees, then turn the result over to you?"

Relaxed, Aaron leaned back. He'd almost forgotten how good it was to haggle. "You'd have the second for nothing. I'd be willing to negotiate on the expenses."

"A flat fee," Jillian said, rising. "We're not talking about dogs, where you can take the pick of the litter."

"I don't need cash," Aaron repeated, lounging back on the couch. "I want a foal, take it or leave it."

Oh, she'd like to leave it. She'd like to have tossed it back in his face. Simmering, she stalked over to the window and stared out. It surprised her that she didn't. Until that moment Jillian hadn't realized just how much she wanted to breed those two horses. Another hunch, she thought, remembering the bull. She could feel that something special would come out of it. Clay had often told her she had a feel. More than once she'd singled out an animal for no other reason than a feeling. Now she had to weigh that with the absurdity of Aaron's suggestion.

She stared hard out of the window into the full night, full dark. Behind her, Aaron remained silent, waiting, watching her with a faint smile. He wondered if she knew just how lovely she was when she was annoyed. It was tempting to keep her that way.

"I get the first foal," she said suddenly. "You get the second. It's my mare who's taking the risk in pregnancy, who won't be any use for working when she's at term and nursing. I'm the one bearing the brunt of the expense."

Aaron considered a moment. She was playing it precisely as he'd have done himself if the situation was reversed. He found it pleased him. "We breed her back as soon as she's weaned the foal."

"Agreed. You pay half the vet bills—on both foalings."

His brows raised. Whatever she knew about cattle, she wasn't a fool when it came to horse trading. "Half," he agreed. "We breed them as soon as she comes in season."

With a nod, Jillian offered her hand on it. "Do you want to draw up the papers or shall I?"

Standing, Aaron took her hand. "I'm not particular. A handshake's binding enough for me."

"Agreed," she said again. "But it never hurts to have words written down."

He grinned, skimming his thumb over her knuckles. "Don't you trust me, Jillian?"

"Not an inch," she said easily, then laughed because he seemed more pleased than offended. "No, not an inch. And you'd be disappointed if I did."

"You have a way of cutting through to the heart of things. It's a pity I've been away for five years." He inclined his head. "But I have a feeling we'll be making up for lost time."

"I haven't lost any time," Jillian countered. "Now that we've concluded our business successfully, Murdock, I have a long day tomorrow."

He tightened his fingers on hers before she could turn away. "Not all our business."

"All I came for." Her voice was cool, even when he stepped closer. "I don't want to make a habit out of hitting you."

"You won't connect this time." He took her other hand and held both lightly, though not so lightly she could draw away. "I'm going to have you, Jillian."

She didn't try to pull her hands away. She didn't back up. Her eyes stayed level with his and her voice just as matter-of-fact. "The hell you are."

"And when I do," he went on as if she hadn't spoken, "it's not going to be something either one of us is going to forget. You stirred something in me—" he yanked her closer so that the unrelieved white of her skirt flowed against the stark black of his slacks "—from the first minute I saw you. It hasn't settled yet."

"Your problem." She angled her chin, but her voice was breathless. "You don't interest me, Murdock."

"Tell me that again," he challenged, "in just a minute."

He brought his mouth down on hers, harder, rougher than he'd intended. His emotions seemed to have no middle ground with her. It was either all soft tenderness or raw passion. Her arms strained against his hold, her body jerked as if to reject him. Then he felt it—the instant she became as consumed as he. In seconds his arms were around her, and hers around him.

It felt just as she'd wanted it to. Heady, overpowering. She could forget everything but that delicious churning within her own body. The rich flavor of wine that lingered on his tongue would make her drunk, but it didn't matter. Her head could whirl and spin, but she could only be grateful for the giddiness. With unapologetic passion, she met his demand with demand.

When his mouth left hers, she would have protested, but the sound became a moan as his lips raced down her throat. Instinctively she tilted her head back to give him more freedom, and the sharp scent of soap drifted over her, laced with a hint of sandalwood. Then his mouth was at her ear, his teeth tugging and nipping before he whispered something she didn't understand. The words didn't matter, the sound alone made her tremble. With a murmur of desperation, she dragged his lips back to hers.

Jillian was demanding he take more. Aaron could feel the strain of her body against his and knew she was aching to be touched. But his hands were still tangled in her hair as they tumbled onto the couch. Then his hands were everywhere, and he couldn't touch enough fast enough. Her body was so slender under all those yards of thin white cotton. So responsive. Her breast was almost lost under the span of his hand, yet it was so firm. And her heartbeat pounded like thunder beneath it.

His legs tangled with hers before he slipped between them. When she sank into the cushions, he nearly lost himself in the simple give of her body. His mouth ravaged hers—he couldn't prevent it, she didn't protest. She only answered and demanded until he was half mad again. Her scent, part subtle, part sultry, enveloped him so that he knew he'd be able to smell her when she was miles from him. He could hear her breath rush from between her lips into his mouth, where it whispered warm and sweet and promising.

Her body was responding of its own accord while her mind raced off in a dozen directions. His weight, that hard, firm press of his body, felt so good, so natural against hers. Those rough, ruthless kisses gave her everything she needed long before she knew she needed. He threatened her with words of passion that were only whispered madness in a world of color without form.

His cheek grazed hers as his lips raced over her face. No one had ever wanted her like this. But more, she'd never wanted this wildly. Her only taste of lovemaking had been so mild, so quiet. Nothing had prepared her for a violence of need that came from within herself. She wanted to fly with it. Too much.

His hand skimmed up her leg, seeking, and everything that was inside her built to a fever pitch. If it exploded, she'd be lost. Pieces of herself might scatter so that she'd never be strong enough to stand on her own again.

In a panic, she began to struggle while part of her fought to yield. And to take.

"No." Moaning, she pushed against him.

"Jillian, for God's sake." Her name came out in a gasp as he felt himself drowning.

"No!" With the strength of fear, she managed to shove him aside and scramble up. Before either of them could think, she was dashing outside, running away from something that followed much too closely. Aaron was cursing steadily when he caught her.

"What the hell's wrong with you?" he demanded as he whipped her back around.

"Let me go! I won't be pawed that way."

"Pawed?" He didn't even hear her gasp as his fingers tightened. "Damn you," he said under his breath. "You were doing some pawing of your own, if that's what you want to call it."

"Just let me go," she said unsteadily. "I told you I don't like to be touched."

"Oh, you like to be touched," he grated, then caught the glint of fear in her eyes. There was pride there as well, a kind of terrorized pride laced with passion. It reminded him sharply of the eyes of a stallion he'd once tied in a stall. Then he realized his fingers were digging into the flesh of very slender arms.

No, he wasn't a gentle man, but she was the first and only woman who'd caused him to lose control to the point where he'd mark her skin. Carefully he loosened his hold without releasing her. Even as his fingers relaxed, he knew he could drag her back inside and have her willing to give herself to him within moments. But some things you didn't fence.

"Jillian." His voice was still rough, only slightly calmer. "You can postpone what's going to happen between us, but you can't stop it." She opened her mouth, but he shook his head in warning. "No, you'd be much better off not to say anything just now. I want you, and at the moment it's a damned uncomfortable feeling. I'm going to take you home while I've got myself convinced I play by the rules. It wouldn't take me long to remember I've never followed any."

He pulled open the passenger door, then strode around to the driver's seat without another word. They drove away in a silence that remained thick for miles. Because her body was still throbbing, Jillian sat very straight. She cursed Aaron, then when she began to calm, she cursed herself. She'd wanted him, and every time he touched her, her initial restraint vanished within moments.

The hands in her lap balled into fists. There was a name for a woman who was willing and eager one moment and hurling accusations the next. It wasn't pleasant. She'd never played that kind of game and had nothing but disdain for anyone who did.

He had a right to be furious, Jillian admitted, but then, so did she. He was the one who'd come barging into her life, stirring things up she wanted left alone. She didn't want to feel all those hungers, all those aches that raged through her when he held her.

She couldn't give in to them. Once she did, she'd start depending. If that happened, she'd start chipping away at her own self-reliance until he had more of who and what she was than she did. It had happened before and the need had been nothing like this. She'd gotten a hint, during that strangely gentle kiss in his kitchen, just how easily she could lose herself to him. And yet…

Yet when it was all said and done, Jillian was forced to admit, she'd acted like an idiot. The one thing she detested more than anything else was finding herself in the wrong.

A deer bounded over the fence to the left, pausing in the road, as it was trapped in the headlights. Even as Aaron braked, it was sprinting off, slender legs lifting as it took the next fence and disappeared into the darkness. The sight warmed Jillian as it always did. With a soft laugh, she turned back to see the smile in Aaron's eyes. The flood of emotion swamped her.

"I'm sorry." The words came quickly, before she realized she would say them. "I overreacted."

He gave her a long look. He'd wanted to stay angry. Somehow it was easier—now it was impossible. "Maybe we both did. We have a tendency to spark something off each other."

She couldn't deny that, but neither did she want to think about it too carefully just then. "Since we're going to have to deal with each other from time to time, maybe we should come to some kind of understanding."

A smile began to tug at his mouth. "That sounds reasonable. What kind of understanding did you have in mind?"

"We're business associates," she said very dryly because of the amusement in his question.

"Uh-huh." Aaron rested his arm on the back of the seat as he began to enjoy himself.

"Do you practice being an idiot, Murdock, or does it come naturally?"

"Oh, no, no insults, Jillian. We're coming to an understanding."

Jillian fought against a grin and lost. "You have a strange sense of humor."

"A keen sense of the ridiculous," he countered. "So we're business associates. You forgot neighbors."

"And neighbors," she agreed with a nod. "Colleagues, if you want to belabor a point."

"Belabor it," Aaron suggested. "But can I ask you a question?"

"Yes." She drew out the word cautiously.

"What *is* the point?"

"Damn it, Aaron," she said with a laugh. "I'm trying to put things in order so I don't end up apologizing again. I hate apologizing."

"I like the way you do it, very simple and sincere right before you lose your temper again."

"I'm not going to lose my temper again."

"I'll give you five to one."

"Damn it, Aaron." Her laugh rippled, low and smooth. "If I took that bet, you'd go out of your way to make me mad."

"You see, we understand each other already. But you were telling me your point." He pulled into the darkened ranch yard. The light from Jillian's front porch spilled into the car and cast his face in shadows.

"We could have a successful business association *if* we both put a lot of effort into it."

"Agreed." He turned and in the small confines of the car was already touching her. Just the skim of his fingers over her shoulder, the brush of leg against leg.

"We'll continue to be neighbors because neither of us is moving. As long as we remember those things, we should be able to deal with each other without too much fighting."

"You forgot something."

"Did I?"

"You've said what we are to each other, not what we're going to be." He watched her eyes narrow.

"Which is?"

"Lovers." He ran his finger casually down the side of her neck. "I still mean to have you."

Jillian let out a long breath and worked on keeping her temper in check. "It's obvious you can't carry on a reasonable conversation."

"A lot of things are obvious." He put his hand over hers as she reached for the handle. With their faces close, he let his gaze linger on her mouth just long enough for the ache to spread. "I'm not a patient man," Aaron murmured. "But there are some things I can wait for."

"You'll have a long wait."

"Maybe longer than I'd like," he agreed. "But shorter than you think." His hand was still over hers as he pressed down the handle to release the door. "Sleep well, Jillian."

She swung out of the car, then gave him a smoldering look. "Don't cross the line until you're invited, Murdock." Slamming the door, she sprinted up the steps, cursing the low, easy laughter that followed her.

In the days that followed, Jillian tried not to think about Aaron. When she couldn't stop him from creeping into her mind, she did her best to think of him with scorn. Occasionally she was successful enough to dismiss him as a spoiled, willful man who was used to getting what he wanted by demanding it. If she were successful, she could forget that he made her laugh, made her want.

Her days were long and full and demanding enough that she had little time to dwell on him or her feelings. But though the nights were growing shorter, she swore against the hours she spent alone and unoccupied. It was then she remembered exactly how it felt to be held against him. It was then she remembered how his eyes could laugh while the rest of his face remained serious and solemn. And how firm and strong his mouth could be against hers.

She began to rise earlier, to work later. She exhausted herself on the range or in the outbuildings until she could tumble boneless into bed. But still there were dreams.

Jillian was out in the pasture as soon as it was light. The sky was still tipped with the colors of sunrise so that gold and rose tinted the hazy blue. Like most of her men, she wore a light work jacket and chaps as they began the job of rounding up the first hundred calves and cows for corral branding. This part of the job would be slow and easy. It was too common to run twenty-five pounds off a cow with a lot of racing and roping. A good deal of the work could be done on foot, the rest with experienced horses or four wheels. If they hazed the mothers along gently, the babies would follow.

Jillian turned Delilah, keeping her at a walk as she urged a cow and calf away from a group of heifers. She looked forward to a long hard morning and the satisfaction of a job well done. When she saw Joe slowly prodding cows along on foot, she tipped her hat to him.

"I always thought branding was a kind of stag party," he commented as he came alongside of her.

Looking down, she laughed. "Not on Utopia." She looked around as punchers nudged cows along with soft calls and footwork. "When we brand again in a couple of days, the plane should be in. God knows it'll be easier to spot the strays."

"You've been working too hard. No, don't give me that look," he insisted. "You know you have. What's up?"

Aaron sneaked past her defenses, but now she just shook her head. "Nothing. It's a busy time of year. We'll be haying soon, first crop should come in right after the spring branding. Then there's the rodeo." She glanced down again as Delilah shifted under her. "I'm counting on those blue ribbons, Joe."

"You've been working from first light to last for a week," he pointed out. "You're entitled to a couple days off."

"The boss is the last one entitled to a couple days off." Satisfied that her cows had joined the slowly moving group headed for the pasture, she wheeled Delilah around. She spotted a calf racing west, spooked by the number of men, horses, and trucks. Sending Delilah into an easy lope, Jillian went after him.

Her first amusement at the frantic pace the dogie was setting faded as she saw he was heading directly for the wire. With a soft oath, she nudged more speed out of her mare and reached for her rope. With an expert movement of arm and wrist, she swung it over her head, then shot it out to loop over the maverick's neck. Jillian pulled him up a foot from the wire where he cried and struggled until his mother caught up.

"Dumb cow," she muttered as she dismounted to release him. "Fat lot of good you'd've done yourself if you'd tangled in that." She cast a glance at the sharp points of wire before she slipped the rope from around his head. The mother eyed her with annoyance as she began to recoil the rope. "Yeah, you're welcome," Jillian told her with a grin. Glancing over, she saw Gil crossing to her on foot. "Still think you can beat my time in July?" she demanded.

"You put too much fancy work on the spin."

Though his words were said in his usual rough-and-ready style, something in his eyes alerted her. "What is it?"

"Something you oughta see down here a ways."

Without a word, she gathered Delilah's reins in her hand and began to walk beside him. There was no use asking, so she didn't bother. Part of her mind still registered the sights and sounds around her—the irritated mooing, the high sound of puzzled calves, the ponderous majestic movements of their mothers, the swish of men and animals through grass. They'd start branding by mid-morning.

"Look here."

Jillian saw the small section of broken fence and swore. "Damn it, we just took care of this line a week ago. I rode this section myself." Jillian scowled into the opposite pasture wondering how many of her cattle had strayed. That would account for the fact that though the numbers reported to her were right, her eye had told her differently that morning. "I'll need a few hands to round up the strays."

"Yeah." Reaching over, he caught a strand of wire in his fingers. "Take a look."

Distracted, she glanced down. Almost immediately, Jillian stiffened and took the wire in her own fingers. The break was much too sharp, much too clean. "It's been cut," she said quietly, then looked up and over into the next pasture. Murdock land.

She expected to feel rage and was stunned when she felt hurt instead. Was he capable? Jillian thought he could be ruthless, even lawless if it suited him. But to deliberately cut wire... Could he have found his own way to pay her back for their personal differences and professional enmity? She let the wire fall.

"Send three of the men over to check for strays," she said flatly. "I'd like you to see to this wire yourself." She met Gil's eyes coolly and on level. "And keep it to yourself."

He squinted at her, then spit. "You're the boss."

"If I'm not back by the time the cattle are ready in the corral, get started. We don't have any time to waste getting brands on the calves."

"Maybe we waited a few days too long already."

Jillian swung into the saddle. "We'll see about that." She led Delilah carefully through the break in the wire, then dug in her heels.

It didn't take her long to come across her first group of men. Delilah pulled up at the Jeep and Jillian stared down her nose. "Where's Murdock?" she demanded. "Aaron Murdock."

The man tipped his hat, recognizing an outraged female when he saw one. "In the north section, ma'am, rounding up calves."

"There's a break in the fence," she said briefly. "Some of my men are coming over to look for strays. You might want to do the same."

"Yes, ma'am." But he said it to her back as she galloped away.

The Murdock crew worked essentially the same way her own did. She saw them fanned out, moving slowly, steadily, with the cows plodding along in front of them. A few were farther afield, outflanking the mavericks and driving them back to the herd.

Jillian saw him well out to the right, twisting and turning Samson around a reluctant calf. Ignoring the curious glances of his men, Jillian picked her way through them. She heard them laugh, then shout something short and rude at the calf before he saw her.

The brim of his hat shaded his face from the early morning sun. She couldn't see his expression, only that he watched her come toward him. Delilah pricked up her ears as she scented the stallion and sidestepped skittishly.

Aaron waited until they were side by side. "Jillian." Because he could already see that something was wrong, he didn't bother with any more words.

"I want to talk to you, Murdock."

"So talk." He nudged the calf, but Jillian reached over to grip his saddle horn. His eyes flicked down to rest on her restraining hand.

"Alone."

His expression remained placid—but she still couldn't see his eyes. Signaling to one of his men to take charge of the maverick, Aaron turned his horse and walked farther north. "You'll have to keep it short, I haven't got time to socialize right now."

"This isn't a social call," she bit off, controlling Delilah as the mare eyed the stallion cautiously.

"So I gathered. What's the problem?"

When she was certain they were out of earshot, Jillian pulled up her mount. "There's a break in the west boundary line."

He looked over her head to watch his men. "You want one of my hands to fix it?"

"I want to know who cut it."

His eyes came back to hers quickly. She could see only that they were dark. The single sign of his mood was the sudden nervous shift of his stallion. Aaron controlled him without taking his eyes off Jillian. "Cut it?"

"That's right." Her voice was even now, with rage bubbling just beneath. "Gil found it, and I saw it myself."

Very slowly he tipped back his hat. For the first time she saw his face unshadowed. She'd seen that expression once before—when it had loomed over her as he pinned her to the ground in Samson's corral. "What are you accusing me of?"

"I'm telling you what I know." Her eyes caught the slant of the morning sun and glittered with it. "You can take it from there."

In what seemed to be a very calm, very deliberate motion, he reached over and gathered the front of her jacket in his hand. "I don't cut fence."

She didn't jerk away from him and her gaze remained steady. A single stray breeze stirred the flame-colored curls that flowed from her hat. "Maybe you don't, but you've got a lot of men working your place. Three of my men are in your pasture now, rounding up my strays. I'm missing some cows."

"I'll send some men to check your herd for any of mine."

"I already suggested that to one of your hands in the border pasture."

He nodded, but his eyes remained very intense and very angry. "A wire can be cut from either side, Jillian."

Dumbfounded, she stared at him. Rage boiled out as she knocked his hand away from her jacket. "That's ridiculous. I wouldn't be telling you about the damn wire if I'd cut it."

Aaron watched her settle her moody mare before he gave her a grim smile. "You have a lot of men working your place," he repeated.

As she continued to stare her angry color drained. Hurt and anger hadn't allowed her to think through the logic of it. Some of her men she'd known and trusted for years. Others—they came and they went, earning a stake, then drifting to another ranch, another county. You rarely knew their names, only their faces. But it was her count that was short, she reminded herself.

"You missing any cattle?" she demanded.

"I'll let you know."

"I'll be doing a thorough count in the west section." She turned away to stare at the rising sun. It could've been one of her men just as easily as it could've been one of his. And she was responsible for everyone who was on Utopia's payroll. She had to face that. "I've no use for your beef, Aaron," she said quietly.

"Any more than I do for yours."

"It wouldn't be the first time." When she looked back at him, her chin stayed up. "The Murdocks made a habit out of cutting Baron wire."

"You want to go back eighty years?" he demanded. "There's two sides to a story, Jillian, just like there's two sides to a line. You and I weren't even alive then, what the hell difference does it make to us?"

"I don't know, but it happened—it could happen again. Clay may be gone, but your father still has some bad feelings."

Temper sprang back into his eyes. "Maybe he dragged himself out here and cut the wire so he could cause you trouble."

"I'm not a fool," she retorted.

"No?" Furious, he wheeled his horse so that they were face-to-face. "You do a damn good imitation. I'll check the west line myself and get back to you."

Before she could throw any of her fury back at him, he galloped away. Teeth gritted, Jillian headed south, back to Utopia.

Chapter Six

By the time Jillian galloped into the ranch yard the cattle were already penned. A glance at the sun told her it was only shortly after eight. Cows and calves were milling and mooing in the largest board pen and the workmen had already begun to separate them. No easy task. Listening to the sounds of men and cattle, Jillian dismounted and unsaddled her mare. There wasn't time to brood over the cut wire when branding was under way.

Some of the men remained on horseback, keeping the cows moving as they worked to chase the frantic mothers into a wire pen while the calves were herded into another board corral. The air was already peppered with curses that were more imaginative than profane.

With blows and shouts, a cow and her calf were driven out of the big corral. Men on foot were strung out in a line too tight to allow the cow to follow as the calf slipped through. Relying mostly on arm waving, shrieks, and whistles, the men propelled the cow into the

wire pen. Then the process repeated itself. She watched
Gil spinning his wiry little body and cheering with an
energy that promised to see him through the day despite
his years. With a half laugh, Jillian settled her hat firmly
on her head and went to join them, lariat in hand.

Calves streaked like terriers back into the cow pen.
Dust flew. Cows bullied their way through the line for
a reunion with their offspring. Men ran them back with
shouts, brute force, or ropes. Men might be outnumbered
and outweighed, but the cattle were no match for western ingenuity.

Gil singled a calf out in the cow pen, roped it, and
dragged it to him, cursing all the way. With a swat on
the flank, he sent it into the calf corral, then squinted
at Jillian.

"Fence repaired?" she asked briefly.

"Yep."

"I'll see to the rest myself." She paused, then swung
her lariat. "I'm going to want to talk to you later, Gil."

He removed his hat, swiped the sweat off his brow
with the arm of his dusty shirt, then perched it on his
head again. "When you're ready." He glanced around as
Jillian pulled in a calf. "Just about done—time to gang
up on 'em."

So saying, he joined the line of men who closed in
on the unruly cows to drive the last of them into their
proper place. Inside the smaller corral calves bawled
and crowded together.

"It isn't pleasant," Jillian muttered to them. "But it'll
be quick."

The gate creaked as it was swung across to hold them
in. The rest wasn't a business she cared for, though she
never would've admitted it to anyone but herself. Knife
and needle and iron were used with precision, with a

rhythm that started off uneven, then gained fluidity and speed. Calves came through the chute one at a time, dreaming of liberation, only to be hoisted onto the calf table.

She watched the next calf roll his big eyes in astonishment as the table tilted, leaving him helpless on his side, as high as a man's waist. Then he was dealt with as any calf is at a roundup.

It was hot, dirty work. There was a smell of sweat, blood, smoking hide, and medicine. Throughout the steady action reminiscences could be heard—stories no one would believe and everyone tried to top. Cows surged in the wire pen; their babies squealed at the bite of needle or knife. The language grew as steamy as the air in the pen.

It wasn't Jillian's first branding, and yet each one—for all the sweat and blood—made her remember why she was here instead of on one of the wide busy streets back east. It was hard work, but honest. It took a special brand of person to do it. The cattle milling and calling in the corral were hers. Just as the land was. She relieved a man at the table and began her turn at the vaccinations.

The sun rose higher, heading toward afternoon before the last calf was released. When it was done, the men were hungry, the calves exhausted and bawling pitifully for their mothers.

Hot and hungry herself, Jillian sat on a handy crate and wiped the grime from her face. Her shirt stuck to her with patches of wet cutting through the dirt. That was only the first hundred, she thought as she arched her back. They wouldn't finish with the spring brandings until the end of that week or into the next. She waited until nearly all the men had made their way toward the cookhouse before she signaled to Gil. He plucked two beers out of a cooler and went to join her.

"Thanks." Jillian twisted off the cap, then let the cold, yeasty taste wash away some of the dust. "Murdock's going to check the rest of the line himself," she began without preamble. "Tell me straight—" she held the bottle to her brow a moment, enjoying the chill "—is he the kind of man who'd play this sort of game?"

"What do you think?" he countered.

What could she think? Jillian asked herself. No matter how hard she tried, her feelings kept getting in the way. Feelings she'd yet to understand because she didn't dare. "I'm asking you."

"Kid's got class," Gil said briefly. "Now, the old man…" He grinned a bit, then squinted into the sun. "Well, he might've done something of the sort years back, just for devilment. Give your grandpaw something to swear about. But the kid—don't strike me like his devilment runs that way. Another thing…" He spit tobacco and shifted his weight. "I did a head count in the pasture this morning. Might be a few off, seeing as they were spread out and scattered during roundup."

Jillian took another swig from the bottle, then set it aside. "But?"

"Looked to me like we were light an easy hundred."

"A hundred?" she repeated in a whisper of shock. "That many cattle aren't going to stray through a break in the fence, not on their own."

"Boys got back midway through the branding. Only rounded up a dozen on Murdock land."

"I see." She let out a long breath. "Then it doesn't look like the wire was cut for mischief, does it?"

"Nope."

"I want an accurate head count in the morning, down

to the last calf. Start with the west pasture." She looked down at her hands. They were filthy. Her fingers ached. It was as innate in her to work for what was hers as it was to fight for it. "Gil, the chances are pretty good that someone on the Murdock payroll's rustling our cattle, maybe for the Double M, but more likely for themselves."

He tugged on his ear. "Maybe."

"Or, it's one of our own."

He met her eyes calmly. He'd wondered if that would occur to her. "Just as likely," he said simply. "Murdock might find his numbers light too."

"I want that head count by sundown tomorrow." She rose to face him. "Pick men you're sure of, no one that's been here less than a season. Men who know how to keep their thoughts to themselves."

He nodded, understanding the need for discretion. Rustling wasn't any less deadly a foe than it had been a century before. "You gonna work with Murdock on this?"

"If I have to." She remembered the fury on his face— something she recognized as angry pride. She had plenty of that herself. The sigh came before she could prevent it and spoke of weariness. "Go get something to eat."

"You coming?"

"No." She walked back to Delilah and hefted the saddle. Mechanically she began to hook cinches and tighten them. In the corral the cattle were beginning to calm.

When she'd finished, Gil tapped her on the shoulder. Turning her head, she saw him hold out a thick biscuit crammed with meat.

"You eat this, damn it," he said gruffly. "You're going to blow away in a high wind if you keep it up."

Accepting the biscuit, she took a huge bite. "You mangy old dog," she muttered with her mouth full. Then, because no one was around to see and razz him, she kissed both his cheeks. Though it pleased him, he cursed her for it and made her laugh as she vaulted into the saddle.

Jillian trotted the mare out of the ranch yard, then, turning toward solitude, rode her hard.

To satisfy her own curiosity, she headed for the west pasture first. Riding slowly now, she checked the repaired fence, then began to count the cattle still grazing. It didn't take long for her to conclude that Gil's estimate had been very close to the mark. A hundred head. Closing her eyes, she tried to think calmly.

The winter had only cost her twenty—that was something every rancher had to deal with. But it hadn't been nature who'd taken these cows from her. She had to find out who, and quickly, before the losses continued. Jillian glanced over the boundary line. On both sides cattle grazed placidly, at peace now that man had left them to their own pursuits. As far as she could see there was nothing but rolling grass and the cattle growing sleek on it. A hundred head, she thought again. Enough to put a small but appreciable dent in her herd—and her profit. She wasn't going to sit still for it.

Grimly she sent Delilah into a gallop. She couldn't afford the luxury of panicking. She'd have to take it step by step, ascertaining a firm and accurate account of her losses before she went to the authorities. But for now she was tired, dirty, and discouraged. The best thing to do was to take care of that before she went back to the ranch.

It had been only a week since she'd last ridden out to the pond, but even in that short time the aspen and cottonwood were greener. She could see hints of bitterroot and of the wild roses that were lovely and so destructive when they sprang up in the pastures. The sun was beginning its gradual decline westward. Jillian judged it to be somewhere between one and two. She'd give herself an hour here to recharge before she went back to begin the painstaking job of checking and rechecking the number of cattle in her books, and their locations. Dismounting, she tethered her mare to a branch of an aspen and let her graze.

Carelessly Jillian tossed her hat aside, then sat on a rock to pull off her boots. As her jeans and shirt followed she listened to the sound of a warbler singing importantly of spring and sunshine. Black-eyed Susans were springing up at the edge of the grass.

The water was deliciously cool. When she lowered herself into it, she could forget about the aches in her muscles, the faint, dull pain in her lower back, and the sense of despair that had followed her out of the west pasture. As owner and boss of Utopia, she'd deal with what needed to be dealt with. For now, she needed to be only Jillian. It was spring, the sun was warm. If the breeze was right, she could smell the young roses. Dipping her head back, she let the water flow over her face and hair.

Aaron didn't ask himself how he'd known she'd be there. He didn't ask himself why knowing it, he'd come. Both he and the stallion remained still as he watched her. She didn't splash around but simply drifted quietly so that the water made soft lapping sounds that didn't disturb the birdsong. He thought he could see the fatigue drain from her. It was the first time he'd seen her completely relaxed without the light of adventure or temper or even laughter in her eyes. This was something she did for herself, and though he knew he intruded, he stayed where he was.

Her skin was milky pale where the sun hadn't touched it. Beneath the rippling water, he could see the slender curves of her body. Her hair clung to her head and shoulders and burned like fire. So did the need that started low in his stomach and spread through his blood.

Did she know how exquisite she was with that long, limber body and creamy skin? Did she know how seductive she looked with that mass of chestnut hair sleek around a face that held both delicacy and strength? No, he thought as she sank beneath the surface, she wouldn't know—wouldn't allow herself to know. Perhaps it was time he showed her. With the slightest of signals, he walked Samson to a tree on his side of the boundary.

Jillian surfaced and found herself looking directly up into Aaron's eyes. Her first shock gave way to annoyance and annoyance to outrage when she remembered her disadvantage. Aaron saw all three emotions. His lips twitched.

"What're you doing here?" she demanded. She knew she could do nothing about modesty and didn't attempt to. Instead she relied on bravado.

"How's the water?" Aaron asked easily. Another woman, he mused, would've made some frantic and useless attempt to conceal herself. Not Jillian. She just tossed up her chin.

"It's cold. Now, why don't you go back to wherever you came from so I can finish what I'm doing."

"It was a long, dusty morning." He sat on a rock near the edge of the pool and smiled companionably. Like Jillian's, his clothes and skin were streaked with grime and sweat. The signs of hard work and effort suited him. Aaron tilted back his hat. "Looks inviting."

"I was here first," she said between her teeth. "If you had any sense of decency, you'd go away."

"Yep." He bent over and pulled off his boots.

Jillian watched first one then the other hit the grass. "What the hell do you think you're doing?"

"Thought I'd take a dip." He gave her an engaging grin as he tossed his hat aside.

"Think again."

He rose, and his brow lifted slowly as he unbuttoned his shirt. "I'm on my own land," he pointed out. He tossed the shirt aside so that Jillian had an unwanted and fascinating view of a hard, lean torso with brown skin stretched tight over the rib cage and a dark vee of hair that trailed down to the low-slung waist of his jeans.

"Damn you, Murdock," she muttered, and judged the distance to her own clothes. Too far to be any use.

"Relax," he suggested, enjoying himself. "We can pretend there's wire strung clean down the middle." With this he unhooked his belt.

His eyes stayed on hers. Jillian's first instinct to look away was overruled by the amusement she saw there. Coolly she watched him strip. If she had to swallow, she did it quietly.

Damn, did he have to be so beautiful? she asked herself and kept well to her own side as he slid into the water. The ripples his body made spread out to tease her own skin. Shivering, she sank a little deeper.

"You're really getting a kick out of this, aren't you?"

Aaron gave a long sigh as the water rinsed away dust and cooled his blood. "Have to admit I am. View from in here's no different from the one I had out there," he reminded her easily. "And I'd already given some thought to what you'd look like without your clothes. Most redheads have freckles."

"I'm just lucky, I guess." Her dimple flickered briefly. At least they were on equal ground again. "You're built like most cowboys," she told him in a drawl. "Lots of leg, no hips." She let her arms float lazily. "I've seen better," she lied. Laughing, she tilted her head and let her legs come up, unable to resist the urge to tease him.

He had only to reach out to grab her ankle and drag her to him. Aaron rubbed his itchy palm on his thigh and relaxed. "You make a habit of skinny-dipping up here?"

"No one comes here." Tossing the hair out of her eyes, she shot him a look. "Or no one did. If you're going to start using the pond regularly, we'll have to work out some kind of schedule."

"I don't mind the company." He drifted closer so that his body brushed the imaginary line.

"Keep to your own side, Murdock," she warned softly, but smiled. "Trespassers still get shot these days." To show her lack of concern, she closed her eyes and floated. "I like to come here on Sunday afternoons, when the men are in the ranch yard, pitching horseshoes and swapping lies."

Aaron studied her face. No, he'd never seen her this relaxed. He wondered if she realized just how little space she gave herself. "Don't you like to swap lies?"

"Men tend to remember I'm a woman on Sunday afternoons. Having me around puts a censor on the— ah, kind of lies."

"They only remember on Sunday afternoons?"

"It's easy to forget the way a person's built when you're out on the range or shoveling out stalls."

He let his eyes skim down the length of her, covered by only a few inches of water. "You say so," he murmured.

"And they need time to complain." With another laugh, she let her legs sink. "About the food, the pay, the work. Hard to do all that when the boss is there." She spun her hand just under the surface and sent the water waving all the way to the edge. He thought it was the first purely frivolous gesture he'd ever seen her make. "Your men complain, Murdock?"

"You should've heard them when my sister decided to fix up the bunkhouse six or seven years back." The memory made him grin. "Seems she thought the place needed some pretty paint and curtains—gingham curtains, baby-blue paint."

"Oh, my God." Jillian tried to imagine what her crew's reaction would be if they were faced with gingham. Throwing back her head, she laughed until her sides ached. "What did they do?"

"They refused to wash anything, sweep anything, or throw anything away. In two weeks' time the place looked like the county dump—smelled like it too."

"Why'd your father let her do it?" Jillian asked, wiping her eyes.

"She looks like my mother," Aaron said simply.

Nodding, she sighed from the effort of laughing. "But they got rid of the curtains."

"I—let's say they disappeared one night," he amended.

Jillian gave him a swift appraising look. "You took them down and burned them."

"If I haven't admitted that in seven years, I'm not going to admit it now. It took damned near a week to get that place cleared out," he remembered. She was smiling at him in such an easy, friendly way it took all his willpower not to reach over and pull her to his side. "Did you do the orphan today?"

"Earmarked, vaccinated, and branded," Jillian returned, trailing her hands through the water again.

"Is that all?"

She grinned, knowing his meaning. "In a couple of years Baby's going to be giving his poppa some competition." She shrugged, so that her body shifted and the water lapped close at the curve of her breast. The less she seemed concerned about her body, the more he became fascinated by it. "I have a feeling about him," she continued. "No use making a steer out of a potential breeder." A cloud of worry came into her eyes. "I rode the west fence before I came up here. I didn't see any more breaks."

"There weren't any more." He'd known they had to discuss it, but it annoyed him to have the few moments of simple camaraderie interrupted. He couldn't remember sharing that sort of simplicity with a woman before. "My men rounded up six cows that had strayed to your side. Seemed like you had about twice that many on mine."

She hesitated a moment, worrying her bottom lip. "Then your count balances?"

He heard the tension in her voice and narrowed his eyes. "Seems to. Why?"

She kept her eyes level and expressionless. "I'm a good hundred head short."

"Hundred?" He'd grabbed her arm before he realized it. "A hundred head? Are you sure?"

"As sure as I can be until we count again and go over the books. But we're short, I'm sure of that."

He stared at her as his thoughts ran along the same path hers had. That many cows didn't stray on their own. "I'll do a count of my own herd in the morning, but I can tell you, I'd know if I had that much extra cattle in my pasture."

"I'm sure you would. I don't think that's where they are."

Aaron reached up to touch her cheek. "I'd like to help you—if you need some extra hands. We can take the plane up. Maybe they wandered in the other direction."

She felt something soften inside her that shouldn't have. A simple offer of help when she needed it—and his hand was gentle on her face. "I appreciate it," Jillian began unsteadily. "But I don't think the cattle wandered any more than you do."

"No." He combed the hair away from her face. "I'll go with you to the sheriff."

Unused to unselfish support, she stared at him. Neither was aware that they were both drifting to the line, and each other. "No—I…it isn't necessary, I can deal with it."

"You don't have to deal with it alone." How was it he'd never noticed how fragile she was? he wondered. Her eyes were so young, so vulnerable. The curve of her cheek was so delicate. He ran his thumb over it and felt her tremble. Somehow his hand was at her lower back, bringing her closer. "Jillian…" But he didn't have the words, only the needs. His mouth came to hers gently.

Her hands ran up his back, skimming up wet, cool skin. Her lips parted softly under his. The tip of his tongue ran lazily around the inside of her mouth, stopping to tease hers. Jillian relaxed against him, content for the long, moist kiss to go on and on. She couldn't remember ever feeling so pliant, so much in tune with another's movements and wishes. His lips grew warmer and heated hers. Against her own, she could feel his heartbeat—quick and steady. His mouth left hers only long enough to change the angle before he began to slowly deepen the kiss.

It happened so gradually she had no defense. It was an emptiness that started in her stomach like a hunger, then spread until it was an ache to be loved. Her body yearned for it. Her heart began to tell her he was the one she could share herself with, not without risk, not without pain, but with something she'd almost forgotten to ask for: hope.

But when her mind started to cloud, she struggled to clear it. It wasn't sharing, she told herself even as his lips slanted over hers to persuade her. It was giving, and if she gave she could lose. Only a fool would forget the boundary line that stood between them.

She pulled out of his hold and stared at him. Was she mad? Making love to a Murdock when her fence had been cut and a hundred of her cows were missing? Was she so weak that a gentle touch, a tender kiss, made her forget her responsibilities and obligations?

"I told you to stay on your own side," she said unsteadily. "I meant it." Turning away, she cut through the water and scrambled up the bank.

Breathing fast, Aaron watched her. She'd been so soft, so giving in his arms. He'd never wanted a woman more—never felt just that way. It came like a blow that she was the first who'd really mattered, and the first to throw his own emotion back in his face. Grimly he swam back to his own side.

"You're one tough lady, aren't you?"

Jillian heard the water lap as he pulled himself from it. Without bothering to shake it out, she dragged on her dusty shirt. "That's right. God knows why I was fool enough to think I could trust you." Why did she want so badly to weep when she never wept? she wondered and buttoned her shirt with shaky fingers. "All that talk about helping me, just so you could get what you wanted." Keeping her back to him, she pulled up her brief panties.

Aaron's hands paused on the snap of his jeans. Rage and frustration tumbled through him so quickly he didn't think he'd be able to control it. "Be careful, Jillian."

She whirled around, eyes brilliant, breasts heaving. "Don't you tell me what to do. You've been clear right from the beginning about what you wanted."

Muscles tense, he laid a hand on the saddle of his stallion. "That's right."

The calm answer only filled her with more fury. "I might've respected your honesty if it wasn't for the fact that I've got a cut fence and missing cattle. Things like that didn't happen when you were in Billings waiting for your father to—" She cut herself off, appalled at what she'd been about to say. Whatever apology she might have made was swallowed at the murderous look he sent her.

"Waiting for him to what?" Aaron said softly—too softly.

The ripple of fear made her lift her chin. "That's for you to answer."

He knew he didn't dare go near her. If he did she might not come out whole. His fingers tightened on the rope that hung on his saddle. "Then you'd better keep your thoughts to yourself."

She'd have given half her spread to have been able to take those hateful, spiteful words back. But they'd been said. "And you keep your hands to yourself," she said evenly. "I want you to stay away from me and mine. I don't need soft words, Murdock. I don't want them from

you or anyone. You're a damn sight easier to take without the pretense." She stalked away to grab at her jeans.

He acted swiftly. He didn't think. His mind was still
reeling from her words—words that had stung because
he'd never felt or shown that kind of tenderness to another woman. What had flowed through him in the pond
had been much more than a physical need and complex
enough to allow him to be hurt for the first time by a
woman.

Jillian gave out a gasp of astonishment as the circle of
rope slipped around her, snapping snugly just about her
waist and pinning her arms above the elbows. Whirling
on her heel, she grabbed at the line. "What the hell do
you think you're doing?"

With a jerk, Aaron brought her stumbling forward.
"What I should've done a week ago." His eyes were
nearly black with fury as she fell helplessly against him.
"You won't get any more soft words out of me."

She struggled impotently against the rope, but her
eyes were defiant and fearless. "You're going to pay for
this, Murdock."

He didn't doubt it, but at that moment he didn't give a
damn. Gathering her wet hair in one hand, he dragged her
closer. "By God," he muttered. "I think it'll be worth it.
You make a man ache, Jillian, in the middle of the night
when he should have some peace. One minute you're so
damn soft, and the next you're snarling. Since you can't
make up your mind, I'll do it for you."

His mouth came down on hers so that she could taste
enraged desire. She fought against it even as it found
some answering chord in her. His chest was still naked,
still wet, so that her shirt soaked up the moisture. The
air rippled against her bare legs as he scooped them out
from under her. With her mouth still imprisoned by his,

she found herself lying on the sun-warmed grass beneath him. Her fury didn't leave room for panic.

She squirmed under him, kicking and straining against the rope, cursing him when he released her mouth to savage her neck. But an oath ended on a moan when his mouth came back to hers. He nipped into her full bottom lip as if to draw out passion. Her movements beneath him altered in tone from protest to demand, but neither of them noticed. Jillian only knew her body was on fire, and that this time she'd submit to it no matter what the cost.

He was drowning in her. He'd forgotten about the rope, forgotten his anger and his hurt. All he knew was that she was warm and slender beneath him and that her mouth was enough to drive a man over the line of reason. Nothing about her was calm. Her lips were avid and seeking; her fingers dug into his waist. He could feel the thunder of her heart race to match his. When she caught his lip between her teeth and drew it into her mouth, he groaned and let her have her way.

Jillian flew with the sensations. The grass rubbed against her legs as she shifted them to allow him more intimacy. His hair smelled of the water that ran from it onto her skin. She tasted it, and the light flavor of salt and flesh when she pressed her lips to his throat. Her name shivered in a desperate whisper against her ear. No soft words. There was nothing soft, nothing gentle about what they brought to each other now. This was a raw, primitive passion that she understood even as it was tapped for the first time. She felt his fingers skim down her shirt, releasing buttons so that he could find her. But it was his mouth not his hand that closed over the taut peak, hot and greedy. The need erupted and shattered her.

Lips, teeth, and tongue were busy on her flesh as she lay dazed from the first swift, unexpected crest. While she fought to catch her breath, Aaron tugged on her shirt to remove it, cursing when it remained tight at her waist. In an urgent move his hand swept down. His fingers touched rope. He froze, his breath heaving in his lungs.

Good God, what was he doing? Squeezing his eyes tight, he fought for reason. His face was nuzzled in the slender valley between her breasts so that he could feel as well as hear the frantic beat of her heart.

He was about to force himself on a helpless woman. No matter what the provocation, there could be no absolution for what he was on the edge of doing. Cursing himself, Aaron tugged on the rope, then yanked it over her head. After he'd tossed it aside, he looked down at her.

Her mouth was swollen from his. Her eyes were nearly closed and so clouded he couldn't read them. She lay so still he could feel each separate tremor from her body. He wanted her badly enough to beg. "You can make me pay now," he said softly and rolled from her onto his back.

She didn't move, but looked up into the calm blue sky while needs churned inside her. The warbler was still singing, the roses still blooming.

Yes, she could make him pay—she'd recognized the look of self-disgust in his eyes. She had only to get up and walk away to do it. She'd never considered herself a fool. Deliberately she rolled over on top of him. Aaron automatically put his hands on her arms to steady her. Their eyes met so that desire stared into desire.

"You'll pay—if you don't finish what you've started."

Diving her hands into his hair, she brought her mouth down on his.

Her shirt fluttered open so that her naked skin slid over his. Jillian felt his groan of pleasure every bit as clearly as she heard it. Then it was all speed and fire, so fast, so hot, there wasn't time for thought. Tasting, feeling was enough as they raced over each other in a frenzy of demand. Her shirt fell away just before she pulled at the snap of his jeans.

She tugged them down, then lost herself in the long lean line of his hips. Her fingers found a narrow raised scar that ran six inches down the bone. She felt a ripple of pain as if her own skin had been rent. Then he was struggling out of his jeans and the feel of him, hot and ready against her, drove everything else out of her mind. But when she reached for him, he shifted so she was beneath him again.

"Aaron…" What she would have demanded ended in a helpless moan as he slid a finger under the elastic riding high on her thigh. With a clever, thorough touch of fingertips he brought her to a racking climax.

She was pulsing all over, inside and out. No longer was she aware that she clung to him, her hands bringing him as much torturous pleasure as his brought her. She only knew that her need built and was met time and time again while he held off that last, that ultimate fulfillment. With eyes dazed with passion, she watched his mouth come toward hers again. Their lips met—he plunged into her, swallowing her gasps.

For a long time she lay spent. The sky overhead was still calm. With her hands on Aaron's shoulders, she could feel each labored breath. There seemed to be no peace for them even in the aftermath of passion. Was this the way it was supposed to be? she wondered. She'd known nothing like this before. Needs that hurt and remained unsettled even after they'd been satisfied. She still wanted him—that moment when her body was hot and trembling from their merging.

After all the years she'd been so careful to distance herself from any chance of an involvement, she found herself needing a man she hardly knew. A man she'd been schooled to distrust. Yet she did trust him…that's what frightened her most of all. She had no reason to— no logical reason. He'd made her forget her ambitions, her work, her responsibilities, and reminded her that beneath it all, she was first a woman. More, he'd made her glory in it.

Aaron raised his head slowly, for the first time in his memory unsure of himself. She'd gotten to a place inside him no one had ever touched. He realized he didn't want her to walk away and leave it empty again—and that he'd never be able to hold her unless she was willing. "Jillian…" He brushed her damp, tangled hair from her cheek. "This was supposed to be easy. Why isn't it?"

"I don't know." She held onto the weakness another moment, bringing his cheek down to hers so that she could draw in his scent and remember. "I need to think."

"About what?"

She closed her eyes a moment and shook her head. "I don't know. Let me go now, Aaron."

His fingers tightened in her hair. "For how long?"

"I don't know that either. I need some time."

It would be easy to keep her—for the moment. He had only to lower his mouth to hers again. He remembered the wild mustang—the hell he'd gone through to catch it, the hell he'd gone through to set it free. Saying nothing, he released her.

They dressed in silence—both of them too battered

by feelings they'd never tried to put into words. When Jillian reached for her hat, Aaron took her arm.

"If I told you this meant something to me, more than I'd expected, maybe more than I'd wanted, would you believe me?"

Jillian moistened her lips. "I do now. I have to be sure I do tomorrow."

Aaron picked up his own hat and shaded his face with it. "I'll wait—but I won't wait long." Lifting a hand, he cupped her chin. "If you don't come to me, I'll come after you."

She ignored the little thrill of excitement that rushed up her spine. "If I don't come to you, you won't be able to come after me." Turning away, she untied her mare and vaulted into the saddle. Aaron slipped his hand under the bridle and gave her one long look.

"Don't bet on it," he said quietly. He walked back over the boundary line to his own mount.

Chapter Seven

If you don't come to me, I'll come after you.

They weren't words Jillian would forget. She hadn't yet decided what to do about them—any more than she'd decided what to do about what had happened between her and Aaron. There'd been more than passion in that fiery afternoon at the pond, more than pleasure, however intense. Perhaps she could have faced the passion and the pleasure, but it was the something more that kept her awake at nights.

If she went to him, what would she be going to? A man she'd yet to scratch the surface of—an affair that promised to have more hills and valleys than she knew how to negotiate. The risk—she was beginning to understand the risk too well. If she relaxed her hands on the reins this time, she'd tumble into love before she could regain control. That was difficult for her to admit, and impossible for her to understand.

She'd always believed that people fell in love because

they wanted to, because they were looking for, or were ready for, romance. Certainly she'd been ready for it once before, open for all those soft feelings and heightened emotions. Yet now, when she believed she was on the border of love again, she was neither ready for it, nor was she experiencing any soft feelings. Aaron Murdock didn't ask for them—and in not asking, he demanded so much more.

If she went to him…could she balance her responsibilities, her ambitions, with the needs he drew out of her? When she was in his arms she didn't think of the ranch, or her position there that she had to struggle every day to maintain.

If she fell in love with him…could she deal with the imbalance of feelings between them and cope when the time came for him to go his own way? She never doubted he would. Other than Clay, there'd never been a man who'd remained constant to her.

Indecision tore at her, as it would in a woman accustomed to following her own route in her own way.

And while her personal life was in turmoil, her professional one fared no better. Five hundred of her cattle were missing. There was no longer any doubt that her herd had been systematically and successfully rustled.

Jillian hung up the phone, rubbing at the headache that drummed behind her temples.

"Well?" Hat in lap, Joe Carlson sat on the other side of her desk.

"They can't deliver the plane until the end of the week." Grimly she set her jaw as she looked over at him. "It hardly matters now. Unless they're fools, they've got the cattle well away by this time. Probably transported them over the border into Wyoming."

He studied the brim of his neat Stetson. "Maybe not, that would make it federal."

"It's what I'd do," she murmured. "You can't hide five hundred head of prime beef." Rising, she dragged her hands through her hair. *Five hundred.* The words continued to flash in her mind—a sign of failure, impotence, vulnerability. "Well, the sheriff's doing what he can, but they've got the jump on us, Joe. There's nothing I can do." On a sound of frustration, she balled her fists. "I hate being helpless."

"Jillian…" Joe ran the brim of his hat through his hands, frowning down at it another moment. During his silence she could hear the old clock on her grandfather's desk tick the time away. "I wouldn't feel right if I didn't bring it up," he said at length and looked back at her. "It wouldn't be too difficult to hide five hundred head if they were scattered through a few thousand."

Her eyes chilled. "Why don't you speak plainly, Joe?"

He rose. After more than six months on Utopia, he still looked more businessman than outdoorsman. And she understood it was the businessman who spoke now. "Jillian, you can't just ignore the fact that the west boundary line was cut. That pasture leads directly onto Murdock land."

"I know where it leads," she said coolly. "Just as I know I need more than a cut line to accuse anyone, particularly the Murdocks, of rustling."

Joe opened his mouth to speak again, met her uncompromising look, then shut it. "Okay."

The simplicity of his answer only fanned her temper. And her doubts. "Aaron told me he was going to take a thorough head count. He'd know if there were fifty extra head on his spread, much less five hundred."

It was her tone much more than her words that told him where the land lay now. "I know."

Jillian stared at him. His eyes were steady and compassionate. "Damn it, he doesn't need to steal cattle from me."

"Jillian, you lose five hundred head now and your profit dwindles down to nothing. Lose that much again, half that much again, and…you might have to start thinking about selling off some of your pasture. There're other reasons than the price per head for rustling."

She spun around, shutting her eyes tight. She'd thought of that—and hated herself for it. "He would've asked me if he wanted to buy my land."

"Maybe, but your answer would've been no. Rumor is he was going to start his own place a few years back. He didn't—but that doesn't mean he's content to make do with what his father has."

She couldn't contradict him, not on anything he'd said. But she couldn't live with it either. "Leave the investigating to the sheriff, Joe. That's his job."

He drew very straight and very stiff at the clipped tone of her voice. "All right. I guess I better get back to mine."

On a wave of frustration and guilt, she turned before he reached the door. "Joe—I'm sorry. I know you're only thinking about Utopia."

"I'm thinking about you, too."

"I appreciate it, I really do." She picked up her worn leather work glove from the desk and ran it through her hands. "I have to handle this my own way, and I need a little more time to decide just what that is."

"Okay." He put his hat on and lowered the brim with his finger. "Just so you know you've got support if you need it."

"I won't forget it."

When he'd gone, Jillian stopped in the center of the office. God, she wanted so badly to panic. Just to throw up her hands and tell whoever'd listen that she couldn't deal with it. There had to be someone else, somewhere, who could take over and see her through until everything was back in order. But she wasn't allowed to panic, or to turn over her responsibilities even for a minute. The land was hers, and all that went with it.

Jillian picked up her hat and her other glove. There was work to be done. If they cleaned her out down to the last hundred head, there would still be work to be done, and a way to build things back up again. She had the land, and her grandfather's legacy of determination.

Even as she opened the front door to go out, she saw Karen Murdock drive up in front of the house. Surprised, Jillian hesitated, then went out on the porch to meet her.

"Hello, I hope you don't mind that I just dropped by."

"No, of course not." Jillian smiled, marveling for the second time at the soft, elegant looks of Aaron's mother. "It's nice to see you again, Mrs. Murdock."

"I've caught you at a bad time," she said, glancing down at the work gloves in Jillian's hand.

"No." Jillian stuck the gloves in her back pocket. "Would you like some coffee?"

"I'd love it."

Karen followed Jillian into the house, glancing around idly as they walked toward the kitchen. "Lord, it's been years since I've been in here. I used to visit your grandmother," she said with a rueful smile. "Of course your grandfather and Paul both knew, but we were all very careful not to mention it. How do you feel about old feuds, Jillian?"

There was a laugh in her voice that might have set Jillian's back up at one time. Now it simply nudged a smile from her. "Not precisely the same way I felt a few weeks ago."

"I'm glad to hear it." Karen took a seat at the kitchen table while Jillian began to brew a fresh pot of coffee. "I realize Paul said some things the other day that were bound to rub you the wrong way. I have to confess he does some of it on purpose. Your reaction was the high point of his day."

Jillian smiled a little as she looked over her shoulder. "Maybe he's more like Clay than I'd imagined."

"They were out of the same mold. There aren't many of them," she murmured. "Jillian—we've heard about your missing cattle. I can't tell you how badly I feel. I realize the words *if there's anything I can do* sound empty, but I mean them."

Turning back to the coffeepot, Jillian managed to shrug. She wasn't sure she could deal easily with sympathy right then. "It's a risk we all take. The sheriff's doing what he can."

"A risk we all take," Karen agreed. "When it happens to one of us, all of us feel it." She hesitated a moment, knowing the ground was delicate. "Jillian, Aaron mentioned the cut line to me, though he's kept it from his father."

"I'm not worried about the cut line," Jillian told her quietly. "I know Aaron didn't have any part in it—I'm not a fool."

No, Karen thought, studying the clean-lined profile. A fool you're not. "He's very concerned about you."

"He needn't be." She swung open a cupboard door for cups. "It's my problem, I have to deal with it."

Karen watched calmly as Jillian poured. "No support accepted?"

With a sigh, Jillian turned around. "I don't mean to be rude, Mrs. Murdock. Running a ranch is a difficult, chancy business. When you're a woman you double those stakes." Bringing the coffee to the table, she sat across from her. "I have to be twice as good as a man would be in my place because this is still a man's world. I can't afford to cave in."

"I understand that." Karen sipped and glanced around the room. "There's no one here you have to prove anything to."

Jillian looked up from her own cup and saw the compassion, and the unique bond one woman can have with another. As she did, the tight band of control loosened. "I'm so scared," she whispered. "Most of the time I don't dare admit it to myself because there's so much riding on this year. I've taken a lot of gambles—if they pay off... Five hundred head." She let out a long breath as the numbers pounded in her mind. "It won't put me under, I can't let it put me under, but it's going to take a long time to recover."

Reaching out, Karen covered her hand with her own. "They could be found."

"You know the chances of that now." For a moment she sat still, accepting the comfort of the touch before she put her hand back on her cup. "Whichever way it goes, I'm still boss at Utopia. I have a responsibility to make what was passed on to me work. Clay trusted me with what was his. I'm going to make it work."

Karen gave her a long, thorough look very much like one of her son's. "For Clay or for yourself?"

"For both of us," Jillian told her. "I owe him for the land, and for what he taught me."

"You can put too much of yourself into this land," Karen said abruptly. "Paul would swear I'd taken leave of my senses if he heard me say so, but it's true. Aaron—" She smiled, indulgent, proud. "He's a great deal like his father, but he doesn't have Paul's rigidity. Perhaps he hasn't needed it. You can't let the land swallow you, Jillian."

"It's all I have."

"You don't mean that. Oh, you think you do," she murmured when Jillian said nothing. "But if you lost every acre of this land tomorrow, you'd make something else. You've the guts for it. I recognize it in you just as I've always seen it in Aaron."

"He had other options." Agitated, Jillian rose to pour coffee she no longer wanted.

"You're thinking of the oil." For a moment Karen said nothing as she weighed the pros and cons of what she was going to say. "He did that for me—and for his father," she said at length. "I hope I don't ever have to ask anything like that of him again."

Jillian came back to the table but didn't sit. "I don't understand."

"Paul was wrong. He's a good man and his mistakes have always been made with the same force and vigor as he does everything." A smile flickered on her lips, but her eyes were serious. "He'd promised something to Aaron, something that had been understood since Aaron was a boy. The Double M would be his, if he'd earned it. By God, he did," she whispered. "I think you understand what I mean."

"Yes." Jillian looked down at her cup, then set it down. "Yes, I do."

"When Aaron came back from college, Paul wasn't ready to let go. That's when Aaron agreed to work it his father's way for three years. He was to take over as manager after that—with full authority."

"I've heard," Jillian began, then changed her tack. "It can't be easy for a man to give up what he's worked for, even to his own son."

"It was time for Paul to give," Karen told her, but she held her head high. "Perhaps he would have if…" She gestured with her hands as though she were slowing herself down. "When he refused to stick to the bargain, Aaron was furious. They had a terrible argument—the kind that's inevitable between two strong, self-willed men. Aaron was determined to go down to Wyoming, buy some land for himself, and start from scratch. As much as he loved the ranch, I think it was something he'd been itching to do in any case."

"But he didn't."

"No." Karen's eyes were very clear. "Because I asked him not to. The doctors had just diagnosed Paul as terminal. They'd given him two years at the outside. He was infuriated that age had caught up with him, that his body was betraying him. He's a very proud man, Jillian. He'd beaten everything he'd ever gone up against."

She remembered the hawklike gaze and trembling hands. "I'm sorry."

"He didn't want anyone to know, not even Aaron. I can count the times I've gone against Paul on one hand." She glanced down at her own palms. Something in her expression told Jillian very clearly that if the woman had acquiesced over the years, it had been because of strength and not weakness. "I knew if Aaron went away like that, Paul would stop fighting for whatever time he had left. And then Aaron, once he knew, would never be able to live with it. So I told him." She let out a long sigh and turned her hands over. "I asked him to give up what he wanted. He went to Billings, and though I'm sure he's always thought he did it for me, I know he did it for his father. I don't imagine the doctors would agree, but Aaron gave his father five years."

Jillian turned away as her throat began to ache. "I've said some horrible things to him."

"You wouldn't be the first, I'm sure. Aaron knew what it would look like. He's never given a damn what people think of him. What most people think," she corrected softly.

"I can't apologize," Jillian said as she fought to control herself. "He'd be furious if I told him I knew."

"You know him well."

"I don't," Jillian returned with sudden passion. "I don't know him, I don't understand him, and—" She cut herself off, amazed that she was about to bare her soul to Aaron's mother.

"I'm his mother," Karen said, interpreting the look. "But I'm still a woman. And one who understands very well what it is to have feelings for a man that promise to lead to difficulties." This time she didn't weigh her words but spoke freely. "I was barely twenty when I met Paul, he was past forty. His friends thought he was mad and that I wanted his money." She laughed, then sat back with a little sigh. "I can promise you, I didn't see the humor in it thirty years ago. I'm not here to offer advice on whatever's between you and Aaron, but to offer support if you'll take it."

Jillian looked at her—the enduring beauty, the strength that showed in her eyes, the kindness. "I'm not sure I know how."

Rising, Karen placed her hands on Jillian's shoulders. So young, she thought wistfully. So dead set. "Do you know how to accept friendship?"

Jillian smiled and touched Karen's hands, still resting on her shoulders. "Yes."

"That'll do. You're busy," she said briskly, giving Jillian a quick squeeze before she released her. "But if you need a woman, as we sometimes do, call me."

"I will. Thank you."

Karen shook her head. "No, it's not all unselfish. I've lived over thirty years in this man's world." Briefly she touched Jillian's cheek. "I miss my daughter."

Aaron stood on the porch and watched the moon rise. The night was so still he heard the whisk of a hawk's wings over his head before it dove after its night prey. In one hand he held a can of iced beer that he sipped occasionally, though he wasn't registering the taste. It was one of those warm spring nights when you could taste the scent of the flowers and smell the hint of summer, which was creeping closer.

He'd be damned if he'd wait much longer.

It had been a week since he'd touched her. Every night after the long, dusty day was over, he found himself aching to have her with him, to fill that emptiness inside him he'd become so suddenly aware of. It was difficult enough to have discovered he didn't want Jillian in the same way he'd wanted any other woman, but to have discovered his own vulnerabilities...

She could hurt him—had hurt him. That was a first, Aaron thought grimly and lifted his beer. He hadn't yet worked out how to prevent it from happening again. But that didn't stop him from wanting her.

She didn't trust him. Though he'd once agreed that he didn't want her to, Aaron had learned that was a lie. He wanted her to give him her trust—to believe in him enough to share her problems with him. She must be going through hell now, he thought as his fingers tightened on the can. But she wouldn't come to him, wouldn't let him help. Maybe it was about time he did something about that—whether she liked it or not.

Abruptly impatient, angry, he started toward the steps. The sound of an approaching car reached him before the headlights did. Glancing toward the sound, he watched the twin beams cut through the darkness. His initial disinterest became a tension he felt in his shoulder and stomach muscles.

Aaron set the half-empty beer on the porch rail as Jillian pulled up in front of his house. Whatever his needs were, he still had enough sense of self-preservation to prevent himself from just rushing down the stairs and grabbing her. He waited.

She'd been so sure her nerves would calm during the drive over. It was difficult for her, as a woman who simply didn't permit herself to be nervous, to deal with a jumpy stomach and dry throat. Not once since his mother had left her that morning had Aaron been out of her thoughts. Yet Jillian had gone through an agony of doubt before she'd made the final decision to come. In coming, she was giving him something she'd never intended to—a portion of her private self.

With the moon at her back she stood by her car a moment, looking up at him. Perhaps because her legs weren't as strong as they should've been, she kept her chin high as she walked up the porch steps.

"This is a mistake," she told him.

Aaron remained where he was, one shoulder leaning against the rail post. "Is it?"

"It's going to complicate things at a time when my life's complicated enough."

His stomach had twisted into a mass of knots that

were only tugging tighter as he looked at her. She was pale, but there wasn't a hint of a tremor in her voice. "You took your sweet time coming here," he said mildly, but he folded his fingers into his palm to keep from touching her.

"I wouldn't have come at all if I could've stopped myself."

"That so?" It was more of an admission than he'd expected. The first muscles began to relax. "Well, since you're here, why don't you come a little closer?"

He wasn't going to make it easy for her, Jillian realized. And she'd have detested herself if she'd let him. With her eyes on his, she stepped forward until their bodies brushed. "Is this close enough?"

His eyes skimmed her face, then he smiled. "No."

Jillian hooked her hands behind his head and pressed her lips to his. "Now?"

"Closer." He allowed himself to touch her—one hand at the small of her back rode slowly up to grip her hair. His eyes glittered in the moonlight, touched with triumph, amusement, and passion. "A damn sight closer, Jillian."

Her eyes stayed open as she fit her body more intimately to his. She felt the answering response of his muscles against her own, the echoing thud of his heart. "If we get much closer out here on the porch," she murmured with her mouth a whisper from his, "we're going to be illegal."

"Yeah." He traced her bottom lip, moistening it, and felt her little jerk of breath on his tongue. "I'll post bond if you're worried."

Her lips throbbed from the expert flick of his tongue. "Shut up, Murdock," she muttered and crushed her mouth to his. Jillian let all the passions, all the emotions that had been chasing her around for days, have their way. Even as they sprang out of her, they consumed her. Mindlessly she pressed against him so that he was caught between her body and the post.

The thrill of pleasure was so intense it almost sliced through his skin. Aaron's arm came around her so that he could cup the back of her head and keep that wildly aggressive mouth on his own. Then, swiftly, his arm scooped under her knees and lifted her off her feet.

"Aaron—" Her protest was smothered by another ruthless kiss before he walked across the porch to the door. Though she admired the way he could swing the screen open, and slam the heavy door with his arms full, she laughed. "Aaron, put me down. I can walk."

"Don't see how when I'm carrying you," he pointed out as he started up the narrow steps to the second floor.

"Is this the sort of thing you do to express male dominance?"

She was rewarded with a narrow-eyed glare and smiled sweetly.

"No," Aaron said in mild tones. "This is the sort of thing I do to express romance. Now, when I want to express male dominance…" As he drew near the top of the steps he shifted her quickly so that she hung over his shoulder.

After the initial shock Jillian had to acknowledge a hit. "Had that one coming," she admitted, blowing the hair out of her face. "I think my point was that I wasn't looking for romance or dominance."

Aaron's brow lifted as he walked into the bedroom. The words had been light enough, but he'd caught the sincerity of tone. Slowly he drew her down so that before her feet had touched the floor every angle of her body had rubbed against his. Weakened by the maneuver, she stared up at him with eyes already stormy with desire. "Don't you like romance, Jillian?"

"That's not what I'm asking for," she managed, reaching for him.

He grabbed her wrists, holding her off. "That's too bad, then." Very lightly he nipped at her ear. "You'll just have to put up with it. Do you reckon straight passion's safer?"

"As anything could be with you." She caught her breath as his tongue traced down the side of her throat.

Aaron laughed, then began lazily, determinedly, to seduce her with his mouth alone. "This right here," he murmured, nibbling at a point just above her collar. "So soft, so delicate. A man could almost forget there're places like this on you until he finds them for himself. You throw up that damn-the-devil chin and it's tempting to give it one good clip, but then—" he tilted his head to a new angle and his lips skimmed along her skin "—right under it's just like silk."

He tugged with his teeth at the cord of her neck and felt her arms go boneless. That's what he wanted, he thought with rising excitement. To have her melting and pliant and out of control, if only for a few minutes. Hot blood and fire were rewards in themselves, but this time, perhaps only this time, he wanted the satisfaction of knowing he could make her as weak as she could make him.

He slanted his mouth over hers, teasing her tongue with the tip of his until her breath was short and shallow. Her pulse pounded into his palms. He was going to take his time undressing her, he thought. A long, leisurely time that would drive them both crazy.

Without hurry Aaron backed her toward the bed, then eased her down until she sat on the edge. In the moonlight he could see that her eyes had already misted with need, her skin softly flushed with it. Watching her, he ran a long finger down her throat to the first button on her shirt. His eyes remained steady as he undid it, then the second—then the third. He stopped there to move his hands down her, lightly over her breasts, the nipped waist, and narrow hips to the long, slender thighs. She was very still but for the quiver of her flesh.

Turning, he tucked her leg between his and began pulling off her boot. The first hit the floor, but when he took the other and tugged, Jillian gave him some assistance with a well-placed foot.

Surprised, he glanced back to see her shoot him a cocky smile. She recovered quickly, he thought. It would be all the more exciting to turn her to putty again. "You might do the same for me," Aaron suggested, then dropped on the bed, leaned back on his elbows, and held out a booted foot.

Jillian rose to oblige him and straddled his leg. This—the wicked grin, the reckless eyes—she knew how to deal with. It might light a fire in her, but it didn't bring on that uncontrollable softness. When she'd finally made her decision to come, she'd made it to come on equal terms, with no quiet promises or tender phrases that meant no more than the breath it took to make them. She'd told herself she wouldn't fall in love with him as long as she listened to her body and blocked off her heart.

The minute his second boot hit the floor, Aaron grabbed her around the waist and swung her back so that she fell onto the bed, laughing. "You're a tough guy, Murdock." Jillian hooked her arms around his neck and grinned up at him. "Always tossing women around."

"Bad habit of mine." Lowering his head, he nibbled

idly at her lips, resisting her attempt to deepen the kiss. "I like your mouth," he murmured. "It's another of those soft, surprising places." Gently he sucked on her lower lip until he felt the hands at his neck grow lax.

The mists were closing in again and she forgot the ways and means to hold them off. This wasn't what she wanted...was it? Yet it seemed to be everything she wanted. Her mind was floating, out of her body, so that she could almost see herself lying languorous and pliant under Aaron. She could see the tension and anxieties of the past days drain out of her own face until it was soft and relaxed under the lazy touch of his mouth and tongue. She could feel her heartbeat drop to a light pace that wasn't quite steady but not yet frantic. Perhaps this was what it felt like to be pampered, to be prized. She wasn't sure, but knew she couldn't bear to lose the sensation. Her sigh came slowly with the release of doubts.

When he bent to whisper something foolish in her ear, she could smell his evening shower on him. His face was rough with the stubble of a long day, but she rubbed her cheek against it, enjoying the scrape. Then his lips grazed across the skin that was alive and tingling until they found their way back to hers.

She felt the brush of strong, clever fingers as they trailed down to release the last buttons of her shirt. Then they skimmed over her rib cage, lightly, effortlessly drawing her deeper into the realm of sensation. He barely touched her. The kisses remained soft, his hands gentle. All coherent thought spun away.

"My shirt's in the way," he murmured against her ear. "I want to feel you against me."

She lifted her hands, and though her fingers didn't fumble, she couldn't make them move quickly. It seemed like hours before she felt the press of his flesh against hers. With a sigh, she slid her hands up to his shoulders and back until she'd drawn the shirt away. The ridge of muscle was so hard. As she rubbed her palms over him, Jillian realized she'd only had flashes of impressions the first time they'd made love. Everything had been so fast and wild she hadn't been able to appreciate just how well he was formed.

Tight sinew, taut flesh. Aaron was a man used to using his back and his hands to do a day's work. She didn't stop to reason why that in itself was a pleasure to her. Then she could reason nothing because his mouth had begun to roam.

He hadn't known he could gain such complete satisfaction in thinking of another's pleasure. He wanted her—wanted her quick and fast and furious, and yet it was a heady feeling to know he had the power to make her weak with a touch.

The underside of her breast was so soft…and he lingered. The skin above the waistband of her jeans was white and smooth…and his hand was content to move just there. He felt her first trembles; they rippled under his lips and hands until his senses swam. Denim strained against denim until he pulled the jeans down over her hips to find her.

Jillian wasn't certain when the languor had become hunger. She arched against him, demanding, but he continued to move without haste. She couldn't understand his fascination with her body when she'd always considered it too straight, too slim and practical. Yet now he seemed anxious to touch, to taste every inch. And the murmurs that reached her whispered approval. His hand cupped her knee so that his fingers trailed over the sensitive back. Years of riding, walking, working, had made her legs strong, and very susceptible.

When his teeth scraped down her thigh, she cried out, stunned to be catapulted to the taut edge of the first peak. But he didn't allow her to go over. Not yet. His warm breath teased her, then the light play of his tongue. She felt the threat of explosion building, growing in power and depth. Yet somehow he knew the instant before it shattered her, and retreated. Again and again he took her to the verge and brought her back until she was weak and desperate.

Jillian shifted beneath Aaron, willing him to take anything, all that he wanted—not even aware that he'd removed the last barrier of clothing until he was once more lying full length on her. She felt each warm, unsteady breath on her face just before his lips raced over it.

"This time…" Aaron pulled air into his lungs so that he could speak. "This time you tell me—you tell me that you want me."

"Yes." She locked herself around him, shuddering with need. "Yes, I want you. Now."

Something flashed in his eyes. "Not just now," he said roughly and drove into her.

Jillian slid over the first edge and was blinded. But there was more, so much more.

Chapter Eight

It was the scent of her hair that slowly brought him back to reason. His face was buried in it. The fragrance reminded him of the wildflowers his mother would sometimes gather and place in a little porcelain vase on a window ledge. It was tangled in his hands, and so soft against his skin he knew he'd be content to stay just as he was through the night.

She lay still beneath him, her breathing so quiet and even she might have been asleep. But when he turned his head to press his lips to her neck, her arms tightened around him. Lifting his head, he looked down at her.

Her eyes were nearly closed, heavy. He'd seen the shadows beneath them when she'd first walked toward him on the porch. With a small frown, Aaron traced his thumb over them. "You haven't been sleeping well."

Surprised by the statement, and his tone, she lifted her brows. After where they'd just gone together, she might've expected him to say something foolish or arousing. Instead his brows had drawn together and his tone was disapproving. She wasn't sure why it made her want to laugh, but it did.

"I'm fine," she said with a smile.

"No." He cut her off and cupped her chin in his hand. "You're not."

She stared up, realizing how easy it would be to just pour out her thoughts and feelings. The worries, the fears, the problems, that seemed to build up faster than she could cope with them—how reassuring it would be to say it all out loud, to him.

She'd done too much of that with his mother, but somehow Jillian could justify that. It was one thing to confess fears and doubts to another woman, and another to give a man an insight on your weaknesses. At dawn they'd both be ranchers again, with a boundary line between them that had stood for nearly a century.

"Aaron, I didn't come here to—"

"I know why you came," he interrupted. His voice was much milder than his eyes. "Because you couldn't stay away. I understand that. Now you're just going to have to accept what comes with it."

It was difficult to drum up a great deal of dignity when she was naked and warm beneath him, but she came close to succeeding. "Which is?"

The annoyance in his eyes lightened to amusement. "I like the way you say that—just like my third grade teacher."

Her lips quivered. "It's one of the few things I managed to pick up from my mother. But you haven't answered the question, Murdock."

"I'm crazy about you," he said suddenly and the mouth that had curved into a smile fell open. She wasn't ready to hear that one, Aaron mused. He wasn't sure he was ready for the consequences of it himself, and decided to play it light. "Of course, I've always been partial to nasty-tempered females. I mean to help you, Jillian." His eyes were abruptly sober. "If I have to climb over your back to do it."

"There isn't anything you can do even if I wanted you to."

He didn't comment immediately but shifted, pulling the pillows up against the headboard, then leaning back before he drew her against him. Jillian didn't stiffen as much as go still. There was something quietly possessive about the move, and irresistibly sweet. Before she could stop it, she'd relaxed against him.

Aaron felt the hesitation but didn't comment. When you went after trust, you did it slowly. "Tell me what's been done."

"Aaron, I don't want to bring you into this."

"I am in it, if for no other reason than that cut line."

She could accept that, and let her eyes close. "We did a full head count and came up five hundred short. As a precaution, we branded what calves were left right away. I estimate we lost fifty or sixty of them. The sheriff's been out."

"What'd he find?"

She moved her shoulders. "Can't tell where they took them out. If they'd cut any more wire, they'd fixed it. Very neat and tidy," she murmured, knowing something died inside her each time she thought of it. "It seems as though they didn't take them all at once, but skimmed a few head here and there."

"Seems odd they left the one line down."

"Maybe they didn't have time to fix it."

"Or maybe they wanted to throw your attention my way until they'd finished."

"Maybe." She turned her face into his shoulder—only slightly, only for an instant—but for Jillian it was a large step toward sharing. "Aaron, I didn't mean the things I said about you and your father."

"Forget it."

She tilted her head back and looked at him. "I can't."

He kissed her roughly. "Try harder," he suggested. "I heard you were getting a plane."

"Yes." She dropped her head on his shoulder and tried to order her thoughts. "It doesn't look like it's going to be ready until next week."

"Then we'll go up in mine tomorrow."

"But why—"

"Nothing against the sheriff," he said easily. "But you know your land better."

Jillian pressed her lips together. "Aaron, I don't want to be obligated to you. I don't know how to explain it, but—"

"Then don't." Taking hold of her hair, he jerked it until her face came up to his. "You're going to find I'm not the kind who'll always give a damn about what you want. You can fight me, sometimes you might even win. But you won't stop me."

Her eyes kindled. "Why do you gear me up for a fight when I'm trying to be grateful?"

In one swift move he shifted so that they lay crosswise across the bed. "Maybe I like you better that way. You're a hell of a lot more dangerous when you soften up."

She threw up her chin. "That's not something that's going to happen very often around you."

"Good," he said and crushed his mouth onto hers. "You'll stay with me tonight."

"I'm not—" Then he silenced her with a savage kiss that left no room for thought, much less words.

"Tonight," he said with a laugh that held more challenge than humor, "you stay with me."

And he took her in a fury that whispered of desperation.

The birds woke her. There was a short stretch of time during the summer when the sun rose early enough that the birds were up before her. With a sigh, Jillian snuggled into the pillow. She could always fool her system into thinking she'd been lazy when she woke to daylight and birdsong.

Groggily she went over the day's workload. She'd have to check Baby before she went in to the horses. He liked to have his bottle right off. With one luxurious stretch, she rolled over, then stared blankly around the room. Aaron's room. He'd won that battle.

Lying back for a moment, she thought about the night with a mixture of pleasure and discomfort. He'd said once before that it wasn't as easy as it should've been. But could he have any idea what it had done to her to lie beside him through the night? She'd never known the simple pleasure of sleeping with someone else, sharing warmth and quiet and darkness. What had made her believe that she could have an affair and remain practical about it?

But she wasn't in love with him. Jillian reached over to touch the side of the bed where he'd slept. She still had too much sense to let that happen. Her fingers dug into the sheet as she closed her eyes. Oh, God, she hoped she did.

The birdcalls distracted her so that she looked over at the window. The sun poured through. But it wasn't summer, Jillian remembered abruptly. What was she still doing in bed when the sun was up? Furious with herself, she sat up just as the door opened. Aaron walked in, carrying a mug of coffee.

"Too bad," he commented as he crossed to her. "I was looking forward to waking you up."

"I've got to get back," she said, tossing her hair from her eyes. "I should've been up hours ago."

Aaron held her in place effortlessly with a hand on her shoulder. "What you should do is sleep till noon," he corrected as he studied her face. "But you look better."

"I've got a ranch to run."

"And there isn't a ranch in the country that can't do without one person for one day." He sat down beside her and pushed the cup into her hand. "Drink your coffee."

She might've been annoyed by his peremptory order, but the scent of coffee was more persuasive. "What time is it?" she asked between sips.

"A bit after nine."

"Nine!" Her eyes grew comically wide. "Good God, I've got to get back."

Again Aaron held her in bed without effort. "You've got to drink your coffee," he corrected. "Then you've got to have some breakfast."

After a quick, abortive struggle, Jillian shot him an exasperated look. "Will you stop treating me as though I were eight years old?"

He glanced down to where she held the sheet absently at her breasts. "It's tempting," he agreed.

"Eyes front, Murdock," she ordered when her mouth twitched. "Look, I appreciate the service," Jillian continued, gesturing with her cup, "but I can't sit around until midday."

"When's the last time you had eight hours' sleep?"

He watched the annoyance flicker into her eyes as she lifted the coffee again, sipping rather than answering. "You'd have had more than that last night if you hadn't—distracted me."

She lifted her brows. "Is that what I did?"

"Several times, as I recall." Something in her expression, a question, a hint of doubt, made him study her a bit more carefully. Was it possible a woman like her would need reassurance after the night they'd spent together? What a strange mixture of tough and vulnerable she was. Aaron bent over and brushed his lips over her brow, knowing what would happen if he allowed himself just one taste of her mouth. "Apparently, you don't have to try very hard," he murmured. His lips trailed down to her temple before he could prevent them. "If you'd like to take advantage of me…"

Jillian let out an unsteady breath. "I think—I'd better have pity on you this morning, Murdock."

"Well…" He hooked a finger under the sheet and began to draw it down. "Can't say I've ever cared much for pity."

"Aaron." Jillian tightened her hold on the sheet. "It's nine o'clock in the morning."

"Probably a bit past that by now."

When he started to lean closer, she lifted the mug and held it against his chest. "I've got stock to check and fences to ride," she reminded him. "And so do you."

He had a woman to protect, he thought, surprising himself. But he had enough sense not to mention it to the woman. "Sometimes," he began, then gave her a friendly kiss, "you're just no fun, Jillian."

Laughing, she drained the coffee. "Why don't you get out of here so I can have a shower and get dressed?"

"See what I mean." But he rose. "I'll fix your breakfast," he told her, then continued before she could say it wasn't necessary. "And neither of us is riding fence today. We're going up in the plane."

"Aaron, you don't have to take the time away from your own ranch to do this."

He hooked his hands in his pockets and studied her for so long her brows drew together. "For a sharp woman, you can be amazingly slow. If it's easier for you, just remember that rustling is every rancher's business."

She could see he was annoyed; she could hear it in the sudden coolness of tone. "I don't understand you."

"No." He inclined his head in a gesture that might've been resignation or acceptance. "I can see that." He started for the door, and Jillian watched him, baffled.

"I…" What the devil did she want to say? "I have to drive over and let Gil know what I'm doing."

"I sent a man over earlier." Aaron paused at the door and turned back to her. "He knows you're with me."

"He knows—you sent—" She broke off, her fingers tightening on the handle of the mug. "You sent a man over to tell him I was here, this morning?"

"That's right."

She dragged a hand through her hair and sunlight shimmered gold at the ends. "Do you realize what that looks like?"

His eyes became very cool and remote. "It looks like what it is. Sorry, I didn't realize you wanted an assignation."

"Aaron—" But he was already closing the door behind him. Jillian brought the mug back in a full swing and barely prevented herself from following through. With a sound of disgust, she set it down and pulled herself from bed. That had been clumsy of her, she berated herself. How was he to understand that it wasn't shame, but insecurity? Perhaps it was better if he didn't understand.

Aaron could cheerfully have strangled her. In the kitchen, he slapped a slice of ham into the skillet. His own fault, he thought as it began to sizzle. Damn it, it was his own fault. He'd had no business letting things get beyond what they were meant to. If he stretched things, he could say that she had a wary sort of affection for him. It was unlikely it would ever go beyond that. If his feelings had, he had only himself to blame, and himself to deal with.

Since when did he want fences around him? Aaron thought savagely as he plunged a kitchen fork into the grilling meat. Since when did he want more from a woman, any woman, than companionship, intelligence, and a warm bed? Maybe his feelings had slipped a bit past that, but he wasn't out of control yet.

Pouring coffee, he drank it hot and black. He'd been around too long to lose his head over a firebrand who didn't want anything more than a practical, uncomplicated affair. After all, he hadn't been looking for any more than that himself. He'd just let himself get caught up because of the problems she was facing, and the unwavering manner with which she faced them.

The coffee calmed him. Reassured, he pulled a carton of eggs out of the refrigerator. He'd help her as much as he could over the rustling, take her to bed as often as possible, and that would be that.

When she came into the room, he glanced over casually. Her hair was still wet, her face naked and glowing with health and a good night's sleep.

Oh, God, he was in love with her. And what the hell was he going to do?

The easy comment she'd been about to make about

the smell of food vanished. Why was he staring at her as if he'd never seen her before? Uncharacteristically self-conscious, she shifted her weight. He looked as though someone had just knocked the wind from him. "Is something wrong?"

"What?"

His answer was so dazed she smiled. What in the world had he been thinking about when she'd interrupted him? she wondered. "I said, is something wrong? You look like you've just taken a quick fall from a tall horse."

He cursed himself and turned away. "Nothing. How do you want your eggs?"

"Over easy, thanks." She took a step toward him, then hesitated. It wasn't a simple matter for her to make an outward show of affection. She'd met with too many lukewarm receptions in her life. Drawing up her courage, she crossed the room and touched his shoulder. He stiffened. She withdrew. "Aaron..." How calm her voice was, she mused. But then, she'd grown very adept very early at concealing hurt. "I'm not very good at accepting support."

"I've noticed." He cracked an egg and let it slide into the pan.

She blinked because her eyes had filled. Stupid! she railed at herself. Never put your weaknesses on display. Swallowing pride came hard to her, but there were times it was necessary. "What I'd like to say is that I appreciate what you're doing. I appreciate it very much."

Emotions were clawing him. He smacked another egg on the side of the pan. "Don't mention it."

She backed away. What else did you expect? she asked herself. You've never been the kind of person who inspires tender feelings. You don't want to be. "Fine," she said carelessly. "I won't." Moving to the coffeepot, she filled her mug again. "Aren't you eating?"

"I ate before." Aaron flipped the eggs, then reached for a plate.

She eyed his back with dislike. "I realize I'm keeping you from a lot of pressing matters. Why don't you just send me up with one of your men?"

"I said I'd take you." He piled her plate with food, then dropped it unceremoniously on the table.

Chin lifted, Jillian took her seat. "Suit yourself, Murdock."

He turned to see her hack a slice from the ham. "I always do." On impulse he grabbed the back of her head and covered her mouth in a long, ruthlessly thorough kiss that left them both simmering with anger and need.

When it was done, Jillian put all her concentration into keeping her hands steady. "A man should be more cautious," she said mildly as she cut another slice, "when a woman's holding a knife."

With a short laugh, he dropped into the chair across from her. "Caution doesn't seem to be something I hold on to well around you." Sipping his coffee, Aaron watched her as she worked her way systematically through the meal. Maybe it was too late to realize that intimacy between them had been a mistake, but if he could keep their relationship on its old footing otherwise, he might get his feelings back in line.

"You know, you should've bought a plane for Utopia years ago," he commented, perfectly aware that it would annoy her.

Her gaze lifted from her plate, slow and deliberate. "Is that so?"

"Only an idiot argues with progress."

Jillian tapped her fork against her empty plate. "What

a fascinating statement," she said sweetly. "Do you have any other suggestions on how I might improve the running of Utopia?"

"As a matter of fact—" Aaron drained his coffee "—I could come up with several."

"Really." She set down the fork before she stabbed him with it. "Would you like me to tell you what you can do with each and every one of them?"

"Maybe later." He rose. "Let's get going. The day's half gone already."

Grinding her teeth, Jillian followed him out the back door. She thought it was a pity she'd wasted even a moment on gratitude.

The small two-seater plane gave her a bad moment. She eyed the propellers while Aaron checked the gauges before takeoff. She trusted things with four legs or four wheels. There, she felt, you had some control—a control she'd be relinquishing the moment Aaron took the plane off the ground. With a show of indifference, she hooked her seat belt while he started the engine.

"Ever been up in one of these?" he asked idly. He slipped on sunglasses before he started down the narrow paved runway.

"Of course I went up in the one I bought." She didn't mention the jitters that one ride had given her. As much as she hated to agree with him, a plane was a necessary part of ranch life in the late twentieth century.

The engine roared and the ground tilted away. She'd just have to get used to it, she reminded herself, since she was going to learn to fly herself. She let her hands lie loosely on her knees and ignored the rolling pitch of her stomach.

"Are you the only one who flies this?" This tuna can with propellers, she thought dismally.

"No, two of our men are licensed pilots. It isn't smart to have only one person who can handle a specific job."

She nodded. "Yes. I've had a man on the payroll for over a month who can fly, but I'm going to have to get a license myself."

He glanced over. "I could teach you." Aaron noticed that her fingers were moving back and forth rhythmically over her knees. Nerves, he realized with some surprise. She hid them very well. "These little jobs're small," he said idly. "But the beauty is maneuverability. You can set them down in a pasture if you have to and hardly disturb the cattle."

"They're very small," Jillian muttered.

"Look down," he suggested. "It's very big."

She did so because she wouldn't, for a moment, have let him know how badly she wanted to be safe on the ground. Oddly her stomach stopped jumping when she did. Her fingers relaxed.

The landscape rolled under them, green and fresh, with strips of brown and amber so neat and tidy they seemed laid out with a ruler. She saw the stream that ran through her property and his, winding blue. Cattle were clumps of black and brown and red. Two young foals frolicked in a pasture while adult horses sunned themselves and grazed. She saw men riding below. Now and again one would take off his hat and wave it in a salute. Aaron dipped his wings in answer. Laughing, Jillian looked farther, to the plains and isolated mountains.

"It's fabulous. God, sometimes I look at it and I can't believe it belongs to me."

"I know." He skimmed the border line and banked the plane over her land. "You can't get tired of looking at it, smelling it."

She rested her head against the window. He loves it as much as I do, she thought. Those five years in Billings must have eaten at him. Every time she thought of it, of the five years he'd given up, her admiration for him grew.

"Don't laugh," she told him and watched him glance over curiously. No, he wouldn't laugh, she realized. "When I was little—the first time I came out—I got a box and dug up a couple handfuls of pasture to take home with me. It didn't stay sweet for long, but it didn't matter."

Good God, sometimes she was so totally disarming it took his breath away. "How long did you keep it?"

"Until my mother found it and threw it away."

He had to bite back an angry remark on insensitivity and ignorance. "She didn't understand you," Aaron said instead.

"No, of course not." She gave a quick laugh at the idea. Who could've expected her to? "Look, that's Gil's truck." The idea of waving down to him distracted her so that she missed Aaron's smoldering look. He'd had some rocky times with his own father, some painful times, but he'd always been understood.

"Tell me about your family."

Jillian turned her head to look at him, not quite trusting the fact that she couldn't see his eyes through his tinted sunglasses. "No, not now." She looked back out the window. "I wish I knew what I was looking for," she murmured.

So do I, he thought grimly and banked down his frustration. It wasn't going to work, he decided. He wasn't going to be able to talk himself out of needing her, all of her, any time soon. "Maybe you'll know when you see it. Could you figure if they took more cattle from any specific section?"

"It seems the north section was the hardest hit. I can't figure out how it got by me. Five hundred head, right under my nose."

"You wouldn't be the first," he reminded her. "Or the last. If you were going to drive cattle out of your north section, where would you go with them?"

"If they weren't mine," she said dryly, "I suppose I'd load them up and get them over the border."

"Maybe." He wondered if his own idea would be any harder for her to take. "Packaged beef's a lot easier to transport than it is on the hoof."

Slowly she turned back to him. She'd thought of it herself—more than once. But every time she'd pushed it aside. The last fragile hope of recovering what was hers would be lost. "I know that." Her voice was calm, her eyes steady. "If that's what was done, there's still the matter of catching who did it. They're not going to get away with it."

Aaron grinned in pure admiration. "Okay. Then let's think about it from this angle a minute. You've got the cattle—the cows are worth a lot more than the calves at this point, so maybe you're going to ship them off to greener pastures for a while. Unless we're dealing with a bunch of idiots, they're not going to slaughter a registered cow for the few hundred the calf would bring."

"A bunch of idiots couldn't have rustled my cattle," she said precisely.

"No." He nodded in simple agreement. "The steers, now…it might be a smart choice to pick out a quiet spot and butcher them. The meat would bring in some quick cash while you worked out the deal for the rest." He made a slight adjustment in course and headed north.

"If you were smarter still, you'd have already set up a deal for the cows and the yearlings," Jillian pointed out. "That accounts for nearly half of what I lost. If I were using a trailer, and slipping them out a few head at a time, I'd make use of one of the canyons in the mountains."

"Yeah. Thought we'd take a look."

Her euphoria was gone, though the landscape below was a rambling map of color and texture. The ground grew more uneven, with the asphalt two-lane road cutting through the twists and angles. The barren clump of mountain wasn't majestic like its brothers farther west, but sat alone, inhabited by coyotes and wildcats who preferred to keep man at a distance.

Aaron took the plane higher and circled. Jillian looked down at jagged peaks and flat-bottomed canyons. Yes, if she had butchering in mind, no place made better sense. Then she saw the vultures, and her heart sank down to her stomach.

"I'm going to set her down," Aaron said simply.

Jillian said nothing but began to check off her options if they found what she thought they would. There were a few economies she could and would have to make before winter, even after the livestock auction at the end of the summer. The old Jeep would simply have to be repaired again instead of being replaced. There were two foals she could sell and keep her books in the black. Checks and balances, she thought as the plane bumped on the ground. Nothing personal.

Aaron shut off the engine. "Why don't you wait here while I take a look?"

"My cattle," she said simply and climbed out of the plane.

The ground was hard and dusty from the lack of

rain. She could smell its faintly metallic odor, so unlike the scent of grass and animals that permeated her own land. With no trees for shade, the sun beat down hard and bright. She heard the flap of a vulture's wings as one circled in and settled on a ridge.

It wasn't difficult going over the low rocky ground through the break in the mountain. No problem at all for a four-wheel drive, she thought and angled the brim of her hat to compensate for the glare of sunlight.

The canyon wasn't large and was cupped between three walls of rock, worn gray with some stubborn sage clinging here and there. Their boots made echoing hollow sounds. From somewhere, surprisingly, she heard a faint tinkling of water. The spring must be small, she mused, or she'd smell it. All she smelled here was…

She stopped and let out a long breath. "Oh, God."

Aaron recognized the odor, sickeningly hot and sweet, even as she did. "Jillian—"

She shook her head. There was no longer room for comfort or hope. "Damn. I wonder how many."

They walked on and saw, behind a rock, the bones a coyote had dug up and picked clean.

Aaron swore in a low soft stream that was all the more pungent in its control. "There's a shovel in the plane," he began. "We can see what's here, or go back for the sheriff."

"It's my business." Jillian wiped her damp hands on her jeans. "I'd rather know now."

He knew better than to suggest she wait at the plane again. In her place, he'd have done precisely what she was ready to do. Without another word, he left her alone.

When she heard his footsteps die away, she squeezed her eyes tight, doubled her hands into fists. She wanted to scream out the useless, impotent rage. What was hers had been stolen, slaughtered, and sold. There could be no restitution now, no bringing back this part of what she'd worked for. Slowly, painfully, she brought herself under tight control. No restitution, but she'd have justice. Sometimes it was just a cleaner word for revenge.

When Aaron returned with the shovel, he saw the anger glittering in her eyes. He preferred it to that brief glimpse of despair he'd seen. "Let's just make sure. After we know, we go into town for the sheriff."

She agreed with a nod. If they found one hide, it would be one too many. The shovel bit into the ground with a thud.

Aaron didn't have to dig long. He glanced up at Jillian to see her face perfectly composed, then uncovered the first stack of hides. Though the stench was vile, she crouched down and made out the *U* of her brand.

"Well, this should be proof enough," she murmured and stayed where she was because she wanted to drop her head to her knees and weep. "How many—"

"Let the sheriff deal with it," Aaron bit off, as infuriated by their find as he would have been if the hide had borne his own brand. With an oath, he scraped the shovel across the loosened dirt and dislodged something.

Jillian reached down and picked it up. The glove was filthy, but the leather was quality—the kind any cowhand would need for working with the wire. A bubble of excitement rose in her. "One of them must've lost it when they were burying these." She sprang to her feet, holding the glove in both hands. "Oh, they're going to pay for it," she said savagely. "This is one mistake they're going to pay for. Most of my hands score their initials on the inside." Ignoring the grime, she turned the bottom of the glove over and found them.

Aaron watched her color drain as she stared at the

inside flap of the glove. Her fingers whitened against the leather before she lifted her eyes to his. Without a word, she handed it to him. Watching her, he took the soiled leather in his hand, then glanced down. There were initials inside. His own.

His face was expressionless when he looked back at her. "Well," he said coolly, "it looks like we're back to square one, doesn't it?" He passed the glove back to her. "You'll need this for the sheriff."

She sent him a look of smoldering anger that cut straight through him. "Do you think I'm stupid enough to believe you had anything to do with this?" Spinning around, she stalked away before he had a chance to understand, much less react. Then he stood where he was for another instant as it struck him, forcibly.

He caught her before she had clambered over the last rocks leading out of the canyon. His hands weren't gentle as he whirled her around, his breath wasn't steady.

"Maybe I do." She jerked away only to have him grab her again. "Maybe I want you to tell me why you don't."

"I might believe a lot of things of you, I might not like everything I believe. But not this." Her voice broke and she fought to even it. "Integrity—integrity isn't something that has to be polite. You wouldn't cut my lines and you wouldn't butcher my cattle."

Her words alone would've shaken him, but he saw her eyes were swimming with tears. What he knew about comforting a woman could be said in one sentence: get out of the way. Aaron held on to her and lifted a hand to her cheek. "Jillian…"

"No! For God's sake don't be kind now." She tried to turn away, only to find herself held close, her face buried against his shoulder. His body was like a solid wall of support and understanding. If she leaned against it now, what would she do when he removed it? "Aaron, don't do this." But her hands clutched at him as he held on.

"I've got to do something," he murmured, stroking her hair. "Lean on me for a minute. It won't hurt you."

But it did. She'd always found tears a painful experience. There was no stopping them, so she wept with the passion they both understood while he held her near the barren mountain under the strong light of the sun.

Chapter Nine

Jillian didn't have time to grieve over her losses. Over two hundred hides had been unearthed from the canyon floor, all bearing the Utopia brand. She'd had interviews with the sheriff, talked to the Cattlemen's Association, and dealt with the visits and calls from neighboring ranchers. After her single bout of weeping, her despair had iced over to a frigid rage she found much more useful. It carried her through each day, pushing her to work just that much harder, helping her not to break down when she was faced with sympathetic words.

For two weeks she knew there was little talk of anything else, on her ranch or for miles around. There hadn't been a rustling of this size in thirty years. It became easier for her when the talk began to die down, though it became equally more difficult to go on believing that the investigation would yield fruit. She had accepted the loss of her cattle because she had no choice, but she couldn't accept the total victory of the thieves.

They were clever—she had to admit it. They'd pulled off a rustling as smooth as anything the old-timers in the area claimed to remember. The cut wire, Aaron's glove; deliberate and subtle "mistakes" that were designed to turn her attention toward Murdock land. Perhaps the first of them had worked well enough to give the rustlers just enough extra time to cover their tracks. Jillian's only comfort was that she hadn't fallen for the second.

Aaron had given her no choice but to accept his support. She'd balked, particularly after recovering from her lapse in the canyon, but he'd proven to be every bit as obstinate as she. He'd taken her to the sheriff himself, stood by her with the Cattlemen's Association, and one evening had come by to drag her forty miles to a movie. Through it all he wasn't gentle with her, didn't pamper. For that more than anything else, Jillian felt she owed him. Kindness left her no defense and edged her back toward despair.

As the days passed, Jillian forced herself to take each one of them separately. She could fill the hours with dozens of tasks and worries and responsibilities. Then there wouldn't be time to mourn. For now, her first concern was the breeding of her mare with Aaron's stallion.

He'd brought two of his own men with him. With Gil and another of Jillian's hands, they would hold the restraining ropes on the stallion. Once he caught the scent of Jillian's mare in heat, he'd be as wild as his father had been, and as dangerous.

When Jillian brought Delilah into the paddock, she cast a look at the stallion surrounded by men. A gorgeous creature, she thought, wholly male—not quite tamed. Her gaze flicked over to Aaron, who stood at the horse's head.

His dark hair sprang from under his hat to curl carelessly over his neck and ears. His body was erect and lean. One might look at him and think he was perfectly relaxed. But Jillian saw more—the coiled tension beneath, the power that was always there and came out unexpectedly. Eyes nearly as dark as his hair were half hidden by the brim of his hat as he both soothed and controlled his stallion.

No mount could've suited him more. Her lover, she realized with the peculiar little jolt that always accompanied the thought. Would her nerves ever stop skidding along whenever she remembered what it was like to be with him—or imagined what it would be like to be with him again? He'd opened up so many places inside of her. When she was alone, it came close to frightening her; when she saw him, her feelings had nothing to do with fear.

Maybe it was the thick, heavy air that threatened rain or the half-nervous, half-impatient quiverings of her mare, but Jillian's heart was already pounding. The horses caught each other's scent.

Samson plunged and began to fight against the ropes. With his head thrown back, his mane flowing, he called the mare. One of the men cursed in reflex. Jillian tightened her grip on Delilah's bridle as the mare began to struggle—against the restraint or against the inevitable, Jillian would never be sure. She soothed her with words that weren't even heard. Samson gave a long, passionate whinny that was answered. Delilah reared, nearly ripping the bridle from Jillian's hand. Watching the struggle and flying hooves, Aaron felt his heart leap into his throat.

"Help her hold the mare," he ordered.

"No." Jillian fought for new purchase and got it. "She doesn't trust anyone but me. Let's get it done." A long line of sweat held her shirt to her back.

The stallion was wild, plunging and straining, his coat glossy with sweat, his eyes fierce. With five men surrounding him, he reared back, hanging poised and magnificent for a heartbeat before he mounted the mare.

The horses were beyond any thought, any fear, any respect for the humans now. Instinct drove them, primitive and consuming. Jillian forgot her aching arms and the rivulets of sweat that poured down her sides. Her feet were planted, her leg muscles taut as she pitted all her strength toward keeping the mare from bolting or rearing and injuring herself.

She was caught up in the fire and desperation of the horses, and the elemental beauty. The air was ripe with the scent of sweat and animal passion. She couldn't breathe but that she drew it in. Since she'd been a child she'd seen animals breed, helped with the matings whenever necessary, but now, for the first time, she understood the consuming force that drove them. The need of a woman for a man could be equally unrestrained, equally primitive.

Then it began to rain, slowly, heavily, coolly over her skin. With her face lifted to the mare's, Jillian let it flow over her cheeks. Another of the men swore as the ropes grew wet and slippery.

When her eyes met Aaron's, she found her heart was still in her throat, the beat as lurching and uneven as the mare's would be. She felt the flash of need that was both shocking and basic. He saw and recognized. As the rain poured over him, he smiled. Her thigh muscles went lax so quickly she had to fight to strengthen them again and maintain her control of the mare. But she didn't look away. Excitement was nearly painful, knowledge enervating. As if his hands were on her, she felt the need pulse from him.

Gradually a softer feeling drifted in. There was a strange sensation of being safe even though the safety was circled with dangers. This time she didn't question it or fight against it. They were helping to create new life. Now there was a bond between them.

The horses' sides were heaving when they drew them apart. The rain continued to sluice down. She heard Gil give a cackle of laughter over something one of the men said under his breath. Jillian forgot them, giving her full attention to the mare. Soothing and murmuring, she walked her back into the stables.

The light was dim, the air heavy with the scent of dry hay and oiled leather. After removing the bridle, Jillian began to groom the mare with long slow strokes until the quivering stopped.

"There now, love." Jillian nuzzled her face into Delilah's neck. "There's not much any of us can do about their bodies."

"Is that how you look at it?"

Jillian turned her head to see Aaron standing at the entrance to the stall. He was drenched and apparently unconcerned about it. She saw his eyes make a short but very thorough scan of her face—a habit he'd developed since their discovery in the canyon. She knew he looked for signs of strain and somewhere along the line had stopped resenting it.

"I'm not a horse," she returned easily and patted Delilah's neck.

Aaron came into the stall and ran his hands over the mare himself. She was dry and still. "She all right?"

"Mmmm. We were right not to field breed them," she added. "Both of them are spirited enough to have done damage." Laughing, she turned to him. "The foal's going to be a champion. I can feel it. There was some-

thing special out there just now, something important."
On impulse, she threw her arms around Aaron's neck
and kissed him ardently.

Surprise held him very still. His hands came to her
waist more in instinct than response. It was the first time
she'd given him any spontaneous show of affection or
offered him any part of herself without reluctance. The
ache of need wove through him, throbbing with what
he now understood was connected to passion but not
exclusive of it.

She was still smiling when she drew away, but he
wasn't. Before the puzzlement over what was in his
eyes had fully registered with her, Aaron drew her back
against him and just held on. Jillian found the unexpected
sweetness disconcerting and wonderful.

"Hadn't you better see to Samson?" she murmured.

"My men have already taken him back."

She rubbed her cheek against his wet shirt. They'd
steal some time, she thought. An hour, a moment—just
some time. "I'll fix you some coffee."

"Yeah." He slipped an arm around her shoulders as
they went back into the rain. "Heard anything from the
sheriff?"

"Nothing new."

They crossed the ranch yard together, both too accustomed to the elements to heed the rain as anything
but necessary.

"It's got the whole county in an uproar."

"I know." They paused at the kitchen door to rid
themselves of muddy boots. Jillian ran a careless hand
through her hair and scattered rain. "It might do more
good than anything else. Every rancher I know or've
heard of in this part of Montana's got his eyes open.

And any number over the border, from what I'm told. I'm toying with offering a reward."

"Not a bad idea." Aaron sat down at the table and stretched out long legs as Jillian brewed coffee. The rain was a constant soothing sound against the roof and windows. He found an odd comfort there in the gloomy light, in the warm kitchen. It might be like this if it were their ranch they were in rather than hers, or his. It might be like this if he could ever make her a permanent part of his life.

It took only a second for the thoughts to go through his head, and another for him to be jolted by them. Marriage. He was thinking marriage. He sat for a moment while the idea settled over him, not uncomfortably but inevitably. I'll be damned, he thought and nearly laughed before he brought himself back to what she'd been saying.

"Let me do it," he said briskly. She turned, words of refusal on the tip of her tongue. "Wait," Aaron ordered. "Hear me out. My father got wind of the cut wire." He watched her subside before she turned away for mugs. "Obviously it didn't set well with him. These old stories between the Murdocks and Barons don't need much fanning to come to life again. Some people are going to think, even if they don't say, that he's eating your beef."

Jillian poured the coffee, then turned with a mug in each hand. "I don't think it."

"I know." He gave her an odd look, holding out a hand. She placed a mug in it, but Aaron set it down on the table and lightly took her fingers. "That means a great deal to me." Because she didn't know how to respond to that tone, she didn't respond at all but only continued to look down at him. "Jillian, this has set him back some. A few years ago the idea of people thinking he'd

done something unethical or illegal would probably have
pleased him. He's not as strong as he was. Your grandfather was a rival, but he was also a contemporary, someone he understood, even respected. It would help if he
could do something. I don't like to ask for favors any
more than you like to accept them."

She looked down at their joined hands, both tanned,
both lean and strong, yet hers was so easily swallowed
up by his. "You love him very much."

"Yes." It was said very simply, in the same emotionless tone he'd used to tell her his father was dying. This
time Jillian understood him better.

"I'd appreciate it if you'd stake the reward."

He laced his fingers with hers. "Good."

"Want some more coffee?"

"No." That wicked light of humor shot into his eyes.
"But I was thinking I should help you out of those wet
clothes."

With a laugh, Jillian sat down. "You know I'm still
planning on beating out the Double M on July Fourth."

"I was hoping you were planning on it," Aaron returned easily. "But about doing it…"

"You a gambling man, Murdock?"

He lifted his brow. "It's been said."

"I've got fifty that says my Hereford bull will take
the blue ribbon over anything you have to put against
him."

Aaron contemplated the dregs of his coffee as if con-
sidering. If everything he'd heard about Jillian's bull
was true, he was tolerably sure he was throwing money
away. "Fifty," he agreed and smiled. "And another fifty
that says I beat your time in the calf roping."

"My pleasure." Jillian held out a hand to seal it.

"Are you competing in anything else?"

"I don't think so." She stretched her back, thinking what a luxury it was to sit stone still in the middle of the afternoon. "The barrel racing doesn't much interest me and I know better than to try bronc riding."

"Know better?"

"Two reasons. First the men would do a lot of muttering and complaining if I did. And second—" she grinned and shrugged "—I'd probably break my neck."

It occurred to him that she wouldn't have admitted the second to him even a week before. Laughing, he leaned over and kissed her. But the friendly kiss stirred something, and cupping the back of her neck, he kissed her again, lingeringly. "It's your mouth," he murmured while his fingertips toyed with her skin. "Once I get started on it, I can't find a single reason to stop."

Her breath fluttered unevenly through her lips, through his. "It's the middle of the day."

He smiled, then teased her tongue with the tip of his. "Yeah. Are you going to take me to bed?"

The eyes that were nearly closed opened again. In them he saw desire and confusion, a combination he found very much to his liking. "I have to check the—" His teeth nipped persuasively into her bottom lip.

"The what?" he whispered as her words ended on a little shiver.

"The, uh…" His lips were skimming over hers in something much more provocative than a kiss. The lazy caress of his tongue kept them moist. His fingers were very light on the back of her neck. Their knees were brushing. Somehow she could already feel the press of his body against hers and the issuing warmth the pressure always brought. "I can't think," she murmured.

It was what he wanted. Or he wanted her to think of him and only him. For himself, he needed to know that she put him first this time, or at least her need for him. Over her ranch, her men, her cattle, her ambitions. If he could draw her feelings out to match his once, he might be able to do so again and again until she was as rashly in love with him as he was with her. "Why do you have to?" he asked and, rising, drew her to her feet. "You can feel."

Yes, with her arms around him and her head cradled against his chest, she could feel. Emotions nudging at her, urging her to acknowledge them—needs, pressing and searingly urgent, demanding that she fulfill them. They were all connected to him, the hungers, the tiny fears, the wishes. She couldn't deny them all. Perhaps, just this once, she didn't need to.

"I want to make love with you." She sighed with the words and nuzzled closer. "I can't seem to stop wanting to."

He tilted her head back so that he could see her face, then, half smiling, skimmed his thumb over her jaw. "In the middle of the day?"

She tossed the hair out of her eyes and settled her linked hands comfortably behind his neck. "I'm going to have you now, Murdock. Right now."

He glanced at the tidy kitchen table and his grin was wicked. "Right now?"

"Your mind takes some unusual turns," she commented. "I think I can give you time enough to get upstairs." Releasing him, she walked over and flicked off the coffeepot. "If you hurry." Even as he grinned, she crossed back to him. Putting her hands on his shoulders, she leaped up, locking her legs around his waist, her arms around his neck. "You know where the stairs are?"

"I can find them."

She pressed her lips to his throat. "Top of the stairs, second door on the right," she told him as she began to please herself with his taste.

As Aaron wound through the house Jillian wondered what he would think or say if he knew she'd never done anything quite like this before. She'd come to realize that the man from her youth hadn't been a lover, but an incident. It took more than one night to make a lover. She'd feel much too foolish telling Aaron he was the first— much too inadequate. How could she tell him that the first rush of passion had loosened the locks she'd put on parts of herself? How could she trust her own feelings when they were so muddled and new?

She rested her head on his shoulder a moment and closed her eyes. For once in her life she was going to enjoy without worrying about the consequences. Shifting, she leaned back so that she could smile at him. "You're out of shape, Murdock. One flight of stairs and your heart's pounding."

"So's yours," he pointed out. "And you had a ride up."

"Must be the rain," she said loftily.

"Your clothes're still damp." He moved into the room she'd directed him to and glanced around briefly.

It was consistent with her style—understated femininity, practicality. It was a room without frills or pastels, but he'd have known it for a woman's. It had none of the feminine disorder of his sister's old room at the ranch, nor the subtle elegance of his mother's. Like the woman he still held, Aaron found the room unique.

Plain walls, plain floors, easy colors, no clutter. No, Jillian wasn't a woman to clutter her life. She wouldn't give herself the time. Perhaps it was the few indulgences she'd allowed herself that gave him the most insight.

A stoneware vase with fluted edges held pussy

willow—soft brown nubs that wouldn't quite be considered a flower. There was a small carved box on her dresser he was certain would play some soft tune when the top was lifted. She might lift it sometimes when she was alone, or lonely. On the wall was a watercolor with all the bleeding passion of sunset. How carefully, how painstakingly, he thought, she'd controlled whatever romanticism she was prone to. How surprised she'd be to know that because she did, it only shouted out louder.

Recognizing his survey, Jillian cocked her head. "There's not a lot to see in here."

"You'd be surprised," he murmured.

The enigmatic answer made her glance around herself. "I don't spend a lot of time in here," she began, realizing it was rather sparse even compared to his room in the white frame house.

"You misunderstood me." Aaron let his hands run up her sides as she slid down. "I'd've known this was your room. It even smells like you."

She laughed, pleased without knowing why. "Are you being poetic?"

"Maybe."

Lifting a hand, she toyed with the top button of his shirt. "Want me to help you out of those wet clothes?"

"Absolutely."

She began to oblige him, then shot him an amused look as she slid the shirt over his shoulders. "If you expect me to seduce you, you're going to be disappointed."

His stomach muscles were already knotted with need. "I am?"

"I don't know any tricks." Before he could comment, she launched herself at him, overbalancing him so that they tumbled back onto the bed. "No wiles," she continued. "No subtlety."

"You're a pushy lady, all right." He could feel the heat of her body through her damp shirt.

"I like the way you look, Murdock." She trailed her fingers through his thick dark hair as she studied his face. "It used to annoy the hell out of me, but now it's kind of nice."

"The way I look?"

"That I like the way you look. It's ruthless," she decided, skimming a finger down his jawline. "And when you smile it can be very charming—the kind of charm a smart woman recognizes as highly dangerous."

He grinned, cupping her hips in his hands. "Did you?"

"I'm a smart woman." With a little laugh, she rubbed her nose against his. "I know a rattlesnake when I see one."

"But not enough to keep your distance."

"Apparently not—then I don't always look for a long, safe ride."

But a short, rocky one, he thought as her lips came down to his. He'd be happy to give her the wisps of danger and trouble, he decided, drawing her closer. But she was going to find out he intended it to last.

He started to shift her, but then her lips were racing over his face. Soft, light, but with a heat that seeped right into him. Her long, limber body seemed almost weightless over his, yet he could feel every line and curve. Moisture still clung to her hair and reminded him of the first time, when he'd dragged her to the ground, consumed with need and fury. Now he was helpless against her rapid assault on his senses. No, she had no wiles, nor he the patience for them.

He could hear the rain patter rhythmically against the window. He could smell it on her. When his lips brushed through her hair, he could taste it. It was almost as though they were alone in a quiet field, with the scent of wet grass and the rain slipping over their skin. The light was gray and indistinct; her mouth was vivid wherever it touched him.

She hadn't known it could be so exciting to weaken a man with herself. Feeling the strength drain from him made her almost light-headed with power. She'd met him on equal terms, and from time to time to her disadvantage, but never when she'd been so certain she could dominate. Her laugh was low and confident as it whispered along his skin, warm and sultry as it brushed over his lips.

He seemed content to lie still while she learned of him. She thought the air grew thicker. Perhaps that alone weighed him down and kept him from challenging her control. Her hands were eager, rushing here then there to linger over some small fascination: tight cords of muscle that ran down his upper arms to bunch and gather at her touch; smooth, taut skin that was surprisingly soft over his rib cage; the narrow, raised scar along his hipbone.

"Where'd you get this?" she murmured, outlining it with a fingertip.

"Brahma," he managed as she tugged his jeans down infinitesimally lower. "Jillian—" But her lips drifted over his again and silenced him.

"A bull?"

"Rodeo, when I had more guts than brains."

She heard the sound of pleasure in his throat as her mouth journeyed down. His body was a treasure of delight to her. In the soft rainy light she could see it, brown and hard against the plain, serviceable bedspread.

Rangy and loose limbed, it was made for riding well and long, toughened by physical work, burnished by the elements. Tiny jumping thrills coursed through her as she thought that it was hers to touch and taste, to look at as long as she liked.

She took a wandering route down him, feeling his skin heat and pulse as she stripped him. The room was filled with the sound of rain and quickening breathing. It was all she heard. The sweet scent of passion enveloped her—a fragrance mixed of the essence of both of them. Intimate. She could taste desire on his skin, a heady flavor that made her greedy when she felt the thud of his heart under her tongue. Even when her excitement grew until her blood was racing, she could have luxuriated in him for hours. The sharp urgency she'd once felt had mellowed into a glowing contentment. She pleasured him. It was more than she'd believed she could do for anyone.

There were flames in his stomach, spreading. God, she was like a drug and he was lost, half dreaming while his flesh was burning up. Her fingers were so cool as they tortured him, her mouth so hot. He'd never explored his own vulnerabilities; it had always been more important to work around them or ignore them altogether. Now he had no choice and he found the sensation incredible.

She aroused, teased, and withdrew only to arouse again. Her enervating, openmouthed kisses ranged over him while her hands stroked and explored lazily, finding point after sensitive point until he trembled. No woman had ever made him tremble. Even as this thought ran through his ravaged mind, she caused him to do so again. Then he knew she was driving him mad.

The wind kicked up, hurling rain against the window, then retreating with a distant howl. Something crazed sprang into him. Roughly he grabbed her, rolling over and pinning her, her arms above her head. His breathing was labored as he looked down.

Her chin was up, her hair spread out, her eyes glowing. There was no fear on her face, and nothing of submission. Though her own breathing came quickly, there was challenge in the look she gave him. A dare. He could take her, take her anyway he chose. And when he did so, he'd be taken as well.

So be it, he thought with a muffled oath. His mouth devoured hers.

She matched his urgency, aroused simply by knowing she had taken him to the edge. He wanted her. Her. In some ways he knew her better than anyone ever had, and still he wanted her. She'd waited so long for that, not even knowing that she'd waited at all. She couldn't think of this, or what the effects might be when his long desperate kisses were rousing her, when she could see small, silvery explosions going on behind her closed lids.

She felt him tug at the buttons of her shirt, heard him swear. When she felt the material rip away she knew only that at last she could feel his flesh against hers. As it was meant to be. His hands wouldn't be still and drove her as she had driven him. He pulled clothes from her in a frenzy as his mouth greedily searched. Somewhere in her hazy brain she felt wonder that she could bring him to this just by being.

Their bodies pressed, their limbs entwined. Their mouths joined. He thought the mixing of their tastes the most intimate thing he'd ever known. Under him she arched, more a demand than an offer. He raised himself over her, wanting to see her, wanting her to see him when he made her his.

Her eyes were dark, misted with need. Need for him. He knew he had what he'd wanted: she thought of nothing and no one else. "I wanted you from the first minute," he murmured as he slipped inside her.

He saw the change in her face as he moved slowly, the flicker of pleasure, the softening that came just before delirium. Pushing back the rushing need in his blood, he drew out the sensations with a control so exquisite it burned in his muscles. Lowering his head, he nibbled at her lips.

She couldn't bear it. She couldn't stop it. When she thought she finally understood what passion was, he showed her there was more. Sensation after sensation slammed into her, leaving her weak and gasping. Even as the pressure built inside her, drumming under her skin and threatening to implode, she wanted it to go on. She could have wept from the joy of it, moaned from the ache. Unwittingly it was she who changed things simply by breathing his name as if she knew no other.

The instant his control snapped, she felt it. There was time only for a tingle of nervous excitement before he was catapulting her with him into a dark, frantic sky where it was all thunder and no air.

Chapter Ten

The lengthy, dusty drive into town and the soaring temperatures couldn't dull the spirit. It was the Fourth of July, and the long, raucous holiday had barely begun.

By early morning the fairgrounds were crowded—ranchers, punchers, wives and sweethearts, and those looking for a sweetheart to share the celebration with. Prized animals were on display to be discussed, bragged about, and studied. Quilts and pies and preserves waited to be judged. As always, there was a pervasive air of expectancy.

Cowboys wore their best uniform—crisp shirts and pressed jeans, with the boots and hats that were saved and cherished for special occasions. Belt buckles gleamed. Children sported their finest, which promised to be dirt streaked and grass stained by the end of the long day.

For Jillian, it was the first carefree day in the season, and one she was all the more determined to enjoy because of her recent problems. For twenty-four hours she was going to forget her worries, the numbers in her account books, and the title of boss she worked day after day to earn. On this one sun-filled, heat-soaked day, she was going to simply enjoy the fact that she was part of a unique group of men and women who both lived and played off the land.

There was an excited babble of voices near the paddock and stable areas. The pungent aroma of animals permeated the air. From somewhere in the distance she could already hear fiddle music. There'd be more music after sundown, and dancing. Before then, there'd be games for young and old, the judgings, and enough food to feed the entire county twice over. She could smell the spicy aroma of an apple pie, still warm, as someone passed her with a laden basket. Her mouth watered.

First things first, she reminded herself as she wandered over to check out her bull's competition.

There were six entries altogether, all well muscled and fierce to look at. Horns gleamed, sharp and dangerous. Hides were sleek and well tended. Objectively Jillian studied each one, noting their high points and their weaknesses. There wasn't any doubt that her stiffest competitor would be the Double M's entry. He'd taken the blue ribbon three years running.

Not this year, she told him silently as her gaze skimmed over him. Pound for pound, he probably had her bull beat, but she thought hers had a bit more breadth in the shoulders. And there was no mistaking that her Hereford's coloring and markings were perfect, the shape of his head superior.

Time for you to move over and make room for new blood, she told the reigning champion. Rather pleased with herself, she hooked her thumbs in her back pockets.

First place and that little swatch of blue ribbon would go a long way to making up for everything that'd gone wrong in the past few weeks.

"Know a winner when you see one?"

Jillian turned at the thready voice that still held a hint of steel. Paul Murdock was dressed to perfection, but his hawklike face had little color under his Stetson. His cane was elegant and tipped with gold, but he leaned on it heavily. As they met hers, however, his eyes were very much alive and challenging.

"I know a winner when I see one," she agreed, then let her gaze skim over to her own bull.

He gave a snort of laughter and shifted his weight. "Been hearing a lot about your new boy." He studied the bull with a faint frown and couldn't prevent a twinge of envy. He, too, knew a winner when he saw one.

He felt the sun warm on his back and for a moment, for just a moment, wished desperately for his youth again. Years ate at strength. If he were fifty again and owned that bull... But he wasn't a man to sigh. "Got possibilities," he said shortly.

She recognized something of the envy and smiled. Nothing could've pleased her more. "Nothing wrong with second place," she said lightly.

Murdock glanced over sharply, pinned her eyes with his, then laughed when she didn't falter. "Damn, you're quite a woman, aren't you, Jillian Baron? The old man taught you well enough."

Her smile held more challenge than humor. "Well enough to run Utopia."

"Could be," he acknowledged. "Times change." There wasn't any mistaking the resentment in the statement, but she understood it. Sympathized with it. "This rustling..." He glanced over to see her face, impassive and still. Murdock had a quick desire to sit across a poker table from her with a large, juicy pot in between. "It's a damn abomination," he said with a savagery that made him momentarily breathless. "There was a time a man'd have his neck stretched for stealing another man's beef."

"Hanging them won't get my cattle back," Jillian said calmly.

"Aaron told me about what you found in the canyon." Murdock stared at the well-muscled bulls. These were the life's blood of their ranches—the profit and the status. "A hard thing for you—for all of us," he added, shifting his eyes to hers again. "I want you to understand that your grandfather and I had our problems. He was a stubborn, stiff-necked bastard."

"Yes," Jillian agreed easily, so easily Murdock laughed. "You'd understand a man like that," she added.

Murdock stopped laughing to fix her with a glittering look. She returned it. "I understand a man like that," he acknowledged. "And I want you to know that if this had happened to him, I'd've been behind him, just as I'd've expected him to be behind me. Personal feelings don't come into it. We're ranchers."

It was said with a sting of pride that made her own chin lift. "I do know it."

"It'd be easy to say the cattle could've been driven over to my land."

"Easy to say," Jillian said with a nod. "If you knew me better, Mr. Murdock, you'd know I'm not a fool. If I believed you'd had my beef on your table, you'd already be paying for it."

His lips curved in a rock-hard, admiring smile. "Baron did well by you," he said after a moment. "Though I still think a woman needs a man beside her if she's going to run a ranch."

"Be careful, Mr. Murdock, I was just beginning to think I could tolerate you."

He laughed again, so obviously pleased that Jillian grinned. "Can't change an old dog, girl." His eyes narrowed fractionally as she'd seen his son's do. It occurred to her that in forty years Aaron would look like this—that honed-down strength that was just a little bit mean. It was the kind of strength you'd want behind you when there was trouble. "I've heard my boy's had his eye on you—can't say I fault his taste."

"Have you?" she returned mildly. "Do you believe everything you hear?"

"If he hasn't had his eye on you," Murdock countered, "he's not as smart as I give him credit for. Man needs a woman to settle him down."

"Really?" Jillian said very dryly.

"Don't get fired up, girl," Murdock ordered. "There'd've been a time when I'd have had his hide for looking twice at a Baron. Times change," he repeated with obvious reluctance. "Our land has run side by side for most of this century, whether we like it or not."

Jillian took a moment to brush off her sleeve. "I'm not looking to settle anyone, Mr. Murdock. And I'm not looking for a merger."

"Sometimes we wind up getting things we're not looking for." He smiled as she stared at him. "You take my Karen—never figured to hitch myself with a beauty who always made me feel like I should wipe my feet whether I'd been in the pastures or not."

Despite herself Jillian laughed, then surprised them both by hooking her arm through his as they began to walk. "I get the feeling you're trying to bury the hatchet." When he stiffened, she muffled a chuckle and continued. "Don't *you* get fired up," she said easily. "I'm willing to try a truce. Aaron and I have...we understand each other," she decided. "I like your wife, and I can just about tolerate you."

"You're your grandmother all over again," Murdock muttered.

"Thanks." As they walked Jillian noted the few speculative glances tossed their way. Baron and Murdock arm in arm; times had indeed changed. She wondered how Clay would feel and decided, in his grudging way, he would've approved. Especially if it caused talk.

When Aaron saw them walking slowly toward the arena area, he broke off the conversation he'd been having with a puncher. Jillian tossed back her hair, tilted her head slightly toward his father's, and murmured something that made the old man hoot with laughter. If he hadn't already, Aaron would've fallen in love with her at that moment.

"Hey, isn't that Jillian Baron with your paw?"

"Hmmm? Yeah." Aaron didn't waste time glancing back at the puncher when he could look at Jillian.

"She sure is easy on the eyes," the puncher concluded a bit wistfully. "Heard you and her—" He broke off, chilled by the cool, neutral look Aaron aimed at him. The cowboy coughed into his hand. "Just meant people wonder about it, seeing as the Murdocks and Barons never had much dealings with each other."

"Do they?" Aaron relieved the cowboy by grinning before he walked off. Murdocks, the puncher thought with a shake of his head. You could never be too sure of them.

"Life's full of surprises," Aaron commented as he walked toward them. "No blood spilled?"

"Your father and I've reached a limited understanding." Jillian smiled at him, and though they touched in no way, Murdock was now certain the rumors he'd heard about Jillian and his son were true. Intimacy was something people often foolishly believed they could conceal, and rarely did.

"Your mother's got me judging the mincemeat," Murdock grumbled. This time he didn't feel that twinge of regret for what he'd lost, but an odd contentment at seeing his slice of immortality in his son. "We'll be in the stands later to watch you." He gave Jillian an arch look. "Both of you."

He walked off slowly. Jillian had to stuff her hands in her pockets to keep from helping him. That, she knew, would be met with cold annoyance. "He came over to the pens," Jillian told Aaron when Murdock was out of earshot. "I think he did it on purpose so that he could talk to me. He was very kind."

"Not many people see him as kind."

"Not many people had a grandfather like Clay Baron." She turned to Aaron and smiled.

"How are you?" He couldn't have resisted the urge to touch her if he'd wanted to. His fingertips skimmed along her jaw.

"How do I look?"

"You don't like me to tell you you're beautiful."

She laughed, and the under-the-lashes look she sent him was the first flirtatious move he'd ever seen from her. "It's a holiday."

"Spend it with me?" He held out a hand, knowing if she put hers in it, in public, where there were curious eyes and tongues that appreciated a nice bit of gossip, it would be a commitment of sorts.

Her fingers laced with his. "I thought you'd never ask."

They spent the morning doing what couples had done

at county fairs for decades. There was lemonade to be drunk, contests to be watched. It was easy to laugh when the sky was clear and the sun promised a dry, golden day.

Children raced by with balloons held by sticky fingers. Teenagers flirted with the nonchalance peculiar to their age. Old-timers chewed tobacco and out-lied each other. The air was touched with the scent of food and animals, and the starch in bandbox shirts had not yet wilted with sweat.

With Aaron's arm around her, Jillian crowded to the fence to watch the greased pig contest. The ground had been flooded and churned up so that the state of the mud was perfection. The pig was slick with lard and quick, so that he eluded the five men who lunged after him. The crowd called out suggestions and hooted with laughter. The pig squealed and shot, like a bullet, out of capturing arms. Men fell on their faces and swore good-naturedly.

Jillian shot him a look, then inclined her head toward the pen where the activity was still wild and loud. "Don't you like games, Murdock?"

"I like to make up my own." He swung her around. "Now, there's this real quiet hayloft I know of."

With a laugh, she eluded him. He'd never known her to be deliberately provocative and found himself not quite certain how to deal with it. The glitter in her eyes made him decide. In one smooth move, Aaron gathered her close and kissed her soundly. There was an approving whoop from a group of cowboys behind them. When Jillian managed to untangle herself, she glanced over to see two of her own men grinning at her.

"It's a holiday," Aaron reminded her when she let out a huff of breath.

She brought her head back slowly and took his measure. Oh, he was damn proud of himself, she decided. And two could play. Her smile had him wondering just what she had up her sleeve.

"You want fireworks?" she asked, then threw her arms around him and silenced him before he could agree or deny.

While his kiss had been firm yet still friendly, hers whispered of secrets only the two of them knew. Aaron never heard the second cheer go up, but he wouldn't have been surprised to feel the ground move.

"I missed you last night, Murdock," she whispered, then went from her toes to her flat feet so that their lips parted. She took a step back before she offered her hand, and the smile on those fascinating lips was cocky.

Carefully Aaron drew air into his lungs and released it. "You're going to finish that one later, Jillian."

She only laughed again. "I certainly hope so. Let's go see if Gil can win the pie-eating contest again this year."

He went wherever she wanted and felt foolishly, and appealingly, like a kid on his first date. It was the sudden carefree aura around her. Jillian had dropped everything, all worries and responsibilities, and had given herself a day for fun. Perhaps because she felt a slight twinge of guilt, like a kid playing hooky, the day was all the sweeter.

She would have sworn the sun had never been brighter, the sky so blue. In all of her life, she couldn't remember ever laughing so easily. A slice of cherry pie was ambrosia. If she could have concentrated the day down, section by section, she would have put it into a box where she could have taken out an hour at a time when she was alone and tired. Because she was too practical to believe that possible, Jillian chose to live each moment to the fullest.

By the time the rodeo officially opened, Jillian was nearly drunk on freedom. As the Fourth of July Queen and her court rode sedately around the arena, she still clutched her bull's blue ribbon in her hand. "That's fifty you owe me," she told Aaron with a grin.

He sat on the ground exchanging dress boots for worn, patched riding favorites. "Why don't we wait and see how the second bet comes out?"

"Okay." She perched on a barrel and listened to the crowd cheer from the stands. She was riding high and knew it. Her luck had turned—there wasn't a problem she could be hit with that she couldn't handle.

A lot of cowboys and potential competitors had already collected behind the chutes. Though it all seemed very casual—the lounging, the rigging bags set carelessly against the chain link fence—there was an air of suppressed excitement. There was the scent of tobacco from the little cans invariably carried in the right rear pocket of jeans, and mink oil on leather. Already she heard the jingle of spurs and harnesses as equipment was checked. The bareback riding was first. When she heard the announcement, Jillian rose and wandered to the fence to watch.

"I'm surprised you didn't give this one a try," Aaron commented.

She tilted her head so that it brushed his arm—one of the rare signs of affection that made him weak. "Too much energy," she said with a laugh. "I'm dedicating the day to laziness. I noticed you were signed up for the bronc riding." Jillian nudged her hat back as she looked up at him. "Still more guts than brains?"

He grinned and shrugged. "Worried about me?"

Jillian gave a snort of laughter. "I've got some good liniment—it'll take the soreness out of the bruises you're going to get."

He ran a fingertip down her spine. "The idea tempts me to make sure I get a few. You know—" he turned her into his arms in a move both smooth and possessive "—it wouldn't take much for me to forget all about this little competition." Lowering his head, he nibbled at her lips, oblivious of whoever might be milling around them. "It's not such a long drive back to the ranch. Not a soul there. Pretty day like this—I start thinking about taking a swim."

"Do you?" She drew her head back so their eyes met.

"Mmmm. Water'd be cool, and quiet."

Chuckling, she pressed her lips to his. "After the calf roping," she said and drew away.

Jillian preferred the chutes to the stands. There she could listen to the men talk of other rodeos, other rides, while she checked over her own equipment. She watched a young girl in a stunning buckskin suit rev up her nerves before the barrel racing. An old hand worked rosin into the palm of a glove with tireless patience. The little breeze carried the scent of grilled meat from the concessions.

No, she thought, her family could never understand the appeal of this. The earthy smells, the earthy talk. They'd be just as much out of their element here as she'd always been at her mother's box at the opera. It was times like these, when she was accepted for simply being what she was, that she stopped remembering the little twinges of panic that had plagued her while she grew up. No, there was nothing lacking in her as she'd often thought. She was simply different.

She watched the bull riding, thrilling to the danger

and daring as men pitted themselves against a ton of beef. There were spills and close calls and clowns who made the terrifying seem amusing. Half dreaming, she leaned on the fence as a riderless bull charged and snorted around the arena, poking bad temperedly at a clown in a barrel. The crowd was loud, but she could hear Aaron in an easy conversation with Gil from somewhere behind her. She caught snatches about the little sorrel mare Aaron had drawn in the bronc riding. A fire-eater. Out of the chute, then a lunge to the right. Liked to spin. Relaxed, Jillian thought she'd enjoy watching Aaron pit himself against the little fire-eater. After she'd won another fifty from him.

She thought the day had simply been set aside for her, warm and sunny and without demands. Perhaps she'd been this relaxed before, this happy, but it was difficult to remember when she'd shared the two sensations so clearly. She savored them.

Then everything happened so quickly she didn't have time to think, only to act.

She heard the childish laughter as she stretched her back muscles. She saw the quick flash of red zip through the fence and bounce on the dirt without fully registering it. But she saw the child skim through the rungs of the fence and into the arena. He was so close his jeans brushed hers as he scrambled through after his ball. Jillian was over the fence and running before his mother screamed. Part of her registered Aaron's voice, either furious or terrified, as he called her name.

Out of the corner of her eye Jillian saw the bull turn. His eyes, already wild from the ride, met hers, though she never paused. Her blood went cold.

She didn't hear the chaos as the crowd leaped to their feet or the mass confusion from behind the chutes as she sprinted after the boy. She did feel the ground tremble as the bull began its charge. There wasn't time to waste her breath on shouting. Running on instinct, she lunged, letting the momentum carry her forward. She went down hard, full length on the boy, and knocked the breath out of both of them. As the bull skimmed by them, she felt the hot rush of air.

Don't move, she told herself, mercilessly pinning the boy beneath her when he started to squirm. Don't even breathe. She could hear shouting, very close by now, but didn't dare move her head to look. She wasn't gored. Jillian swallowed on the thought. No, she'd know it if he'd caught her with his horns. And he hadn't trampled her. Yet.

Someone was cursing furiously. Jillian closed her eyes and wondered if she'd ever be able to stand up again. The boy was beginning to cry lustily. She tried to smother the sound with her body.

When hands came under her arms, she jolted and started to struggle. "You *idiot*!" Recognizing the voice, Jillian relaxed and allowed herself to be hauled to her feet. She might have swayed if she hadn't been held so tightly. "What kind of a stunt was that?" She stared up at Aaron's deathly white face while he shook her. "Are you hurt?" he demanded. "Are you hurt anywhere?"

"What?"

He shook her again because his hands were trembling. "Damn it, Jillian!"

Her head was spinning a bit like it had when she'd had that first plug of tobacco. It took her a moment to realize someone was gripping her hand. Bemused, she listened to the tearful gratitude of the mother while the boy wept loudly with his face buried in his father's shirt. The Simmons boy, she thought dazedly. The little Simmons boy, who played in the yard while his mother hung out the wash and his father worked on her own land.

"He's all right, Joleen," she managed, though her mouth didn't want to follow the order of her brain. "I might've put some bruises on him, though."

Aaron cut her off, barely suppressing the urge to suggest someone introduce the boy to a razor strap before he dragged Jillian away. She had a misty impression of a sea of faces and Aaron's simmering rage.

"...get you over to first aid."

"What?" she said again as his voice drifted in and out of her mind.

"I said I'm going to get you over to first aid." He bit off the words as he came to the fence.

"No, I'm fine." The light went gray for a moment and she shook her head.

"As soon as I'm sure of that, I'm going to strangle you."

She pulled her hand from his and straightened her shoulders. "I said I'm fine," she repeated. Then the ground tilted and rushed up at her.

The first thing she felt was the tickle of grass under her palm. Then there was a cool cloth, more wet than damp, on her face. Jillian moaned in annoyance as water trickled down to her collar. Opening her eyes, she saw a blur of light and shadow. She closed them again, then concentrated on focusing.

She saw Aaron first, grim and pale as he hitched her up to a half-sitting position and held a glass to her lips. Then Gil, shifting his weight from foot to foot while he ran his hat through his hands. "She ain't hurt none," he told Aaron in a voice raised to convince everyone, including himself. "Just had herself a spell, that's all. Women do."

"A lot you know," she muttered, then discovered what Aaron held to her lips wasn't a glass but a flask of neat brandy. It burned very effectively through the mists. "I didn't faint," Jillian said in disgust.

"You did a damn good imitation, then," Aaron snapped at her.

"Let the child breathe." Karen Murdock's calm, elegant voice had the magic effect of moving the crowd back. She slipped through and knelt at Jillian's side. Clucking her tongue, she took the dripping cloth from Jillian's brow and wrung it out. "Men'll always try to overcompensate. Well, Jillian, you caused quite a sensation."

Grimacing, Jillian sat up. "Did I?" She pressed her forehead to her knees a minute until she was certain the world wasn't going to do any more spinning. "I can't believe I fainted," she mumbled.

Aaron swore and took a healthy swig from the flask himself. "She almost gets herself killed and she's worried about what fainting's going to do to her image."

Jillian's head snapped up. "Look, Murdock—"

"I wouldn't push it if I were you," he warned and meticulously capped the flask. "If you can stand, I'll take you home."

"Of course I can stand," she retorted. "And I'm not going home."

"I'm sure you're fine," Karen began and shot her son a telling look. For a smart man, Karen mused, Aaron was showing a remarkable lack of sense. Then again, when love was around, sense customarily went out the window. "Trouble is, you're a seven-day wonder," she told Jillian with a brief glance at the gathering crowd. "You're going to be congratulated to death if you stay around here." She smiled as she saw her words sink in.

Grumbling, Jillian rose. "All right." The bruises were beginning to be felt. Rather than admit it, she brushed at the dust on her jeans. "There's no need for you to go," she told Aaron stiffly. "I'm perfectly capable of—"

His fingers were wrapped tight around her arm as he dragged her away. "I don't know what your problem is, Murdock," she said through her teeth. "But I don't have to take this."

"I'd keep a lid on it for a while if I were you." The crowd fell back as he strode through. If anyone considered speaking to Jillian, Aaron's challenging look changed their minds.

After wrenching open the door of his truck, Aaron gave her a none-too-gentle boost inside. Jillian pulled her hat from her back and, taking the brim in both hands, slammed it down on her head. Folding her arms, she prepared to endure the next hour's drive in absolute silence. As Aaron pulled out it occurred to her that she had missed not only the calf roping, but also her sacred right to gloat over her bull's victory at the evening barbecue. The injustice of it made her smolder.

And just what's he so worked up about? Jillian asked herself righteously. He hadn't scared himself blind, wrenched his knee, or humiliated himself by fainting in public. Gingerly she touched her elbow where she'd scraped most of the skin away. After all, if you wanted to be technical, she'd probably saved that kid's life. Jillian's chin angled as her arm began to ache with real enthusiasm. So why was he acting as though she'd committed some crime?

"One of these days you're going to put your chin out like that and someone's going to take you up on it."

Slowly she turned her head to glare at him. "You want to give it a shot, Murdock?"

"Don't tempt me." He punched on the gas until the speedometer hovered at seventy.

"Look, I don't know what your problem is," she said tightly. "But since you've got one, why don't you just spill it? I'm not in the mood for your nasty little comments."

He swung the truck over to the side of the road so abruptly she crashed into the door. By the time she'd recovered, he was out of his side and striding across the tough wild grass of a narrow field. Rubbing her sore arm, Jillian pushed out of the truck and went after him.

"What the hell is all this about?" Anger made her breathless as she caught at his shirtsleeve. "If you want to drive like a maniac, I'll hitch a ride back to the ranch."

"Just shut up." He jerked away from her. Distance, he told himself. He just needed some distance until he pulled himself together. He was still seeing those lowered horns sweeping past Jillian's tumbling body. His rope might've missed the mark, and then— He couldn't afford to think of any *and thens*. As it was, it had taken three well-placed ropes and several strong arms before they'd been able to drag the bull away from those two prone bodies. He'd nearly lost her. In one split second he'd nearly lost her.

"Don't you tell me to shut up." Spinning in front of him, Jillian gripped his shirtfront. Her hat tumbled down her back as she tossed her head and rage poured out of her. "I've had all I'm going to take from you. God knows why I've let you get away with this much, but no more. Now you can just hop back in your truck and head it in whatever direction you like. To hell would suit me just fine."

She whirled away, but before she could storm off she was spun back and crushed in his arms. Spitting mad, she struggled only to have his grip tighten. It wasn't until she stopped to marshal her forces that she realized he was trembling and that his breathing came fast and uneven. Emotion ruled him, yes, but it wasn't anger. Subsiding, she waited. Not certain what she was offering comfort for, she stroked his back. "Aaron?"

He shook his head and buried his face in her hair. It was the closest he could remember to just falling apart. It hadn't been distance he'd needed, he discovered, but this. To feel her warm and safe and solid in his arms.

"Oh, God, Jillian, do you know what you did to me?"

Baffled, she let her cheek rest against his drumming heart and continued to stroke his back. "I'm sorry," she offered, hoping it would be enough for whatever she'd done.

"It was so close. Inches—just inches more. I wasn't sure at first that he hadn't gotten you."

The bull, Jillian realized. It hadn't been anger, but fear. Something warm and sweet moved through her. "Don't," she murmured. "I wasn't hurt. It wasn't nearly as bad as it must've looked."

"The hell it wasn't." His hands came to her face and jerked it back. "I was only a few yards back when I got the first rope around him. He was more'n half crazy by then. Another couple of seconds and he'd've scooped you right up off that ground."

Jillian stared up at him and finally managed to swallow. "I—I didn't know."

He watched as the color her temper had given her fled from her cheeks. And I just had to tell you, he thought furiously. Taking both her hands, he brought them to his lips, burying his mouth in one palm, then the other. The gesture alone was enough to distract her. "It's done," Aaron said with more control. "I guess I overreacted.

It's not easy to watch something like that." Because she needed it, he smiled at her. "I wouldn't have cared for it if you'd picked up any holes."

Relaxing a bit, she answered the smile. "Neither would I. As it is, I picked up a few bruises I'm not too fond of."

Still holding her hands, he bent over and kissed her with such exquisite gentleness that she felt the ground tilt for the second time. There was something different here, she realized dimly. Something... But she couldn't hold on to it.

Aaron drew away, knowing the time was coming when he'd have to tell her what he felt, whether she was ready to hear it or not. As he led her back to the truck he decided that since he was only going to bare his heart to one woman in his life, he was going to do it right.

"You're going to take a hot bath," he told her as he lifted her into the truck. "Then I'm going to fix you dinner."

Jillian settled back against the seat. "Maybe fainting isn't such a bad thing after all."

Chapter Eleven

By the time they drove into the ranch yard, Jillian had decided she'd probably enjoy a few hours of pampering. As far as she could remember, no one had ever fussed over her before. As a child, she'd been strong and healthy. Whenever she'd been ill, she'd been treated with competent practicality by her doctor father. She'd learned early that the fewer complaints you made the less likelihood there was for a hypodermic to come out of that little black bag. Clay had always treated bumps and blood as a routine part of the life. Wash up and get back to work.

Now she thought it might be a rather interesting experience to have someone murmur over her scrapes and bruises. Especially if he kissed her like he had on the side of the road…in that soft, gentle way that made the top of her head threaten to spin off.

Perhaps they wouldn't have the noise and lights and music of the fairgrounds, but they could make their own fireworks, alone, on Utopia.

All the buildings were quiet, bunkhouse, barns, stables. Instead of the noise and action that would accompany any late afternoon, there was simple, absolute peace over acres of land. Whatever animals hadn't been taken to the fair had been left to graze for the day. It would be hours before anyone returned to Utopia.

"I don't think I've ever been here alone before," Jillian murmured when Aaron stopped the truck. She sat for a moment and absorbed the quiet and the stillness. It occurred to her that she could cup her hands and shout if she liked—no one would even hear the echo.

"It's funny, it even feels different. You always know there're people around." She stepped out of the truck, then listened to the echo of the slam. "Somebody in the bunkhouse or the cookhouse or one of the outbuildings. Some of the wives or children hanging out clothes or working in the gardens. You hardly think about it, but it's like a little town."

"Self-sufficient, independent." He took her hand, thinking that the words described her just as accurately as they described the ranch. They were two of the reasons he'd been drawn to her.

"It has to be, doesn't it? It's so easy to get cut off— one bad storm. Besides, it's what makes it all so special." Though she didn't understand the smile he sent her, she answered it. "I'm glad I've got so many married hands who've settled," she added. "It's harder to depend on the drifters." Jillian scanned the ranch yard, not quite understanding her own reluctance to go inside. It was as if she were missing something. With a shrug, she put it down to the oddity of being alone, but she caught herself searching the area again.

Aaron glanced down and saw the lowered-brow look of concentration. "Something wrong?"

"I don't know… It seems like there is." With another shrug, she turned to him. "I must be getting jumpy." Reaching up, she tipped back the brim of his hat. She liked the way it shadowed his face, accenting the angle of bone, adding just one more shade of darkness to his eyes. "You didn't mention anything about scrubbing my back when I took that hot bath, did you?"

"No, but I could probably be persuaded."

Agreeably she went into his arms. She thought she could catch just a trace of rosin on him, perhaps a hint of saddle soap. "Did I mention how sore I am?"

"No, you didn't."

"I don't like to complain…" She snuggled against him.

"But?" he prompted with a grin.

"Well, now that you mention it—there are one or two places that sting, just a bit."

"Want me to kiss them and make them better?"

She sighed as he nuzzled her ear. "If it wouldn't be too much trouble."

"I'm a humanitarian," he told her, then began to nudge her slowly toward the porch steps. It was then Jillian remembered. With a gasp, she broke out of his arms and raced across the yard. "Jillian—" Swearing, Aaron followed her.

Oh, God, how could she've missed it! Jillian raced to the paddock fence and leaned breathlessly against it. Empty. *Empty.* She balled her hands into fists as she looked at the bottle she'd left hanging at an angle in the shade. The trough of water glimmered in the sun. The few scoops of grain she'd left were barely touched.

"What's going on?"

"Baby," she muttered, tapping her hand rhythmically against the fence. "They've taken Baby." Her tone started out calm, then became more and more agitated. "They walked right into my backyard, right into my backyard, and stole from me."

"Maybe one of your hands put him back in the barn."

She only shook her head and continued to tap her hand on the fence. "The five hundred weren't enough," she murmured. "They had to come here and steal within a stone's throw of my house. I should've left Joe—he offered to stay. I should've stayed myself."

"Come on, we'll check the barn."

She looked at him, and her eyes were flat and dark. "He's not in the barn."

He'd rather have had her rage, weep, than look so— resigned. "Maybe not, but we'll be sure. Then we'll see if anything else was taken before we call the sheriff."

"The sheriff." Jillian laughed under her breath and stared blindly into the empty paddock. "The sheriff."

"Jillian—" Aaron slipped his arms around her, but she drew away immediately.

"No, I'm not going to fall apart this time." Her voice trembled slightly, but her eyes were clear. "They won't do that to me again."

It might be better if she did, Aaron thought. Her face was pale, but he knew that expression by now. There'd be no backing down. "You check the barn," he suggested. "I'll look in the stables."

Jillian followed the routine, though she knew it was hopeless. Baby's stall was empty. She watched the little motes of hay and dust as they floated in the slant of sunlight. Someone had taken her yearling. Someone. Her hands balled into fists. Somehow, some way, she was going to get a name. Spinning on her heel, she strode back out. Though she itched with impatience, she waited until Aaron crossed the yard to her. There wasn't any need for words. Together, they went into the house.

She's not going to take this one lying down, he decided, with as much admiration as concern. Yes, she was still pale, but her voice was strong and clear as she spoke to the sheriff's office. Resigned—yes, she was still resigned that it had been done. But she didn't consider it over.

He remembered the way she'd nuzzled the calf when it'd been newborn—the way her eyes had softened when she spoke of it. It was always a mistake to make a pet out of one of your stock, but there were times it happened. She was paying for it now.

Thoughtfully he began to brew coffee. Aaron considered it a foolish move for anyone to have stolen Utopia's prize yearling. For butchering? It hardly seemed worth the risk or effort. Yet what rancher in the area would buy a young Hereford so easily identified? Someone had gotten greedy, or stupid. Either way, it would make them easier to catch.

Jillian leaned against the kitchen wall and talked steadily into the phone. Aaron found himself wanting to shield, to protect. She took the coffee from him with a brief nod and continued talking. Shaking his head, he reminded himself he should know better by now. Protection wasn't something Jillian would take gracefully. He drank his own coffee, looking out of the kitchen window and wondering how a man dealt with loving a woman who had more grit than most men.

"He'll do what he can," she said as she hung up the phone with a snap. "I'm going to offer a separate reward for Baby." Jillian drank down half the coffee, hot and black. "Tomorrow I'll go see the Cattlemen's Association again. I want to put the pressure on, and put it on

hard. People are going to realize this isn't going to stop
at Utopia." She looked into her coffee, then grimly finished it off. "I kept telling myself it wasn't personal.
Even when I saw the hides and bones in the canyon. Not
this time. They got cocky, Aaron. It's always easier to
catch arrogance."

There was relish in the tone of her voice, the kind
of relish that made him smile as he turned to face her.
"You're right."

"What're you grinning at?"

"I was thinking if the rustlers could see you now,
they'd be shaking the dust of this county off their boots
in a hurry."

Her lips curved. She hadn't thought it possible.
"Thank you." She gestured with the cup, then set it back
on the stove. "I seem to be saying that to you quite a bit
these days."

"You don't have to say it at all. Hungry?"

"Hmmm." She put her hand on her stomach and
thought about it. "I don't know."

"Go get yourself a bath, I'll rustle up something."

Walking to him, Jillian slipped her arms around
his waist and rested her head on his chest. How was
it he knew her so well? How did he understand that
she needed a few moments alone to sort through her
thoughts and feelings?

"Why are you so good to me?" she murmured.

With a half laugh, Aaron buried his face in her hair.
"God knows. Go soak your bruises."

"Okay." But she gave in to the urge to hug him
fiercely before she left the room.

She wished she knew a better way to express gratitude. As she climbed the stairs to the second floor, Jillian wished she were more clever with words. If she

were, she'd be able to tell him how much it meant that he offered no more than she could comfortably take. His support today had been steady but unobtrusive. And he was giving her time alone without leaving her alone. Perhaps it had taken her quite some time to discover just how special a man he was, but she had discovered it. It wasn't something she'd forget.

As Jillian peeled off her clothes she found she was a bit more tender in places than she'd realized. Better, she decided, and turned the hot water on in the tub to let it steam. A few bruises were something solid to concentrate on. They were easier than the bruises she felt on the inside. It might have been foolish to feel as though she'd let her grandfather down, but she couldn't rid herself of the feeling. He'd given her something in trust and she hadn't protected it well enough. It would have soothed her if he'd been around to berate her for it.

Wincing a bit, she lowered herself into the water. The raw skin on her elbow objected and she ignored it. One of her own men? she thought with a grimace. It was too possible. Back up a truck to the paddock, load up the calf, and go.

She'd start making a few discreet inquiries herself. Stealing the calf would've taken time. Maybe she could discover just who was away from the fair. Perhaps they'd be confident enough to throw a little extra money around if they thought they were safe and then… Then they'd see, she thought as she relaxed in the water.

Poor Baby. No one would spend the time scratching his ears or talking to him now. Sinking farther in the water, she waited until her mind went blank.

It was nearly an hour before she came downstairs again. She'd soaked the stiffness away and nearly all the depression. Nothing practical could be done with depression. She caught the aroma of something spicy that had her stomach juices churning.

Aaron's name was on the tip of her tongue as she walked into the kitchen, but the room was empty. A pot simmered on the stove with little hisses and puffs of steam. It drew her, irresistibly. Jillian lifted the lid, closed her eyes, and breathed deep. Chili, thick, and fragrant enough to make the mouth water. She wouldn't have to give it any thought if he asked if she was hungry now.

Picking up a spoon, she began to stir. Maybe just one little taste…

"My mother used to smack my hand for that," Aaron commented. Jillian dropped the lid with a clatter.

"Damn, Murdock! You scared me to—" Turning, she saw the clutch of wildflowers in his hand.

Some men might've looked foolish holding small colorful blooms in a hand roughened by work and weather. Other men might've seemed awkward. Aaron was neither. Something turned over in her chest when he smiled at her.

She looked stunned—not that he minded. It wasn't often you caught a woman like Jillian Baron off-balance. As he watched, she put her hands behind her back and gripped them together. He lifted a brow. If he'd known he could make her nervous with a bunch of wildflowers, he'd have dug up a field of them long before this.

"Feel better?" he asked and slowly crossed to her.

She'd backed into the counter before she'd realized she made the defensive move. "Yes, thanks."

He gave her one of his long, serious looks while his eyes laughed. "Something wrong?"

"No. The chili smells great."

"Something I picked up at one of the line camps a few

years back." Bending his head, he kissed the corners of her mouth. "Don't you want the flowers, Jillian?"

"Yes, I—" She found she was gripping her fingers together until they hurt. Annoyed with herself, she loosened them and took the flowers from his hand. "They're very pretty."

"It's what your hair smells like," he murmured and saw the cautious look she threw up at him. Tilting his head, he studied her. "Hasn't anyone ever given you flowers before?"

Not in years, she realized. Not since—florist boxes, ribbons, and soft words. Realizing she was making a fool of herself, she shrugged. "Roses," she said carelessly. "Red roses."

Something in her tone warned him. He kept his touch very light as he wound her hair around his finger. It was the color of flame, the texture of silk. "Too tame," he said simply. "Much too tame."

Something flickered inside her—acknowledgment, caution, need. With a sigh, she looked down at the small bold flowers in her hand. "Once—a long time ago—I thought I could be too."

He tugged on her hair until she looked up at him. "Is that what you wanted to be?"

"Then, I—" She broke off, but something in his eyes demanded an answer. "Yes, I would've tried."

"Were you in love with him?" He wasn't certain why he was hacking away at a wound—his and hers—but he couldn't stop.

"Aaron—"

"Were you?"

She let out a long breath. Mechanically she began to fill a water glass for the flowers. "I was very young. He was a great deal like my father—steady, quiet, dedicated. My father loved me because he had to, never because he wanted to. There's a tremendous difference." The sharp, clean scent of the wildflowers drifted up to her. "Maybe somewhere along the line I thought if I pleased him, I'd please my father. I don't know, I was foolish."

"That isn't an answer." He discovered jealousy tasted bitter even after it was swallowed.

"I guess I don't have one I'm sure of." She moved her shoulders and fluffed the flowers in the glass. "Shouldn't we eat?" She went very still when his hands came to her shoulders, but she didn't resist when he turned her around.

She had a moment's fear that he would say something gentle, something sweet, and undermine her completely. She saw something of it in his eyes, just as he saw the apprehension in hers. Aaron tugged her against him and brought his mouth down hard on hers.

She could understand the turbulence and let go. She could meet the desire, the violence of needs, without fear of stumbling past her own rules. Her arms went around him to hold him close. Her lips sought his hungrily. If through the relief came a stir of feeling, she could almost convince herself it was nothing more complex than passion.

"Eat fast," Aaron told her. "I've been thinking about making love with you for hours."

"Didn't we eat already?"

With a chuckle he nuzzled her neck. "No, you don't. When I cook for a woman, she eats." He gave her a companionable smack on the bottom as he drew away. "Get the bowls."

Jillian handed him two and watched him scoop out generous portions. "Smells fabulous. Want a beer?"

"Yeah."

Unearthing two from the refrigerator, she poured them into glasses. "You know, if you ever get tired of ranching, you could have a job in the cookhouse here at Utopia."

"Always a comfort to have something to fall back on."

"We've got a woman now," Jillian went on as she took her seat. "The men call her Aunt Sally. She's got a way with biscuits—" She broke off as she took the first bite. Heat spread through her and woke up every cell in her body. Swallowing, she met Aaron's grin. "You use a free hand with the peppers."

"Separates the men from the boys." He took a generous forkful. "Too hot for you?"

Disdainfully she took a second bite. "There's nothing you can dish out I can't take, Murdock."

Laughing, he continued to eat. Jillian decided the first encounter had numbed her mouth right down to the vocal cords. She ate with as much relish as he, cooling off occasionally with sips of cold beer.

"Those people in town don't know what they're missing," she commented as she scraped down to the bottom of the bowl. "It isn't every day you get battery acid this tasty."

He glanced over as she ate the last forkful. "Want some more?"

"I want to live," she countered. "God, Aaron, a steady diet of that and you wouldn't have a stomach lining. It's fabulous."

"We had a Mexican foreman when I was a boy," Aaron told her. "Best damn cattleman I've ever known. I spent the best part of a summer with him up at the line camp. You should taste my flour tortillas."

The man was a constant surprise, Jillian decided as she rested her elbows on the table and cupped her chin in her hand. "What happened to him?"

"Saved his stake, went back to Mexico, and started his own spread."

"The impossible dream," Jillian murmured.

"Too easy to lose a month's pay in a poker game."

She nodded, but her lips curved. "Do you play?"

"I've sat in on a hand or two. You?"

"Clay taught me. We'll have to arrange a game one of these days."

"Any time."

"I'm counting on a few poker skills to bring me out of this rustling business."

Aaron watched her rise to clear the table. "How?"

"People get careless when they think you're ready to fold. They made a mistake with the yearling, Aaron. I'm going to be able to find him—especially if nobody knows how hard I'm looking. I'm thinking about hiring an investigator. Whatever it costs, I'd rather pay it than have the stealing go on."

He sat for a moment, listening to her run water in the sink—a homey, everyday sound. "How hard is all this hitting your books, Jillian?"

She cast a look over her shoulder, calm and cool. "I can still raise the bet."

He knew better than to offer her financial assistance. It irked him. Rising, he paced the kitchen until he'd come full circle behind her. "The Cattlemen's Association would back you."

"They'd have to know about it to do that. The less people who know, the more effective a private investigation would be."

"I want to help you."

Touched, she turned and took him into her arms. "You have helped me. I won't forget it."

"I have to hog-tie you before you'll let me do anything."

She laughed and lifted her face to his. "I'm not that bad."

"Worse," he countered. "If I offered you some men to help patrol your land…"

"Aaron—"

"See." He kissed her before she could finish the protest. "I could work for you myself until everything was straightened out."

"I couldn't let you—" Then his mouth was hard and bruising on hers again.

"I'm the one who has to watch you worry and struggle," he told her as his hands began to roam down. "Do you know what that does to me?"

She tried to concentrate on his words, but his mouth—his mouth was demanding all her attention. The hot, spicy kiss took her breath away, but she clung to him and fought for more. Each time he touched her it was only seconds until the needs took over completely. She'd never known anything so liberating, or so imprisoning. Jillian might have struggled against the latter if she'd known how. Instead she accepted the bars and locks even as she accepted the open sky and the wind. He was the only man who could tempt her to.

This was something he could do for her, Aaron knew. Make her forget, thrust her problems away from her, if only temporarily. Even so, he knew, if she had a choice, she would have kept some distance there as well. She'd been hurt, and her trust wasn't completely his yet. The frustration of it made his mouth more ruthless, his hands more urgent. There was still only one way that she was

his without question. He swept her up, then silenced her
murmured protest.

Jillian was aware she was being carried. Some inner
part of her rebelled against it. And yet... He wasn't
taking her anywhere she wouldn't have gone willingly.
Perhaps he needed this—romance he'd once called it.
Romance frightened her, as the flowers had frightened
her. It was so easy to lie in candlelight, so easy to de-
ceive with fragrant blossoms and soft words. And she
was no longer sure the defenses she'd once had were
still there. Not with him.

"I want you." The words drifted from her to shimmer against his lips.

He would've taken her to bed. But it was too far. He
would have given her the slow, easy loving a cherished
woman deserves. But he was too hungry. With his mouth
still fused to hers, he tumbled onto the couch with her
and let the fire take them both.

She understood desperation. It was honest and real.
There could be no doubting the frantic search of his
mouth or the urgent pressure of his fingers against her
skin. Desire had no shadows. She could feel it pulsing
from him even as it pulsed from her. His curses as he
tugged at her clothes made her laugh breathlessly. *She*
made him clumsy. It was the greatest compliment she'd
ever had.

He was relentless, spinning her beyond time and
space the moment he could touch her flesh. She let herself go. Every touch, every frenzied caress, every deep,
greedy kiss, took her further from the strict, practical
world she'd formed for herself. Once she'd sought solitude and speed when she'd needed freedom. Now she
needed only Aaron.

She felt his hair brush over her bare shoulder and savored even that simple contact. It brought a sweetness flowing into her while the burn of his mouth brought the fire. Only with him had she realized it was possible to have both. Only with him had she realized the great, yawning need in herself to have both. Her moan came as much from the revelation as from the passion.

Did she know how giving she was? How incredibly arousing? Aaron had to fight the need to take her quickly, ruthlessly, while they were both still half dressed. No woman had ever sapped his control the way she could. One look, one touch, and he was hers so completely— How could she not know?

Her body flowed, fluid as water, heady as wine, under his hands. Her lips had the punch of an electric current and the texture of silk. Could any woman remain unaware of such a deadly combination?

As if to catch his breath, he took his lips to her throat and burrowed there. He drew in the fragrance from her bath, some subtle woman's scent that lingered there, waiting to entice a lover. It was then he remembered the bruises. Aaron shook his head, trying to clear it.

"I'm hurting you."

"No." She drew him back, close. "No, you're not. You never do. I'm not fragile, Aaron."

"No?" He lifted his head so that he could see her face. There was the delicate line of bone she couldn't deny, the honey-touched skin that remained soft after hours in the sun. The frailty that came and went in her eyes at the right word, the right touch. "Sometimes you are," he murmured. "Let me show you."

"No—"

But even as she protested, his lips skimmed hers, so gentle, so reassuring. It did nothing to smother the fire, only banked it while he showed her what magic there could be with mouth to mouth. With his fingers he traced her face as though he might never see it with his eyes again—over the curve of cheekbone, down the slim line of jaw.

Patient, soft, murmuring, he seduced where no seduction was needed. Tender, thorough, easy, he let his lips show her what he hadn't yet spoken. The hand on his shoulder slid bonelessly down to his waist. He touched the tip of her tongue with his, then went deeper, slowly, in a soul-wrenching kiss that left them both limp. Then he began a careful worship of her body. She floated.

Was there any kind of pleasure he couldn't show her? Jillian wondered. Was this humming world just one more aspect to passion? She wanted desperately to give him something in return, yet her body was so heavy, weighed down with sensations. Sandalwood and leather—it would always bring him to her mind. The ridge of callus on his hand where the reins rubbed daily—nothing felt more perfect against her skin. He shifted so that she sank deeper into the cushions, and he with her.

She could taste him—and what she realized must be a wisp of herself on his lips. His cheek grazed hers, not quite smooth. She wanted to burrow against it. He whispered her name and generated a new layer of warmth.

Even when his hands began to roam, the excitement stayed hazy. She couldn't break through the mists, and no longer tried. Her skin was throbbing, but it went deeper, to the blood and bone. His mouth was light at her breast, his tongue clever enough to make her shudder, then settle, then shudder again.

He kept the pace easy, though she began to writhe under him. Time dripped away as he gave himself the pleasure of showing her each new delight. He knew afternoon was ending only by the way the light slanted over her face. The quiet was punctuated only with murmurs and sighs. He'd never felt more alone with her.

He took her slowly, savoring each moment, each movement, until there could be no more.

As she lay beneath him, Jillian watched the light shift toward dusk. It had been like a dream, she thought, like something you sigh over in the middle of the night when your wishes take control. Should it move her more than the fire and flash they usually brought each other? Somehow she knew what she'd just experienced had been more dangerous.

Aaron shifted, and though she made no objection to his weight, sat up, bringing her with him. "I like the way you stay soft and warm after I make love to you."

"It's never been just like that before," she murmured.

The words moved him; he couldn't stop it. "No." Tilting back her head, he kissed her again. "It will be again."

Perhaps because she wanted so badly to hold on, to stay, to depend, she drew away. "I'm never sure how to take you." Something warned her it was time to play it light. She was out of her depth—far, far out of her depth.

"In what way?"

She gave in to the urge to hold him again, just to feel the way his hand slid easily up and down her bare back. Reluctantly she slipped out of his arms and pulled on her shirt. "You're a lot of different people, Aaron Murdock. Every time I think I might get to know who you are, you're someone else."

"No, I'm not." Before she could button it, Aaron took her shirtfront and pulled her back to him. "Different moods don't make different people."

"Maybe not." She disconcerted him by kissing the back of his hand. "But I still can't get a handle on you."

"Is that what you want?"

"I'm a simple person."

He stared at her a moment as she continued to dress. "Are you joking?"

Because there was a laugh in his voice, she looked over, half serious, half embarrassed. "No, I am. I have to know where I stand, what my options are, what's expected of me. As long as I know I can do my job and take care of what's mine, I'm content."

He watched her thoughtfully as he pulled on his jeans. "Your job's what's vital in your life?"

"It's what I know," she countered. "I understand the land."

"And people?"

"I'm not really very good with people—a lot of people. Unless I understand them."

Aaron pulled his shirt on but left it open as he crossed to her. "And I'm one you don't understand?"

"Only sometimes," she murmured. "I guess I understand you best when I'm annoyed with you. Other times..." She was sinking even deeper and started to turn away.

"Other times," Aaron prompted, holding on to her arms.

"Other times I don't know. I never expected to get involved with you—this way."

He ran his thumbs over the pulses at the inside of her elbows. They weren't steady any longer. "This way, Jillian?"

"I didn't expect that we'd be lovers. I never expected—" Why was her heart pounding like this again, so soon? "To want you," she finished.

"Didn't you?" There was something about the way she looked at him—not quite sure of herself when he knew she was fighting to be—that made him reckless. "I wanted you from the first minute I saw you, riding hell for leather on that mare. There were other things I didn't expect. Finding those soft places, on you, in you."

"Aaron—"

He shook his head when she tried to stop him. "Thinking of you in the middle of the day, the middle of the night. Remembering just the way you say my name."

"Don't."

He felt her start to tremble before she tried to pull away. "Damn it, it's time you heard what I've been carrying around inside of me. I love you, Jillian."

Panic came first, even when she began to build up the reserve. "No, you don't have to say that." Her voice was sharp and fast. "I don't expect to hear those kinds of things."

"What the hell are you talking about?" He shook her once in frustration, and a second time in anger. "I know what I have to say. I don't care if you expect to hear it or not, because you're going to."

She hung on to her temper because she knew it was emotion that brought on betrayal. If she hadn't had her pride, she would have told him just how much those words, that easily said empty phrase hurt her. "Aaron, I told you before I don't need the soft words. I don't even like them. Whatever's between us—"

"What is between us?" he demanded. He hadn't known he could be hurt, not like this. Not so he could all but feel the blood draining out of him where he stood. He'd just told a woman he loved her—the only woman, the first time. And she was answering him with ice. "You tell me what there is between us. Just this?" He swung a hand toward the couch, still rumpled from their bodies. "Is that it for you, Jillian?"

"I don't—" There was a tug-of-war going on inside of her, so fierce she was breathless from it. "It's all I thought you—" Frightened, she dragged both hands through her hair. Why was he doing this now, when she was just beginning to think she understood what he wanted from her, what she needed from him? "I don't know what you want. But I—I just can't give you any more than I already have. It's already more than I've ever given to anyone else."

His fingers loosened on her arms one by one, then dropped away. They were a match in many ways, and pride was one of them. Aaron watched her almost dispassionately as he buttoned his shirt. "You've let something freeze inside you, woman. If all you want's a warm body on a cold night, you shouldn't have much trouble. Personally, I like a little something more."

She watched him walk out of the door, heard the sound of his truck as it broke the silence. The sun was just slipping over the horizon.

Chapter Twelve

He worked until his muscles ached and he could think about little more than easing them. He probably drank too much. He rode the cattle, hours in the saddle, rounded strays, and ate more dust than food. He spent the long, sweaty days of summer at the line camp, driving himself from sunup to sundown. Sometimes, only sometimes, he managed to push her out of his mind.

For three weeks Aaron was hell to be around. Or so his men mumbled whenever he was out of earshot. It was a woman, they told each other. Only a woman could drive a man to the edge, and then give him that gentle tap over. The Baron woman's name came up. Well, Murdocks and Barons had never mixed, so it was no wonder. No one'd expected much to come of that but hot tempers and bad feelings.

If Aaron heard the murmurs, he ignored them. He'd come up to the camp to work—and he was going to do just that until she was out of his system. No woman was going to make him crawl. He'd told her he loved her, and she'd shoved his words, his emotions, right back in his face. Not interested.

Aaron dropped a new fence post into the ground as the sweat rolled freely down his back and sides. Maybe she was the first woman he'd ever loved—that didn't mean she'd be the last. He came down hard on the post with a sledgehammer, hissing with the effort.

He hadn't meant to tell her—not then, not that way. Somehow, the words had started rolling and he hadn't been able to stop them. Had she wanted them all tied up with a ribbon, neat and fancy? Cursing, he came down with the hammer again so that the post vibrated and the noise sang out. Maybe he had more finesse than he'd shown her, and maybe he could've used it. With someone else. Someone who didn't make his feelings come up and grab him by the throat.

Where in God's name had he ever come up with the idea that she had those soft parts, that sweet vulnerability under all that starch and fire? Must've been crazy, he told himself as he began running fresh wire. Jillian Baron was a cold, single-minded woman who cared more about her head count than any real emotion.

And he was almost sick with loving her.

He gripped the wire hard enough so that it bit through the leather of his glove and into his hand. He cursed again. He'd just have to get over it. He had his own land to tend.

Pausing, he looked out. It rolled, oceans of grass, high with summer, green and rippling. The sky was a merciless blue, and the sun beat down, strong and clean. It could be enough for a man—these thousands of acres. His cattle were fat and healthy, the yearlings growing strong. In a few weeks they'd round them up, drive them into Miles City. When those long days were over, the men would celebrate. It was their right to. And so would he, Aaron told himself grimly. So, by God, would he.

He'd have given half of what was his just to get her out of his mind for one day.

At dusk he washed off the day's sweat and dirt. He could smell the night's meal through the open windows of the cabin. Good red meat. Someone was playing a guitar and singing of lonely, lamented love. He found he wanted a beer more than he wanted his share of the steak. Because he knew a man couldn't work and not eat, he piled food on his plate and transferred it to his stomach. But he worked his way through one beer, then two, while the men made up their evening poker game. As they grew louder he took a six-pack and went out on the narrow wood porch.

The stars were just coming out. He heard a coyote call at the moon, then fall silent. The air was as still as it had been all day and barely cooler, but he could smell the sweet clover and wild roses. Resting his back against the porch rail, Aaron willed his mind to empty. But he thought of her…

Fully dressed and spitting mad, standing in the pond—crooning quietly to an orphaned calf—laughing up at him with her hair spread out over the earth of the corral—weeping in his arms over her butchered cattle. Soft one minute, prickly the next—no, she wasn't a temperate woman. But she was the only one he wanted. She was the only one he'd ever felt enough for to hurt over.

Aaron took a long swig from the bottle. He didn't care much for emotional pain. The poets could have it. She didn't want him. Aaron swore and scowled into the dark. The hell she didn't—he wasn't a fool. Maybe her needs weren't the same as his, but she had them. For the first time in weeks he began to think calmly.

He hadn't played his hand well, he realized. It wasn't like him to fold so early—then again, he wasn't used to being soft-headed over a woman. Thoughtfully he tipped back his hat and looked at the stars. She was too set on having her own way, and it was time he gave her a run for her money.

No, he wasn't going back on his knees, Aaron thought with a grim smile. But he was going back. If he had to hobble and brand her, he was going to have Jillian Baron.

When the screen door opened he glanced around absently. His mood was more open to company.

"My luck's pretty poor."

Jennsen, Aaron thought, running through a quick mental outline of the man as he offered him a beer. A bit jittery, he mused. On his first season with the Double M, though he wasn't a greenhorn. He was a man who kept to himself and whose past was no more than could be seen in a worn saddle and patched boots.

Jennsen sat on the first step so that his lantern jaw was shadowed by the porch roof. Aaron thought he might be anywhere from thirty-five to fifty. There was age in his eyes—the kind that came from too many years of looking into the sun at another man's land.

"Cards aren't falling?" Aaron said conversationally while he watched Jennsen roll a cigarette. He didn't miss the fact that the fingers weren't quite steady.

"Haven't been for weeks." Jennsen gave a brief laugh as he struck a match. "Trouble is, I've never been much good at staying away from a gamble." He shot Aaron a sidelong look as he drank again. He'd been working his way up to this talk for days and nearly had enough beer in him to go through with it. "Your luck's pretty steady at the table."

"Comes and goes," Aaron said, deciding Jennsen was feeling his way along for an advance or a loan.

"Luck's a funny thing." Jennsen wiped his mouth with the back of his hand. "Had some bad luck over at the Baron place lately. Losing that cattle," he continued when Aaron glanced over at him. "Somebody made a pretty profit off that beef."

He caught the trace of bitterness. Casually he twisted the top from another bottle and handed it over. "It's easy to make a profit when you don't pay for the beef. Whoever skimmed from the Baron place did a smooth job of it."

"Yeah." Jennsen drew in strong tobacco. He'd heard the rumors about something going on between Aaron Murdock and the Baron woman, but there didn't seem to be anything to it. Most of the talk was about the bad blood between the two families. It'd been going on for years, and it seemed as though it would go on for years more. At the moment he needed badly to believe it. "Guess it doesn't much matter on this side of the fence how much cattle slips away from the Baron spread."

Aaron stretched out his legs and crossed them at the ankles. The lowered brim of his hat shadowed his eyes. "People have to look out for themselves," he said lazily.

Jennsen moistened his lips and prodded a bit further. "I've heard stories about your grandpaw helping himself to Baron beef."

Aaron's eyes narrowed to slits, but he checked his temper. "Stories," he agreed. "No proof."

Jennsen took another long swallow of beer. "I heard that somebody waltzed right onto Baron land and loaded up a prize yearling, sired by that fancy bull."

"Did a tidy job of it." Aaron kept his voice expressionless. Jennsen was testing the waters all right, but he wasn't looking for a loan. "It'd be a shame if they took it for baby beef," he added. "The yearling has the look of his sire—a real moneymaker. 'Course, in a few months he'd stand out like a sore thumb on a small spread. Hate to see a good bloodline wasted."

"Man hears things," Jennsen mumbled, accepting the fresh beer Aaron handed him. "You were interested in the Baron bull."

Aaron took a swig from his bottle, tipped back his hat, and grinned agreeably. "I'm always interested in good stock. Know where I can get my hands on some?"

Jennsen searched his face and swallowed. "Maybe."

Jillian slowed down as she passed the white frame house. Empty. Of course it was empty, she told herself. Even if he'd come back, he wouldn't be home in the middle of the morning. She shouldn't be here on Murdock land when she had her hands full of her own work. She couldn't stay away. If he didn't come back soon, she was going to make a fool of herself and go up to the line camp and...

And what? she asked herself. Half the time she didn't know what she wanted to do, how she felt, what she thought. The one thing she was certain of was that she'd never spent three more miserable weeks in her life. It was perilously close to grief.

Something had died in her when he'd left—something she hadn't acknowledged had been alive. She'd convinced herself that she wouldn't fall in love with him. It would be impossible to count the times she'd told herself it wouldn't happen—even after it already had. Why hadn't she recognized it?

Jillian supposed it wasn't always easy to recognize something you'd never experienced before. Especially when it had no explanation. A woman so accustomed to getting and going her own way had no business falling for a man who was equally obstinate and independent.

Falling in love. Jillian thought it an apt phrase. When it happened you just lost your foothold and plunged.

Maybe he'd meant it, she thought. Maybe they had been more than words to him. If he loved her back, didn't it mean she had someone to hold on to while she was falling? She let out a long breath as she pulled up in front of the ranch house. If he'd meant it, why wasn't he here? Mistake, she told herself with forced calm. It was always a mistake to depend too much. People pulled back or just went away. But if she could only see him again...

"Going to just sit there in that Jeep all morning?"

With a jerk, Jillian turned to watch Paul Murdock take a few slow, measured steps out onto the porch. She got out of the Jeep, wondering which of the excuses she'd made up before she'd set out would work the best.

"Sit," Murdock ordered before she could come to a decision. "Karen's fixing up a pitcher of tea."

"Thank you." Feeling awkward, she sat on the edge of the porch swing and searched for something to say.

"He hasn't come down from the camp yet," Murdock told her bluntly as he lowered himself into a rocker. "Don't frazzle your brain, girl," he ordered with an impatient brush of his hand. "I may be old, but I can see what's going on under my nose. What'd the two of you spat about?"

"Paul." Karen carried a tray laden with glasses and an iced pitcher. "Jillian's entitled to her privacy."

"Privacy!" he snorted while Karen arranged the tray on a table. "She's dangling after my son."

"Dangling!" Jillian was on her feet in a flash. "I

don't dangle after anything or anyone. If I want something, I get it."

He laughed, rocking back and forth and wheezing with the effort as she glared down at him. "I like you, girl, damn if I don't. Got a fetching face, doesn't she, Karen?"

"Lovely." With a smile, Karen offered Jillian a glass of tea.

"Thank you." Stiffly she took her seat again. "I just stopped by to let Aaron know that the mare's doing well. The vet was by yesterday to check her out."

"That the best you could do?" Murdock demanded.

"Paul." Karen sat on the arm of the rocker and laid a hand on his arm.

"If I want manure, all I have to do is walk my own pasture," he grumbled, then pointed his cane at Jillian. "You going to tell me you don't want my boy?"

"Mr. Murdock," Jillian began with icy dignity, "Aaron and I have a business arrangement."

"When a man's dying he doesn't like to waste time," Murdock said with a scowl. "Now, you want to look me in the eye and tell me straight you've got no feelings for that son of mine, fine. We'll talk about the weather a bit."

Jillian opened her mouth, then closed it again with a helpless shake of her head. "When's he coming back?" she whispered. "It's been three weeks."

"He'll come back when he stops being as thickheaded as you are," Murdock told her curtly.

"I don't know what to do." After the words had tumbled out, she sat in amazement. She'd never in her life said that out loud to anyone.

"What do you want?" Karen asked her.

Jillian looked over and studied them—the old man

and his beautiful wife. Karen's hand was over his on top of the cane. Their shoulders brushed. A few scattered times in her life she'd seen that kind of perfect intimacy that came from deep abiding love. It was easy to recognize, enviable. And a little scary. It came as a shock to discover she wanted that for herself. One man, one lifetime. But if that was ultimately what love equaled for her, she understood it had to be a shared dream.

"I'm still finding out," she murmured.

"That Jeep." Murdock nodded toward it. "You wouldn't have any trouble getting up to the line camp in a four-wheel drive."

Jillian smiled and set her glass aside. "I can't do it that way. It wouldn't work for me if I didn't meet him on equal terms."

"Stubborn young fool," Murdock grumbled.

"Yes." Jillian smiled again as she rose. "If he wants me, that's what he's going to get." The sound of an engine had her glancing over. When she recognized Gil's truck, she frowned and started down the steps.

"Ma'am." He tipped his hat to Karen but didn't even open the door of the truck. "Mr. Murdock. Got a problem," he said briefly, shifting his eyes to Jillian.

"What is it?"

"Sheriff called. Seems your yearling's been identified on a spread 'bout hundred and fifty miles south of here. Wants you to go down and take a look for yourself."

Jillian gripped the bottom of the open window. "Where?"

"Old Larraby spread. I'll take you now."

"Leave your Jeep here," Murdock told her, getting to his feet. "One of my men'll take it back to your place."

"Thanks." Quickly she dashed around to the other side of the truck. "Let's go," she ordered the moment the door shut beside her. "How, Gil?" she demanded as they drove out of the ranch yard. "Who identified him?"

Gil spit out the window and felt rather pleased with himself. "Aaron Murdock."

"Aaron—"

Gil was a bit more pleased when Jillian's mouth fell open. "Yep." When he came to the fork in the road, he headed south at a steady, mile-eating clip.

"But how? Aaron's been up at his line camp for weeks, and—"

"Maybe you'd like to settle down so I can tell you, or maybe you wouldn't."

Seething with impatience, Jillian subsided. "Tell me."

"Seems one of the Murdock men had a hand in the rustling, fellow named Jennsen. Well, he wasn't too happy with his cut and gambled away most of it anyhow. Decided if they could slice off five hundred and get away with it, he'd take one more for himself."

"Baby," Jillian muttered and crossed her arms over her chest.

"Yep. Had himself a tiger by the tail there. Knew the makings of a prize bull when he saw it and took it over to Larraby. Used to work there before Larraby fell on hard times. Anyhow, he started to get nervous once the man who headed up the rustling got wind of who took the little bull, figured he better get it off his hands. Last night he tried to sell him to Aaron Murdock."

"I see." That was one more she owed him, Jillian thought with a scowl. It was hard to meet a man toe to toe when you were piling up debts. "If it is Baby, and this Jennsen was involved, we'll get the rest of them."

"We'll see if it's Baby," Gil said, then eased a cautious look at her. "The sheriff's already rounding up the rest of them. Picked up Joe Carlson a couple hours ago."

"Joe?" Stunned, she turned completely around in her seat to stare at Gil. "Joe Carlson?"

"Seems he bought himself a little place over in Wyoming. From the sound of it, he's already got a couple hundred head of your cattle grazing there."

"Joe." Shifting, Jillian stared straight ahead. So much for trust, she thought. So much for her expert reading of character. Clay hadn't wanted to hire him—she'd insisted. One of her first major independent decisions on Utopia had been her first major mistake.

"Guess he fooled me too," Gil muttered after a moment. "Knew his cattle front and back." He spit again and set his teeth. "Shoulda known better than to trust a man with soft hands and a clean hat."

"I hired him," Jillian muttered.

"I worked with him," Gil tossed back. "Side by side. And if you don't think that sticks in my craw, then you ain't too smart. Bamboozled me," he grumbled. *"Me!"*

It was his insulted pride that made her laugh. Jillian propped her feet up on the dash. What was done was over, she told herself. She was going to get a good chunk of her cattle back and see justice done. And at roundup time her books would shift back into the black. Maybe they'd have that new Jeep after all. "Did you get the full story from the sheriff?"

"Aaron Murdock," Gil told her. "He came by right before I set out after you."

"He came by the ranch?" she asked with a casualness that wouldn't have fooled anyone.

"Stopped by so I'd have the details."

"Did he—ah—say anything else?"

"Just that he had a lot of things to see to. Busy man."

"Oh." Jillian turned her head and stared out the window. Gil took a chance and grinned hugely.

* * *

She waited until it was nearly dark. It was impossible to bank down the hope that he'd come by or call, if only to see that everything had gone well. She worked out a dozen opening speeches and revised them. She paced. When she knew that she'd scream if she spent another minute within four walls, Jillian went out to the stables and saddled her mare.

"Men," she grumbled as she pulled the cinch. "If this is all part of the game, I'm not interested."

Ready for a run, Delilah sniffed the air the moment Jillian led her outside. When Jillian swung into the saddle, the mare danced and strained against the bit. Within moments they'd left the lights of the ranch yard behind.

The ride would clear her head, she told herself. Anyone would be a bit crazed after a day like this one. Getting Baby back had eased the sting of betrayal she'd felt after learning Joe Carlson had stolen from her. Methodically stolen, she thought, while offering advice and sympathy. He'd certainly been clever, she mused, subtly, systematically turning her attention toward the Murdocks while he was slipping her own cattle through her own fences. Until she found a new herdsman, she'd have to add his duties to her own.

It would do her good, she decided, keep her mind off things. Aaron. If he'd wanted to see her, he'd known where to find her. Apparently, she'd done them both a favor by pushing him away weeks before. If she hadn't, they'd have found themselves in a very painful situation. As it was, they were each just going their own way— exactly as she'd known they would from the beginning. Perhaps she'd had a few moments of weakness, like the one that morning on the Double M, but they wouldn't last. In the next few weeks she'd be too busy to worry about Aaron Murdock and some foolish dreams.

Jillan told herself she hadn't deliberately ridden to the pond, but had simply let Delilah go her own way. In any case, it was still a spot she'd choose for solitude, no matter what memories lingered there.

The moon was full and white, the brush silvered with it. She told herself she wasn't unhappy, just tired after a long day of traveling, dealing with the sheriff, answering questions. She couldn't be unhappy when she finally had what was hers back. When the weariness passed, she'd celebrate. She could have wept, and hated herself.

When she saw the moon reflected on the water, she slowed Delilah to an easy lope. There wasn't a sound but the steady hoofbeats of her own mount. She heard the stallion even as her mare scented him. With her own heart pounding, Jillian controlled the now skittish Delilah and brought her to a halt. Aaron stepped out of the shadow of a cottonwood and said nothing at all.

He'd known she'd come—sooner or later. He could've gone to her, or waited for her to come to him. Somehow he'd known they had to meet here on land that belonged to them both.

It was better to face it all now and be done with it, Jillian told herself, then found her hands were wet with nerves as she dismounted. Nothing could've stiffened her spine more effectively. In thrumming silence she tethered her mare. When she turned, she found Aaron had moved behind her, as silently as the wildcat she'd once compared him to. She stood very straight, kept her tone very impassive.

"So, you came back."

His eyes were lazy and amused as he scanned her face. "Did you think I wouldn't?"

Her chin came up as he'd known it would. "I didn't think about it at all."

"No?" He smiled then—it should have warned her. "Did you think about this?" He dragged her to him, one hand at her waist, one at the back of her head, and devoured the mouth he'd starved for. He expected her to struggle—perhaps he would've relished it just then—but she met the demands of his mouth with the strength and verve he remembered.

When he tore his mouth from hers, she clung, burying her face in his shoulder. He still wanted her—the thought pounded inside her head. She hadn't lost him, not yet. "Hold me," she murmured. "Please, just for a minute."

How could she do this to him? Aaron wondered. How could she shift his mood from crazed to tender in the space of seconds? Maybe he'd never figure out quite how to handle her, but he didn't intend to stop learning.

When she felt her nerves come back, she drew away. "I want to thank you for what you did. The sheriff told me that you got the evidence from Jennsen, and—"

"I don't want to talk about the cattle, Jillian."

"No." Linking her hands together, she turned away. No, it was time they put that aside and dealt with what was really important. What was vital. "I've thought about what happened—about what you said the last time we saw each other." Where were all those speeches she'd planned? They'd all been so calm, so lucid. She twisted her fingers until they hurt, then separated them. "Aaron, I meant it when I said that I don't expect to be told those things. Some women do."

"I wasn't saying them to some women."

"It's so easy to say," she told him in a vibrating whisper. "So easy."

"Not for me."

She turned slowly, warily, as if she expected him to make a move she wasn't prepared for. He looked so calm, she thought. And yet the way the moonlight hit his eyes… "It's hard," she murmured.

"What is?"

"Loving you."

He could have gone to her then, right then, and pulled her to him until there was no more talk, no more thought. But her chin was up and her eyes were swimming. "Maybe it's supposed to be. I'm not offering you an easy road."

"No one's ever loved me back the way I wanted." Swallowing, she stepped away. "No one but Clay, and he never told me. He never had to."

"I'm not Clay, or your father. And there's no one who's ever going to love you the way I do." He took a step toward her, and though she didn't back up, he thought he could see every muscle brace. "What are you afraid of?"

"I'm not afraid!"

He came closer. "Like hell."

"That you'll stop." It wrenched out of her as she gripped her hands behind her back. Once started, the words rushed out quickly and ran together. "That you'll decide you never really loved me anyway. And I'll have let myself want and start depending and needing you. I've spent most of my life working on not depending on anyone, not for anything."

"I'm not anyone," he said quietly.

Her breath came shuddering out. "Since you've been gone I haven't cared about anything except you coming back."

He ran his hands up her arms. "Now that I am?"

"I couldn't bear it if you didn't stay. And though I think I could stand the hurt, I just can't stand being afraid." She put her hands to his chest when he started to draw her to him.

"Jillian, do you think you can tell me things I've been waiting to hear and have me keep my hands off you? Don't you know there's risk on both sides? Dependence on both sides?"

"Maybe." She made herself breathe evenly until she got it all out. "But people aren't always looking for the same things."

"Such as?"

This time she moistened her lips. "Are you going to marry me?" The surprise in his eyes made her muscles stiffen again.

"You asking?"

She dragged herself out of his hold, cursing herself for being a fool and him for laughing at her. "Go to hell," she told him as she started for her horse.

He caught her around the waist, lifting her off the ground as she kicked out. "Damn, you've got a short fuse," he muttered and ended by pinning her to the ground. "I have a feeling I'm going to spend the best part of my life wrestling with you." Showing an amazing amount of patience, he waited until she'd run out of curses and had subsided, panting. "I'd planned to put the question to you a bit differently," he began. "As in, will you. But as I see it, that's a waste of time." As she stared up at him, he smiled. "God, you're beautiful. Don't argue," he warned as she opened her mouth. "I'm going to tell you that whenever I please so you might as well start swallowing it now."

"You were laughing at me," she began, but he cut her off.

"At both of us." Lowering his head, he kissed her, gently at first, then with building passion. "Now…" Cautiously he let her wrists go until he was certain she wasn't going to take a swing at him. "I'll give you a week to get things organized at your ranch."

"A week—"

"Shut up," he suggested. "A week, then we're both taking the next week off to get married."

Jillian lay very still and soaked it in. It was pure joy. "It doesn't take a week to get married."

"The way I do it does. When we get back—"

"Get back from where?"

"From any place where we can be alone," he told her. "We're going to start making some plans."

She reached for his cheek. "So far I like them. Aaron, say it again, while I'm looking at you."

"I love you, Jillian. A good bit of the time I like you as well, though I can't say I mind fighting with you."

"I guess you really mean it." She closed her eyes a moment. When she opened them again, they were laughing. "It's hard to take a Murdock at his word, but I'm going to gamble."

"What about a Baron?"

"A Baron's word's gold," she said, angling her chin. "I love you, Aaron. I'm going to make you a frustrating wife and a hell of a partner." She grinned as his lips pressed against hers. "What about those plans?"

"You've got a ranch, I've got a ranch," he pointed out as he kissed her palm. "I don't much care whether we run them separately or together, but there's a matter of living. Your house, my house—that's not going to work for either of us. So we'll build our house, and that's where we're going to raise our children."

Our. She decided it was the most exciting word in

the English language. She was going to use it a dozen times every day for the rest of her life. "Where?"

He glanced over her head, skimming the pool, the solitude. "Right on the damn boundary line."

With a laugh, Jillian circled his neck. "What boundary line?"

* * * * *

REQUEST YOUR
FREE BOOKS!

2 FREE NOVELS
FROM THE ROMANCE COLLECTION
PLUS 2 FREE GIFTS!

YES! Please send me 2 FREE novels from the Romance Collection and my 2 FREE gifts (gifts are worth about $10). After receiving them, if I don't wish to receive any more books, I can return the shipping statement marked "cancel." If I don't cancel, I will receive 4 brand-new novels every month and be billed just $5.99 per book in the U.S. or $6.49 per book in Canada. That's a saving of at least 25% off the cover price. It's quite a bargain! Shipping and handling is just 50¢ per book in the U.S. and 75¢ per book in Canada.* I understand that accepting the 2 free books and gifts places me under no obligation to buy anything. I can always return a shipment and cancel at any time. Even if I never buy another book, the two free books and gifts are mine to keep forever.

194/394 MDN FELQ

Name	(PLEASE PRINT)

Address	Apt. #

City	State/Prov.	Zip/Postal Code

Signature (if under 18, a parent or guardian must sign)

Mail to the **Reader Service:**
IN U.S.A.: P.O. Box 1867, Buffalo, NY 14240-1867
IN CANADA: P.O. Box 609, Fort Erie, Ontario L2A 5X3

Not valid for current subscribers to the Romance Collection
or the Romance/Suspense Collection.

Want to try two free books from another line?
Call 1-800-873-8635 or visit www.ReaderService.com.

* Terms and prices subject to change without notice. Prices do not include applicable taxes. Sales tax applicable in N.Y. Canadian residents will be charged applicable taxes. Offer not valid in Quebec. This offer is limited to one order per household. All orders subject to credit approval. Credit or debit balances in a customer's account(s) may be offset by any other outstanding balance owed by or to the customer. Please allow 4 to 6 weeks for delivery. Offer available while quantities last.

Your Privacy—The Reader Service is committed to protecting your privacy. Our Privacy Policy is available online at www.ReaderService.com or upon request from the Reader Service.

We make a portion of our mailing list available to reputable third parties that offer products we believe may interest you. If you prefer that we not exchange your name with third parties, or if you wish to clarify or modify your communication preferences, please visit us at www.ReaderService.com/consumerschoice or write to us at Reader Service Preference Service, P.O. Box 9062, Buffalo, NY 14269. Include your complete name and address.

NORA ROBERTS

28597	LOVE BY DESIGN	__ $7.99 U.S.	__ $9.99 CAN.
28595	WINDFALL	__ $7.99 U.S.	__ $8.99 CAN.
28594	O'HURLEY'S RETURN	__ $7.99 U.S.	__ $9.99 CAN.
28592	O'HURLEY BORN	__ $7.99 U.S.	__ $9.99 CAN.
28590	SWEET RAINS	__ $7.99 U.S.	__ $9.99 CAN.
28588	NIGHT TALES:		
	NIGHT SHIELD & NIGHT MOVES	__ $7.99 U.S.	__ $9.99 CAN.
28587	NIGHT TALES:		
	NIGHTSHADE & NIGHT SMOKE	__ $7.99 U.S.	__ $9.99 CAN.
28586	NIGHT TALES: NIGHT SHIFT &		
	NIGHT SHADOW	__ $7.99 U.S.	__ $9.99 CAN.
28583	WORTH THE RISK	__ $7.99 U.S.	__ $9.99 CAN.
28580	THE MacKADE BROTHERS:		
	DEVIN AND SHANE	__ $7.99 U.S.	__ $8.99 CAN.
28575	THE MacKADE BROTHERS:		
	RAFE AND JARED	__ $7.99 U.S.	__ $7.99 CAN.
28574	CHARMED & ENCHANTED	__ $7.99 U.S.	__ $7.99 CAN.
28569	THE MacGREGOR GROOMS	__ $7.99 U.S.	__ $7.99 CAN.
28568	WAITING FOR NICK &		
	CONSIDERING KATE	__ $7.99 U.S.	__ $7.99 CAN.
28565	TREASURES	__ $7.99 U.S.	__ $9.50 CAN.
28151	IRISH DREAMS	__ $7.99 U.S.	__ $9.99 CAN.
28150	IRISH HEARTS	__ $7.99 U.S.	__ $9.99 CAN.
28137	PERFECT HARMONY	__ $7.99 U.S.	__ $9.99 CAN.
28134	THE MacGREGORS:		
	ALAN & GRANT	__ $7.99 U.S.	__ $9.99 CAN.
28133	THE MacGREGORS:		
	SERENA & CAINE	__ $7.99 U.S.	__ $9.99 CAN.

(limited quantities available)

TOTAL AMOUNT	$ _____
POSTAGE & HANDLING	$ _____
($1.00 FOR 1 BOOK, 50¢ for each additional)	
APPLICABLE TAXES*	$ _____
TOTAL PAYABLE	$ _____

(check or money order—please do not send cash)

To order, complete this form and send it, along with a check or money order for the total above, payable to Harlequin Books, to: **In the U.S.:** 3010 Walden Avenue, P.O. Box 9077, Buffalo, NY 14269-9077; **In Canada:** P.O. Box 636, Fort Erie, Ontario, L2A 5X3.

Name: _____

Address: _____ City: _____

State/Prov.: _____ Zip/Postal Code: _____

Account Number (if applicable): _____

075 CSAS

*New York residents remit applicable sales taxes.
*Canadian residents remit applicable GST and provincial taxes.

Silhouette®
Where love comes alive™

Visit Silhouette Books at www.Harlequin.com

PSNR1011BL